在家就能進行的雙語教育

全新！美國家庭萬用親子英文

全MP3一次下載

http://www.booknews.com.tw/mp3/9789864542727.htm

此為ZIP壓縮檔，請先安裝解壓縮程式或APP，
iOS系統請升級至iOS 13後再行下載。
此為大型檔案（約353M），建議使用WIFI連線下載，以免占用流量，
並確認連線狀況，以利下載順暢。

前言
獻給希望小孩英文流暢的「家長們」

我從事的 suksuk 網站（www.suksuk.com 編注：此網站內容為韓文，懂韓文的閱讀者可至此網站蒐集大量幼兒英文教育資料）是跟小孩是從幼兒到小中學的父母們一起討論英文教育方向的「英文教育社群網站」。從 2000 年開創以來，會員人數已經達到 150 萬名。只要是苦惱小孩英文的人，至少都曾經進來看過這個充滿父母親愛的地方。去年五月，suksuk 網站計畫要出這本「為爸媽準備的萬用生活英語」的書。因為過去十年間，suksuk 的家長們最苦惱的領域就是「生活英語」。為了讓小孩不只是「學習」英文，而是從「生活」中自然地學會英文，這就一定需要經歷從生活中熟悉英文的過程。也就是說，爸媽無論何時都要讓孩子有學習生活英語的機會。因此，這本書是為對英文很頭疼的「家長們」而策劃的。

本書誕生了一個「共同計畫」。這是由六名 suksuk 的媽媽們一起製作，其目的是為了孩子覺得英文很容易親近，簡單的表達可以直接用英文說出。其中有的媽媽讓子女從嬰兒時就生活在英文的環境中，也有的媽媽努力地給小孩讀英文故事書，讓孩子慢慢地熟悉名詞。這種情況下，大家常遇到太多「這句話用英文要怎麼說？」這種苦惱的狀況，而這些媽媽們就將這些狀況整理出來。因此，這本書網羅了所有父母跟子女之間最可能說的對話。

本書的表達分成不同的小標題，就像特定場合的台詞一般，創造出許多可以想像的空間。對話並不只是單方面的表達而已，而是雙方有意義的相互反應。因此，請家長從說 「媽媽先說英文，你也這樣回答」開始。在類似的情況下進行練習的話，就可以引起孩子的好奇心。

不要只是根據書上出現的表達逐字逐句地學習，一定要在家中說出英文來產生一個「有意義的結果」。例如，準備晚餐時，可以說 Dinner's ready, Honey!（寶貝，晚餐準備好了！）；洗碗時，可以說 Can you help me to do the dishes?（你要幫我洗碗嗎？）。又或是當小孩要點心時，可以跟小孩說「用英文說一次看看吧。Can I have a snack?」之後，再給準備點心給他。

即使到了小學高年級，學校的英文還是停留在解題的階段。在學習日常生活中所需的英文之前，光解題和背單字就已經把所有時間用光了。以現場長期教授英文的經驗來看， 如果有學習過「有意義的溝通英文」，「童話和影片出現的有趣英文」的小孩在上中學和高中時，都可以輕鬆地消化大量的習題量。那麼，從今天開始就在家中進行簡單的英文對話吧。爸爸媽媽跟子女輕鬆地溝通，有點像是在玩小遊戲，小孩子都會很容易吸收。同時，借此契機可以真正說出英文。因此，即使覺得害羞，也要鼓起用勇氣試試看。

感謝我們 suksuk 的媽媽們一直一起討論到這本書出版為止。感謝歷經數月辛苦地寫英文句子的兒子 Yun Jaewon。同時，也感謝一起分享了無數討論和想法的編輯，還要感謝鼓勵和幫助這次出書的 suksuk 全體會員們。在此，把這本書獻給 suksuk 150 萬的會員們。

suksuk 網站 英文研究所所長

參與本書製作

媽咪六人組的真心推薦

為了出版這本爸媽和小孩在現實生活中會使用到的英文表達書，六名好幾年直接教小孩英文的媽媽們一起參與了這次製作。過去一年間，六名媽媽從目錄選定、表達的收集，到英文原稿的討論都相當認真地一起完成。託這六名媽媽的福，這本書終於可以出版了。下面是一起討論原稿的六名媽咪的真心推薦。

這本書是英文完全不拿手的家長們的聖經！《美國家庭萬用親子英文》除了有家人之間每天都會用到的表達，連媽媽本身經常使用、但卻不易找到適當英文表達的用語都一併告訴大家。這本書收集到這樣的程度，真的具有收藏的價值。有了這本書，我可以保證執行親子英文教育的過程中，出現過的所有英文難題都可以一次解決。

- Byeon Gyeongsuk（小孩 7 歲，《普通媽媽的初級英文》（韓文書）的作者）

對教育兩個小孩的我來說，這是一本應用性很高的書。它把過去要分成好幾本的教室英文，幼稚園英文，教養英文，遊戲英文等內容都網羅在一起。因此，雖然還很早，但是我想把這本書傳給我的兒媳婦。^^

-Go Sugyeong（小孩一個 5 歲，一個 7 歲）

有個地方很癢，但是卻沒有抓癢的方法的話，那會有多不爽呀！想跟小孩用英文來對話，卻不知道生活英語嗎？這本書就是要來解決那種癢癢的心情！當想知道「這種時候，用英文要怎麼說呢？」的話，就可以馬上從書中找出，根據不同的情況一個個來熟悉英文表達。這樣的話，媽媽和小孩的英文實力都會快速提高。

- I Jiyeong（小孩一個 8 歲，一個 10 歲）

雖然下決心要用英文來教小孩，但是一開始就連跟小孩用英文說一兩句，對我來說都已經是很不簡單的苦行（>_<）了。但是，如今有這樣好的一本書出現了，媽咪們就可以少吃一點我吃過的苦。因為這本書可以一次性地解決像我這種媽媽的所有苦惱。特別，這本書是經過實際執行過英文教育的媽咪們好幾次的篩選和討論之後而誕生的。我相信這個本會比任何一本表達集更具有應用性。

- Yeon Gyusun（小孩一個 6 歲，一個 10 歲）

在進行英文教育時，最沒信心的部分就是「生活會話」。不過，很意外的是，要找到有完全的生活英語表達的教材卻很難。但是這本書經過親自執行過英文教育的媽媽們嚴格挑選，所以有相當多家長對小孩使用的例句。與其死記硬背，還不如就把這本書放在附近，和小孩一起生活時，找出相對應的表達來經常使用。這不就是最好的方法了嗎？好的開始是成功的一半，用這本書中出現的表達一句句跟小孩子對談的話，不知不覺中家長和小孩就在會在自然的環境中養成英文對話的習慣。

- Go Eunyeong（小孩一個 7 歲，一個 9 歲）

以媽媽的身分執行英文教育的八年來，我讀了很多本英文會話書。但是，總是覺得有某一個部分是很可惜的。以幼兒為主要對象的書，對小學生來說不適合；以會話為中心的書的話，又少了遊戲的表達。但是，這本書除了有每天的生活會話之外，還有基本的英文日記寫作、英文書讀後感發表，以及與外籍老師面談等等英文。同時，也收集了學期末的感謝信，真的是無所不有。只要有了這一本，就不需要其他本書了。這不是一本讀完一次之後，就擺在書架上當裝飾的書，我保證它是一本每天都可以拿出來讀的生活必讀品。

- Jo Yangsu（小孩 8 歲）

讓小孩的英文越來越流利的

親子英文教育四階段的學習法

網路上有很多對小孩學習英文的建議，如「跟英文兒歌一起唱」，「不是，一定要先學字母」，「多看些 DVD」等等。這些建議只會讓跟子女一起學習英文的爸媽們更加手忙腳亂。還有，對一部份小孩很有用的方法不見得適合自己的小孩。不過，請不用太煩惱了。因為不管當下流行哪一種學習法，總是有些共同的基本原則。小孩子在學習英文時，都會經歷以下四個階段，只要留意不同階段的注意事項，讓小孩能獲得學英語的成就感的話，不論是把小孩送去英語幼兒園或是媽媽自己教，小孩的英文都會變得很熟練。

1 階段 先熟悉英文的「聲音」！

對於完全不認識字，即使認得字母，也不知道準確發音的幼兒來說，最重要的是熟悉「英文」的「聲音（sounds）」。這時候，可以讓他們聽有節奏感的歌曲和童謠，或是看有趣的 DVD。不過，比起這個方法，最好的方法還是媽媽經常讀以日常生活為主題的英文繪本給小孩聽。

「熟悉聲音」的過程對幼兒來說也是熟悉「口語（oral language）」的機會。像這樣聽聲音後，用嘴巴說出來的話，可以同時熟悉詞彙和表達。以

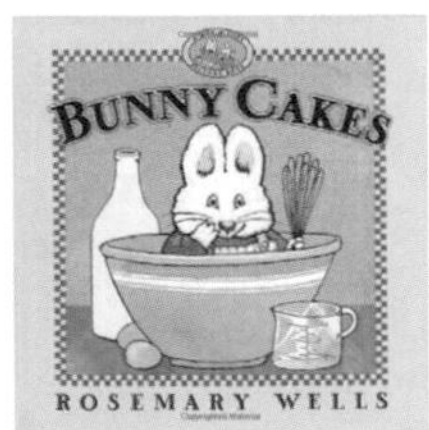

▶《Max & Ruby》、《Timothy Goes to School》、《Caillou》都是對幼兒很親切的主題和生活內容，因此是人氣很高的系列。《Mother Goose Club》在它的 YouTube 頻道上（https://www.youtube.com/MotherGooseClub）提供各種影片。

後學習文字後，並開始閱讀時，已經有了背景知識，就可以更容易地學習語言。媽媽們可以閱讀英文繪本中出現的反覆句型和單字，或是通過有趣的童話和圖片來說明故事情節。具有日常話題的生活童話是很好的選擇。

在小孩子還不懂閱讀樂趣的時候，就太積極地叫他記單字，或是讀小孩子根本就不感興趣的書給他聽的時候，只會產生反效果。讓小孩子覺得書這種東西也是跟玩具那樣好玩是最優先的課題。

2階段 為了正式的閱讀，要開始學習字母！

懂得字母，但是文字和發音沒辦法準確地連接起來，或是知道個別的發音，但是還看不出它在單字中規律的字母組合，這時候就可以先專注於自然發音法。自然發音法是只看字母組合，就能很流利發音的能力。

首先孩子要可以輕鬆地讀出單字，才能把注意力放在故事內容上，進而掌握文章的意思。因此，除了要挑選有故事情節的繪本之外，還要看書中有沒有相類似的句型或是相關聯的單字等等。（如：train, tree, trick, try 以 tr 開頭，或是 train, pain, rain, again 以 ain 結尾等）

不過，自然發音法並不是閱讀教育的全部，長期只注重學習自然發音的話，學習就會變得枯燥無味。如果自然發音法中出現的單字在閱讀的書籍當中也有出現的話，就會讓閱讀變得更有趣。這時，可以讓小孩在聽著名作者的繪本 CD 之後，鼓勵小孩自己來讀看看，或是在那本書中找出學過的單字，又或是找出有相同初音或尾音的單字。

▶《I Can Read Phonics》、《Sightword Readers》、《Leap Frog》不是傳統的學習素材，而是以有趣的方式來學習發音。如果小孩已經可以自己移動滑鼠的話，推薦一個自然發音法的網站 Starfall.com。

3階段 透過反覆朗讀來培養流暢性！

看到單字時，可以根據自然發音法讀出來，但是讀文章時卻總是結結巴巴，讀完之後也不能理解文意的話，就一定得做「流暢性（fluency）訓練」。「流暢性」是指可以準確順暢地唸出文章，同時有表達力可以讓聽者了解意思的朗讀能力。

可以流暢地朗讀的話，就證明在讀出來的同時也就理解了文章的內容。單字一個接一個地讀出來的話，不僅僅是聲音很不自然，也沒有掌握內容的空暇。如果可以大聲流暢朗讀的話，對口語表達也會產生信心，同時也能提高閱讀能力。因此，大聲地反覆朗讀同一本書是很好的方法。遇到較難的句子時，可以分成幾個小段，反覆讀4遍。等到比較流暢時，就可以整篇文章朗讀4遍。有一個更好的方法是邊聽錄音邊大聲地跟讀。這個方法叫做聽讀（audio assisted reading），它可以幫助練習語調和重音，進而讓發音夠準確，同時也可以提高閱讀能力。

練習流暢性的核心是「反覆朗讀（repeated reading）」，但是它的缺點是很容易感到無聊。因此，可以要多試試各種方法。如，選擇小孩感興趣的書，或是在書上畫畫，又或是每次小孩大聲朗讀時，就給於相同次數的貼紙等等。根據年齡別選擇不同類型的書籍來進行階段性的訓練。

▶《An I Can Read》、《Oxford Reading》有許多不同程度的系列讀物，讓小孩可以增進他的閱讀能力。而 Arthur 系列有《Arthur Starter》、《Arthur Adventure》、《Arthur Chapter Book》等以 Arthur 為主角的各種不同年齡層的讀物。

4階段 多讀培養理解能力，精讀學習詞彙！

如果小孩到了沒有圖片，只有文字也可以理解的階段的話，那麼就要開始做一些難度更高的閱讀練習。閱讀理解能力（reading comprehension）是指「看了部分內容之後，推測接下去的內容」、「替整體的內容做摘要」、「掌握作者的意圖」、「掌握核心內容」等能力，不再只是單純地記住內容。閱讀過後，可以用自己的話來說明，這裡指的是可以做比較和評價的思考能力。

從這時開始，要指導小孩集中所學的詞彙來閱讀，並且訂出目標，挑出幾個詞彙和例句一起來作練習。或是如果出現不認識的單字時，根據前後文的提示來練習推測意思。還有，寫出如 why、how 等需要思考的問題也是很重要的。在這個過程中，思考和寫作的練習是可以同步進行的。因此，閱讀之後，練習寫出主觀性問題的答案，或是做其他各種閱讀練習。章節較短的橋梁書和讓人感動的紐伯瑞兒童小說都是很好的選擇。經過這些訓練的小孩接觸到為考試而準備的閱讀習作本、單字書、文法書等等時，就不會覺得很困難。

不過，也不要提出太多閱讀的問題，以免讓閱讀變成苦差事。所謂的想法其實是相當困難的思考過程。不可以沒有什麼根據，就直接說出答案。媽媽要先做好模範，例如，先說「我認為作者是這樣想的，因為書中有這樣的內容。」接著，再讓小孩說出自己的想法。

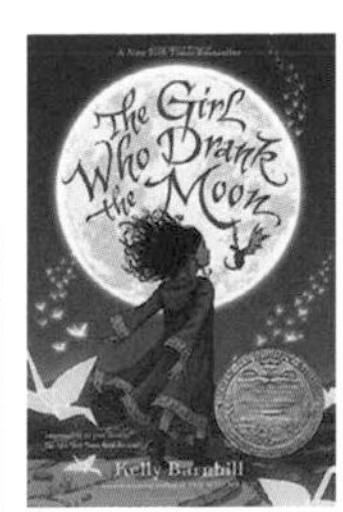

▶較早期的橋樑書《Magic Tree House》系列、紐伯瑞兒童小說和父母親最想讓子女閱讀的英文原文書《哈利波特》系列。

以美國家庭的方式學英文！

爸媽就是最好的英文老師！

讓說到「英文」就很灰心的家長們，也能輕鬆在家營造全美語環境！

「一天幾句也好！」很想讓小孩自然地說出英文，但是一說起英文就很沒信心的家長們。這是一本收集了親子生活各種英文表達的萬用會話書，可以幫助父母親有自信地說出英文的生活用語，進而跟小孩用英文交談。現在，當小孩無時無刻在問「爸爸媽媽，OOO的英文是什麼？」請利用本書自信地回答他們！永遠記住，「父母親主動講，小孩子就敢開口說英文」這個重要觀念！

收集了 150 萬爸媽們最想知道的 8000 句生活用語

這本書網羅了過去十年間 150 萬爸媽們在「生活用語留言板」、「幼兒英文留言板」、「小學生英文留言板」等 suksuk 網站中討論的 8000 句生活用語表達。除了「想尿尿嗎？」、「不可以挑食！」、「爸爸來了。」等每天都會用到的表達外，連像「不要挖鼻屎！」、「誰放屁了？」等小孩子在生活中也想知道的英文表達也都有收錄。

洪賢珠博士及六名媽媽們嚴格撰寫編輯 連爸媽都能用本書跟外籍老師對談

身為suksuk 網站英文研究所所長的洪賢珠博士，根據過去 20 年所學，挑出家長們英文表達。同時六名媽媽也以測試員的身分，嚴格確認是否有任何遺漏，因此連與外師交談的狀況，都可以在本書中找到！媽媽們會審視英文句子寫得好不好。如果對家長來說是很長很困難的表達，就會再次進行認真地討論。讓英文不是很好的爸爸媽媽也可以很輕鬆使用本書。

適用各個年齡層，不需多買教材，全家用這一本就足夠了！

不用為了老大買一本「小學英文」，再為老么買一本「幼兒英文」了！這本書收集了從懷孕、嬰兒、幼兒到小學，爸爸媽媽及小孩子們會用到的英文表達，讓孩子的英語力，從懷孕時期就建立！同時，還包含了小孩英文幼稚園或是英文補習班的作業中所需的英文日記，英文讀後感等基本表達，學期末的英文感謝信等表達。就這一本書，就可以確實地解決所有全家大小的英文難題。

本書使用方法

試著跟小孩說英文，找出不知道的表達

Chapter 01
忙碌的早晨
Time to wake up!
起床的時間到了！
Can I sleep some more?
我可以再多睡一會嗎？
起床

「我的小孩為什麼在家不會主動說英文？」很多重視孩子英文教育的家長常有這樣的煩惱，但如果家長擔心本身的英文能力，不敢主動對孩子說英文，卻要求孩子主動開口說，這不是很奇怪嗎？其實只要從每天幾句話開始，父母先做「勇敢的示範」，就能逐漸影響孩子學英文的態度。本書根據美國家庭經常使用的會話為模仿對象，提供了8000句不同情況的日常生活英文。父母跟小孩進行英文對話時，碰到問題就可以隨時查找，不用擔心「不知道怎麼說」的窘境。

讓小孩直接找出想知道的英文表達方式

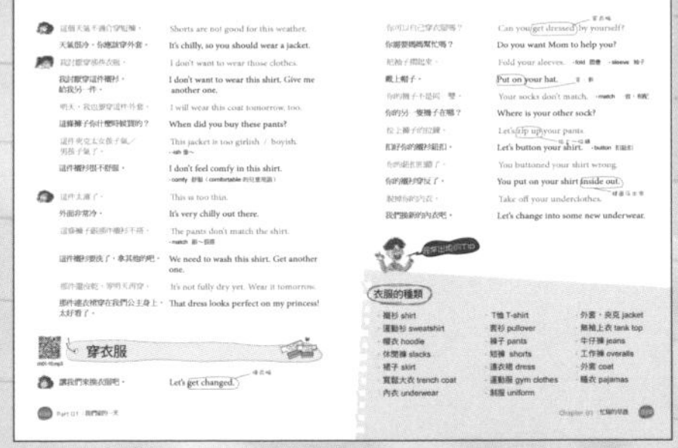

小孩懂得中文，也有了某種程度的英文能力後，可以讓小孩直接找出想知道的英文說法。當小孩子說：「爸爸媽媽，OO的英文怎麼說？」的時候，父母可以說：「我也不知道耶，我們一起找找看吧？」進而間接訓練小孩尋找答案的能力。小孩和爸媽反覆幾次這種練習之後，有一天小孩就會養成自己找答案的習慣。

Step 3

以「扮演美國家庭」的方式來練習英文會話

透過角色扮演跟小孩練習本書的某個場景也是很好的方法。每天透過本書中媽媽、爸爸、兒子、女兒的角色來進行對話練習，讓英文學習好像玩扮家家酒一樣有趣。這樣持續下去的話，有一天就會突然發現，不只是小孩，全家的英文實力都變好了。同時，本書的專業錄音員都為英文母語人士，透過聲音表情來錄音，讓英文更加有趣。不管是隨意聽或是集中注意力聽，這本書都是很容易使用的教材。

本書美國家庭會話 QR 碼音檔（約10小時）

隨書附贈約10小時的QR碼音檔隨掃隨聽，皆由母語為英文的專業配音員錄製。透過活潑、生動、有聲音表情的方式扮演媽媽、爸爸、兒子、女兒等角色，可以更確實地鍛鍊小孩的聽力。

簡單明瞭的目錄

詳細分類
的目錄

Part 2 每天用的稱讚和嘮叨

Part 3 和媽媽一起玩 Let's Play!

Part 8 年齡別英文表現：從出生到小學

爸媽最常使用的50句英文

ch00-01.mp3

01	該起床了！	Time to wake up!
02	早安	Good morning!
03	睡得好嗎？	Did you sleep well?
04	快來吃早餐吧。	Come and eat your breakfast.
05	不要挑食。	Don't be picky about your food.
06	洗臉刷牙。	Wash your face and brush your teeth.
07	爸爸要出門了，說再見。	Daddy is leaving. Say goodbye.
08	來穿衣服吧。	Let's get dressed.
09	今天你想要穿什麼呢？	What do you want to wear today?
10	我來幫你梳頭。	Let me comb your hair.
11	你的臉上擦乳液了嗎？	Did you put some lotion on your face?
12	快點，寶貝！要遲到了。	Hurry up, Honey! You'll be late.
13	電梯來了。我們進去吧。	Here's the elevator. Let's get in.
14	按一樓。	Push button one.
15	我們出去吧。	Let's get out.
16	祝你有個美好的一天。	Have a nice day.
17	小心車子。	Watch out for cars.
18	今天學校如何？	How was school today?
19	你餓了嗎？	Are you hungry?
20	去洗手。	Go wash your hands.
21	我們吃點心吧。	Let's have a snack.
22	還想要多吃點嗎？	Do you want some more?
23	休息時間結束了。	Recess is over!
24	該學習了。	It's time to study!

25 坐好。 Sit properly.
26 你有作業嗎？ Do you have any homework?
27 你作業都做完了嗎？ Are you done with your homework?
28 考試考得好嗎？ Did you do well on your test?
29 你考了幾分？ What score did you get on the test?
30 你做得很好！ Good job!
31 從電視那裡往後退。 Move back from the TV.
32 現在關掉電視。 Turn off the TV now.
33 是誰弄得這麼髒的？ Who made such a mess?
34 把你的玩具收拾好。 Put your toys away.
35 你不舒服嗎？ Are you sick?
36 你要尿尿／便便嗎？ Do you want to pee / poop?
37 要我背你嗎？ Do you want a piggy-back ride?
38 要我抱你嗎？ Do you want me to hold you?
39 親一下！ Give me a kiss!
40 不要跟弟弟／妹妹打架。 Don't fight with your little brother / sister.
41 不可以打弟弟／妹妹。 Don't hit your brother / sister.
42 不要打擾你的姊姊。 Don't bother your sister.
43 要跟朋友好好玩。 Play nicely with your friends.
44 不要再嘀嘀咕咕了。 Stop whining.
45 不要頂嘴！ Don't talk back!
46 對不起。我們和好吧。 I'm sorry. Let's make up.
47 我來唸個故事給你聽。 Let me read you a story.
48 該睡覺了喔。 It's time to go to bed.
49 晚安！祝你做個好夢！ Good night! Sweet dreams!
50 不要忘記我愛你。 Don't forget that I love you.

孩子最常使用的50句英文

ch00-02.mp3

01	爸爸媽媽，早安！	Good morning, Mom and Dad!
02	我醒了。（爸媽叫起床時）	I'm awake.
03	爸，祝你有個美好的一天！	Have a nice day, Dad!
04	我要穿這件襯衫。	I want to wear this shirt.
05	我可以自己完成它。	I can do it by myself.
06	媽，我現在都長大了。	Mom, I'm all grown up now.
07	媽，我美／帥嗎？	Do I look good, Mom?
08	請幫我綁頭髮。	Tie my hair, please.
09	再見！我要出門了。	Goodbye! I'm leaving.
10	媽，我回來了。	I'm home, Mom.
11	媽，可以給我剪刀嗎？	Can you get me the scissors, Mom?
12	媽，看這個。	Look at this, Mom.
13	媽，我很無聊。	Mom, I'm bored.
14	媽，跟我玩。	Play with me, Mom!
15	幫我畫車子。	Draw me a car.
16	我可以看電視嗎？	Can I watch TV?
17	請播放《Caillou》。	Please play *Caillou*.
18	等這個節目結束。	After this TV show.
19	我可以玩一會電腦遊戲嗎？	Can I play computer games for a little bit?
20	我可以去外面玩嗎？	Can I go play outside?
21	我可以去吉娜家玩嗎？	Can I go play at Jina's house?
22	媽咪，我想試試看。	I want to try it, Mommy!
23	敏基打我。	Minji hit me.
24	不是我的錯。	It was not my fault.

25	是他先開始的。	He started it.
26	不要生氣。	Don't get angry.
27	對不起。我不會再這樣了。	I'm sorry. It won't happen again.
28	我真的生氣了。	I'm really angry.
29	我不是在頂嘴。	I'm not talking back.
30	我很高興你誇獎我。	I'm glad you praised me.
31	你可以把牛奶拿給我嗎？拜託啦。	Can you get me milk, please?
32	我可以再要一些嗎？	Can I have some more?
33	我可以吃些冰淇淋嗎？	Can I have some ice cream?
34	我討厭蘑菇。	I hate mushrooms.
35	我沒心情吃飯。	I don't feel like eating.
36	我要尿尿。	I need to pee.
37	我要便便。	I need to poop.
38	媽，我好了。	I'm done, Mom.
39	我累了。	I'm tired.
40	我睏了。	I'm sleepy. / I'm tired.
41	我餓了。	I'm hungry / I'm starving.
42	我腿痛。	My legs hurt.
43	給我一個（大大的）擁抱。	Hold me (tight). / Give me a (big) hug.
44	背我。	Give me a piggy-back ride.
45	我可以休息一下嗎？	Can I take a break?
46	媽，等我。	Wait for me, Mom.
47	爸，你什麼時候回來？	Dad, when are you coming?
48	媽，可以讀個故事給我聽嗎？	Can you read me a story, Mom?
49	你愛誰多一點，我還是敏基？	Who do you love more, me or Minji?
50	在這個世界上，我最愛妳了。	I love you the most in the world.

Part 1 我們家的一天

Chapter 01

忙碌的早晨

Time to wake up!
起床的時間到了！

Can I sleep some more?
我可以再多睡一會嗎？

ch01-01.mp3

起床

該起床了！	Time to wake up! ★ It's time to 的簡略表達。
起床了，你這個貪睡鬼	Wake up, you sleepyhead! (Wake up：起床，醒來) ・sleepyhead 貪睡鬼
太陽都曬屁股了！	Rise and shine!
快點起床！該去學校／幼稚園了！	Get up, please! Time to go to school. (Get up：（從睡覺中）醒來) ★「幼稚園」也常被說成 school。
還在睡夢中嗎？	Still dreaming? ★ 句子的前面省略了Are you。

再不起床的話，我要搔癢了喔。 I'll tickle you if you don't wake up.

• tickle 癢，使發癢

你要早睡早起。 **You should go to bed early to get up early.**

還想睡嗎？ Want to sleep more?

★ 句子的前面省略了 Do you。

我可以多睡一會嗎？ **Can I sleep some more?**

我太累了，起不來。 I'm so tired that I can't get up.

• so 形容詞 that 主詞 + 動詞 因為太～，所以～

媽，我睜不開眼睛！ **Mom, I can't keep my eyes open!**

只能再睡五分鐘。 Just five more minutes.

我數到三。快點起床！ **I'll count to three. Come on!**

快點，否則你要遲到了。 Hurry up, or you will be late.

• 命令句, or 主詞 will 動詞 做～，不然的話，你將～

我醒了。 **I'm awake.**

你不用叫我也沒關係。我已經醒了。 You don't have to wake me up. I'm already up.

（don't have to：不做～也可以）

哇！你自己起床的嗎？ **Wow! Did you get up by yourself?**

• by oneself 自己，獨自

你沒有聽到鬧鐘響嗎？ Did you not hear the alarm?

• alarm 鬧鐘

不要打瞌睡。坐好。 **Don't doze off. Sit right up.**

（doze off：打瞌睡）

看看誰先起床了？ Let's see who gets up first.

你還在沉睡。 **You're still sound asleep.**

（sound asleep：睡得很沉（sound: 深深地，完全地））

伸展一下你的身體。 Stretch your body.

• stretch 伸懶腰，舒展（肢體）

以後我不會再叫你起床了。 I'm not going to wake you up anymore.

ch01-02.mp3

早晨打招呼

爸爸媽媽，早安！ Good morning, Mom and Dad!

你睡得好嗎？ Did you sleep well?

早！晚上睡得好嗎？ Hey! Did you get a good night's sleep?

寶貝，睡得好嗎？ Did you sleep tight, my sweetie?
睡得好 (sleep tight)
• sweetie 寶貝（對小孩的愛稱）

你睡懶覺了。 You slept in.
睡懶覺 (slept in)

晚上不冷吧？ Was it not chilly at night? • chilly 涼，冷

你已經醒了喔？為什麼這麼早起呢？ You're already awake? Why so early?

哇！太陽打西邊出來了。 Whoa! I've never seen this before!

我剛睜開眼睛。 My eyes just opened.

看起來你的心情很好。 Seems like you're in a good mood.
心情很好 (in a good mood)
★ 句子的前面省略了主詞 It。

睡個好覺後，你看起來心情很好。 You look happy after a good night's sleep.

為什麼今天早上你看起來心情不太好？ Why do you look grumpy this morning?
• grumpy 脾氣壞的

我還想睡覺。 I'm still sleepy.

起床後，你應該先打招呼。 You should say hello first thing in the morning.
早晨要先做的事 (first thing in the morning)

你應該說：「早安！」

You should say, "Good morning!"

親一下，說「早安」吧。

Let's kiss and say, "Good morning!"

你做了好夢嗎？

Did you have sweet dreams?

媽媽，要聽聽我做的夢嗎？

Mom, want to hear about my dreams?

你可以叫你弟弟起床嗎？

Can you wake up your brother?

ch01-03.mp3

洗臉

起床洗臉了喔。

Get up to wash your face.

★ 也可以說成 Get up and wash your face。

洗臉刷牙。

Wash your face and brush your teeth.

脖子也要洗喔。

Wash your neck, too.

誰要先洗？

Who wants to wash up first?

需要媽媽幫你嗎？

Want Mom to help you?

★ 句子的前面省略了 Do you。

媽媽，你可以幫我嗎？

Can you help me, Mom?

自己洗的話，我會弄濕衣服的。

If I do it by myself, I will get my clothes wet.

get ~ wet 弄濕～

• by oneself 自己

我不想洗臉！

I don't want to clean my face!

我要吃飯後再洗。

I'll wash myself after I eat.

都洗好了嗎？

Are you done? • be done 結束，完成

我正在洗，媽咪。

I'm working, Mommy.

拿一條乾淨的毛巾。 Get a clean towel.

媽，沒有毛巾。 **Mom, there's no towel.**

媽，可以拿條毛巾給我嗎？ Mom, can you get me a towel?

• get A B 拿 B 給 A

洗好後，你看起好美喔。 **You look pretty after cleaning.**

廁所的地板很滑，要小心喔。 Watch out (小心) for the slippery floor.

• slippery 滑

ch01-04.mp3

刷牙

一天要刷三次牙。 **You should brush your teeth three times a day.** (一天三次)

好好地刷牙。 Brush your teeth properly.

• properly 正確地，好好地

刷牙要上下刷。 **Brush up and down.** (上下)

不要忘記也要刷裡面。 Don't forget to brush deep inside. (裡面深處)

牙和牙床都要徹底地刷乾淨。 **Clean your teeth and gums thoroughly.**

• gum 牙床 • thoroughly 徹底地

不要忘記刷舌頭。 Don't forget to brush your tongue.

• tongue 舌頭

嗽口，然後吐掉。 **Gargle and spit.** • gargle 漱口 • spit 吐

牙刷上要沾點牙膏。 Put only a little toothpaste on your toothbrush. • toothpaste 牙膏 • toothbrush 牙刷

媽媽，幫我擠牙膏。 **Mom, squeeze the toothpaste for me.**

• squeeze 擠

我們沒有牙膏了。

We're out of toothpaste.

沒有～ (out of)

一定要刷三分鐘。

Brush for three minutes.

三分鐘到了嗎？

Has it been three minutes yet?

不要忘記關水。

Don't leave the water running.

• leave A -ing 使 A 保持～狀態

我討厭刷牙。

I hate brushing my teeth.

• hate -ing 討厭做～

媽媽，幫我刷牙。

Brush my teeth for me, Mom.

要好好刷牙，不然的話，
你的牙齒會變黑喔。

Brush your teeth well, or they will turn black.

如果你不好好照顧你的
牙齒的話，你會蛀牙。

If you don't take care of your teeth, you'll get cavities.

• cavity 蛀洞

不好好刷牙地話，會有口臭。

If you don't brush well, you'll have bad breath.

有口臭 (have bad breath)

不要用錯誤的方法刷牙。

Don't brush your teeth the wrong way.

ch01-05.mp3

吃早餐

該吃早餐了。

It's time for breakfast.

來吃早餐吧。

Come and eat your breakfast.

坐餐桌旁。

Sit at the table.

爸爸，來和我們一起吃早餐。

Dad, come and eat with us.

你可以也叫一下你弟弟嗎？

Can you call your brother, too?

誰可以幫媽媽擺餐桌？	Who wants to help me set the table? (set the table: 擺餐桌) ・help A 動詞　幫助 A 做～
你可以把湯匙擺在餐桌上嗎？	Can you put the spoons on the table?
吃飯前，先來禱告吧。	Let's say grace before we eat. (say grace: 吃飯前說感恩的話)
吃早餐吧。	Let's have breakfast.
味道如何？好吃嗎？	How is it? Isn't it good?
你不喜歡嗎？	Don't you like it? ★這句話比 taste bad（不好吃）更常使用。
沒胃口嗎？	Don't you feel like eating? ・feel like -ing　想做～
你為什麼不吃？	Why aren't you eating?
我不怎麼想吃。	I don't feel like eating much.
我在早上不要吃東西。	I can't eat in the morning.
吃早餐會讓你更健康。	Eating breakfast makes you strong.
再多吃一口。	Just take one more bite.　・bite　一口
先吃一口看看好不好吃。	Just try and see if it's good. (see if: 看看是否～)
要遲到了。快吃。	You'll be late. Hurry up and eat.
喝點水。	Let's drink some water.
不要讓牛奶灑出來。	Don't spill the milk.　・spill　溢出
我夾不到菜。	I can't reach that dish.　・reach　碰到～
飯太多了。	There is too much rice.
我來餵你。	I'll feed you.　・feed　餵
太燙了。	It's too hot.

吹一下，讓它冷一點。
Blow on your food to cool it off.
• cool off 使變冷

都吃完了嗎？
Are you finished?

不要再吃了。
Stop eating now.

我再也吃不下了。
I can't eat anymore.

我飽了。
I'm full. • full 飽

不可以剩一點嗎？
Can't I leave some?

可以不要全部吃完嗎？
Is it okay if I don't finish it all?

我幾乎都吃了。
I'm almost done eating.

看起來好好吃。謝謝！
Looks good. Thank you!

感謝你這麼好吃的一餐。
Thank you for the nice meal.
• meal 飯，一餐

食物相當好吃。謝謝。
The food was fabulous. Thanks.
• fabulous 極好的

ch01-06.mp3

用餐習慣和禮節

不要挑食。
Don't be picky with your food.
• picky 挑剔

吃飯的時候，不要走來走去。
Don't walk around while you eat.
• while ～的時候

食物不可以剩下。
Don't leave your food uneaten. • leave 留下

你要自己吃。
You should eat by yourself.

小心食物不要弄掉。
Be careful not to drop your food.

哎呀！你弄掉食物了。 Oops! You dropped your food.

沒關係。我來收拾。 **It's okay. I'll clean it.**

慢慢吃。不要急。 Eat slowly and don't rush. ・rush 急

好好咀嚼。 **Chew well.** ・chew 咀嚼

正確使用筷子。 Use your chopsticks right. ・chopsticks 筷子

不要把食物吐出來。 **Don't spit out the food.** 吐出來

要坐在餐桌吃飯。 Sit down and eat at the table.

好好坐在餐桌旁。 **Sit properly at the table.**
・properly 恰當地，正確地

嘴巴內有東西時，不要說話。 Don't talk with your mouth full.
・with one's mouth full 嘴巴內塞滿食物

把碗放在洗碗槽內。 **Put your bowl in the sink.**
・bowl 碗 ・sink 洗碗槽

來幫媽媽收拾餐桌吧。 Help me clean up the table.

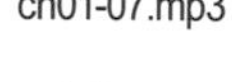
ch01-07.mp3

上廁所

我要去尿尿。 **I have to pee.** ・pee 小便，尿尿

我要去便便。 I have to poop. ・poop 便便

我快要大出來了。 **I'm about to poop.** ・be about to 正要做～

先把你的褲子脫下來。 Take off your pants first. 脫下

不要忘記沖水。 **Don't forget to flush.** ・flush（馬桶）沖水

不要用太多的衛生紙。 Don't use too much toilet paper. 衛生紙

唷！好臭喔！	**Phew! It stinks!** ‧stink 發出惡臭，充滿惡臭
如果你要尿尿的話，要告訴我。	Tell me if you have to pee.
尿不出來嗎？	**Is it not coming out?**
不要忍。去尿。	Don't hold it. Go pee. ‧hold 忍
憋尿是不好的。	**It's not good to hold your pee.** (It's not good to：做～是不好的)
 我討厭坐馬桶。	I don't want to sit on the toilet. ‧toilet 馬桶
 你可以自己尿尿嗎？	**Can you pee by yourself?**
便便後，要洗手。	Wash your hands after you poop.
水沖一次就好。	**Flush the toilet only once.**
好了叫我喔。	Call me when you're done.
 媽，我好了。	**I'm done, Mom.**
你可以幫我擦屁股嗎？	Can you wipe my bottom? ‧wipe 擦 ‧bottom 屁股，臀部
我一直要放屁。捏住你的鼻子。	**I keep farting. Hold your nose.** ‧fart 放屁 ‧hold 捏
 噁，誰放屁了？	Ugh, who cut the cheese? (cut the cheese：放屁)
放屁在我臉上的話， 我會抓住你。	**Fart in my face, and I'll get you!** ‧get（為了懲罰）抓
你尿在褲子上了嗎？	Did you pee in your pants?
看起來你很急。	**It looks like you were in a rush.** (in a rush：急)
你肚子痛嗎？	Does your tummy ache? ‧tummy 肚子 ‧ache 痛
下次，不可以忍到尿在褲子上。	**Don't hold it till you have to pee in your pants next time.**

ch01-08.mp3

爸爸去上班

爸爸要去上班了。	Daddy is going to work.
爸爸要出門了，說再見。	Daddy is leaving. Say goodbye.
說再見，甜心。	Say bye-bye, Sweetie.

爸爸，祝你有美好的一天。	Have a good day, Dad!
爸爸，祝你好運。	Good luck, Dad!

親一下爸爸。	Give Daddy a kiss. ・give a kiss 給一個吻
寶貝，要幫爸爸擦皮鞋嗎？	Honey, want to polish Dad's shoes? ・polish one's shoes 擦皮鞋

爸爸，我幫你拿鞋子。	Let me get your shoes ready, Dad. ・get A ready 把 A 準備好

晚的話，打個電話回來。	Call us if you're going to be late.
你要跟同事去聚餐嗎？	Are you eating out with your coworkers? ・coworker 同事　(eating out：在外用餐)

早點回來。	Come home early.
不要太晚，爸爸。	Don't be too late, Dad.
你什麼時候回來？	When are you coming back?
我想跟爸爸一起出門！	I want to go with you, Dad!
早點回來跟我玩。	Come home early to play with me.
不要喝酒，早點回家。	Don't drink and come home early.
爸爸，一會見！	See you later, Dad!

回來時，要買好吃的給我。 Bring me some goodies when you get back.
・goodies 好吃的東西
get back — 回來

爸爸，你看起來很帥！ Dad, you look great!
look great — 看起來很帥

甜心，今天也玩得開心。 Have fun all day, Sweetie.
Have fun — 玩得開心

爸爸要去上班了。 Dad will go to work.

當我在上班時，我會想你的。 I'll miss you while I work.

午餐時，我會打電話給你。 Dad will call you at lunch hour.

我可以買什麼好東西給你呢？ Shall I bring you something good?

跟媽媽好好玩。 Have fun with Mommy.

下班後，我會盡可能早回家。 I'll come back from work as fast as I can.
as fast as I can — 盡可能早點～

ch01-09.mp3

挑衣服

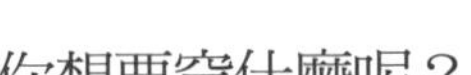
你想要穿什麼呢？ What do you want to wear?

挑一件你想穿的吧。 Choose what you want to wear.
・what 主詞 + 動詞 做～

今天我要穿裙子。 I want to wear a skirt today.

今天你需要穿什麼？ What do you need to wear today?

今天，你需要穿學校制服。 Today, you need to wear your school uniform.

今天，你需要穿體育服。 Today, you need to wear your PE clothes.
★ 美國的小學沒有體育服。 體育（= physical education）

給我運動服。 Get me my gym clothes.

這個天氣不適合穿短褲。 Shorts are not good for this weather.

天氣很冷，你應該穿外套。 It's chilly, so you should wear a jacket.

我討厭穿那些衣服。 I don't want to wear those clothes.

我討厭穿這件襯衫，給我另一件。 I don't want to wear this shirt. Give me another one.

明天，我也要穿這件外套。 I will wear this coat tomorrow, too.

這條褲子你什麼時候買的？ When did you buy these pants?

這件夾克太女孩子氣／男孩子氣了。 This jacket is too girlish / boyish.

• -ish 像～

這件襯衫很不舒服。 I don't feel comfy in this shirt.

• comfy 舒服（comfortable 的兒童用語）

這件太薄了。 This is too thin.

外面非常冷。 It's very chilly out there.

這條褲子跟那件襯衫不搭。 The pants don't match the shirt.

• match 跟～很搭

這件襯衫要洗了，拿其他的吧。 We need to wash this shirt. Get another one.

那件還沒乾，等明天再穿。 It's not fully dry yet. Wear it tomorrow.

那件連衣裙穿在我們公主身上，太好看了。 That dress looks perfect on my princess!

ch01-10.mp3

穿衣服

讓我們來換衣服吧。 Let's get changed.

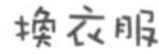

你可以自己穿衣服嗎？	Can you get dressed by yourself? 穿衣服
你需要媽媽幫忙嗎？	Do you want Mom to help you?
把袖子摺起來。	Fold your sleeves. ・fold 摺疊 ・sleeve 袖子
戴上帽子。	Put on your hat. 穿，戴
你的襪子不是同一雙。	Your socks don't match. ・match 一致，相配
你的另一隻襪子在哪？	Where is your other sock?
拉上褲子的拉鍊。	Let's zip up your pants. 拉上～拉鍊
扣好你的襯衫鈕扣。	Let's button your shirt. ・button 扣鈕扣
你的鈕扣扣錯了。	You buttoned your shirt wrong.
你的襯衫穿反了。	You put on your shirt inside out. 裡面反出來
脫掉你的內衣。	Take off your underclothes.
我們換新的內衣吧。	Let's change into some new underwear.

衣服的種類

- 襯衫 shirt
- 運動衫 sweatshirt
- 帽衣 hoodie
- 休閒褲 slacks
- 裙子 skirt
- 寬鬆大衣 trench coat
- 內衣 underwear
- T恤 T-shirt
- 套衫 pullover
- 褲子 pants
- 短褲 shorts
- 連衣裙 dress
- 運動服 gym clothes
- 制服 uniform
- 外套，夾克 jacket
- 無袖上衣 tank top
- 牛仔褲 jeans
- 工作褲 overalls
- 外套 coat
- 睡衣 pajamas

你可以幫我穿上這件嗎？　Can you help me put this on?

你可以幫我解開襯衫的扣子嗎？　Can you unbutton my shirt?
• unbutton 解鈕扣

你可以幫我拉開拉鍊嗎？　Can you unzip me?　• unzip 拉開拉鍊

這太小／大件了。　This is too small / large.

這件褲子現在太小了。　These pants are too small now.

你長大了，這些衣服都不能穿了。　You have outgrown these clothes.
• outgrow 長大後，衣服不能穿

媽，我看起來好看嗎？　Do I look good, Mom?

ch01-11.mp3

自己穿衣服

去換衣服。　Change your clothes.

我要穿哪一件？　What should I wear?

在你的衣櫃裡找找。　Look in your closet.　• closet 壁櫥；衣櫃

換上舒服一點的衣服。　Change into some comfortable clothes.
• comfortable 舒服

換上乾淨的衣服。　Change into some clean clothes.

穿你想穿的衣服。　Wear what you want to wear.

換上居家服。　Change into what you wear at home.

我可以穿這件嗎？　Can I wear this?

不會太熱嗎？穿其他件。　Isn't that too hot? Wear something else.

我只要穿這些衣服。　I'll just stay in these clothes.

那件髒了，要換掉。 That's dirty. Change now.

把髒衣服放進洗衣籃內。 Put your dirty clothes in the laundry basket.

內衣也要換。 Change your underwear, too.

換上準備好的衣服。 Put on the clothes that are ready.

媽媽，我要穿的衣服在哪？ Mom, where are the clothes ready to wear?

你不穿衣服，還在做什麼？ What are you doing not getting dressed?

你自己可以穿衣服了。現在你是大男孩／女孩了。 You got dressed by yourself. Now you're a big boy / girl.

ch01-12.mp3

梳頭髮

我們來梳頭髮吧。 Let's comb your hair. ·comb 梳頭髮

我會把你的頭髮綁得很漂亮。 I will tie your hair pretty. ·tie 綁

你要綁成馬尾？還是辮子？ Do you want it tied in a ponytail or pigtails? ·ponytail 馬尾 ·pigtails 辮子

讓我來幫你把頭髮分邊。 Let me part your hair.

不要動。 Don't move.

你的頭髮長很多了。 Your hair has grown a lot.

你的頭髮很蓬鬆。 Your hair is fluffy. ·fluffy 蓬鬆，毛茸茸

你需要去美容院剪頭髮。 You need a haircut at a beauty shop. 美容院

你要別個髮夾嗎？ Do you want a hairpin?

你要綁髮帶嗎？ Do you want a hairband?

你想要綁哪一個髮帶？	**Which hairband do you want?**
你的頭髮都打結了，我梳不開。	Your hair is tangled up, so I can't comb it. 打結
輕輕地幫我梳頭髮。	**Brush my hair softly.** ·brush（用梳子）梳頭
媽媽，好痛！	Mom, that hurts!
要我幫你綁辮子嗎？	**Want me to braid your hair?** ·braid 綁辮子
我來把你的頭髮梳起來。	Let me put your hair up.
你能把髮夾拿給我嗎？	**Can you hand me the hairpin?** ·hand 拿給
請把梳子拿給我。	Please bring me the comb.
你能幫我綁頭髮嗎？	**Can you tie my hair?**
你能幫我剪掉瀏海嗎？我的頭髮戳到眼睛了。	Can you cut my bangs? My hair is poking me in my eyes. ·bangs 瀏海 ·poke 戳
可以幫我綁跟昨天一樣的嗎？	**Can you tie my hair like you did yesterday?**
我不喜歡這個髮型。	I don't like this hairstyle.
請幫我重新綁，好嗎？	**Can you tie it again, please?**
今天，我要把頭髮放下來。	I want to untie my hair today. ·untie 解開
請把我的頭髮綁成馬尾。	**Tie my hair in a ponytail.**
請把我的頭髮綁成辮子。	Tie my hair in pigtails.
請不要綁太緊。	**Don't tie it too hard.**
你要把瀏海留長嗎？	Do you want your bangs to grow?

ch01-13.mp3

準備學校用品

今天的學校用品是什麼？ What are your supplies for school today?
• supplies 用品（school supplies 的簡稱）

你整理好書包了嗎？ Did you pack your bag?

教科書放進去了嗎？ Did you get your books?

作業放進去了嗎？ Did you get your homework?

便當和水瓶都準備好了嗎？ Do you have your lunchbox and water bottle?

室內鞋準備好了嗎？ Do you have your indoor shoes?
★ 美國的教室並沒有使用室內鞋。

啊，我忘了。 Oops, I forgot. • oops 〈感嘆詞〉啊，咦

我忘記我要帶什麼了。 I can't remember what I should bring.

我應該要帶美術用具。 I should bring some art supplies.

這份考卷需要簽名。 I need to get this paper signed.

我都準備好了。 I got everything ready.

老師叫你要帶什麼呢？ What did your teacher ask you to bring?

今天有美術課嗎？ Do you have art class today?

你應該事先準備好學校用品。 You should have your supplies prepared in advance. 事先
• have A prepared 準備好 A.

從明天開始，要事先準備。 Starting tomorrow, have it ready beforehand. • beforehand 事先

你準備好了嗎？ Are you ready?

確認你有沒有都帶了。	Make sure you have everything.
我忘記裝你的便當了。	I forgot to pack your lunchbox.
你還需要其他的嗎？	Do you need anything else? 其他東西
哇，你都準備好了。很棒！	Wow, you got it ready. Good job!
 今天沒有作業／學校用品。	I have no homework / supplies today.
我不知道要帶什麼去學校。	I don't know what to bring to school.
我們老師從不跟我們說任何事。	My teacher never told us anything.
媽，我的學校用品在哪？	Where are my supplies, Mom?
我以為我已經把它們放進你書包了。	I thought I put them in your backpack. • backpack 書包（也可以叫做 bookbag）
準備學校用品是你自己的事情。	It's your job to get your supplies.
去學校時順道去一下文具店。	You should stop by the stationery store on your way to school. stop by 順道進去；stationery store 文具店

美國小學的學校用品

在美國，學期初的時候就會分發需要的學校用品目錄，並且可以把學校用品放在個人的儲藏櫃內，因此在學期中就不需要每天帶學校用品來上學。特別活動時，如果需要特別用品，老師會用信件通知爸媽要讓孩子們帶什麼來學校。

ch01-14.mp3

催促 ch01-14.mp3

快點，寶貝！	**Hurry up, Honey!**
媽媽在等喔。	Mom's waiting.
你要遲到了。	**You'll be late.**

我們還有時間，媽咪。	We still have time, Mommy.

如果你不快點的話，你上學就會遲到。	**You'll be late for school if you don't hurry.**
一天都要結束了。	The day will be over soon. ‧over 結束
喔，不，太晚了。	**Oh, no! It's too late.**
你會錯過校車的。	You're going to miss the school bus. ‧miss 錯過

你能開車送我去嗎？	**Can you give me a ride?** ‧give a ride 開車接送

看一下時鐘，你能告訴我幾點了嗎？	Look at the clock. Can't you tell the time? （tell the time：判讀時鐘顯示的時間）
你知道你晚了多久了嗎？	**Do you know how late you are?**
五分鐘把它完成。	Finish in five minutes.

現在幾點了？	**What time is it now?**
我正在盡全力。	I'm doing my best. ‧do one's best 盡全力
不好意思，我會快點。	**I'm sorry. I'll speed up.** （speed up：加速）

我不等你了。	I'm not waiting for you any longer.
我要先走了。	**I'm leaving before you.**
如果你一直遲到的話，	If you keep on being late, it will be

這個習慣將很難改掉。 **a hard habit to break.** ‧keep on -ing 持續~

媽媽在外面等你。 I'll be outside waiting for you.

我數到三之前要完成。 **Finish before I count to three.** ‧count 數數

現在我們一定要出發了。 We need to leave now.

你的時間已經不夠了。 **You don't have enough time.** ‧enough 足夠

時間飛快過去了。 Time is ticking away.（ticking away：時間飛快流逝）

為什麼每天早上都要這樣混亂？ **Why should this happen every morning?**
‧happen 發生

對不起，不會再這樣了。 Sorry. It won't happen again.

ch01-15.mp3

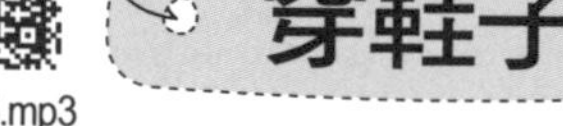

穿鞋子

穿上你的鞋子。 **Put on your shoes.**

背好背包，穿好鞋子。 Get your bag and put on your shoes.

換上運動鞋。 **Change your shoes to sneakers.**
‧sneakers 運動鞋

你的鞋子穿錯腳了。 Your shoes are on the wrong feet.

鞋子交換穿一下。 **Switch shoes.** ‧switch 交換

不要踩到鞋後跟。 Don't step on the back of your shoes.（step on：踩~）

如果你要跑步的話，你需要穿運動鞋。 **You need your sneakers if you want to run.**

你的鞋子現在舊了。 Your shoes are old now.

這雙鞋子又舊又破。 **These shoes are old and torn.** ‧torn 破的

我還是很喜歡這雙鞋子。不要丟掉它們。 I still love these shoes. Don't throw them away. ·throw away 丟掉

媽媽，我的鞋帶鬆開了。 **My shoelaces are untied, Mom.**
·shoelaces 鞋帶 ·untied 鬆開

我的鞋帶一直鬆開。 My shoelaces won't stay tied. ·tied 綁著的

你能幫我綁鞋帶嗎？ **Can you tie my shoes?**

我喜歡魔鬼氈鞋。 I like Velcro shoes.
·Velcro 魔鬼氈（一種尼龍刺黏扣，兩面一碰即黏合。）

那雙鞋子跟你的衣服不搭。 **Those shoes don't match your clothes.**

把鞋子放在該放的位置上。 Put your shoes in the right place.

把鞋子放在鞋架上。 **Put your shoes on the shoe rack.** 鞋架

它們應該放在鞋架上。 They must be on the shoe rack.

你鞋子的大小是 130 公釐。 **Your shoe size is 130mm.**

鞋子合腳嗎？ Do the shoes fit? ·fit（大小）合適

鞋子太大／小？ **Are they not too big / small?**

你已經長到鞋子穿不下了。 You've outgrown your shoes.

鞋子的種類

- 皮鞋 dress shoes
- 涼鞋 sandals
- 靴子 boots
- 運動鞋 sneakers, sports shoes
- 拖鞋 slippers, flip-flops
- 有跟的女鞋 pumps

讓我買雙新的給你吧。 Let me buy you a new pair.
（Let me：讓我～）

新鞋讓我的腳好痛。 These new shoes hurt my feet.

我要穿我的皮鞋。 I want to wear my dress shoes.
（dress shoes：皮鞋）

媽媽，我要穿哪雙鞋？ What shoes should I wear, Mom?

它們都好髒喔，要洗一洗了。 They are very dirty. They need to be washed.

ch01-16.mp3

上學前的打招呼

祝你有個美好的一天。 Have a good day.

祝你渡過美好的時光。 Have a good time.

跟朋友們好好玩喔。 Have fun with your friends.

一整天都要快樂喔。 Be happy all day long.
（all day long：一整天）

要禮貌地鞠躬打招呼，寶貝。 Bow your head politely, Honey.

• bow one's head 低頭，鞠躬 • politely 禮貌地

你應該說再見。 You should say goodbye.

你不該跟爸爸說再見嗎？ Shouldn't you say bye to Dad?

親一下，寶貝。 Give me a kiss, Honey.

你沒有忘了什麼嗎？（意思是要親我一下） Didn't you forget something?

再見，我走了。 Goodbye! I'm leaving.

在學校好好用功。 Study hard at school.

好好待在學校，要聽話！ Be good at school. Behave!

★ 比起說「要好好用功」，美國的媽媽更常說的是這句話。

放學後，打電話給我。 Call me after school. / Call me after you're done. ‧be done 結束，完成

等一下下午見。 I'll see you later in the afternoon.

放學後，立刻回家。 Come home right after school. （right after ～之後，馬上）

我會準備好吃的點心等你。 I'll be waiting with a tasty snack ready.

‧tasty 好吃的 ‧snack 點心

我回來時，你會在家嗎？ Will you be home when I come back?

等一下開車來接我。 Come pick me up later. ‧pick up 開車去接～

我會去接你。 I'll go pick you up. （go pick = go and pick）

ch01-17.mp3

媽媽的叮嚀

要小心車。 Watch out for cars. （Watch out for 小心～）

不要走到車道上。 Don't walk on the road.

穿越馬路一定要走在斑馬線上。 Always cross at crosswalks.

‧cross 穿越，橫越 ‧crosswalk 行人穿越道，斑馬線

你過馬路時，要小心。 Be careful when you cross the street.

走路時，要注意看旁邊。 Look sideways while you are walking.

‧sideways 旁邊

要看紅綠燈。 Watch for the traffic lights. （traffic lights 紅綠燈）

確定是綠燈時，你才能走。 Make sure you walk when the light is green. （Make sure 確定，確認）

過馬路上，要舉起你的手。	Raise your hand when you cross the street. ・raise one's hand 舉手
不要在路上玩你的手機。	Don't play with your cell phone on the street. (cell phone：手機)
不要跑，慢慢走。	Don't run. Walk slowly.
不要趕。	Don't rush.
直接去學校。	Go straight to school. (Go straight：直接)
絕對不可以跟陌生人走。	Don't ever follow strangers. ・follow 跟
要走在大馬路上。	Go along the broad street. ・broad 寬的
不可以走到狹窄的巷弄。	Don't go down the narrow back street. (back street：小路) ・narrow 狹窄的
要聽老師的話。	Listen to your teacher.
如果你要去廁所，你要跟老師說一聲。	Ask your teacher if you want to go to the bathroom.
要跟朋友們好好相處。	Be nice to your friends.
在學校時要關掉手機。	Turn off your cell phone at school. (Turn off：（電源）關掉)
午餐要吃飽。	Eat plenty for lunch. ・plenty 充分地
不要在遊戲機前停留，走過去就好。	Don't stop at the game machine. Just pass by it. (pass by：經過)
當有惡霸時，你應該怎麼做？	What should you do when there is a bully? ・bully 惡霸
如果你看到有人被欺負，要立刻告訴我。	If you meet a bully, tell me at once. (at once：馬上，立刻)

ch01-18.mp3

使用電梯／樓梯

去按一下電梯。	Go and call the elevator. ★ 按下按鈕後，等待的這個過程用 call 來表達。

電梯上來／下來了。	The elevator is going up / down.
我來按按鈕。	Let me push the button. ・push 按
電梯來了。	The elevator is here.

按鈕讓電梯停住。	Hold the elevator.
進電梯吧。	Let's get on the elevator. (get on 坐上～)
等到所有人出來。	Wait until everyone gets off. (gets off 出來)
你能按一下一樓嗎？	Can you press the first floor? ・press 按 ・floor 樓
我們應該要按哪一樓呢？	What floor should we press?
按一下開門／關門鈕。	Press the open / close button.
在裡面請安靜。	Be calm inside here. ・calm 平靜，沉默
不要靠在電梯門上。	Don't lean on the elevator door. (lean on 靠～)
不要在電梯內搗蛋。	Don't goof around in the elevator.
不要在電梯內跳來跳去。	Don't jump inside the elevator.
小心！你會被門夾住的。	Be careful! You might get stuck in the door. (get stuck 夾住，不能動)

這台電梯太慢了。	This elevator moves too slowly.
哇，好快喔。	Wow, it's moving fast.
你要去幾樓？	What floor are you going to?

我們出去吧。 **Let's get out.** ★ 也經常使用 get off。

當電梯門完全打開後，再出去。 Get off when the elevator is completely open. ‧completely 完全地

出去時要小心。 **Be careful when you get off.**

出去之前，要看一下是幾樓。 Always look at what floor you're leaving.

我們走樓梯吧。 **Let's take the stairs.** ‧stairs 樓梯

我們比賽誰先到一樓吧。 Let's have a race to the first floor. (have a race 比賽)

絕對不可以在樓梯上跑。 **Don't ever run on the stairs.**

不要握住欄杆不放。 Don't hang on the handrail. (hang on 握住不放) ‧handrail 欄杆

一次走一個階梯。 **Go down one step at a time.** (at a time 一次) ‧step 一個階梯

不可以在樓梯搗蛋，你會受傷的。 Don't goof around on the steps. You might get hurt. (goof around 搗蛋；get hurt 受傷)

ch01-19.mp3

搭校車

公車要來的時間到了。 **It's about time for the bus.**

校車馬上就要來了，快點！ Your school bus will be here very soon. Let's hurry!

我喜歡搭校車。 **I like riding on the school bus.** ‧ride 搭

去好好排隊等公車。 Go line up nicely for the bus. (line up 排隊)

我們來早了。一個人也沒有耶。 **We're early. No one's here yet.**

已經有很多小朋友在排隊了。	There are a lot of kids already waiting in line. 排隊等待
下次我們再快點吧。	**Let's hurry up the next time.**
今天公車提早／晚到了。	The bus is early / late today.
我們再多等一會。	**Let's wait a little longer.** 更久一點
馬上就會來了。	It will be here soon.
公車準時來了。	**The bus came on time.** 準時，按時
喔，公車已經來了。	Oh, the bus is already here.
我會排在第一個。	**I'll be the first in line.**
公車來了。	There's the bus. / I see the bus coming.
要等公車停好喔。	**Wait until the bus has stopped.**
跟老師問好。	Say hello to the teacher.
好，現在讓我們上公車吧。	**Okay, let's get on the bus now.** 搭上～
按順序一個一個上公車。	Get on the bus one after another. / Get on the bus one by one. 一個接一個
上下公車都要很小心。	**Be careful when you get on and off the bus.**
不要插隊。	Don't cut in line. 插隊
不要推擠，慢慢上車。	**Don't push. Get on slowly.**
今天媽媽會送你去學校。	Mommy will take you to school today. • take 接送
繫好安全帶。	**Fasten your seatbelt.** • fasten 繫上 • seatbelt 安全帶
準備下車了。	Get ready to get off.

Chapter 02

做家事

I want to try, Mom.
媽，我想試試看。

Let's clean up.
我們來打掃吧！

ch02-01.mp3

用吸塵器

該是打掃的時間了。 It's time to clean up.

打掃，整理

你能幫媽媽嗎？ Can you help Mommy?

你想用吸塵器嗎？ Will you try to use the vacuum?

• vacuum (cleaner) 吸塵器

試試看，這很好玩喔。 Try it. It's fun.

媽咪，我想試試看。 I want to try, Mommy!

我會一直幫你打掃。 I'll help you clean all the time. 一直

打開窗戶讓新鮮空氣進來。 Open the window and let the fresh air in. • let A in 使 A 進來 新鮮的空氣

打開窗戶時，要小心喔。 Be careful when you open the window.

你能把這個搬開一點嗎？ Can you move a little bit?

你能移開你的玩具，讓我用一下吸塵器嗎？ Can you move your toys so I can vacuum? • toy 玩具 • vacuum 用吸塵器吸

你必須把地板上的東西移開。 You need to move the stuff on the floor. • stuff 東西

讓我們把鞋子放整齊。 Let's tidy up the shoes. 整理整齊（= organize）

我只是要拍掉灰塵。 I just want to get the dust off. • dust 灰塵

吸塵器很重吧？拿給媽媽吧。 Isn't the vacuum heavy? Give it to Mommy.

我要整理我的房間。 I want to clean up my room.

看！有很多頭髮。 Look! Lots of hair.

咦，好噁心！ Ew, gross! • gross 噁心

你要休息一下嗎？ Want to take a little break? 休息一下

打掃後，變得好乾淨。 It's clean after we clean up.

親愛的，因為有你幫忙，打掃提前結束了。 We finished early because of you, my darling.

你們都長大了，可以幫媽媽打掃房子了。 You're all grown up helping Mommy clean the house. 長大，變成大人

你不累嗎？ Aren't you tired?

ch02-02.mp3

掃地／擦地板

我們來擦地板吧。	**Let's wipe the floor.** •wipe 用布擦拭
今天我要掃地。	I'm going to sweep the floor today. •sweep 用掃把掃
我們要用抹布擦房間。	**We're going to wipe the room with a rag.** •rag 抹布
先掃之後再擦。	I wipe after sweeping.
我們在擦地之前，要先用吸塵器吸過。	**We need to use the vacuum before we wipe the floor.**
你能幫我打掃房間嗎？	Can you help me clean the room?
你能幫我拿抹布嗎？	**Can you get me the rag?**
把抹布翻過來，然後清潔地板。	Turn it over and clean the floor. •turn over 翻過來
哎呀，這抹布好髒喔。	**Ugh, the rag's too dirty.**
我們要洗一下抹布。	We need to wash the rag.
打掃每個地方，並讓每個東西都乾淨整潔。	**Clean everywhere and make everything nice and neat.**
用全力去擦。	Clean with all your strength. •with all one's strength 使上全部的力量
看起來你打掃得很漫不經心。	**It looks like you're cleaning carelessly.** •carelessly 漫不經心
媽媽，這邊還沒有打掃。	Mom, this isn't all clean yet.
我想這應該讓爸爸做吧。	**I think Daddy should do it.**

快點擦，把抹布給我。 Clean quickly and get me the rag.

擦地很累人，對吧？ Wiping the floor is tiring, isn't it?
• tiring 累人的

跪完之後，我的膝蓋好痛喔。 My knees hurt after kneeling down.
• knees 膝蓋 • kneel down 跪下

用拖把代替抹布吧。 Use the mop instead of a rag.
• mop 拖把
instead of 代替

ch02-03.mp3

整理玩具

地板上的玩具很凌亂。 The toys on the floor are a mess.
• mess 混亂，凌亂的狀態

是誰弄得這麼亂的？ Who made such a mess?
such a 這麼，很

為什麼這麼亂？ Why is there such a mess?

玩完之後，你應該整理的。 You should clean up after you play.

當你不玩時，你應該對你的玩具做什麼呢？ What should you do with your toys when you finish playing with them?
• finish -ing 完成～

去收好你的玩具，媽媽才能打掃房間。 Go put away your toys so Mommy can clean the room.
put away 將東西放回原位

我正打算要整理。 I was just about to clean that up.
• be about to 正打算做～

我可以再玩一會嗎？ Can I play a bit longer?

我等一下會整理。 I'll clean up after a little while.

我不想整理，就這樣放著吧。拜託啦。 | I don't want to clean it up. Just leave it there, please. •leave 放著

你能自己整理嗎？ | **Can you clean up by yourself?**

收拾積木和其他玩具。 | Pick up the blocks and the other toys. (撿起，收拾)

請把地板上的玩具收拾一下。 | **Please pick up your toys from the floor.**

你應該把書放在書架上。 | You should put the books back on the shelves. •(book)shelf 書架 cf. 複數形 (book)shelves

把那個放在玩具箱內。 | **Put it in the toy box.**

把那個放回原位。 | Put it back where it was.

這些玩具應該放哪裡呢？ | **Where should these toys go?**

你應該收拾自己的玩具。 | You should put away your own toys.

哇！你收拾得好好喔。 | **Wow! You cleaned up so nicely.**

因為你都收拾好了，你應該得到一張貼紙。 | You deserve a sticker for cleaning up. •deserve 應得到～

媽媽很高興你幫了我。 | **Mommy feels so happy because you're helping me.**

這些玩具想回到它們的家。 | The toys want to go back to their home.

還在地板上的這個玩具，我可以丟掉嗎？ | **Can I get rid of this since it's still on the floor?** (丟掉～)

呃，我們什麼時候把這些都收拾乾淨？ | Ugh, when are we going to clean up all of this?

現在我可以把這個玩具給其他小朋友嗎？ | **Should we give away the toys to other babies now?** (給，捐)

不要把他們送走，我會收拾的。 | Don't give them away. I'll clean them up.

ch02-04.mp3

打掃房間及整理書桌

請把房間清乾淨。	Please clean up your room.
請把書桌清乾淨。	Please clear off your desk.
書架已經亂得不像樣了。	The bookshelves are all messed up.
請把垃圾桶清空。	Please empty the trash can. ‧empty 倒空
你的床太髒亂了。	Your bed is so messy. ‧messy 髒亂的，混亂的

我要自己清我的書桌。	I want to clean my desk by myself.
媽，請幫我打掃房間。	Please clean up my room for me, Mom.
不好意思，我現在馬上打掃。	I'm sorry. I'll clean it up right away.
這太髒亂了，我一個人沒辦法打掃。	It is so messy that I can't clean it by myself.
下次，我不會再弄得這樣髒亂了。	I won't mess it up the next time. ‧mess up 弄髒亂

ch02-05.mp3

洗碗

媽媽在洗碗。	Mommy is doing the dishes. —洗碗
我們應該去洗碗。	We should do the dishes.
今天有很多碗要洗。	There are a lot of dishes today.
你能清理餐桌嗎？	Can you clear the table?
你能去擦餐桌嗎？	Can you wipe the table?

把碗盤放在洗碗槽內。 Put the dishes in the sink.

請把你自己用的碗拿走。 Please put away the dishes you used.

請把碗從餐桌上拿走。 Please put away the dishes from the table.

你能幫我洗碗嗎？ Can you help me do the dishes?

今天誰要洗碗呢？ Who will do the dishes today?

我今天可以洗碗嗎？ Can I do the dishes today?

我想試試洗碗。 I want to try doing the dishes.
• try -ing 試試做～

海綿／洗碗精在哪裡？ Where is the sponge / liquid soap? (液體肥皂，洗潔精)

以後，碗都由我來洗。 Let me do the dishes from now on. (從今以後)

現在你能幫我洗碗，真的長大了。 You're a big boy / girl now helping me do the dishes.

等你再大一點後，再做吧。 You can do that when you are older.

戴上橡膠手套，再把洗碗精擠在海棉上。 Put on the rubber gloves (橡膠手套) and put some liquid soap on the sponge.

要小心洗碗，不要把碗打破了。 Wash the dishes carefully so they won't break. • break 打破

仔細清洗，就不會有食物殘渣。 Wash them carefully so there is no food left.

碗乾淨得閃閃發光。 They are sparkling clean. • sparkling 閃閃發光的

要把水龍頭關好。 Turn off the water.

上面還有些泡泡，很滑喔。 There is still some soap on it. It's slippery.
• slippery 滑的

油垢很難洗掉。 Oily residue is hard to get off.
• residue 殘留物，殘渣 get off 弄掉

用熱水把油垢洗掉。 Use hot water to wash off the grease.
• grease 油垢 wash off 洗掉

請把濕的碗倒過來放在架子上。 Place the dripping bowls upside down on the rack.
• dripping 濕淋淋的 upside down 顛倒

用洗碗的毛巾把盤子擦乾。 Dry the plates with a dish towel.

有很多碗要洗，那讓我們用洗碗機吧。 We've got a lot to clean, so let's use the dishwasher.
• dishwasher 洗碗機

把碗放進洗碗機。 Load the dishes in the dishwasher.
• load （將衣服，碗等）放入機器內

把洗潔劑放進這裡。 The detergent should go in here.
★ 洗碗機的「洗潔劑」叫做 detergent，「廚房的洗碗精」叫做 liquid soap。

好，把門關起來，然後按下按鈕。 Okay, close the door and push this button.

ch02-06.mp3

洗衣服

我要去用洗衣機了。 I'm going to use the washing machine.

我要去洗衣服了。 I'm going to do the laundry.

把要洗的衣服放進洗衣機內。 Let's put the laundry in the machine.

把襪子都放一起。 Get the socks all together.
• get A together 把 A 放一起

有顏色的衣服放這裡，白色的衣服放那裡。 Put the colored clothes here and the whites over there.
• colored 有顏色的

這條褲子也要洗嗎？
Should these pants be washed?

啊！爸爸的襪子好臭！
Gosh! Dad's socks smell bad!
‧Gosh〈感嘆詞〉啊，糟了

媽媽，你能洗這件襯衫嗎？
Mom, can you wash this shirt?

這件襯衫沾上汙漬了。
There are stains on the shirt. ‧stain 汙漬

我們來燙白衣服和毛巾吧。
We're going to boil the whites and towels. ‧boil 水煮，將水加熱燙物品

有好多衣服要洗。
There is a lot of laundry to do.

放洗衣粉。
Put in the detergent.

這個我會用手洗。
I'll hand-wash this.

不要把那些衣服放進洗衣機。
Don't put those clothes in the machine.

那些衣服必須乾洗。
We have to dry-clean those clothes.
‧dry-clean 乾洗

衣服洗好了。
The laundry is done.

洗衣服結束！
Laundry's done!

ch02-07.mp3

晾衣服

我們把衣服晾在晾衣架上吧。
Let's hang the clothes on the rack.
‧hang 晾，掛 ‧(drying) rack 晾衣架

你能幫我晾這些衣服嗎？
Will you help me hang the clothes?

試著自己晾晾看你的衣服。
Try hanging your clothes by yourself.

我想要晾襪子。
I want to hang the socks.

晾在晾衣架上。
Put it on the drying rack.

這是誰的襪子？
Whose sock is this?

你能晾這些襪子嗎？
Can you hang the socks?

一件件抖開之後，
再把它們晾上去。
Shake each item and put it on the rack.
• shake 抖動

晾上去之前，要先把衣服抖好。
Shape the clothes before you hang them.
• shape 使成形

這是我的內褲。
These are my briefs. • briefs 內褲

哇，爸爸的四角褲好大件！
Wow, Dad's trunks are super big!
• trunks 四角內褲

媽媽，你的內衣好漂亮。
Your bra is pretty, Mom. • bra 內衣，胸罩

確認衣服不會碰到地上。
Make sure the clothes don't hit the ground.
確保，確認

把襯衫掛在衣架上。
Put the shirt on the hanger. • hanger 衣架

我們需要一些衣夾。
We will need some clothespins.
• clothespin 衣夾

衣夾在這裡。
Here's a clothespin.

汙漬沒有完全洗掉。
The stain's not completely out.

到明天，一定都全乾了。
It will be all dry tomorrow.

沒有空間可以晾了。
There's no room anymore. • room 空間

天氣應該會很好。
The weather should be nice.

因為天氣好，衣服會很快乾。
The laundry's going to dry well because it's sunny.

晴天就是好的洗衣日。
A sunny day is a good laundry day.

下雨的話，衣服不太會乾。 If it rains, the laundry won't dry well.

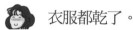

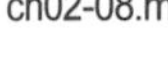
ch02-08.mp3

摺衣服

 衣服都乾了。	The laundry is all dry.
衣服還沒有全乾。	The laundry's not completely dry yet.
 衣服都乾了。	The clothes are well dried.
我們應該把乾的衣服收一收。	We should get the dry clothes.
我們把衣服從晾衣架拿下來吧。	Let's take the clothes off the rack.
你能幫我收衣服嗎？	Can you help me get the clothes off?
你能幫我摺衣服嗎？	Can you help me fold the clothes? • fold 摺
我們來好好摺衣服吧。	Let's fold these clothes neatly. • neatly 好好地，整齊地
試著摺整齊一點。	Try to fold it neatly.
像這樣對半摺。	Fold it in half like this. in half 對半
把襪子放在襪子箱內。	Put the socks in the sock bin. • bin 箱
你能把衣服放回原處嗎？	Can you put the clothes back in the right places?
你應該摺自己的衣服。	You should fold your own clothes.
 我的衣服我自己來摺。	Let me fold mine by myself.
 那是爸爸的。	That's Daddy's.
 另一隻襪子在哪裡？	Where is the other sock?

你能找到另一隻嗎？ Can you find the other pair?

這是誰的衣服？ Whose is this?

把爸爸的衣服放在同一個地方。 Get Daddy's clothes in one place.

把它們放抽屜。 Put them in the drawer. ·drawer 抽屜

襯衫要用衣架掛起來。 Hang the shirts on the coat hanger.

你要像這樣摺衣服。 This is how you fold clothes.
（This is how 這是～的方法）

媽媽，這件太大，我摺不了。 Mom, this is too big for me to fold.
·too 形容詞 to 動詞 太～而不能～

我摺這些衣服摺得好嗎？ Did I do a good job folding those clothes?
（do a good job 做得很好）

ch02-09.mp3

燙衣服

我們要燙爸爸的襯衫。 We need to iron Dad's shirt. ·iron 熨，熨斗

這件襯衫都皺皺的。 The shirt's all wrinkled. ·wrinkled 皺皺的

想看媽媽燙衣服嗎？ Want to see Mommy ironing?

這熨斗看起來好像一艘船。 The iron looks like a boat.
（looks like 看起來像）

熨斗太燙，很危險。 The iron's too hot. It's dangerous.

不要碰。 Don't touch it.

你不可以自己燙衣服。 You shouldn't iron by yourself.

不要靠太近，因為很燙。 Don't come near it since it's hot.
·since 因為～

我在燙衣服的時候去坐那邊。 Go sit over there while I'm ironing.
·while ～的時候

媽，小心。

Watch out, Mom.

我們需要先噴點水。

We need to spray it with water first.

• spray 用噴霧器噴灑

你能拿噴霧器給我嗎？

Will you get me the spray bottle?

我們是為了弄平皺褶才燙衣服的。

We need to straighten out the wrinkles by ironing. • by -ing 透過～

(straighten out：使～平坦)

看！變平了。

Look. It's straightening out.

皺褶都不見了。好酷喔。

The wrinkles are gone. That's cool!

(are gone：消失)

• cool 棒，酷

這是蒸汽熨斗。

This is a steam iron. • steam 蒸氣

等一下！你應該要等我們燙完褲子再穿。

Wait! You should wear your pants after we iron them.

我們應該燙一下媽咪的圍裙。

We should iron Mommy's apron.

百褶裙很難燙。

Pleated skirts are hard to iron.

• pleated 打褶的

我們應該燙到沒有皺褶。

We need to iron it so there are no wrinkles.

我們應該讓線條更工整。

We need to make the lines neat.

現在這個衣領很挺吧。

The collar's straight now.

燙過後，衣服不是很整齊嗎？

Isn't it neat after ironing?

剛剛燙好的衣服很溫暖。

It's warm since we just ironed it.

我幫你在襯衫上噴水。

Let me spray water on the shirt for you.

拔掉插頭後，還是有一段時間會很燙。

It's still hot after we pull the cord out.

• pull out 拔掉，抽掉 • cord 電線

ch02-10.mp3

照顧花草

我們放點水到花盆裡吧。	Let's put some water in the flower pots. 花盆
我們來澆花吧。	Let's water the flowers. ·water 澆水
這些土都乾了。	The soil is all dry. ·soil 土
這些花都枯了。	The flower's withered. ·withered 枯萎
這些花看起來很乾枯。	Seems like the flowers are thirsty. 看起來～（It seems like 的簡略用法）
我們要給它們澆水，以便讓花不會枯萎。	Let's give them some water so the flowers won't wither. ·wither 枯萎

我來澆這花。	I'll water this flower.
我現在想給它澆點水。	I want to give it some water now.
我可以澆多少？	How much should I pour? ·pour 灌，注

把澆水壺再傾斜一點。	Tilt the watering can more. ·tilt 傾斜 澆水壺
用澆水壺慢慢地把水澆在花上。	Slowly pour the water in the watering can on the flower.
如果天氣很熱，我們要澆更多的水。	If the weather's hot, we need to give it more water.
澆太多水，植物也有可能會死掉。	Giving too much water might make the plant die.
確認水沒有直接碰到花。	Make sure the water doesn't actually touch the flower.
灰塵和蟲子也能藉由澆水被沖掉。	By pouring water, the dust and bugs are washed away. ·bug 蟲子
這是什麼花呢？	What flower is this?

這花好香喔。聞聞看。
This flower has a strong scent. Smell it.
•scent 香氣

花園讓屋子的空氣更清淨。
Flower gardens make the air in the house cleaner.

花都全開了。
The flowers are in full blossom.
in full blossom 花朵盛開

這棵樹結果實了。
This tree bears fruit.
bears fruit 結果實

發芽了。
The sprouts have come up. •sprout 芽

這植物是不開花的。
This plant has no flowers growing.

你能照顧花嗎？
Can you take care of the flowers?
take care of 照顧～

葉子上的灰塵也要洗掉。
Clean the dust on the leaves.

喔！這棵樹會死嗎？
Oh my! Will this tree die?

現在讓我來照顧這些花草。
Let me take care of these plants now.

這棵將成為我的樹。
This is going to be my tree.

ch02-11.mp3

修東西

這好像故障了。
Looks like it's broken. •broken 故障
Looks like 好像～（= It looks like）

媽，這個不能動了。
Mom, it's not working. •work 動，運作

媽媽，你會修這個嗎？
Mom, can you fix this? •fix 修理

我不小心弄破了。
I broke it by accident.
by accident 失手，意外地

這個還能再用嗎？
Can it be used again?

我會試試看。
I'll try.

看起來我可以修好的樣子。
Looks like I can handle it. •handle 操作，處理

明天我來修。 I'll fix it tomorrow.

你回來的時候，它就會動喔。 **When you come back, it will be working.**

我會把它修得像全新的一樣。 I'll fix it so that it will be like it's brand new.（brand new 全新的）

這個因為故障了，才不能動。 **It doesn't work because it is broken.**

如果變得更糟，怎麼辦？ What if it gets worse?（gets worse 變得更壞）

這個我好像不會修。 **This looks like I can't fix it.**

即使修好了，也不會像之前那樣好用。 It won't be as good as it used to be even if we fix it.（even if 即使～）

抱歉。我們不得不等爸爸回來。 **Sorry. We're going to have to wait till Dad gets here.**

拜託爸爸修這個。 Ask Daddy to fix this. • ask A to 拜託 A 做～

爸爸會修任何東西。 **Daddy can fix anything.**

我們能把它丟掉買新的嗎？ Can we throw it away and get a new one?

• throw away 丟掉 • get 買，購得

不可以只是丟掉，我們修修看。 **We shouldn't just get rid of it. Let's try to fix it.**（get rid of 丟掉）

它壞掉了，我好傷心。 I'm so sad that it's broken.

謝謝你修好它。 **Thank you for fixing it.**

• Thank you for -ing 謝謝你做～

ch02-12.mp3

吃午餐

媽媽，我餓了。 **Mom, I'm hungry.**

我餓死了。

I'm starving (to death).

・starving (to death) 餓

等一下，我馬上把午餐準備好。

Wait a second. I'll have lunch ready soon.

午餐是什麼？

What is for lunch?

三明治如何？

What about sandwich?

～如何？

要在家吃，還是出去吃？

Want to eat at home or out? ・eat out 外食

午餐要不要叫外送？

Want to order something for lunch?

・order 訂餐

我可以吃拉麵嗎？

Can I eat ramen?

我想吃披薩

I want some pizza.

如果你吃糖果的話，
午餐會沒有味道。

If you eat candy, lunch won't taste good.

我來拿掉魚刺。

I'll get the fishbones out.

・get out 拿掉 ・fishbone 魚刺

太大了嗎？我來切一下。

Is it too big? Let me cut it off.

即使你不想吃，也要吃一點。

Eat just a little bit even though you don't feel like eating.

即使～也

速食對身體不好。

Fast food isn't good for you.

你很快吃完一整盤了。

You finished an entire plate very quickly.

・entire 全部的 ・plate 盤，碟

甜心，你吃夠了嗎？

Did you eat enough, Sweetheart?

多吃一點，變壯一點。

Eat a lot and get strong.

我會做好午餐再出門。

I'll get lunch ready and then leave.

Chapter 03 下課後孩子回家

I'm home, Mommy!
媽，我回來了！

Oh, Honey, glad you're back!
噢，親愛的，歡迎回家！

ch03-01.mp3

小孩回家

我回來了。	I'm home.
 寶貝，你回來了。	You're home, Honey.
你回來得很早。	You're home early.
今天過得如何？	How was your day?
今天在學校過得如何？	How was school today?
 很好玩。	It was fun.

還好。 It was all right. 還可以

你今天有點晚，有什麼事嗎？ You're a little late. Did something happen?

放學後，我跟朋友玩了一會。 I played with my friend after school.

甜心，我很擔心你。 I was worried about you, Sweetie.

下次，要直接回家。 Next time, come straight home.

・straight 直接

你看起來很開心。 You look happy.

你好像玩得很開心。 You seem to have had fun. 好像～

你看起來很累。 You look tired.

姐姐回來了嗎？ Is Sister here?

★ 在英文系國家，兄弟姊妹間主要用姓名稱呼。

還沒，她快回來了。 Not yet. She'll be home soon.

是呀，她已經回來了。 Yes. She's already here.

當然，她在等你了。 Of course. She is waiting for you. 等～

她正在睡覺，安靜點。 She's sleeping, so be quiet.

不熱嗎？ Wasn't it hot?

媽，好熱喔！可以喝點水嗎？ Mom, it's so hot! Can I have some water?

啊！今天好冷。 Brrr! It's cold today. ・brrr〈發抖的聲音〉簌簌

你跟朋友們處得好嗎？ Do you get along with your friends all the time? 和～和睦相處

你在學校做／學了什麼？ What did you do / learn at school?

午餐，你吃了什麼？ What did you have for lunch?

ch03-02.mp3

接小孩

甜心，媽媽在這裡！	**Sweetheart, I'm here!**
媽媽，為什麼你來接我？	Why did you come to pick me up, Mom?
因為我想快一點看到你。	**Because I wanted to see you sooner.**
你為什麼這樣晚？我正等著你。	Why are you so late? I've been waiting for you.
我很晚吃午餐。	**I had lunch late.**
如果媽媽晚到的話，我們可能就錯過彼此了。	If Mommy had been late, we could have missed each other. • could have + 過去分詞　也有可能～　• miss　錯過
把書包給我，我來拿。	**Give me your bookbag. I'll carry it for you.**
下雨的時候，等我拿雨傘給你。	When it's raining, wait for me to bring an umbrella.
今天公車晚了。	**The bus is late today.**
媽媽來接你，高興嗎？	Are you happy that Mommy came?
我真的很高興你能來接我。	**I'm really happy that you came for me.**
媽媽也很高興能來。	Mommy feels happy to come here, too.
明天你也能來接我嗎？	**Can you pick me up again tomorrow?**
明天，我在這裡等你。	I'll be waiting here tomorrow.
抱歉，我晚了一點。	**Sorry I was a little late.**
每週一，我都會來接你。	I'll come and pick you up every Monday.

你等我一會了嗎？	Were you waiting for me for a while?（for a while：一會）
即使媽媽晚到，也一定要在這等。	Even if Mommy's late, wait here.

洗手

ch03-03.mp3

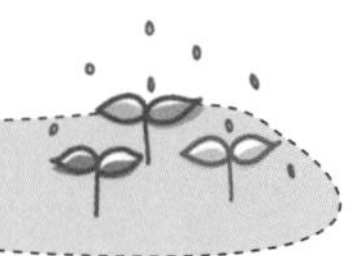

看看你的手！好髒。	Look at your hands! They're dirty.
去洗手，快！	Go wash your hands. Quickly!（Go wash：Go and wash）
回到家時，你應該洗一下手。	When you come home, you should wash your hands.
用肥皂擦洗你的手。	Scrub your hands with soap. •scrub 擦洗

媽媽，洗不掉。	It won't come off, Mommy.（come off：去除）
你能幫我捲起袖子嗎？	Can you roll up my sleeves?（roll up：捲起來）

把肥皂都洗掉。	Wash off all the soap.
你的手上還有泡沫。	There's still foam on your hands. •foam 泡沫
你的手上有很多細菌。	There are a lot of germs on your hands. •germ 細菌

我看不到細菌。	I can't see the germs.

你沒辦法看到細菌。	You can't see germs.
你能自己洗嗎？	Can you wash yourself alone? •alone 單獨

不，你能幫我嗎？	No. Can you help me?

不要這樣隨便，要徹底地洗乾淨。	Don't be careless. Wash them thoroughly. •careless 隨便 •thoroughly 徹底地，完全地

手指間也要擦洗。	Scrub between your fingers.
手腕也要洗。	Wash your wrist, too. ‧wrist 手腕
不要把水放著一直流。	Don't leave the water on.
洗到雙手都明顯乾淨為止。	Wash until your hands are visibly clean. (visibly clean 明顯很乾淨)
我在你說之前就已經洗好了。	I washed them before you told me to.
我洗好了！	I'm done washing!

ch03-04.mp3

肚子餓的時候

我餓了。請給我點心。	I'm hungry. Please get me a snack. ‧snack 點心
等一下，就快好了。	Wait a little bit. It's almost ready.
你一定很餓了吧？	You must be hungry.
我拿點心給你。	I'll give you a snack.
你在學校沒有把飯吃完嗎？ 為什麼會餓呢？	Didn't you finish your lunch at school? Why are you hungry?

今天的飯不好吃，所以我沒有都吃完。	The food today was bad, so I didn't eat it all.

你渴了嗎？	Are you thirsty?
你要喝的嗎？	Want something to drink? (something to drink 喝的東西)
要來點吃的嗎？	Want something to eat?
你會餓因為你只吃了一點早餐。	You're hungry because you had little breakfast.

我今天什麼都還沒吃。 I haven't eaten anything today.

還沒到吃晚餐的時間嗎？ Is it time for dinner yet?

你又餓了嗎？ Are you hungry again?

吃點什麼吧。 Eat something.

去冰箱找找看。 Get something from the fridge.
‧fridge 冰箱（refrigerator 的簡寫）

你想吃什麼？ What do you want to eat?

要媽媽做好吃的給你嗎？ Want Mommy to make you something tasty? ‧tasty 好吃的

等一下，我做好吃的給你。 Wait a little bit. I'll make you something good.

因為今天我玩了好一陣子，所以很餓。 I'm hungry because I played for a while.

ch03-05.mp3

吃點心

我們來吃點心吧。 Let's have a snack.

寶貝，來吃點心了。 Come and have a snack, Honey.

你想吃什麼點心？ What do you want for a snack?

請給我麵包和牛奶。 Bread and milk, please.

媽媽，我的點心是什麼？ What's my snack, Mom?

是你最喜歡的鬆餅。 It's your favorite. Waffles.

沒有其他的了嗎？ Is there anything else?

你想吃什麼？ What do you want to eat?

跟你弟弟一起分享。 **Share it with your brother.** ‧share 分享

留一些給你弟弟。 Leave some for your brother. ‧leave 留下

花生多一點？你要多一點嗎？ **Want more peanuts? Do you want more?**

不，不用了。我很飽。我已經吃很多了。 No, I'm fine. I'm full. I've had enough.

你要多一點牛奶或果汁嗎？ **Want more milk or juice?**

好吃嗎？ Does it taste good? （taste good 好吃）

嗯，很好吃。 **Yeah, it's delicious.** ‧delicious 好吃

媽，我可以再要一些嗎？ Mom, can I have some more?

試著不要吃太多。 **Try not to eat too much.** （Try not to 試著不要～）

如果你吃太多餅乾，你會吃不下晚餐。 If you eat too many cookies, you can't have dinner.

如果你吃太多甜食，你的牙齒會爛掉。 **If you eat too many sweets, your teeth will rot!** ‧sweets 甜食 ‧rot 爛

西方小孩經常吃的點心

- macaroni and cheese 起司通心麵（美國小孩最愛的點心）
- grilled cheese 烤起司三明治（在吐司上放上起司後烤成）
- pretzel 椒鹽蝴蝶餅 （蝴蝶的模樣，有點鹹的餅乾）
- popsicle 冰棒（經常叫做 hard）
- cookie 小餅乾
- chips 洋芋片
- candy 糖果
- ice cream 冰淇淋

那對你不好。
That's bad for you.

焦糖不是對身體很好的點心。
Caramel is not a healthy snack. / Caramel is not good for your health.

我可以吃些冰淇淋嗎？
Can I have some ice cream?

如果你吃太多冰的食物，會讓你生病的。
Eating too much cold food will make you sick. ·sick 病

如果你吃太多炸的食物，你會變胖。
If you eat too much fried food, you will gain weight. —變胖

吃太多辣的食物，你的胃會受傷。
Too much spicy food can hurt your stomach. ·spicy 辣的

如果你喝太多碳酸飲料，你的身體會出問題。
You'll get in trouble (有問題) if you drink too much soda. ·soda 碳酸飲料

漢堡是一種垃圾食物。
Hamburgers are a kind of junk food. —垃圾食物

路邊賣的烤雞沒有正確地煮好。
The barbecued chicken sold on the street is not properly cooked. ·properly 正確地

不要吃那麼多披薩了。
Stop eating so much pizza.

ch03-06.mp3

聊幼稚園／學校生活

學校有趣嗎？
Was school fun? ·fun 有趣

嗯，很有趣。
Yeah, it was fun.

什麼最有趣？
What was the most fun?

在戶外玩的時候最有趣了。
Playing outside was the best.

我發生了不好的事情。
Something bad (壞事) happened to me.

什麼意思？發生什麼事了？ What do you mean? What happened?

你跟老師起糾紛了嗎？ Did you get in trouble (捲入麻煩) with your teacher?

我在休息時間跑來跑去，所以被罵了。 I got in trouble because I ran during recess. ・recess 休息時間

不要問，我不想說。 Don't ask. I don't want to talk about it.

媽，金宏因為不舒服沒有來。 Mom, Jinhong didn't come because he was sick.

喔，希望他快點好起來。 Oh, I hope he gets well (好起來) soon.

告訴我你在學校學了什麼。 Tell me what you learned in school.

你在幼稚園／學校玩了什麼？ What did you play in school?

你在幼稚園學了什麼歌？ What songs did you learn in school?

你能唱你學的歌嗎？ Can you sing the song you learned?

今天你有聽老師的話嗎？ Did you listen to your teacher today?

你的老師問了什麼問題？ What questions did your teacher ask?

今天老師稱讚我了。 The teacher praised me today. ・praise 稱讚

你跟朋友們好好玩了嗎？ Did you have a good time with your friends?

你今天跟誰一起坐？ Who did you sit with today?

我的同桌是敏基。 My seatmate is Minji. ・seatmate 同桌的人

今天我們換座位了。 We changed seats today. ・seat 座位

嗯…我記不起她的名字。 Hmm... I can't remember her name.

ch03-07.mp3

做作業

 你有回家作業嗎？ Do you have any homework?

 是的，我有。／不，我沒有。 Yes, I do. / No, I don't.

 你有很多作業嗎？ Do you have a lot of homework?

你的作業是什麼？ What's your homework?

給我看你的作業簿。 Show me your assignment notebook.

・assignment 作業 ・notebook 筆記本，簿子

做完作業再玩。 Play after you do your homework.

你把作業做完了嗎？ Did you get your homework done?

先做作業。 Do your homework first.

 我先玩一會再做。 I'll do it after playing for a little bit.

再等一下下。 After a little while.

等這個電視節目看完。 After this TV show.

 不可以把它往後拖延。 Don't put it off until later.（put it off：拖延）

如果你一直往後延，你就不會想做了。 If you keep putting it off, you won't want to do it.

想要媽媽幫你嗎？ Want Mommy to help you?

 不，我可以自己做。 No, I can do it by myself.

 作業都做完了嗎？ Did you finish your homework? / Are you done with your homework?

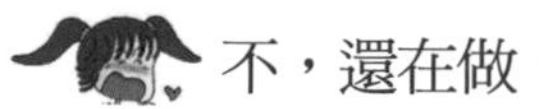 不，還在做。 No, I'm still doing it. / No, I'm still working on it.

是的，我都做完了。 Yes, I'm done.

媽，你能幫我嗎？ Mom, can you help me?

這個要怎麼做？ How do I do this?

你應該自己做作業。 You should do your homework by yourself.

如果你需要幫忙，就叫我喔。 If you need help, call me out.

媽，這個太難了。 Mom, this is too hard.

回家後，你應該立刻做作業。 You should do your homework right after you come back.

這個作業什麼時候要做完？ When is this homework due? ‧due 到期的

你應該要在什麼時候完成？ When should you get this done?
‧get A done 完成 A

如果你做完作業，把它放進書包。 If you're done with your homework, put it in the bag.

我做這項勞作作業有困難。 I have trouble working on this craft homework.
‧have trouble -ing 做～有困難 ‧craft 手工藝，勞作

老師給我們出了一些很難的數學作業。 My teacher gave us some difficult math homework. ‧difficult 困難的

這是小組作業。 This is a group project.

今天的作業是做家庭報紙。 Today's homework is making a family newspaper.

我必須讀三遍的教科書。 I have to read my textbook three times.
‧textbook 教科書，教材

這週的作業是參觀博物館。 This week's homework is to visit a museum.

我明天必須交出一份讀書報告。	I have to turn in a book report by tomorrow. 交出 讀書報告

ch03-08.mp3

整理書包

把明天的書整理好。	Pack your bookbag for tomorrow. •pack 包裝
整理好書包再玩。	Play after you pack your bag.
從學校回來後，要先整理書包。	Pack your bag after you come back from school.
睡覺前，先整理書包。	Pack your bag before you go to sleep.
明天你需要的東西都準備好了嗎？	Do you have anything you need for tomorrow?
媽媽，我每週的行程表在哪裡？	Mom, where is my weekly schedule?
在書桌上找找看。	Look on your desk.
你整理好書包了嗎？	Did you pack your backpack?
我需要買一些文具用品。	I need to buy some supplies.
我整理好書包了。	I finished packing my bag.
確認東西有沒有都帶了。	Check if you have everything.
削好你的鉛筆。	Sharpen your pencils. •sharpen 削尖
你沒有放進你的數學課本。	You don't have your math book.
我把社會課本放在我的置物櫃內了。	I put my social studies book in my locker. •locker 有鎖的置物櫃 社會
把你不需要的東西都拿出來。	Take everything out that you don't need. •take out 拿出

不要帶任何玩具去學校。	Don't take any toys to school.
讓我檢查是不是都帶齊了。	Let me check if everything's okay.
你把作業都放進去了嗎？	Do you have all of your homework?
為什麼你的作業出現在客廳？	Why is your homework out in the living room? 客廳
你的書包太重了。	Your bag's too heavy.
把彩色鉛筆放在置物櫃。	Put the color pencils in your locker.
媽媽，你能幫我看一下都帶齊了嗎？	Can you check if everything's ready, Mom?

ch03-09.mp3

跑腿

你能幫我一個忙嗎？	Can you do me a favor? • do A a favor 幫 A 一個忙
抱歉，我現在有事。	I'm sorry. I have something to do.
我做完這個再去。	I'll do it after I'm done with this.
為什麼老是我去做？	Why do I always have to do it?
請恩紀去做。	Ask Enji to do it.
誰要幫我跑腿？	Who wants to do an errand for me? 跑腿
媽媽很忙，請幫我跑腿一下。	Mom's busy. Please do me a favor.
我會給幫我做的人 5 元。	Whoever does it for me will get 5 dollars.
幫忙的話，你會給我獎賞嗎？	Will you give me a reward for that? • reward 獎賞
那麼給我一些錢作為獎賞吧。	Then give me some money for a reward.

 好吧。 Yes, I will.

 好，什麼差事？ Okay, what errand? ・errand 差事

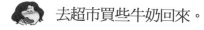

 去超市買些牛奶回來。 Go buy some milk at the supermarket.

這裡有 100 元。 Here's 100 dollars.

不要忘記找錢。 Don't forget to get the change. ・change 零錢

出門要小心。 Always be careful outside.

 不用擔心。 Don't worry.

媽媽！我回來了。牛奶在這裡。 Mom! I'm back. Here's the milk.

 可以幫忙跑腿，現在你完全長大了。 Running an errand, you're all grown up now.

做得好！ Good job.

謝謝。你有拿回零錢嗎？ Thank you. Did you get the change?

 有，這裡是找回來的錢。 Yeah, here's the money.

 零錢就給你了。 Keep the change.

 謝謝。下次我還要做。 Thanks. I'll do it again next time.

媽媽，我做得很好，不是嗎？ Mom, I did a good job, didn't I? （did a good job 做得很好）

ch03-10.mp3

在外面玩

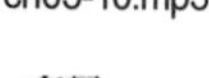 媽，我可以去外面玩嗎？ Mom, can I go play outside?

我要去遊樂場玩。 I'm going to the playground.
・playground 遊樂場，運動場

媽媽，我可以騎腳踏車嗎？ **Mom, can I ride my bike?**

・ride a bike 騎腳踏車

去外面玩。 Go and play outside.

一小時候後要回來。 **Come back in an hour.**

晚餐前要回來。 Come back before dinner.

只能在房子附近玩。 **Just stay around the house.**

不要走到公寓社區外。 Don't go out of the apartment area.

out of ～的外面

不要去太遠。 **Don't go too far.** ・far 遠

我會去看你是否在遊樂場。 I'll see if you stay in the playground.

帶你的弟弟／妹妹去。 **Take your brother / sister.**

跟媽媽一起去。 Let's go with Mommy.

要下雨了。今天不要出去。 **It's going to rain. Don't go out today.**

今天太熱了。在家裡玩。 It's too hot today. Play inside.

你已經出去玩過了。 **You've already been outside.**

不要再出去了。 Don't go out again.

你要去哪裡？ **Where are you going to go?**

為什麼你總是要出去呢？ How come you always want to go out?

How come 為什麼（= Why ~?）

ch03-11.mp3

去才藝班

甜心，該去才藝班了。 **It's time for the after-school club, Sweetie.**

去才藝班。 Go to the after-school club.

不要忘記去才藝班。 Don't forget to go to the after-school club.

整理好你的書包。 Get your bag ready.

快點，公車要走了。 Hurry up. The bus is leaving.

媽媽，今天我不想去。 Mom, I don't want to go today.

你昨天沒有去，今天你必須去。 You missed it yesterday. You need to go today.

・miss 失去，缺席

週一是美術課。 Monday is art class.

美術課

我真很不想去上美術課。 I really don't want to go to art class.

我可以停止去上美術課嗎？ Can I stop going to art class, please?

是你說要去的。我們再上一段時間看看。 You asked for it. Let's see for a little longer.

要求～，拜託

才藝班的課不有趣嗎？ Is the after-school club not fun?

才藝班的課結束後，我會去接你。 When the after-school club is over, I will come pick you up.

要提早五分鐘到才藝班。 Arrive at the after-school club 5 minutes early.

才藝班的課結束後，要直接回家。 Come straight home after the after-school club.

你在才藝班學了什麼？ What did you learn in the club?

才藝班的課為什麼這樣晚結束？ Why did the after-school club end so late?

你今天過得很辛苦。 You had a long day today.

（時間過得很慢）辛苦的一天

週五是最忙的一天。 Friday is my busiest day.

ch03-12.mp3

接待家教老師

	老師要來了。	The teacher's going to come.
	媽，你可以叫老師晚點來嗎？	Mom, can't you ask the teacher to come a little late?
	不行，你跟老師約好時間了。	No. You set up the time with the teacher. 約定，設定 (set up)
	整理好你的書／書桌。	Get your books / desk ready.
	你的作業都完成了嗎？ 也練習好了嗎？	Did you finish your homework? Finish practicing? ·practice 練習
	等一下，媽！我完成這個後再做。	Wait, Mom! I'll do it after I'm done with this.
	不要散漫。要好好聽老師的話。	Don't get distracted. Listen to your teacher. 散漫，想其他事情 (get distracted)
	老師今天似乎會比較晚到。	Seems like the teacher's going to be late today.
	我來準備點心。	I'll get the snacks ready.
	上課要專心。	Concentrate in class. ·concentrate 集中
	不要問奇怪的問題。	Don't ask weird questions. ·weird 奇怪的
	老師來了。	The teacher's here.
	希望你上課愉快。	Hope you have a good time. ★ 省略了第一人稱的 I。
	不要漏掉每天的功課。 你會落後的。	Don't miss the daily work. 每天的功課 (daily work) You'll fall behind. 落在後面 (fall behind)
	你要確實做好每天的功課。	Make sure you do your daily work.

每天的學習單我可以不做嗎？ Can't I stop doing the daily worksheets?
‧worksheet 活頁練習題

我收集到很多貼紙，所以從老師那裡得到了禮物。 I've collected a lot of stickers, so I got a present from the teacher. ‧collect 收集

ch03-13.mp3

休息時間

媽，我累了。我要休息。 Mom, I'm tired. I want to rest. ‧rest 休息

好，休息一下。 Okay. Rest for a little.

好好休息吧。 Rest for a long time.

媽，我需要休息。 Mom, I need to take a rest. (take a rest 休息)

你做了什麼？ What did you do?

休息一個小時。 Take a break for an hour. (take a break 休息)

休息之後，你會沒事的。 You'll be all right after resting.

不要想任何事，好好休息吧。 Don't think about anything. Just rest.

現在，休息時間結束了。 Rest time is over now.

下週開始，是考試期間。 The test period is beginning next week.
‧period 期間

我沒有休息很久。 I haven't rested that long. (that long 那樣長)

我可以看漫畫書嗎？ Can I read some comic books? (comic books 漫畫書)

我想小睡一下。 I want to take a nap. (take a nap 打盹)

玩電腦遊戲並不是休息。 Playing computer games isn't resting.

ch03-14.mp3

獨自在家

我要外出一下，不過會馬上回來。 I'm going out, but I'll be right back.

你要去哪裡？ Where are you going?

我去一下雜貨店。 I'm going to the grocery store.（grocery store 雜貨店）

你是說我必須單獨在家嗎？ Are you saying I need to be alone?

你不能自己單獨在家嗎？ Can't you be by yourself?

你為什麼會害怕呢？只是一會兒而已。 Why are you scared? It's only for a while.
• scared 害怕

快點回來。 Be back soon.

我有可能會有點晚。 I might be a little late.

不要給陌生人開門。 Don't open the door for strangers.
• stranger 陌生人

媽媽回來之前，都不可以出去。 Don't go outside until Mommy comes back.

好好照顧弟弟／妹妹。 Watch over your brother / sister.（Watch over 照顧，照看）

要聽哥哥／姊姊的話。 Listen to your brother / sister.

如果你有任何需要的東西，打電話給媽媽。 Call Mommy if there's anything you need.

你知道媽媽的電話，對吧？ You know Mommy's number, right?

不用擔心。 Don't worry.

謝謝。我會很快回來。 Thanks. I'll be back soon.

媽媽回來了。 Mommy's back.

為什麼你這麼晚回來？ Why are you so late?

一切都還好吧？ **Was everything okay?**

我好害怕，但是我有忍住。 I was scared, but I tried not to be.

喔？你已經回來了？ **Eh? You're back already?**

一個人看家，現在你是個大男孩囉。 Being home alone, you're a big boy now.

Chapter 04 從傍晚到晚上

When are you coming, Daddy?
爹地，你什麼時候回來？

I'm on my way. Coming right up!
我正在路上，馬上就回家！

ch04-01.mp3

爸爸要下班了

 爸爸什麼時候回家？ When is Daddy coming home?

我不知道。你要打給他嗎？ I don't know. Want to call him?

你記得爸爸的電話嗎？ Do you remember Daddy's number?

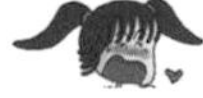 是的，我來打電話。 Yes, I'll dial it. •dial 打電話

現在電話中。 The line is busy.

爸爸沒有接。 Daddy's not answering.

爸，你什麼時候回來？ **Dad, when are you coming?**

我在回家的路上！ I'm on my way! / I'm coming!

我快到了。 **I'll be right there in a minute.**

爸爸，我想你。 I miss you, Daddy.

爸爸，不要喝酒。 **Don't drink, Dad.**

爸爸，早點回來。 Come home early, Dad.

爸爸，早點回來跟我玩。 **Come early to play with me, Daddy.**

爸爸，你回來的時候，要買冰淇淋給我。 Dad, get me some ice cream when you're back.

他快到家了。 **He's almost home.**

我想知道是不是爸爸回來了。 I wonder if Dad's here.

（I wonder if：我想知道）

是爸爸。 **It's Daddy.**

孩子們，快去跟爸爸打招呼。 Go greet your daddy, kids.

• greet 打招呼

你今天過得好嗎？ **Did you have a good day?**

爸爸，好高興再看到你！ Dad, good to see you again!

親愛的，去洗一洗吧。 **Go wash up, Honey.**

你很累了吧？ Did you have a long day?

去換衣服吧。 **Go change, please.**

親愛的，你一定很餓了吧。 Honey, you must be hungry.

（must be：一定～）

你今天為什麼晚了？ **Why were you late today?**

你幫我買冰淇淋了嗎？ Did you get me the ice cream?

爸爸，你能跟我玩嗎？ Can you play with me, Dad?

爸爸有點累。 Daddy's a little tired.

親愛的，孩子們等你很久了。 Honey, the kids really waited for you.

爸爸，你累了嗎？ Are you tired, Dad?

甜心，爸爸好想你喔。 Sweetie, Daddy missed you a lot.

ch04-02.mp3

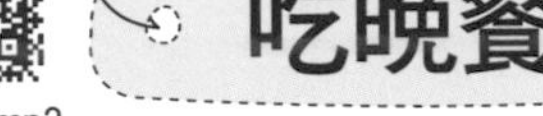

吃晚餐

晚餐你想吃什麼？ What do you want for dinner?

我想吃義大利麵。 I want pasta.

要吃晚餐了。 It's time for dinner.

晚餐好了。 Dinner's ready.

來吃晚餐吧。 Come and have dinner.

吃晚餐前要先洗手。 Wash your hands before dinner.

寶貝，叫爸爸來吃晚餐。 Honey, tell Dad to come and eat.

你能告訴爸爸晚餐好了嗎？ Can you tell Dad that dinner's ready?

媽，我幫你準備餐桌。 Mom, I'll help you set the table.

謝謝。你能把湯匙拿來嗎？ Thank you. Can you get the spoons?

哇，看起來好好吃喔！ Wow, it looks delicious!

嗯，味道很香。 Hmm, that smells so good.

媽，感謝你準備晚餐。 Mom, thank you for the food.

好，多吃一點。 Okay. Help yourself. •help oneself 盡情享用

我的寶貝，你很能吃喔。	**You're eating well, my baby.**
媽，今天的晚餐是什麼？	Mom, what's for dinner?
 我做了韓式烤肉。	**I made some bulgogi.** ・bulgogi 韓式烤肉
 哇！那是我的最愛。	Wow! That's my favorite.
 好吃嗎？	**Is it good?**
 韓式烤肉好好吃。	The bulgogi tastes good.
媽媽做的食物最棒了。	**Mommy's food is the best.**
 不要只吃肉，也要吃點蔬菜。	Don't just eat the meat. Eat some vegetables, too. ・meat 肉 ・vegetable 蔬菜
 媽媽，我可以再多吃一點嗎？	**Mom, can I eat some more?**
 你不會太飽嗎？	Aren't you full already?
不要吃太多。	**Don't eat too much.**
 你都吃完了。好棒！	You're finished. Good job!
 媽媽，我都吃完了。	**Mom, I'm done.**
我太飽了，再也吃不下了。	I can't eat anymore because I'm stuffed. ・be stuffed 被充滿
我幫你洗碗。	**I'll help you do the dishes.**
 你吃太少了。	You eat like a bird. 吃太少
你吃太快了。	**You're eating too fast.**
你吃太久了。	You take forever to eat.

ch04-03.mp3

看電視

今天晚上我們要看什麼節目呢？ **What program should we watch tonight?**

我要看《Star King》。 I'm going to watch *Star King* today.

媽媽也想看。 **Mom wants to watch it, too.**

快來這裡，要開始了。 Come here. It's going to start.

哇，好好笑喔！ **Wow, it's really fun!**

這是我最喜歡的節目。 It's my favorite show. ‧show 電視節目

嘿，你喜歡的歌出現了。 **Hey, it's your favorite song.**

往後一點。你的眼睛會壞掉的。 Back off a little. Your eyes will get bad.
Back off 往後退

看的時候要坐正。 **Sit straight while watching.**
Sit straight （挺直）坐正

甜心，坐好。 Sit properly, Sweetie. ‧properly 正確地

你能把音量調低嗎？ **Will you turn down the volume?**
turn down （聲音等）變低

這個結束後，我就會關掉。 I'll turn it off after it's finished.
‧turn off （電源）關掉

結束了。現在把電視關掉。 **It's finished. Turn off the TV now.**

媽，我可以多看一會電視嗎？ Mom, can I watch a little more TV?

你已經看了一個小時的電視了。不要再看了。 **You've watched TV for an hour. Stop watching.**

你已經看超過一個小時的電視了。 You've been watching TV for over an hour. ‧have been -ing 持續～

今天不能再看電視了。 **No more TV today.**

看太多電視，對眼睛不好。 It's not good to watch too much TV.

不要看了，去玩吧　**Stop watching. Go and play.**

現在關掉電視去睡覺。　Turn it off and go to sleep now.

那不是小孩子看的節目。　**That show's not for children.**

那是給大人看的。　It's for adults.　• adult 大人

如果你不遵守約定，之後你都不能再看電視。　**If you don't keep your promises, you can't watch TV anymore!**
• keep one's promise 遵守約定

媽媽，還沒有結束。　Mom, it's not over yet.

媽媽，你一直都在看電視劇。　**You always watch dramas, Mom.**

是連續劇的時間耶！現在電視是媽媽的了。　Soap opera time! The TV's mine now.
（Soap opera：連續劇，電視劇）

ch04-04.mp3

吃宵夜

媽，你能幫我做宵夜嗎？　Mom, can you fix me a snack?　• fix 做

電視節目的英文？

電視節目叫做 program，即使如此大體上也可以叫做 show。

drama、children、talk、comedy、music、reality、sports 等單字後面也可加上 show、當然也可以只是稱為 show。除此之外，還有 documentary、news、report、interview 等等。

媽，我餓到睡不著。	Mom, I can't sleep because I'm hungry.
媽，你能給我些水果嗎？	**Mom, can you give me some fruit?**
你晚餐吃那麼多，還會餓喔？	You ate that much dinner, but you're still hungry?
你不久前才吃了晚餐。	**You had dinner just a while ago.**
因為你只吃了一點點，餓了吧。	You're hungry because you ate a little.
你要吃些番薯嗎？	**Want some sweet potatoes?** 番薯
除了番薯外，還有其他的嗎？	Is there anything else besides sweet potatoes? ・besides ～之外
韓式烤肉還有剩嗎？	**Isn't there any leftover bulgogi?** ・leftover 吃剩的飯菜
不要吃太多。	Don't eat too much.
寶貝，你吃太多了。	**You eat like a horse, Honey.** 吃太多
晚上吃東西不太好。	It's not good to eat at night. 晚上
睡前吃東西對你的胃不好。	**It's not good for your tummy to eat before going to sleep.** ・tummy （幼兒用語）肚子，胃（= stomach）
你甚至比媽媽吃得還多。	You even eat more than Mommy.
睡前吃東西，你會變胖的。	**You're going to get fat if you eat before you go to sleep.** 變胖
慢慢吃。	Slow down. 放慢速度
如果你睡不著，就喝點牛奶。	**Drink some milk if you can't sleep.**
你不可以吃拉麵。	You can't eat ramen.
要我做三明治給你嗎？	**Do you want me to make a sandwich?**

我來餵你，媽咪。說「啊」。 Let me get you some, Mommy. Say "Ah."

先給爸比。 Give Daddy some first.

ch04-05.mp3

跟爸爸玩

爸，跟我玩。 Please play with me, Dad.

爸，起來跟我玩。 Get up and play, Dad.

爸，我們去公園踢足球。 Dad, let's play soccer at the park.

爸，不要看電視了。跟我玩。 Dad, stop watching TV. Play with me.

好，我們要玩什麼呢？ Okay, what should we play?

我要玩騎馬。 I want to play horse.

我們來玩捉迷藏。 Let's play hide and seek. 捉迷藏

爸，你當鬼。 You're it, Dad. • it （捉迷藏的）鬼

爸，你現在應該躲起來。 Dad, you should hide now.

爸，來捉我。 Catch me, Dad!

爸比來當馬。 Daddy will be the horse.

爸爸很忙，你能等一下嗎？ Dad's busy. Could you wait?

你每天都那樣說，但是你從來沒跟我玩過。 You say that every day, but you don't ever play with me.

• ever〈使用在否定句〉一次也，一直

爸爸累了，跟媽媽玩吧。 Dad's tired, so play with Mommy.

不，我想跟爸爸玩。 No. I want to play with Daddy.

跟爸爸玩最有趣了。 Playing with Daddy is the most fun.

跟你玩，也是最有趣的。 **Playing with you is fun for me, too.**

要跟我去遊樂場嗎？ Want to go to the playground with me?

你能教我如何騎腳踏車嗎？ **Can you teach me how to ride a bike?**

我要丟球了喔。試著接球。 I'll throw the ball. Try to catch it!

爸，你為什麼這麼厲害？ **Why are you so good at this, Dad?**
• be good at 擅長～

跟著爸爸做。 Follow what Daddy does. / Just do as I do.

ch04-06.mp3

洗澡

到洗澡的時間了。 **It's time to take a bath.**
洗澡（= have a bath）

洗澡睡覺喔。 Go to sleep after your bath.

脫掉衣服。 **Take off your clothes.**

要先洗頭嗎？ Want to wash your hair first?

我討厭洗頭。 **I don't want to wash my hair.**

我只想淋浴。 I just want to take a shower.

先用肥皂洗手。 **First, wash your hands with soap.**

媽媽，我想要自己洗澡。 Mom, I want to take a bath by myself.

浴缸的水都滿了。 **The tub is filled now.** • (bath)tub 浴缸 • fill 裝滿

現在要進去浴缸了嗎？ Want to get into the tub now?

水是溫溫的嗎？ **Is the water warm?**

媽媽，水溫溫的／很冷。 Mom, the water's warm / cold.

多加一些溫／冷水。 Let's add some more warm / cold water.

拿玩具給我。 Bring my toys to me.

這個像船一樣浮在水上。 This is floating like a boat. ·float 浮

不要搗蛋了。洗澡了。 Don't fool around. Wash yourself. 胡搞，搗蛋

我們趕快淋個浴吧。 Let's take a quick shower.

搓一下肥皂，會有泡泡喔。 Rub the soap and make some foam.

讓我好好幫你洗澡。 Let me wash you well.

把你的身體徹底地洗乾淨。 Wash your body thoroughly.

弄點沐浴乳在海綿上。 Get some body cleanser on the sponge.

搓揉海綿，把泡泡弄出來。 Rub the sponge to make some foam.
·rub 搓，摩擦 ·foam 泡沫

用這些肥皂泡沫好好洗澡。 Clean yourself well using the soap foam.

肥皂跑進我眼睛了。 The soap got into my eyes.

我們把你身上的汙垢搓掉吧。 Let's rub the dirt off your body.

你的脖子好髒喔。 Your neck is so dirty.

看！我身上的肥皂泡泡。 Look! I've got soap bubbles. ·bubble 泡沫

媽，很痛耶！ Mom, it hurts!

哎唷！我的眼睛很刺痛。 Ouch! My eyes sting. ·sting 感覺刺痛

我們把肥皂洗掉吧。 Let's wash off the soap now.

最後再沖一下水。 Give yourself a final rinse. ·rinse 沖洗，清洗

好了。用毛巾擦乾。 It's done. Let's dry you with a towel.

洗澡後，有沒有覺得很清爽？ Don't you feel fresh since you bathed? 覺得清爽
·bathe 洗澡

好，我覺得好清爽。 Yes, I feel fresh.

我可以在浴缸內多玩一會嗎？ **Can I play in the tub a little longer?**

要小心，因為地板很滑。 Be careful because the floor's slippery.

• slippery 滑的

不要把水濺到媽媽身上。 **Don't splash water on Mom.**

• splash 濺，潑灑

ch04-07.mp3

洗頭

我頭好癢。 **My head is itchy.** • itchy 癢

來洗頭吧。 Let's wash your hair.

我拿不下髮帶，請幫我。 **My hairband won't come off. Help me.** (come off：拿下，去除)

我昨天也有洗，為什麼還要再洗一次？ I washed it yesterday, but I have to do it again?

你必須每天洗頭。 **You need to wash your hair every day.**

你的頭髮臭臭的。來洗頭吧。 Your hair smells. Let's wash it.

把洗髮精搓出泡泡來。 **Let's make some foam with the shampoo.**

洗髮精跑進我的眼睛了啦，好痛喔。 The shampoo got in my eye, and it stings.

媽媽幫你洗。 **Mommy will wash you.**

閉上眼睛。 Close your eyes.

把頭髮沖乾淨吧。 **Let's rinse your hair.**

潤髮乳會讓你的頭髮更柔順喔。 The hair conditioner will make your hair softer. (hair conditioner：潤髮乳)

你的頭髮太長，好難洗喔。
It's hard to wash your hair because it's too long.

用毛巾把頭髮擦乾吧。
Let's dry your hair with a towel.

我用吹風機來吹乾你的頭髮。
I'll dry your hair with a blow dryer.

如果你頭髮濕濕的就睡覺的話，會臭臭的。
If you sleep with your hair wet, it will smell bad.

梳頭髮吧。
Comb your hair.

你現在看起來很乾淨。
You look very clean now.

你的頭髮聞起來很香。
Your hair smells so good.

ch04-08.mp3

擦乳液

我們來擦乳液吧。
Let's put on some lotion.（put on 擦）

聞一下香味。
Smell the scent. ・scent 香氣，味道

我可以自己擦。
I can put it on by myself.

媽，你可以擠一點在我手上嗎？
Can you put some on my hand, Mom?

推開它，充分地搓一搓。
Spread it out well and rub it well. ・rub 搓

感覺如何？
How does it feel?

滑滑軟軟的。
It's slippery and soft.

把乳液擦在你的身體和臉上。
Put the lotion on your body and face.

我不要擦任何乳液。
I don't want to put on any lotion.

乳液很容易跑進眼睛裡面
It easily gets into my eyes.

試著避開眼睛周遭。	Try to avoid the area around your eyes. • avoid 避開
小心，不要讓乳液跑進眼睛。	Be careful not to get any lotion in your eyes.
不要擠太多。	Don't squeeze out too much.
一定要確實把蓋子蓋回去。	Make sure you put the cap back on.
你需要擦些乳液，這樣你的皮膚才不會乾燥。	You need to put on some lotion so your skin won't get dry.
乳液會讓你的皮膚濕潤滑順，寶貝。	The lotion makes your skin moist and soft, Honey. • moist 濕潤
因為你擦了乳液，現在你看起來很好看。	You look pretty now because you put on some lotion.
你看起來棒極了。	You look fabulous. • fabulous 棒極了

ch04-09.mp3

穿睡衣

穿上你的睡衣。	Put on your pajamas.
換上你的睡衣。	Change into your pajamas.
你的睡衣在這裡，穿上吧。	Here are your pajamas. Put them on.
睡衣已經拿出來了。	There are the pajamas.

我太累了。我沒辦法換睡衣。	I'm too tired. I can't change into my pajamas.

睡覺時穿睡衣比較舒服。	It's comfortable to wear pajamas when sleeping.

媽，我的藍色睡衣在哪？	Mom, where are my blue pajamas?

那件還沒乾。穿別件吧。 They are not dry yet. Wear something else.

我就穿這樣去睡了。 **I'll just go to sleep with this on.**

• with A on 穿著 A

媽，幫我穿上睡衣。 Mom, help me put on my pajamas.

你穿睡衣好可愛。 **You look cute in your sleepwear.**

ch04-10.mp3

寫日記

寫你的日記。 **Write in your diary.** (Write in：寫在，寫入)

你寫日記了嗎？ Did you write in your diary?

你的日記本在哪？ **Where is your diary?**

我明天會寫。 I'll write in it tomorrow.

我今天可以不寫嗎？ **Can I not write today?**

你應該每天寫日記。 You should keep a diary every day. (keep a diary：寫日記)

要把每天寫日記變成一個習慣。 **Make it a rule to write in your diary every day.** (Make it a rule to：使～成為習慣或規則)

媽媽，沒有什麼好寫的。 Mom, there's nothing to write about.

我可以寫很短嗎？ **Can I write something short?**

至少寫一行。 Write at least one line. (at least：至少)

我要在日記上寫什麼呢？ **What should I write in my diary?**

想想今天發生了什麼事。 Think about what happened today.

想想你今天做了什麼。 **Think about what you did today.**

你記得什麼？ What can you remember?

寫寫你的同桌同學。 Write about your seatmate in school.
‧seatmate 同桌的人

你要寫標題嗎？ Will you make a title? ‧title 標題

不想寫的話，就畫畫吧。 Draw if you don't want to write.

你可以寫你的想法和感覺。 You can write about your thoughts and feelings. ‧thoughts 想法，思考 ‧feelings 感覺

用英文寫吧。 Let's write in English.

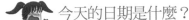

今天的日期是什麼？ What is today's date? ‧date 日期

今天的天氣如何？ What was the weather like today?

今天是星期幾？ What day is today? ‧day 星期，日子

我今天幾點起床？ When did I get up today?

我完成我的日記了。 I'm done writing in my diary.

你忘記了日期。 You forgot the date.

很好。 Nice job!

你的書寫沒有很好看。 Your handwriting is not that good.
‧handwriting 書寫

不要看我的日記。 Don't look at my diary.

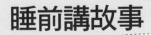

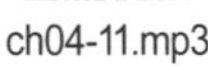

ch04-11.mp3

睡前講故事

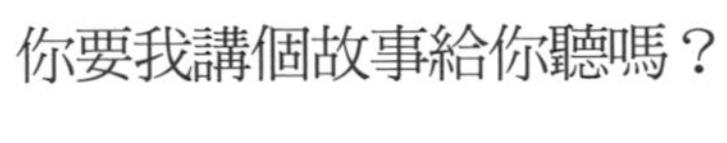

你要我講個故事給你聽嗎？ Do you want me to read a story for you?

我給你講個故事吧。 Let me read you a story.

媽咪會一直講故事，直到你睡著。
Mommy will read to you until you fall asleep. (fall asleep 睡著)

你喜歡哪種故事？
What story would be good?

選一本你想聽的故事書吧？
Choose a book you want to read.

我來選。
I'll choose.

你選了一本很有趣的書。
You picked a good one. •pick 選

你選太多了。
You chose too many.

你今天要講哪個故事呢？
What are you going to read to me today?

我要講《月亮，晚安》。
I'll read *Good Night, Moon*.

仔細聽喔。
Listen carefully.

媽媽，我想睡了。
I'm sleepy, Mom.

想睡的話，就睡吧。
You can sleep if you feel sleepy.

閉上眼睛聽吧。
Listen with your eyes closed.
•with one's eyes closed 閉著眼睛

媽，再講一個。
Read me one more, Mom.

你還沒睡嗎？我只會再講一個喔。
You're still awake? I'll read to you just one more. •awake 醒著

媽，我睡不著。
Mom, I'm not sleepy.

媽媽的喉嚨也痛了，就到此為止吧。
Mom's throat hurts, too. Let's stop now.
•throat 喉嚨 •hurt 痛

明天可以再唸那本故事書給我聽嗎？
Will you read me the book again tomorrow?

我好想知道接下去的故事喔。
I really want to know the next story.

我們昨天讀到哪裡了呢？
Where did we read to yesterday?

你根本沒在聽。	You're not listening.
不讀了，去睡吧。	Stop reading and go to bed now.
現在去睡，怎麼樣？	How about going to sleep now? How about ～如何？
我明天會再講給你聽。	I'll read to you tomorrow again.
明天你可以講剩下的嗎？	Can you read the rest tomorrow? • rest 剩餘
媽媽今天太累了。現在不講了。	Mommy's too tired today. Let's just stop reading for now.

ch04-12.mp3

各自睡

去你的房間睡吧。	Go to sleep in your room.
既然你長大了，就去自己的房間睡吧。	Now that you're grown up, go to sleep in your room. Now that 既然～　grown up 長大
既然你已經讀小學了，去自己的房間睡。	Now that you're in elementary school, go to sleep in your room.
媽，可以陪我直到我去睡覺嗎？	Mom, will you stay with me until I go to sleep?
媽，我好害怕喔。我要跟媽媽一起睡。	Mom, I'm scared. I want to sleep with you.
媽，今天是最後一次我想跟你一起睡。	Mom, I want to sleep with you for the last time today. for the last time 最後一次

要我唱歌哄你睡嗎？	Want me to sing you to sleep?

媽，不要關燈。	Mom, don't turn off the light.
媽，我沒辦法自己一個人睡。	Mom, I can't go to sleep by myself.

不用擔心，媽咪會跟你在一起。 Don't worry. Mommy will be with you.

這個娃娃會跟你在一起。 This doll will be with you. ‧doll 娃娃

我會把門開著，你就能聽到我的聲音了。 I'll leave the door open so you can hear me.

我會來看你睡了沒，不用擔心。 I'll check if you're asleep. Don't worry.

你能自己睡嗎？ Can you sleep by yourself?

我可以自己睡。 I can sleep by myself.

媽媽，我現在都長大了。 Mom, I'm all grown up now.

ch04-13.mp3

睡前打招呼

上床睡覺的時間到了。 It's time to go to bed.

外面很暗了，該去睡覺了。 It's dark outside. It's time to go to sleep.

媽，我還不睏。 Mom, I'm not tired yet.

★ 要表達「睏」的時候，比起 sleepy，更常使用 tired。

已經超過 10 點了，上床睡覺。 It's past 10 o'clock. Go to bed.

睡前，要去一下廁所。 Go to the bathroom before you go to sleep.

我不用尿尿。我已經去過了。 I don't have to pee. I already went.

媽媽親一下，晚安！ Mommy will kiss you. Good night!

給媽媽一個晚安吻。 Give Mommy a goodnight kiss.

晚安！祝你做個好夢！ Good night! Sweet dreams!

讓我幫你蓋好被子 Let me tuck you in. ‧tuck in（躺在床上）蓋被子

媽，明天早點叫我起床。 **Mom, wake me up early tomorrow.**

媽，七點叫我起床。 Mom, wake me up at 7.

當我叫醒你之後，你要立刻起床。 **You have to get right up when I wake you up.**

媽，我睡不著。我要晚點睡。 Mom, I can't sleep. I want to go to sleep later.

你要早睡早起。 **You need to go to sleep early to wake up early.**

不可以太晚睡。 Don't go to bed too late.

不要躺在床上說話。 **Stop talking in bed.**

現在給我安靜。 Be quiet now.

爸爸媽媽，晚安！ **Good night, Mom and Dad!**

媽，明天見！ See you tomorrow, Mom!

ch04-14.mp3

睡覺中醒來

你怎麼醒了？ **Why did you wake up?**

寶貝，你怎麼了嗎？ What's wrong, Honey?

媽，我做了個惡夢。 **Mom, I had a nightmare.** ·nightmare 惡夢

我想喝水，所以醒了。 I woke up because I needed some water.

我想去廁所。 **I want to go to the bathroom.**

我想去尿尿，所以醒了。 I woke up because I want to pee.

媽，我尿床了。 **Mom, I wet the bed.** —— 尿床

我想你尿床了。
I think you wet the bed.

噢！你尿床了，寶貝。
Eeek! You wet the bed, Honey.

換好衣服後回去睡。
Get changed and go back to sleep. 回去睡覺

我在黑暗中醒來，我好害怕。
I woke up in the dark, and I was scared.

現在不是早晨嗎？
Isn't it the morning right now?

不，再多睡一會。
No, sleep some more.

蚊子一直打擾我。
The mosquitoes are annoying me.
• mosquito 蚊子 • annoy 打擾

我來噴防蚊液。
I'll get the repellent. • repellent 防蚊液，驅蟲劑

我夢到我被怪物追趕。
I had a dream I was getting chased by a monster. • monster 怪物
追趕

我的寶貝一定被嚇壞了吧。
My sweetie must have been scared.
• must have 過去分詞 一定～

現在沒關係了，媽媽就在這裡。
You're okay now. Mommy's right here.

我的寶貝一定是做惡夢了。
My baby must have had a nightmare.

那不是真的，只是一個夢而已。
That wasn't real. It was just a dream.
• real 真的

抱著你最喜歡的熊寶寶睡吧。
Sleep with your favorite bear in your arms.

現在你可以再睡了，對吧？
You can go back to sleep now, right?

我要睡在你旁邊。
I want to sleep next to you.
旁邊～

媽媽幫你入睡。
I'll put you to bed. • put A to bed 使 A 入睡

我唱首歌給你聽。／
我唱搖籃曲給你聽。
I'll sing you a song. /
I'll sing you a lullaby. • lullaby 搖籃曲

不要覺得害怕。	Don't be scared.
媽媽抱著你的話，就沒事了。	**It will be all right if I hold you.** ・hold 抱
今天和媽媽一起睡吧。	Sleep with me tonight.
現在試著回去睡覺	**Try to go back to sleep now.**
媽媽再幫你蓋被子。	I'll tuck you in again.

稱呼「媽媽」的時候

越小的小孩越是無時無刻都要叫媽媽。找東西時，叫 「媽媽」；無聊時，大聲叫 「媽媽」。聽到叫媽媽時，國內的媽媽就會回答說，「怎麼了？」或是「媽媽在這裡。」那麼，你知道美國的媽媽聽到 Mommy 時，又是如何回答的嗎？她們會答說 Yes, Honey! What?

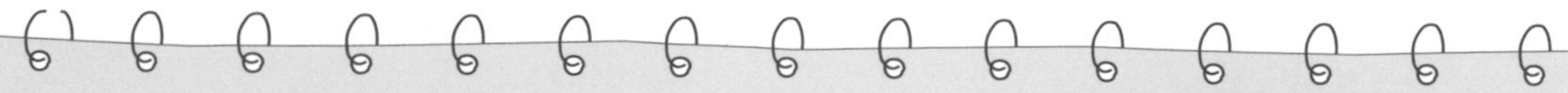

復活節 Easter

在美國，復活節具有紀念耶穌復活的宗教性色彩，同時也是迎接春天的慶典。最能代表復活節的就是復活節彩蛋（Easter egg）和復活節兔子（Easter Bunny）了。傳說中復活節的兔子會送復活節籃子給好孩子，所以對小孩來說，復活節兔子就像是聖誕老公公。復活節的籃子裡放滿了巧克力、糖果、玩具等等。復活節活動中的撿復活節彩蛋（Easter egg hunt）是最具代表性的。大人們會把復活節彩蛋（或是塑膠蛋內放糖果和果凍等等）藏在各個地方，然後小孩各自提著復活節籃子去把彩蛋找出來。

★ 常用的會話句子

· 我們來彩繪雞蛋吧。	**Let's decorate the Easter eggs.**
· 我已經把彩蛋藏在某個地方了。現在，開始撿彩蛋吧！	**I've hidden the eggs somewhere. Let's start the Easter egg hunt now!**
· 要放什麼在籃子裡呢？	**What will be in the basket?**
· 那邊有復活節兔子耶。來跟兔子打招呼吧。	**There's the Easter Bunny over there. Let's say hello to the bunny.**

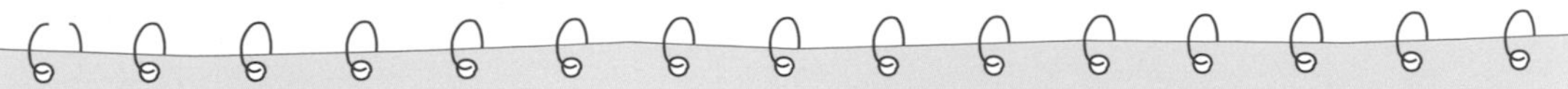

萬聖節前夕 Halloween

萬聖節前夕是每年的10月31日，也是小孩子特別喜歡的節日。這天，小孩子們都會穿上魔女、幽靈、精靈、黑貓等流行的卡通人物的奇特服裝（costume），然後去社區內的家家戶戶叫喊 Trick or treat！（不給糖就搗蛋）。鄰居就會把準備好的糖果、零食、巧克力等等拿出來分享。還有把南瓜挖空，鑽出眼睛、鼻子和嘴巴後，放入燈泡或蠟燭的 jack -o' -lantern（傑克燈籠）也是一大樂趣。在城市，不只是小孩子，連大人都穿上萬聖節的服裝參加遊行。

★常用的會話句子

・我們一起來做傑克燈吧。	Let's make a jack-o'-lantern together.
・在莖的周圍用刀劃一圈，然後拿起來。	Cut a circle around the stem and lift it off.
・用大湯匙把籽和黏稠的內容物都挖出來。	Scoop out the seeds and sticky interior by using a big spoon.
・用筆在南瓜上畫臉。	Draw the features on the pumpkin by using a pen.
・用刀子小心地挖出臉。	Cut the face. Use the knife carefully.
・把南瓜內側粗糙的邊緣整理一下。	Clear away the rough edges inside the pumpkin.
・放入點亮的蠟燭後，蓋上蓋子。	Put a lit candle in and close the lid.
・傑克燈看起來真可怕。	The lantern looks really scary.

每天用的稱讚和嘮叨

Chapter 05

表達稱讚

I love my Jenny the most.
我最愛我的珍妮了。

Who do you love the most in the world?
這個世界上妳最喜歡誰？

ch05-01.mp3

親密的稱呼

我愛你，達令。	I love you, my darling.
小可愛。	You cutie.
喔，我的甜心。	Oh, my sweetie.
 你是讓人多麼驚奇的寶貝呀。	You're such an amazing baby.
我的小甜心。	My little sweetheart.

我的美人兒。 You pretty thing.

來這裡，我的公主。 **Come here, my princess.**

ch05-02.mp3

說我愛你

媽咪，你有多愛我？ **How much do you love me, Mommy?**

我對你的愛像宇宙那麼大。 My love for you is as big as the universe.

・universe 宇宙

你是我的寶藏。 **You are my treasure.** ・treasure 寶藏

你知道我有多愛你，對吧？ You know how much I love you, right?

在這個世界上，媽媽最愛你了。 **Mommy loves you the most in the entire world.**

很感謝你是我的兒子／女兒。 Thanks so much for being my son / daughter.

我要親你一下。 **I'll give you a kiss.**

我太愛你了，已經不能用言語來表達。 I love you more than words can say.

比言語所能表達的還要～

達令，沒有你，我活不下去。 **I can't live without you, Darling.**

・without 沒有～

沒有我心愛的兒子／女兒的話，我怎麼能活下去呢？ How could I live without my loving son / daughter?

我就愛這樣的你。 **I love you just the way you are.**

因為你，我很幸福。 I'm so happy because of you.

你是我歡樂的泉源。 **You are my joy.** ・joy 歡樂

你愛誰多一點，我還是爸爸？ Who do you love more, me or Daddy?

當然是愛你多一點。 **Of course I love you more.**

兩個人，一樣愛。 I love you both the same.

ch05-03.mp3

稱讚外貌

媽咪，我看起來如何？ **How do I look, Mommy?**

媽咪，我看起來漂亮嗎？ Do I look good, Mommy?

哇，你看起來棒極了！ **Wow, you look fabulous!** ・fabulous 棒極了

你看起來很棒。 You look so great!

你看起來像個小王子／小公主。 **You look like a prince / princess.**

你好漂亮。是誰家的女兒長得這樣美呢？ You're so pretty. Whose daughter is this pretty?

太讓人驚訝了！你的朋友看到你，一定會很吃驚的。 **Amazing! Your friends will be surprised to see you.**
・amazing （到達相當感嘆的程度）令人驚訝的

你很完美！ You're perfect!

今天你看起來更美了！ **You look prettier today!**

我快認不出你了。 I don't even recognize you. ・recognize 認出

我的美人兒，你看起來像誰呢？ **Who do you look like, you pretty thing?** （look like：看起來像～）

我很漂亮，因為我看起來像你。 I'm pretty because I look like you.

我聽說媽媽和我長得很像。 **I heard you and I look alike.** （look alike：看起來相像的）

ch05-04.mp3

稱讚

好厲害！／了不起！	Great! / Terrific!
你做得非常好。	You did so well.
到現在為止都做得很好。	Nice work so far.
你的努力得到了好結果，對吧？	Your hard work pays off, right? （pays off 取得成果）

媽咪，我做得好嗎？	Did I do well, Mommy?

給你兩個讚！	Two thumbs up! ★舉起大拇指，表示稱讚。
很好，下次你也可以做得這樣好嗎？	Good job. Can you do this well the next time, too?
哇，你真是個好男孩。連媽媽都要向你學習了。	Wow, you're a nice boy. Even Mommy should learn from you.
太棒了！了不起！	Super! Just fantastic!
看到你像那樣的表現，媽媽好開心。	Mommy's happy to see you behave like that. •behave 行為舉止
你也為自己感到自豪吧？	Don't you feel proud of yourself? （proud of 為～感到光榮）

你認為我會做不好嗎？	Did you think I wouldn't do well?
你認為我會做不來嗎？	Did you think I wouldn't make it?

這已經超過我期待的。	This was better than I had expected. （better than 比～更好） •expect 期待
我猜你的努力得到回報了。	I guess your efforts were rewarded. •effort 努力 •reward 獎賞

下次我會更努力。	I'm going to try harder next time.

寶貝，你真的長大了。 You're all grown up, Honey.

你怎麼想出那個方法的？ How did you get the idea?

你好有創意。 You're very creative. ・creative 有創意的

你真的很謙虛。 You're really modest. ・modest 謙虛的

你獨自完成這件事讓我很驕傲。 I'm so proud you did it all by yourself.

這應該可以成為別人的模範。 It should be an example for others.
・example 例子，模範

恭喜

ch05-05.mp3

恭喜！ Congratulations! ・congratulations 恭喜

恭喜！你得到第一名。 Congratulations! You won first place.

恭喜你得獎了！ Congratulations on your award!

恭喜你進步了！ Congratulations on your improvement!

恭喜你得到好成績！ Congratulations on your good grades!
・grade 分數

我為你感到驕傲。 I'm so proud of you.

耶！優勝者來了！ Yay! Here's the winner!

萬歲！你成功了！ Hooray! You made it!
（made it：成功，完成）

今天你是冠軍！ You are the champ today!
・champ 冠軍（champion 的簡稱）

我知道你一定行的。 I knew you could do it.

你很開心吧？媽媽也好開心。
Aren't you happy? Mommy feels happy, too.

我們來打電話給爸爸，告訴他這個好消息吧。
Let's call Daddy and tell him the good news.

媽媽該做什麼當作你的禮物呢？
What should Mommy do as a gift for you?

快過來。我要抱抱你。
Come here. I'll give you a hug.

我覺得很棒。
I feel great.

大家拍手鼓掌！
Let's give a round of applause!
• applause 拍手

媽媽請你吃好吃的晚餐作為獎勵。
I'll treat you to a wonderful dinner as a reward.

我們辦個派對慶祝一下。
Let's have a party to celebrate this.

你的阿姨想要恭喜你。
Your aunt wants to congratulate you.

ch05-06.mp3

認同

我想你是對的。
I think you're right.

一點也沒錯。／當然。
Absolutely! / Certainly!

你說的沒錯。
You can say that again.

就是說嘛！
Tell me about it! ★請注意此句非字面意思。

嗯…我想你是對的。
Yeah... I guess you're right.

我能理解你的感受。
I understand your feelings.
• feeling 心情，感受

我知道你的心情。 I know how you feel.

所以這就是你要說的，對吧？ So what you're saying is this, right?

對，你當然會那樣想。 You're right. You should think like that.

我的想法如何？ What about my idea?

那是個好主意！ That's a great idea!

媽媽，你也認同我嗎？ Do you agree with me, Mommy?

agree with 認同～

當然。 Of course.

我也是這樣想。 I agree with you.

也是有可能會那樣。 That could happen.

站在你的立場，那是有可能的。 From your point of view, that could be.

point of view 觀點，見解

那種事情也曾發生在我身上。 That has happened to me, too.

我以前也是那樣覺得。 I've felt that way before.

that way 那樣

ch05-07.mp3

抒解壓力

媽媽，我想我是個膽小鬼。 Mom, I think I'm a scaredy pants.

scaredy pants 「膽小鬼」的可愛表達

我可以不做嗎？ Can I not do this?

我好緊張。 I'm so nervous.

・nervous 緊張

你很害怕嗎？ Are you scared?

要我牽你的手嗎？ Want me to hold your hand?

要有勇氣。 Be brave.

不要害怕。 Don't be afraid.

你不需要感到害怕。	You don't have to be scared.
深呼吸。	Take a deep breath. 深呼吸
我會在你旁邊。	I'll be next to you.
做錯也沒關係，盡你的全力吧。	It's okay if you make a mistake. Try your best. • try / do one's best 全力以赴
你會做得很好的。	You will do fine.
你在害怕什麼？	What are you afraid of?
媽媽在你的年紀時也是這樣。	Mommy was just like you when I was your age.
我會看著你的。	I'll be watching over you.
我在這裡，寶貝。	I'm here for you, Honey.
你不是個膽小鬼。	You're not a coward. • coward 膽小鬼
像個男子漢。	Be a man.
下定決心，這完全取決於你。	Make up your own mind. It's up to you. • Make up one's own mind 下決心 • be up to 取決於～

ch05-08.mp3

鼓勵

祝你好運！	Good luck!
打起精神。	Cheer up.
有什麼不順的事嗎？	Is there anything wrong?

我又搞砸了。	I didn't make it again. / I messed up again. 成功 / 搞砸

我肯定你心情不好。	I'm sure you feel bad.
為什麼這麼沮喪？	Why are you so down? ・down 沮喪的
你不需要那麼沮喪。	You don't have to be so down.
你可以的。我相信你。	You can do it. I trust in you. 相信～
去做吧！我永遠站在你這一邊。	Go for it! I'm always on your side. 去做吧 ・on one's side 在～的一邊

因為我沒拿到獎，所以很傷心。	I feel bad I couldn't win the award. ・award 獎
我像個傻瓜，犯了同樣的錯誤。	I am such a fool to have made the same mistake. ・fool 傻瓜
下次會更好的。	It will be better next time.
我不會再試了。	I'm not going to try that again.
我覺得很丟臉。	I feel ashamed. ・ashamed 羞愧的，難為情
太丟臉了！我沒能做完它。	It's a shame I could not make it through. ・shame 丟臉的事 完成
不要放棄。	Don't give up. 放棄
我會讓你振作起來。	I'll cheer you up.
做你想做的。	Do as you please.
你現在覺得好一點了嗎？	Do you feel better now?
如果你吃點東西，會感覺更好一些。	If you eat something, you'll feel better.
怎樣做才能讓你心情變好呢？	What can make you feel better?
不會再更糟了。等著看看吧。	It could've been worse. Just wait and see. 有可能更糟糕（could have 過去分詞：會有～）

Chapter 06

偶爾也會挨罵

Don't hit your brother.
不要打你弟弟。

Peter started it.
彼得開始的。

ch06-01.mp3

和朋友吵架

你跟朋友發生什麼事了嗎？ Did something happen with your friend?

我真的討厭記溯。 I really don't like Jisu.

我再也不要跟他說話了。 I'm never going to talk to him again.

我再也不要跟他玩了。 I don't want to play with him anymore.

記溯打了我。 Jisu hit me.

朋友之間是不可以打架的。	Friends shouldn't fight.
朋友是不可以互相罵對方的。	Friends shouldn't curse at each other. 互相 • curse 罵，詛咒
朋友應該和睦相處。	Friends should get along well. 和睦相處
如果你們一直吵架， 我不會再讓你們一起玩。	If you keep fighting, I won't let you hang out together. 朋友一起消磨時間，一起玩
跟你的朋友道歉。	Apologize to your friend. • apologize 道歉
你說對不起了嗎？	Did you say sorry?
你的朋友可能也後悔了。	Your friend is probably regretting it, too. • probably 可能 • regret 後悔
你的朋友讓你心煩了。	Your friend made you upset. • upset 生氣，心煩
他為什麼那樣做？	Why did he do that?
但是你不可以討厭你的朋友。	But you shouldn't hate your friend.
跟你的朋友說說你的感受， 怎麼樣？	How about talking to your friend about your feelings?
為什麼你不試著先跟他談談呢？	Why don't you try talking to him first?
站在他／她的立場想一想。	Put yourself in his / her shoes. • Put oneself in one's shoes. 站在～的立場

ch06-02.mp3

兄弟姊妹吵架

你們兩個在幹什麼？ 你們在吵架嗎？	What are you two doing? Are you fighting?

他先開始的。 | He started it.

誰先開始的不是重點。 | It doesn't matter who started it.
• matter 重要，成為個問題

互相說對不起。 | Apologize to each other.

你們吵架的話，媽媽會很心痛的。 | If you guys argue, Mommy feels hurt.
• argue 爭吵

你不可以打自己的妹妹。 | You shouldn't hit your sister.

我跟你說過你不可以打你妹妹。 | I told you that you should not hit your sister.

你應該好好對待你的妹妹。 | You should be nice to your sister.

你應該照顧你的妹妹 | You should look after your sister.

你比較大，你應該讓你的弟弟。 | You are older, so let your brother do it.

不可以對你的哥哥無禮，還那樣說話。 | Don't be rude to your brother and talk like that. • rude 無禮

不要吐口水。 | Don't spit. • spit 吐口水

如果你再吐口水，你就給我去面壁思過。 | You'll get a timeout if you spit again.
• timeout 面壁思過

媽媽真的很生氣。 | Mommy is really mad. • mad 生氣

跟你的姊姊握手。 | Shake hands with your sister. (握手)

給他一個抱抱。 | Give him a hug. • give a hug 擁抱

你們兩個都想受罰嗎？ | You both want to get punished? (受罰，挨罰)

現在你們兩個都要受罰。不可以看電視。 | You both are grounded now. You can't watch TV.
• grounded 被處罰不能外出、遊戲等

你們不能馬上停止嗎？ | Won't you stop right this minute? (馬上)

誰在尖叫？	Who just screamed? •scream 尖叫
你們還要這樣嗎？	**Are you going to do it again?**
跟你姊姊吵架是對的嗎？	Does it seem right to argue with your older sister? •right 對的 （argue with：跟～吵架）
你不可以命令，要用請求的。	**You shouldn't demand but ask.** •demand 要求
你是哥哥，請表現成熟點。	You are a big brother. Please act mature. •mature 成熟的
你身為姊姊，怎麼沒有責任感。	**You are not responsible as a big sister.** •responsible 有責任感的
你們不是說好再也不吵架了嗎？	Didn't you promise you wouldn't fight?
你知道你可能被處罰，知道吧？	**You know you might get a timeout, huh?** （get a timeout：受罰）
我不會再打架了。	I won't ever fight again.
你們兩個都有錯。	**You two both were wrong.**
兄弟／姊妹間應該友好相處。	Brothers / Sisters should be friends.

timeout 是處罰（punishment）的其中一種，指的是制止某些行為，在角落暫時反省的時間，類似中文的「面壁思過」。「受罰」的其他表達還有 get grounded，它指的是不可以外出或是玩遊戲等等。英語系國家是禁止父母對小孩進行體罰的，但是以教養（discipline）為由打幾下屁股，因此 spanking 還是被允許的。當然不可以打得太過分。

ch06-03.mp3

吵著要買東西

	媽媽，我要買這個。	I want this, Mom.
	你能買這個給我嗎？拜託啦！	Can you buy me this? Please!
	媽媽買不起。	Mommy can't afford it.
	我沒有帶錢出來。	I didn't bring any money.
	你不能有這麼多要求。	You should not be demanding. •demanding 要求很多
	太貴了！	It's too expensive! •expensive 貴
	這個對一個小學生來說太超過了。	It's too much for an elementary school student.
	為什麼你的要求這麼多？	Why are you so demanding?
	家裡有一樣的。	You have the same thing at home.
	不要說傻話！	Don't be silly! •silly 傻
	我知道你想要，但是現在不行。	I know you want it, but not now.
	說不行就是不行。	No means no! •mean 表示~的意思
	什麼時候要買給我？	When can I get it?
	下次買吧。	Let's get it next time.
	媽，你每次都說下次。	Mom, you always say next time.
	媽咪，你自己要的都買了。	Mommy, you buy everything you want.
	你總是買東西給弟弟，但都沒有買給我。	You always buy things for my brother but not for me.

就這一次。這是最後一次。我保證。	Only this time. This is the last time. I promise.

媽媽也沒有什麼都買。	Mommy doesn't get everything.
你為什麼不用你的零用錢買呢？	Why don't you buy it with your allowance? • allowance 零用錢
這不是小孩子用的東西。	These aren't for kids.
這種食物對你不好。	This food isn't good for you.
我們今天不是為了這個才來的。	We didn't come here for this today.
我們來想想是不是真的需要。	Let's think if it's actually that necessary.
可是，我們現在沒有足夠的錢可以買。	Well, we don't have enough money for that right now.
大家都在看我們呢。停止！	People are staring at (盯著看～) us. Stop!
不要再看了，走吧。	Stop looking at it. Let's leave now.
買這個給你後，金額會從零用錢中扣除，可以嗎？	The amount will be taken out of (扣除～ (= deduct)) your allowance after I buy you this. Okay? • amount 金額
如果你能集到 30 個獎勵貼紙的話，我就買給你。	You can get this when you collect 30 good job stickers.

ch06-04.mp3

不專心

你在想什麼？	What are you thinking about?
你在做什麼？	What are you doing?
注意這邊。	Pay attention.

你在看什麼？ What are you looking at?

快點做，寶貝。 Go ahead, Honey.

快點做！ Speed up! / Hurry up!

你恍神了嗎？ Are you getting distracted?

• distracted 注意力分散的

為什麼你那樣在意呢？那不關你的事。 Why do you care? It's not your business.

• care 關心，在意

我想你不知道你在做什麼吧。 I think you're lost.

你為什麼這樣散漫呢？ Why are you so distracted?

寶貝，我們在做什麼呢？ What were we doing, Honey?

停下來！看著我。 Stop! Look at me.

不要跑來跑去。坐下來聽我說。 Don't move around. Sit here and listen.

你要我說幾次呢？ How many times should I tell you?

集中精神完成它。 Let's focus and finish this. • focus 集中

至少專心做 10 分鐘。 Stay on that for at least 10 minutes.

你知道你在做什麼嗎？ Do you know what you're doing?

什麼事在煩你呢？ What's bothering you?

• bother 使費心，使煩惱

不要玩你的手。 Don't play with your hands.

坐好！ Sit up straight!

這是你現在要做的事情嗎？ Is this what you should be doing?

你不想做這個嗎？你要下次再做嗎？ Do you not want to do this? Do you want to do it next time?

我知道我要去做， 但結果不是很好。	**I know I have to, but it doesn't work out well.**
我一直想到其他事情。	I can't stop thinking about other things.
我可以看完這本漫畫書後 再去做嗎？	**Can I do it later after finishing this comic book?**
我也相當努力在試。	I am trying really hard.
集中注意力真的是太難了。	**It's too difficult to stay focused.**
對我來說，一小時太長了。	One hour is too long for me.

ch06-05.mp3

說謊

那是謊話。	**That's a lie.** • lie 說謊，謊言
你為什麼說謊？	Why did you lie?
我想知道你為什說謊。	**I wonder why you lied.**
我不會責備你，告訴我實話。	I won't scold you, so tell me the truth. • scold 責備 • tell the truth 說實話

對不起，我說謊了。	**I'm sorry that I lied.**
我是無意中說謊的。	I accidentally told a lie. • accidentally 無意地
我害怕被你責罵，所以才說了謊。	**I lied because I was afraid I would get in trouble.** 責罵

你還會說謊嗎？	Are you going to lie again?
媽媽相信你，你不會再這樣了， 對吧？	**Mommy trusts you. You won't do it again, right?** • trust 相信

我再也不會說謊了。	I won't do it again.

謝謝你告訴我實話。	Thanks for telling the truth.
一個小謊言會變成大謊言的。	A small lie becomes a big lie.
因為你說謊，媽媽很不開心。	Mommy's upset because you lied.
你也不想成為一個說謊的人，對吧？	You don't want to be a liar, do you? • liar 說謊的人
說實話也是很有勇氣的。	It's brave to tell the truth.
我希望你不會再對我說謊。	I hope you won't ever lie to me.
看看你做了什麼。	Look what you did.
那樣做是不對的。	It was wrong to do that.
那是不正確的。	It was not appropriate. • appropriate 適當的，恰當的
你可能會不自覺地說謊。	You could be lying without knowing it.
反省是很重要的。	It's important to repent. • repent 反省，悔改
如果你說謊，你都不會覺得羞愧嗎？	If you tell a lie, don't you feel ashamed of yourself? • ashamed of oneself 覺得羞愧
我知道你在說謊。	I can tell you are lying. • tell 知道，區分
有人對我撒謊時，我很討厭。	I really hate when people lie to me.
說謊是世界上最糟的事。	Lying is the worst thing in the world.
沒有人會想跟說謊的人在一起。	Nobody wants to be with a liar.

ch06-06.mp3

拖拖拉拉

時間都已經到了吧？	Time's already up?

時間幾乎快到了。 It's almost time.

我正在做。 **I'm doing it.**

還沒好。 Not yet.

我可以留下你先走嗎？ **Can I leave without you?**

等我啦。 Wait for me.

我再給你 10 分鐘。 **I'll give you ten minutes.**

為什麼你老是這樣呢？ Why do you do this all the time?

我已經跟你說了一千次要快點了。 **I've told you to hurry up a thousand times.**

我已經厭煩了。 I'm sick of it! / I'm tired of it!

• be sick / tired of 對～疲倦，對～厭煩

大家都在等你。 **Everyone's waiting for you.**

唉，你慢得跟蝸牛一樣。 Gosh, you're as slow as a snail! • snail 蝸牛

我快好了。 **I'm almost done.**

好，我能按時完成。 It's okay. I can make it on time.

你能準時完成嗎？ **Can you make it on time?**

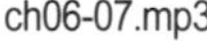
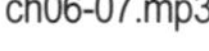

ch06-07.mp3

頑皮搗蛋

喂喂，鎮定一下。 **Hey, hey... Calm down.** （Calm down 鎮定下來）

停下來，你會受傷的。 Stop. You could get hurt. （get hurt 受傷）

你的朋友會不喜歡的。 **Your friend doesn't like it.**

太過分了。你必須停止。 That's too much. You should stop.

替其他人想一想。 Think about others. •others 其他人，別人

這太有趣了，所以停不下來。 It's too fun to stop.

我要懲罰你。 I'm going to punish you. •punish 懲罰，責罵

你的弟弟快哭了。 Your brother might cry soon.

不要惹麻煩。 Don't get into trouble. 惹上麻煩

你打擾到其他人了。 You're disrupting the other people. •disrupt 擾亂

ch06-08.mp3

吵鬧

太吵了！ It's too loud! •loud 吵

不要那麼吵。 Don't be so loud.

安靜，孩子們！ Be quiet, you guys!

太吵了，安靜地玩。 That's too loud. Play quietly.

你需要平靜一下。 You need to settle down. 平靜下來

安靜點，聽我說。 Be quiet and listen to me.

你可以安靜嗎？ Can you be quiet?

你就不能安靜一點嗎？ Can't you quiet down a bit? 安靜下來

說話不要太大聲。 Stop talking too loud.

坐著好好玩。 Sit down and play.

小聲說話。 Use your inside voice. 輕聲細語

我在講電話，你不能安靜一點嗎？ Could you be quiet since I'm on the phone? 講電話中

我都聽不到對方的聲音了。 I can't hear the other person.

媽媽很不舒服，你能安靜點玩嗎？ Can you play quietly because Mommy's sick?

是誰講話這麼大聲？ Who's talking so loudly?

真的讓人很煩。 It's distracting. •distracting 令人分心的

我耳朵都痛了。 My ears are hurting. •hurt 疼痛

要我說多少次安靜點？ How many times do I have to tell you to be quiet?

ch06-09.mp3

頂嘴

你剛才說了什麼？ What did you just say?

不要跟媽媽頂嘴。 Don't talk back to Mom. (talk back to 對～頂嘴)

不要回嘴。 Stop talking back.

你又這樣了！ You're doing it again!

不要招惹我。 Don't start with me.

你應該管好自己的嘴巴。 You should control your mouth. •control 控制，管制

你覺得你應該那樣說話嗎？ Do you think you should talk like that?

你還繼續頂嘴。 You keep talking back.

媽媽，你不明白。 Mom, you don't understand.

為什麼我不能跟你說我想說的？ Why shouldn't I tell you what I want?

你應該跟我說要小心。 You should have warned me. •warn 告誡

你從哪學到那種態度的？ Where did you learn that attitude?
• attitude 態度

我不是在頂嘴。 I'm not talking back.

能讓我把話講完嗎？ Can I finish?

你讓我很生氣。 You're making me mad. • mad 非常憤怒的

如果你再多一句話，我就不再忍耐了。 I'm not going to hold back if you say one more word.
hold back：忍耐，耐著性子

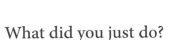

ch06-10.mp3

沒禮貌

剛剛你做了什麼？ What did you just do?

那是沒禮貌的。 That's not polite. • polite 有禮貌的

真的是非常無禮。 That's very rude. • rude 無禮的，沒禮貌的

不要那麼沒禮貌。 Don't be rude.

媽媽可不是你的朋友。 Mom's not your friend.

要有禮貌。 Please behave. • behave 行為舉止有禮貌

你怎麼可以做那樣的事呢？ How could you do such a thing?
such a thing：那樣的事情

你應該要更懂事。 You should know better than that.

要怎麼做才是對的？ What's the right way to do it?

你的老師是那樣教的嗎？ Did your teacher teach you like that?

媽媽教你那樣的嗎？ Did Mommy teach you that way?

我可不想你長大像那樣。 I don't want you to grow up like that.

你知道你哪裡做錯了嗎？ Do you know what you did wrong?

現在，給我好好做。
Now get it right.

你也不想成為一個沒禮貌的小孩，對吧？
You don't want to be a rude child, right?

你要對你的行為道歉。
Apologize for your behavior.
• behavior 行為

在大人面前不可以說那樣的話。
Don't use that word in front of adults.
• adult 大人
in front of：～的前面

如果你是他／她的話，你會開心嗎？
Would you be happy if you were him / her?

ch06-11.mp3

鬧彆扭

你為什麼不開心？
Why are you annoyed? • annoyed 生氣的
★ 也經常使用 feel upset、feel bad。

有什麼不好的事情嗎？
Is there something wrong?

停止。這真的讓我很煩。
Stop it. It's really bugging me. • bug 使煩心

有什麼問題嗎？
What's the problem?

你在煩什麼？
What's troubling you?

不要再嘀嘀咕咕的了。
Stop whining. • whine 嘀嘀咕咕，發牢騷

我不想聽到你發牢騷。
I don't want to hear you whine.

發牢騷是沒有用的。
It's no use whining.
It's no use：做～沒有用

我跟你說過不要那麼容易生氣。
I told you not to get upset so easily.

為什麼你在生媽媽的氣呢？
Why are you getting angry at Mommy?

請冷靜地說。
Please speak calmly.

你好好說的話，我會聽的。 I'm going to listen if you speak properly.

告訴我你有什麼不滿。 Tell me if there's something wrong.

沒有人關心我。 Nobody pays attention to me. 關心，注意

我只是不開心。 I'm just annoyed. / I just don't feel well.

我也不知道為什麼不開心。 I don't know why I feel annoyed.

當你生氣時，臉色很難看。 When you're angry, you look ugly.

如果你感覺差，沒有事會順利。 If you feel bad, nothing goes right.

那不是你要生氣的事情。 That's not something you felt bad about.

ch06-12.mp3

處罰

我再也忍不下去了！ I can't stand it! •stand 忍受

你一定要被處罰。 You should be grounded.

你應該受罰，不是嗎？ You deserve punishment, don't you?
•deserve 應該受到～ •punishment 處罰

告訴我你做錯了什麼。 Tell me what you did wrong.

這不是我的錯。 It was not my fault. •fault 錯誤

這是處罰！坐到反省的椅子上。 Timeout! Sit in the Thinking Chair.

你知道你做錯了什麼，對吧？ You know what you did wrong, right?

媽媽也不想要處罰你。 Mommy doesn't want to punish you.

但是你應該對你的行為負責。 But you should be responsible for your actions. •responsible 負責任的

媽媽，對不起。 Mom, I'm sorry.

請原諒我。	Please forgive me. ・forgive 原諒
我不會再這樣做了。	I won't ever do it again.
 因為你犯錯了，所以你不能看電視。	You can't watch TV because of your wrongdoing. ・wrongdoing 做壞事
因為你今天做的事情，你被禁足了，而且不能玩電腦。	You're grounded and can't use the computer because of what you did today. ・be grounded 被禁足
不要只是說對不起。	Don't just say sorry.
去寫道歉信。	Go write an apology letter. 道歉信
這都是為了你好。	It's all for your own good.

ch06-13.mp3

道歉

 互相說對不起。	Say sorry to each other.
誰要先道歉？	Who wants to apologize first? ・apologize 道歉
 對不起。	I'm sorry.
我是誠心地道歉。	I mean it.
我下次會小心的。	I'll be careful next time.
 互相握手吧。	Shake hands with each other.
看著對方的眼睛說對不起。	Look at each other in the eyes and say sorry.
不要因此指責別人。	Don't blame others for that. ・blame 指責

誠心地說對不起。 Say sorry sincerely.

讓我們確認這種事以後都不會再發生，好嗎？ Let's make sure this never happens again. All right?

我們和好吧。 Let's get along.

我不是故意那樣的。 I didn't do it on purpose.

on purpose 故意，特意

我不是那個意思。 I didn't mean it that way.

我錯了。真的很對不起。 It was a mistake. I'm really sorry.

你欠我一個正式的道歉。 You owe me a big apology.

• owe 欠 • apology 道歉

ch06-14.mp3

和解

那個，真的很對不起。 I'm so sorry for that.

你真的很傷心吧？ Were you really upset?

自己想一想，這是你的錯。 Think for yourself. It was your fault.

因為我責備你，所以你討厭我了嗎？ Did you hate me because I scolded you?

• scold 責罵，責備

媽媽也很不開心。 Mommy was really upset, too.

為什麼嘆那樣大的氣？ Why did you let out a huge sigh?

let out 發出（呻吟等）

• sigh 嘆氣

這很令人失望嗎？ Is it very disappointing?

你一定很震驚吧？ You must have been devastated.

• devastated 極度震驚的

我希望你能成為很棒的人。	I want you to grow up to be a wonderful person.
現在我可以抱你嗎？	Can I hug you now?
來這裡，媽媽親你一下。	Come here. I'll give you a kiss.
你知道媽媽的心情，對吧？	You know how Mommy feels, right?
不要再不開心了。	Don't be upset anymore.
現在我可以相信你吧？	Can I trust you now?
媽媽相信你。	Mommy trusts you.
要不要吃點好吃的呢？	Want to eat something delicious?
要不要去散步？	Want to go for a walk? 散步
 媽咪，當你生氣時我好害怕哦。	I was scared when you were mad, Mommy.
 我不是因為討厭你才那樣做。	I didn't do it because I hated you.
媽媽太暴躁了，對不起。	Mommy was too mean. I'm sorry. • mean 脾氣暴躁的
但是你還是我的心愛寶貝。	But you are still my loving baby.

Chapter 07

勸告

Who's running in the house?
誰在房子裡跑來跑去的呀？

OK. I won't.
好啦！我不會再跑了。

ch07-01.mp3

指出錯誤

等一下。	Wait.
那不是正確的行為。	That's not the right thing to do.
那是你應該做的嗎？	**Is that what you should be doing?**
做你應該做的事情。	Do what you are supposed to do.（are supposed to：應該做～）
那是我不喜歡的行為。	**That's what I'm not pleased with.**

這是不該發生的事。 This is not what should happen.

我叫你停止了。 I told you to stop.

為什麼你總是認為我做錯呢？ Why do you always think I'm wrong?

我做錯了什麼？ What did I do wrong?

那樣做好像是不行的。 It seems like you shouldn't do that.

那麼，我應該怎樣做呢？ Then what should I do?

想想其他方法。 Think of something else.

我希望你不要那樣做。 I hope you won't do it.

沒有那個必要。 That's not necessary. • necessary 必要

告訴我你哪裡做錯了。 Tell me what you did wrong.

為什麼你還繼續那樣做？ Why do you keep doing that?

你認為你做對了嗎？ Do you think you did the right thing?

那不是個好的想法。 That's not a good idea.

ch07-02.mp3

發脾氣時的教訓

不要大叫。 Don't shout.

不要發脾氣。 Stop being angry.

停止發脾氣。 Stop taking out your anger.
• take out one's anger 發脾氣

不要馬上發脾氣，那樣不好。 Don't lose your temper so quickly. That's not good. • lose one's temper 發脾氣

不要把脾氣發在別人身上。 Don't take out your anger on others.

那是不好的話。不可以那樣說！ That's a bad word. Don't say that!

如果你不能管好自己的話，我就會處罰你。 If you can't control yourself, I'm going to punish you. ‧control oneself 自我克制

忍一下！ Be patient!

誰能忍住脾氣，誰就是贏家。 The one who controls his anger wins.

你需要控制你的脾氣。 You need to get your anger under control.

你為什麼發脾氣呢？ Why are you taking out your anger?

不要皺眉頭了，笑一笑。 Don't frown. Smile. ‧frown 皺眉頭

我只是太生氣，所以不知道該做什麼。 I'm just so mad I don't know what to do.

我不想跟你說話。 I don't want to talk to you.

你幹嘛在意？ Why do you care?

那麼，我也要對你發脾氣了。 Then I'm going to get mad at you, too.

ch07-03.mp3

告誡不要在戶外亂跑

不要跑，你會跌倒的。 Don't run. You could trip and fall. ‧trip 跌倒，絆倒

車子很多。 There are a lot of cars.

危險。車子來了。 It's dangerous. There's a car coming.

在轉彎處，要特別小心。 Be extra careful on a curve. ‧extra 特別，外加

要四周看看是否有車子來。 Look around to see if there are any cars.

走在人行道內側。
Walk on the inner side of the sidewalk.
・sidewalk 人行道

牽住我的手。
Hold my hand.

跟我一起走，寶貝。
Walk with me, Honey.

路上很危險，不要跑。
The road's dangerous. Don't run.

要好好看著前面走。
Look straight ahead and walk.

小心！前面有人。
Be careful! There's someone in your way.

不要在人很多的地方跑來跑去。
Don't run where there are a lot of people.

等一下！這裡不是寫著停止嗎？
Wait! It is telling you to stop.
It is telling：（標示板，看板等）寫著～

你上次也是那樣才跌倒的。
You fell down doing that the last time.

你怎麼跑到我們前面去了？
How come you ran ahead of us?
ahead of：～的前面

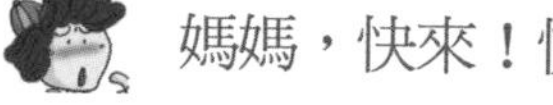

媽媽，快來！快點！
Come on, Mommy! Hurry up!

我以為跟你走丟了，嚇了一跳。
I was shocked because I thought I had lost you.

我跟你說的一樣差點跌倒了。
I almost fell down like you warned me.

哦，千鈞一髮。
Oh, gosh! It was a close call.
close call：千鈞一髮

ch07-04.mp3

告誡不要在室內亂跑

地板在震動了。
The floor is shaking. ・shake 震動

去外面跑。
Go outside and run.

你在屋內要用走的。
You walk in the house.

踮起腳尖走。
Walk on your tiptoes. ・tiptoe 腳尖

是誰在房子裡面跑？ Who's running in the house?

我沒有亂跑。 I didn't run much.

因為你在跑，連你弟弟也一起跑了。 Your brother's running because you're running.

不可以，不可以那樣跳。 No. Don't jump like that.

不要從沙發上跳下來。 Don't jump off the couch. ‧couch 沙發

不可以在沙發上跳，到處都是灰塵。 Don't jump on the couch. There's dust everywhere. ‧dust 灰塵

警衛要上來了。 The janitor is going to come up. ‧janitor 管理員，警衛

你絕對不可以在晚上跑！ You should never run at night!

現在鄰居們都在睡覺了。 The neighbors are sleeping now.

樓下的人會抗議太大聲了。 The people downstairs are going to say it's loud. ‧downstairs 在樓下的

你會喜歡聽到從樓上的鄰居傳來跺腳的聲音嗎？ Do you like it if you hear stomping from the upstairs neighbor? ‧stomp 跺腳

ch07-05.mp3

阻止危險的行動

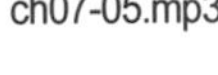

不可以！危險！ No! It's dangerous!

離遠一點。 Move far away.

往後退！ Step back! / Move back!

你會流血的。 You could bleed.

不要靠近過來。 Don't come near.

如果我碰到這個，會怎樣呢？	What happens if I touch this?
碰到的話，你會有麻煩喔。	**If you touch it, you'll get in trouble.**
我不希望你去碰它。	I don't want you to touch it.
不要碰它，因為很危險。	**Don't touch it because it's dangerous.**
不要讓你弟弟碰到。	Don't let your brother touch it. • Don't let A 動詞　不要讓 A 做～

為什麼我不能碰？	**Why can't I touch it?**
你可能會受傷。	You could get hurt.
這很燙／很銳利。	**It's hot / sharp.**
還不行。等你長大後才可以碰。	Not yet. You can touch it when you grow up.
我把這個放在你拿不到的地方。	**Let me put this out of your reach.** • out of one's reach　在～拿得到的範圍之外
如果你受傷了，媽媽會難過的。	If you get hurt, Mommy will be sad.
答應我絕對不可以碰。	**Let's promise never to touch it.**
你那時應該先問過媽媽。	You should've asked Mommy first. • should have 過去分詞　當時應該要做～
那也有可能很危險。	**That could have been dangerous.** （could have been：也有可能～）

ch07-06.mp3

不要碰哥哥姊姊的東西

你最好不要碰那個。	**You'd better not touch it.** • had better not　最好不做～（強烈警告）
這是哥哥的東西，不要碰喔。	**Don't touch it because it's your brother's.**

如果你碰了這個東西，你姊姊會不開心喔。

Your sister is not going to like it if you touch it.

你姊姊真的很珍惜那個東西。

Your sister really cares about that.（cares about 對～關心）

我只是想看看而已。

I just want to look at it.

我看完後就會把它放回原位。

I'll leave it right after I see it.

你會喜歡有人碰你的東西嗎？

Do you like when someone touches your stuff?
• stuff 東西

你姊姊同意讓你碰了嗎？

Did your sister allow you to touch it?

先去問，再來跟它玩。

Ask first and then play with it.

如果你姊姊生氣的話，我不會幫你的。

I won't help you if your sister gets mad.（gets mad 生氣）

小心地拿，然後放回原位。

Handle it carefully and then put it back.
• handle 對待　• put back 放回原位

媽媽，你能幫我保密嗎？

Mom, can you keep it a secret?（keep it a secret 保密）

請不要告訴姊姊我玩了這個。

Please don't tell her I played with this.

萬一壞了怎麼辦？

What if it broke?（What if 萬一～怎麼辦？）

你姊姊肯定會生氣。

Your sister will get mad for sure.（for sure 肯定）

姊姊也會拿我的東西。

She touched mine, too.

你能把這個讓你的妹妹玩一會嗎？

Can't you let your little sister play with it for a while?（for a while 一會兒）

ch07-07.mp3

勸告不要塗鴉

這是什麼？誰做的？

What's this? Who did this?

是誰亂塗鴉整個牆壁？ Who scribbled all over the wall?
・scribble 亂塗亂畫

你為什麼在這裡畫畫？ Why did you draw here? ・draw 畫畫

你應該要在紙上畫畫。 Drawing should be done on paper.

我想要畫畫。 I want to draw.

我等一下會擦掉。 I'll erase it later. ・erase 擦掉

這是擦不掉的。 This won't come off. 擦掉

你應該跟媽媽要紙張。 You should have asked Mommy for paper. ・ask for 要求～

下次要跟我拿紙張，知道嗎？ Ask for paper next time. Okay?

這是你畫的，你要負責擦掉。 Since you drew it, you should erase it.

弄得這樣髒，現在你高興了嗎？ Are you happy now since it's so dirty?

你不可以在任何地方亂塗鴉。 You shouldn't just be scribbling everywhere.

媽媽很不高興，因為地板被弄得很髒。 Mommy's upset because the floor is so dirty.

在這上面畫。 Draw on this.

ch07-08.mp3

小心陌生人

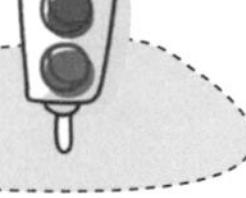

不要跟陌生人說話。 Don't talk to strangers. ・stranger 陌生人

即使有人要求，你也不可以跟他一起走。 Don't follow anyone even if they ask. 即使～
・follow 跟隨

不要告訴陌生人你的姓名或電話號碼。	Don't tell a stranger your name or number.
如果發生奇怪的事，要告訴老師或媽媽。	Tell your teacher or mom if something weird happens. ·weird 怪異的
有奇怪的人出現時，要請求幫忙。	Ask for help when a stranger comes.
不要靠近陌生人的車子。	Don't go near a stranger's car.
不可以坐陌生人的車。	Don't get in a stranger's car.
要堅決地說不。	Just say no firmly.
只能走熱鬧的街道。	Only walk on busy streets. ·busy 繁華，熱鬧
走在有人可以看到你的地方。	Walk where people can see you.
覺得不對勁時，絕對要跑開。	Just run if something feels wrong.

ch07-09.mp3

身體很髒時

太髒了。	It's so dirty.
你的身體沾到什麼了？	What's on your body?
照照鏡子。	Look at the mirror.
你聞起來很臭。	You smell bad.
你不是應該洗一下嗎？	Shouldn't you wash up?

我沒有那麼髒。	I'm not that dirty.

進去浴室。	Go to the bathroom.
有髒東西在你身上，要我把它洗掉嗎？	There's dirt on you. Want me to wash it off?

如果你更乾淨，你會更好看的。	You would look better if you were cleaner.
去換衣服。	Go change.
你在哪裡弄得這麼髒呢？	Where did you get so dirty?
你的新襯衫發生了什麼事？	What happened to your new shirt?
細菌會喜歡跟你一起住的。	Germs will love to live in you. ・germ 細菌，病菌
這麼髒的話，你會生病的。	You could get sick if you're so dirty. get sick 生病

ch07-10.mp3

房間髒亂時

 你能整理一下房間嗎？	Can you clean your room?
整理一下書桌吧。	Clear up the desk.
你的房間太髒了。	Your room's too dirty.
 我剛整理好。	I just cleaned up.
 你應該整理自己的房間。	You should clean your own room.
我連走都走不過去。	I can't even walk by.
連可以走的空間都沒有了。	There's no room to walk. ・room 空間
這個應該放在哪裡？	Where should this go?
這是人住的房間嗎？	How can a person live in here?
整個地方都是垃圾。	Junk is all over the place. ・junk 垃圾
現在這樣很難找東西。	It's hard to find things now.

你髒亂的房間快把我搞瘋了。	Your messy room drives me crazy. • messy 髒亂的　• drive A crazy 使 A 瘋狂
我 10 分鐘後再來。	I'll come by in 10 minutes. come by 過來
到時，我希望它被整理好。	I want it to be clean by then.
 弟弟也有弄亂，為什麼只有我要整理呢？	My brother did it, too. Why should I clean it alone?
這個髒亂不是我弄的。	I didn't make this mess.
 幫你弟弟整理一下。	Help your brother clean up.
想要比賽看誰比較快整理好嗎？	Want to have a match to see who can clean up faster? have a match 比賽
你的老師快來了，我們來整理它吧。	Your teacher's coming soon, so let's clean it.
你整理好後，叫媽媽一下。	Call Mommy when you're done cleaning.
當你不玩時，應該要做什麼？	What do you do when you're done playing?
 我需要整理。	I need to clean up.
 我們按照顏色整理它們。	Let's organize them by color. • organize 整理
根據大小把它們放好。	Place them according to their size. • place 放　according to 根據～
 媽媽，這個玩具要放哪？	Mom, where does this toy go?

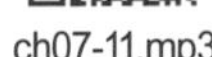

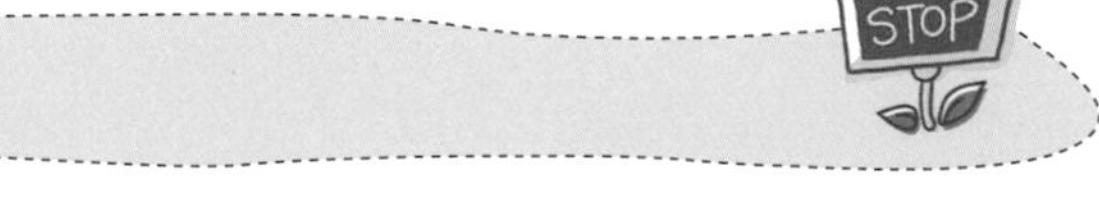

ch07-11.mp3

打人時

 打人是不好的。	It's bad to hit others.

絕對不可以打別人。 Never hit others.

你不應該傷害其他的人。 **You shouldn't hurt other people.**

即使你想打他，也要忍下來。 Hold it even if you want to hit him. ‧hold 忍耐

我太討厭他了，以致於我不知道該怎麼做。 **I hate him so badly that I don't know what to do.** ‧hate 討厭 ‧badly 非常

是他先打我的。 He hit me first.

不要用打的，要用說的。 **Don't hit him. Talk to him.**

如果你打回去，你也是不對的。 You will do the wrong thing, too if you hit him back.

你打他的話，你朋友會受傷的。 **Your friend's going to be hurt if you hit him.**

我告訴過你絕對不可以那樣做。 I told you never to do that!

你需要被處罰。 **You need to get in trouble.** 受罰

你要我去叫警察嗎？ Want me to call the cops? ‧cop 警察

你不可以打女孩。 **You must not hit girls.**

現在你的朋友不會想跟你玩。這樣你也可以嗎？ Your friend's not going to want to play with you now. Are you fine with it?

Chapter 08

習慣養成

Don't watch TV while lying down.
不要躺著看電視

Alright!
好啦！

ch08-01.mp3

正確坐姿

坐好。	Sit properly.
坐得舒服點。	Sit comfortably.
盤腿坐。	Sit crisscross. ★ Sit with your legs crisscrossed. 的簡單說法。
腰挺直。	Straighten your back. / Keep your back straight.

屁股貼著椅子。	**Sit on your bottom.** ・bottom 屁股
整個坐下去。	Sit all the way down.
不要靠著坐。	**Don't just perch on the chair.** ・perch 靠著坐
這張椅子／書桌不舒服。	This chair / desk is uncomfortable.
這張椅子太高／低了。	**The chair is too high / low.**
媽媽，這張書桌／椅子太晃。	Mom, the desk / chair is too wobbly. ・wobbly 擺動的，不穩的
 停止搖晃書桌。	**Stop shaking the desk.** ・shake 搖動
不要趴在書桌上。	Don't put your head on your desk.
手不要托住下巴。	**Don't put your hand under your chin.** ・chin 下巴
把腰挺直坐好。	Sit in a chair with your back up.
背要靠著椅背。	**Lean against the back of the chair.** (Lean against：靠著～)
為什麼你一直從椅子上起來？	Why do you keep getting out of the chair?
媽媽把椅子推到屁股下給你坐。	**Mommy will push the chair in for you.**
不要站在旋轉椅上。	Don't stand on the swivel chair. (swivel chair：旋轉椅)
不要轉椅子。	**Don't spin on the chair.** ・spin 轉動
不要跪坐。	Don't sit on your knees.
不要躺著。	**Don't lie down.**
不要抖腳。	Don't shake your legs.
這樣坐著更舒服。	**It's more comfortable to sit like this.**
以後你的背會彎曲的。	Your back might be bent later. ・bent 彎曲的

你那樣坐的話，你的腰會彎曲的。
If you sit like that, your waist will be bent.

確保你的腰不會太彎。
Make sure not to bend too much at your waist. •bend 彎曲

我怕你會有脊椎彎曲的問題。
I'm afraid you'll have a swayback.
•swayback 脊椎彎曲

我不希望你跟老太太一樣彎腰。
I don't want you to get bent over like an old lady.

ch08-02.mp3

拿鉛筆

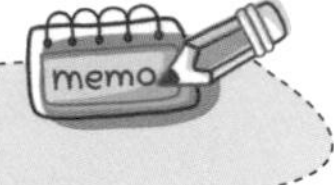

拿好鉛筆。
Hold your pencil right.

不要握得太用力。
Don't hold on it too hard.

像媽媽一樣拿著。
Hold it like Mommy.

你鉛筆拿得太短／長了。
You hold the pencil too short / long.

用右手寫寫看。
Write with your right hand.

我比較會用左手。
I use my left hand better.

你的鉛筆斷了。
Your pencil's broken.

媽媽，你能幫我削鉛筆嗎？
Mom, will you sharpen my pencil?
•sharpen 削尖

ch08-03.mp3

寫字

字母寫太小／大了。
The letters are too small / large.

你的字要寫大一點。 You want them bigger.

試著沿著線寫。 Try to write along the line.

你寫的字太潦草了。 Your handwriting is sloppy.

・sloppy 潦草，隨便

把你的字母寫得一樣大。 Make your letters the same size.

不要寫得太用力。 Don't write too hard.

用橡皮擦擦掉。 Erase it with an eraser.

・erase 擦掉 ・eraser 橡皮擦

試著再寫一次。 Try to write again.

寶貝，要寫正確。 Get it right, Honey.

慢慢寫。 Write slowly.

媽，我可以像這樣寫嗎？ Should I write like this, Mom?

這個要怎麼寫？ How do you write this?

你寫字要留間隔。 You have to space the words.

・space 留間隔

你的尾音拼錯了。 The ending sound is misspelled.

・misspelled 拼錯

這個是大寫 K／小寫 k。 It's a capital K / a lower case k.

寫下一行。 Go to the next line.

單字之間要留間隔。 Put a space between the words.

我想你用錯標點符號了。 I think you got the punctuation wrong.

・punctuation 標點符號

你拼錯字了。 You spelled the word wrong.

檢查你的拼字。 Check your spelling.

我喜歡你寫的字。 I like your handwriting. •handwriting 筆跡

寫字時要坐正。 Sit properly when writing.

媽媽，我的手指痛。 **Mom, my fingers hurt.**

沒有線條的紙張很難寫。 It's hard to write on unlined paper.
•unlined 沒有線的 (= unruled)

ch08-04.mp3

看電視

離電視遠一點。 Back off from the TV.

再往後一點。 Back off a little more.

不要躺著看電視。 Don't watch TV while lying down.

你電視看得太近囉。 You're watching too close.

關掉電視。 Turn off the TV.

看完電視後一定要關掉。 Be sure to turn it off after watching it.

那樣看的話，對眼睛不好。 It's not good for your eyes to watch it like that.

你好好坐著嗎？ Are you sitting properly?

你又躺下來了。 You're lying down again.

如果你那樣坐的話，我會關掉電視。 I'll turn off the TV if you sit like that.

如果你不往後一點的話，我會關掉電視。 I'll turn off the TV if you don't move back.

你答應我只看 30 分鐘！ You promised to watch for 30 minutes!

這是你最後能看的了。 This will be the last thing you watch.

這看完後你一定要把電視關掉。	Make sure you turn it off after this.
靠在後面的靠墊。	**Lean on** the cushion behind you. 靠～

媽媽，這個沙發不舒服。	Mom, the sofa's uncomfortable.
媽媽，你能給我一個靠墊嗎？	**Mom, will you get me a cushion?**
媽媽，你能給我一個可以靠的東西嗎？	Mom, will you get me something to lean on?

不要一直按遙控器。	**Don't press the remote on and on.** • remote 遙控器 (= remote control)
寫完功課後，再看電視。	Watch TV after finishing your homework.
先完成你要做的事情。	**Finish what you need to do first.**
不要看電視，去做你的功課。	Stop watching TV and do your homework.
你一直在換頻道。	**You keep flipping through the channels.** 快速轉過～
我想你電視中毒了。	I think you're obsessed with TV. • be obsessed with 著迷～，執著～

ch08-05.mp3

把東西放回原位

地板滿滿地都是東西。	**There are lots of things on the floor.**
把它放進抽屜。	Put it in the drawer.
把它們放上架子。	**Put them in the shelf.**
好好整理你的東西。	Organize your things well. • organize 整理
你應該收拾你自己的東西。	**You should clear up your things.** 收拾

這個之前放在哪裡？ Where was this before?

這個不是放在這裡的東西。 This doesn't belong here. • belong 屬於～

把這個放在它應該在的地方。 Put this where it is supposed to be.

把它物歸原位。 Put it where it belongs.

把用過的東西放回原處。 Put the used things back into their place.

把東西放在原位，這樣你能很容易找到。 Put the things where they belong so you can find them easily.

你當時應該把它們放在正確的地方。 You should have put them in the right place.

媽媽，這個我要放哪？ Mom, where should I put this?

媽媽，我把這個放在這裡。 Mom, I'll put this here.

我現在要用這個。 I'm going to use this now.

媽媽跟你說過要把這個放哪？ Where did Mommy tell you to put this?

整理好之後，不就很容易找到嗎？ Isn't it easy to find things since you cleaned up?

ch08-06.mp3

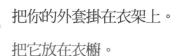

整理衣服

把你的外套掛在衣架上。 Hang your jacket on the hanger. • hanger 衣架

把它放在衣櫥。 Put it in the closet. • closet 衣櫥

媽媽，沒有地方可以放了。 Mom, there's nowhere to put this.
• nowhere 任何地方都沒有

媽媽，現在這件太小了。 Mom, this is too small now.

把你不穿的衣服拿出來。 Take out what you're not going to wear.
Take out 拿出來

這邊有個洞。	There's a hole here. ‧hole 洞
 我來幫你把這個縫好。	I'll sew this for you. ‧sew 縫
把髒的襪子放進洗衣籃內。	Put your dirty socks in the laundry.
這些襪子為什麼在這裡？	Why are these socks here?
我告訴過你不要把襪子反過來了。	I told you not to turn the socks inside out. 裡面的翻到外面
這些抽屜滿了。	The drawers are full. ‧drawer 抽屜
我們把春／夏／秋／冬季的衣服整理好吧。	Let's organize our spring / summer / fall / winter clothes.
這些衣服已經過季了，把它們放回去吧。	These clothes are out of season, so let's put them back. 季節已過
我們把你不穿的衣服放進箱子內吧。	Let's put the clothes that you don't wear in the box.
把你不穿的衣服捐出去，如何？	How about donating the clothes that you don't wear? ‧donate 捐贈
我們把舊衣服送給表妹吧。	Let's give away the old clothes to your cousin. 贈送

有關收納用品的表達

- 抽屜 drawer / dresser
- 壁櫥 closet
- 衣架 clothes hanger
- 架子 shelf
- 掛衣服的衣夾或木釘 peg
- 大衣衣架 coat hanger
- 整理箱 storage container
- 洗衣籃 hamper

吃飯禮儀

ch08-07.mp3

吃飯前洗好手了嗎？	Did you wash your hands before eating?
吃飯前，要好好洗手。	Wash your hands well before eating.
等大人們先開動，你才能吃。	Start eating once the adult starts.
不要同時拿筷子和湯匙。	Don't hold the spoon and chopsticks together. •chopsticks 筷子
好好地使用筷子。	Use your chopsticks right.
像這樣拿筷子。	Hold your chopsticks like this.
嘴裡有食物時，不要說話。	Don't talk with food in your mouth. / Don't talk with your mouth full.
不可以剩下食物。	Don't leave any food uneaten. / Don't leave any food on your plate.
吃飯時，不可以咂嘴唇。	Don't smack your lips when you eat. •smack one's lips 咂嘴唇
咳嗽時，一定要轉過頭去。	Turn your head when coughing. •cough 咳嗽
不要把它吐得到處都是。	Don't spit it out everywhere!
吃飯時，不要離開位子。	Do not leave the table while you're eating.
小心不要把食物弄掉。	Be careful not to drop the food.
不要把湯灑出來。	Don't spill your soup. •spill 灑
吃飯的時候，要坐正。	Sit properly when eating.
喝湯時，不要發出聲音。	Don't make noises when you eat soup.

不可以用手抓食物。
Don't pick at the food with your hand. / Do not use your hands to pick at the food.

不可以邊看電視邊吃飯。
Don't watch TV while eating.

閉上嘴巴咀嚼。
Chew with your mouth closed.

吃飯的時候，不要跑來跑去。
Don't move around while eating.

不要舔手指頭，要用紙巾擦。
Don't lick your fingers. Use a napkin.
• lick 舔

把食物吹涼時，不要吹太用力。
Don't blow on your food too hard to cool it off.

把你的雙腳好好放在桌子下面。
Keep your legs still under the table.

不要在餐桌上打嗝。
Don't ever burp at the table. • burp 打嗝

噁，爸爸，你打嗝了。
Yuck. You burped, Daddy.

吃飯的時候，不可以講髒的東西。
Don't talk about dirty things while eating.

在餐桌上擤鼻涕是沒禮貌的行為。
It's not polite to blow your nose at the table.
• blow one's nose 擤鼻涕

Chapter 09

孩子們常用的表達

I'll do it after I do this.
我玩完這個後會去做。

Do your homework, Honey!
作功課囉，親愛的。

ch09-01.mp3

找東西

媽媽，我的尺在哪裡？ Mom, where is my ruler?

• ruler 尺

媽媽，我找不到。 I can't find it, Mom.

找仔細一點。 Look for it carefully.

試著想想你放在哪了。 Try to think where you left it.

我確定我把它放在這了。 I'm sure I put it here.

媽媽，你能找到我的筆記本嗎？ Mom, can you find my notebook?

我以為我把它放在這了。	I thought I left it here.
我都找遍了，可是還是沒看到。	I've looked all over (到處) for it, but I can't see it.
媽媽，你把它丟掉了嗎？	Did you throw it away (把它丟掉), Mom?
那邊你找過了嗎？	Did you look over there?
它在那邊。	It's over there.

在這裡！	Here it is!
我找到了。	I found it.
為什麼會在那裡呢？	Why is it there?
我沒有把它放在那裡。	I didn't leave it there.
媽媽，我的鉛筆盒不見了。	Mom, I lost my pencil case.
敏基把它拿走了。	Minji took it.

你上次是在哪裡看到的？	Where did you see it last?
你上次用是什麼時候？	When was the last time you used it?
你沒有把它放在學校嗎？	Didn't you leave it at school?
我告訴過你要把東西放在原位。	I told you to put your things in their places.

ch09-02.mp3

要東西

媽媽，給我一些水。	Get me some water, Mom.
這不夠。	It isn't enough.
我還要更多。	I want more.

這樣就夠了。	This is enough.
我要點心。	I want a snack.
我餓了！我能吃晚餐了嗎？	I'm hungry! Can I have dinner?
你能把書拿給我嗎？	Will you hand me the book?
你能把玩具給我嗎？	Will you pass me the toys?
那個高度，我搆不到。	I can't reach that high.
你能把那邊的那個東西給我嗎？	Can you get me that over there?
你可以幫我拿遙控器嗎？	Will you get me the remote?
 你有手，自己拿。	You have hands. Take it yourself.
怎麼一直要這要那？	How come you keep asking?
那不是媽媽的工作，你自己做。	That's not Mommy's job. Do it yourself.
你不能自己做嗎？	Can't you do it on your own?
 我忘記我的鞋袋了。	I forgot my shoe bag.
媽媽，我忘記帶學校用品了。	Mom, I forgot to bring my supplies.
你能把學校用品帶來學校嗎？	Will you take my supplies to school?
 好的。	It's done!
媽媽很忙，你自己做。	Mom's busy. Do it by yourself.
這次媽媽幫你做， 但是下次你要自己做。	I'm doing this for you now, but do it yourself next time.

ch09-03.mp3

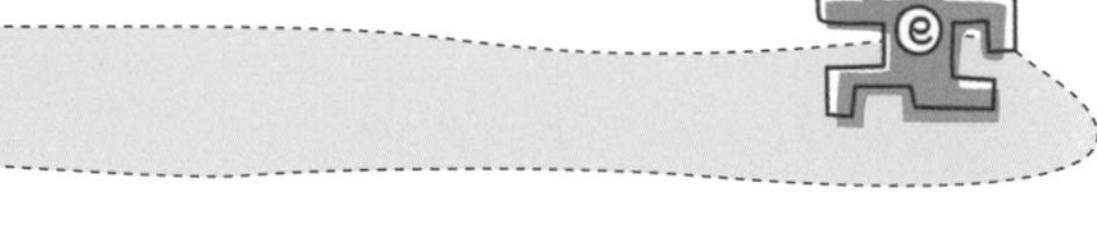

做事拖拉時

這個我能明天做嗎？	Can I do it tomorrow?

這個我五分鐘後再做。 I'll do it in 5 minutes.

不要催我。 **Don't push me.** ‧push 催促

我快做好了，再等一下。 I'm almost done. Wait a little.

我累了。 **I'm tired.**

我累垮了。 I'm all tired out. —累垮了

我頭好痛。 **I have a headache.** ‧headache 頭痛

我可以休息一下後再做嗎？ Can I do it after I get some rest?

我做完這個再做。 **I'll do it after I do this.**

我已經沒有力氣去做了。 I have no more strength to do it. ‧strength 力氣

媽媽，我需要休息。 **Mom, I need some rest.**

好，好，我待會一定會把它完成。 Okay, okay. I'll definitely get it done later. ‧definitely 肯定，當然

還有剩很多時間。 **There's still a lot of time left.**

你不需要那麼急嘛。 You don't have to rush. ‧rush 急著做～

我會做，我保證！ **I'll do it. Promise!**

媽，為什麼你都不讓我休息？ Why do you never let me rest, Mom?

你總是說等一下。 **You always say later.**

現在就把它完成！ Finish it right this minute!

做你必須做的事情。 **Do what you have to do.**

這已經拖了一個禮拜了。 It's been pushed back a week. —往後推

沒有時間。不要再拖延了。 **There's no time. Stop pushing it back.**

ch09-04.mp3

要求再多玩一會

我不能再玩一會嗎？	**Can't I play a little more?**
我想要多玩 30 分鐘。	I want to play for 30 more minutes.
我還沒玩完。	**I'm not done playing.**
我還沒玩完。	I'm not done yet.
我沒有好好玩夠。	**I didn't play well enough.**
我們甚至還沒開始玩。	We haven't even gotten started.
我剛才開始玩。	**I just started.**
為什麼時間過得這麼快？	Why does time fly?
已經那麼晚了嗎？	**It's already that late?**

才開始覺得好玩的說。	It's starting to get fun.
讓我再多玩一會。	**Allow me to play a little more.**
如果你讓我多玩一會，我會努力讀書的。	I'll study hard if you let me play more.
我完成我的事情了，所以我可以多玩一會嗎？	**I finished my work. So can I play more?**
沒有足夠的時間去玩。	There's not enough time to play.
我希望我能多玩一會。	**I wish I could play more.** （I wish：我希望～）
我才剛開始玩 5 分鐘而已。	It's been only 5 minutes since I started the game.
答應我下次會讓我玩久一點。	**Promise you'll let me play longer next time.**

我明白你的心情，但是你不能一直玩了。	I know how you feel, but you can't play all the time. 總是
我想你已經玩得差不多了。	You had enough fun, I guess.
玩耍時間結束，去準備睡覺。	Play time is over. Get ready to go to bed. • over 結束

ch09-05.mp3

表示討厭

我累了。	I'm tired.
那不好玩。	That's not fun.
那個太幼稚了，我不喜歡。	I hate it because it's too childish. • childish 幼稚的
那是小孩子的玩意兒。	It's a childlike thing. • childlike 孩子般的
這不符合我的年齡。	It's not something for my age. • age 年齡
我只是不想要做。	I just don't want to do it.
沒有時間。	There's no time.
我不知道要怎麼做。	I don't know how to do it.
那太難了。	That's too hard.
那不是我能做到的事情。	That's not something I can do.

我能不做嗎？	Can I not do it?
我一定要做這個嗎？	Should I do this?
我能把它停止嗎？	Can I stop it?
弟弟不能做嗎？	Can't my brother do it?

又要做一遍嗎？	Do it again?
其他小孩也沒有做那個啊。	Other kids don't even do that.
媽媽總是叫我做事！	Mom always makes me do work!
爸爸媽媽甚至也沒做。	Mom and Dad don't even do it.
我的朋友會取笑我的。	My friends will make fun of me. 取笑～
不要叫我做我不想做的事情。	Don't make me do what I don't want to do.
我今天的狀況不好。	I'm not feeling good today.
我不想做。	I don't feel like doing it. ･feel like -ing 不想做～
 可是，那也是你的事。	It's your job, though. ･though 可是，然而
為什麼你一直說不要？	How come you always say no?
這是你一定要做的事，你也知道的。	You need to be doing this, and you know it.
抱歉，沒有人可以幫你做。	I am sorry. Nobody can do that for you.

ch09-06.mp3

生氣

 走開！	Go away!
為什麼你那樣對我？	Why do you do that to me?
不要再惹我了。	Stop bothering me. ･bother 打擾
再給我說話試試看。	Don't say a word.
不要那樣說話。	Don't talk like that.
你一直都是那樣！	You're always like that!

這是我的。不要碰。
It's mine. Don't touch it.

誰准你碰的？
Who told you to touch it?

如果你再那樣做的話，我會動手的！
I'm going to get you if you do it again!

天啊，沒有人聽我說話。
Gosh, nobody's listening to me.

媽，我不要跟你說話。
I don't want to talk to you, Mom!

你不知道我在說什麼嗎？
Don't you know what I'm saying?

媽媽，你總是那樣！
You're always like that, Mommy!

那媽媽，你也自己做做看啊！
Then try it by yourself, Mom!

爸，你總是照自己的意思去做！
You always do it your way, Dad!

我現在不要聽媽媽的話。
I'm not going to listen to Mommy now.

我要照我的方式去做！
I'm going to do it my way!

不要跟我說話。
Don't talk to me.

那樣說真的很不禮貌。
It's not polite to say that.

是什麼讓你這麼生氣呢？
What made you this angry?

生氣也是沒有用的。
It's no use getting angry.

一直生氣的話，有什麼好處呢？
What good is it to stay angry?

ch09-07.mp3

表示不公平

媽媽總是指責我。
Mom always blames me. ·blame 指責

你總是對我嘮叨！
You always nag me! ·nag 嘮叨

為什麼你只罵我？ Why do you only scold me?

這不公平。 It's not fair.

他的更大。 His is bigger.

她的比我的更好。 Hers is better than mine.

她先說的。 She said it first.

他做的。 He did it.

你對吉娜偏心。 You favor Jina over me.
• favor A over B 偏愛 A 勝過 B

為什麼你喜歡吉娜比我多？ Why do you like Jina more than me?

也給我買些東西。 Buy me something, too.

我不要別人穿過的舊衣服。 I don't want hand-me-downs.
• hand-me-down 別人穿過的舊衣服

不要把我跟她做比較。 Don't compare me with her.
• compare A with B 比較 A 和 B

我不是你的兒子嗎？ Am I not your son?

為什麼記溯總是拿走好的？ Why does Jisu always get the good one?

我比她更需要那個。 I need it more than her.

你總是先想到她。 You always think of her first.

不是那樣的。 That's not true.

我對你們兩個的愛都是一樣的。 I love you both the same.

我不喜歡你說話的方式。 I don't like the way you talk.

如果有什麼事在煩你，告訴我。不要忍住不說。 If something bothers you, tell me. Don't hold back. • hold back 抑制

Chapter 10

爸爸正在講理由

Where are you, Dad? You're not home, yet.
爸，你在哪？你還沒回家喔。

I'm afraid I'm running late.
抱歉，我會晚一點。

ch10-01.mp3

說晚回家／很忙

爸，你什麼時候回家？	When are you coming, Dad?
因為我還有會議，我想會很晚。	I think I'll be late because I have a meeting.
現在塞車。我想會晚一點。	There's traffic. I think I'm running a little late. ・traffic 交通流量
我可能會晚回去。寶貝，你先睡。	I might be late. Go to sleep, Honey.

不要等我。	**Don't wait for me.**
有客戶要來。	I have a guest. ·guest 客人
我突然有事情要做。	**I suddenly have something to do.**
我要跟同事去吃晚餐。	I have to eat dinner with my coworkers. ·coworker 同事
我必須把事情處理掉。	**I have to finish something.**
我在工作。	I'm working.
爸爸還在工作。	**Dad is still at work.**
我忙著在期限內完成工作。	I'm busy keeping my deadline. ·deadline 截止期限
我真的很忙。	**I'm really busy.**
我必須去見朋友。	I have to meet my friend.
我會吃過晚餐後再回家。	**I'll come home after eating dinner.**
我沒有時間跟你聊了。	I have no time to talk.
我晚一點再打給你。	**I'll call later.**
你又要晚回來了嗎？	Are you going to be late again?
孩子們正在等你呢。	**The kids are waiting for you.**
爸，我想你。	Dad, I miss you.
早點回家。	**Come home early.**
一結束，我就立刻回家。	I'll come right home when it is over.
我會盡可能早點回去。	**I'll try to go in as early as I can.** 盡可能早

ch10-02.mp3

媽媽的嘮叨

為什麼你現在才回來？	Why did you come home now?
脫下衣服去睡吧。	Take off your clothes and go to sleep.
你能把你要洗的衣服放進洗衣籃嗎？	Will you put your laundry in the laundry bin? ‧bin 箱，容器
不要把你的衣服到處亂放！	Don't just leave your clothes everywhere!
為什麼我要在你後面幫你撿？	How come I should pick up after you?
你不能停止看電視嗎？	Can't you stop watching TV?
你晚餐一定要總是吃外面嗎？	Do you always have to eat dinner out?
不要喝太多酒。	Stop drinking too much.
你需要去做些運動。	You need to get some exercise. ‧exercise 運動
你應該消除你的腰間贅肉。	You should get rid of (消除～) your love handles. (腰間贅肉)
注意你的健康。	Think about your health.
不要抽菸了。	Stop smoking. ‧smoke 抽菸
你能幫我打掃家裡嗎？	Will you help me clean the house?
你忘了我們結婚前的約定了嗎？	Did you forget the promise we made before we got married? (結婚)
親愛的，你可以洗碗嗎？	Will you do the dishes, Darling?
不要在孩子面前躺著。	Don't lie down when the kids are around.
親愛的，你能幫我做嗎？	Will you do it for me, Darling?
請跟孩子們玩。	Play with the kids, please.

ch10-03.mp3

爸爸的週末約定

好好期待週末吧！	**Wait for the weekend!**
你可以相信我的話。	You can take my word for it. (相信我的話)
我會遵守這週末的諾言。	**I'll keep my promise this weekend.** (遵守我的諾言)
這個週末你想做什麼呢？	What do you want to do this weekend?
這個週末要看電影嗎？	**Want to watch a movie this weekend?**
我帶你去兜風。	I'll take you on a drive. • take A on a drive 開車帶 A 兜風
這次我將為你達成這件事。	**I'll try to make it work for you this time.** (把事情辦成)
計畫一下週末要做什麼吧。	Plan on something for the weekend.
這個週末跟爸爸一起學習吧。	**Let's study with Daddy this weekend.**
這個週日我們一起去踢足球吧。	Let's play soccer together this Sunday.
這個週末，我會陪你玩。	**I'll play with you this weekend.**
抱歉！我這個週末再來做。	Sorry! I'll do it this weekend.
抱歉！我這個禮拜會做。	**Sorry! I'll do it during this week.**
我們去吃些好吃的吧。	Let's go to eat something delicious.
我們只有週末有時間。	**We only have time on weekends.**
我在平日沒有時間。	I have no time on weekdays.
連假時，我們去旅行吧。	**Let's go on a trip during the long holiday.** (連續假日)
我會在週六跟週日哄你入睡。	I'll tuck you into bed on Saturdays and Sundays. • tuck A into bed 哄 A 睡覺

這個週末我會幫你打掃房子。	**I'll help you clean up the house this weekend.**
這個週末我來洗碗。	I'll do the dishes this weekend.
我來照顧孩子，你休息一下吧。	**I'll take care of the kids, so get some rest.**
親愛的，這個週末你什麼也不需要做。	You don't have to do a thing this weekend, Honey.
今天事情都由我來做。	**I'll do everything today.**

ch10-04.mp3

爸爸的解釋

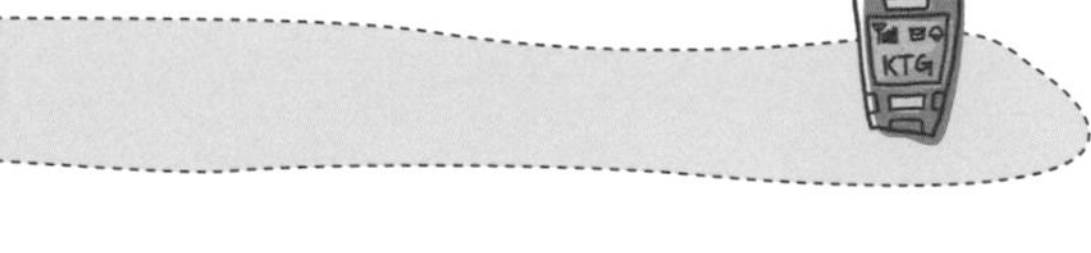

抱歉，我忘了。	**Sorry that I forgot.**
我不是要那樣做的。	I wasn't trying to do that.
我一直有事情要忙。	**Something kept me busy.**
你能理解嗎？	Will you understand?
你知道我的意思嗎？	**You know what I mean?**
我也很想去。	I wanted to go, too.
我本來想要幫你做的。	**I wanted to do it for you.**
我確定下次我一定會做。	I'll make sure I do it next time.
我本來打算補償你的。	**I was trying to make it up to you.** (make it up：補償，挽回)
結果變成這樣，我也很難受。	I'm also sad it didn't work out well.
這次我真的想要履行約定的。	**I was trying to keep my word this time.**
它並沒有按計畫進行。	It didn't work as planned. (as planned：按已計畫的)
我下次不會再這樣了。	**I won't do it next time.**

這種事不會再發生了。 This won't happen again.

我們下次再做吧。 Let's do it next time.

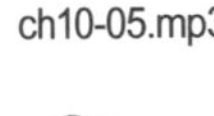

ch10-05.mp3

安慰疲憊的爸爸

親愛的，你一定很累吧。	You must be tired, Honey.
你知道全家都很愛你，對吧？	You know our family loves you, right?
我愛你，爸爸！	I love you, Dad!
爸，提起精神來！	Cheer up, Dad!
爸，我幫你按摩。	I'll give you a massage, Dad.
我會給你親親。	I'll give you a kiss.

爸，我們一直在背後支持你。	Dad, we're always behind you.
不要灰心。	Don't let yourself down. • let oneself down 使～灰心、失望
挺直肩膀。	Straighten your shoulders. • straighten 挺直

看吧，爸爸是最厲害的！	See? Daddy's the best!
我長大後會照顧你的。	I'll take good care of you when I grow up.

休息一下再做吧。	Do it after resting a little.
為了你的健康，我希望你能慢慢來。	I hope you slow down for your health. （slow down：放鬆，放慢）
即使很忙，也不要忘了吃飯喔。	Even if you're busy, don't forget to eat.

我做了很多好吃的菜幫你打氣。	**I made a lot of good food, so you can cheer up.**
你知道我們很需要你，對吧？	**You know we really need you, right?**

Praise 讚美單字怎麼說

爸爸媽媽有沒有常常誇獎自己的孩子做得很好，做得很棒呢？其實孩子是需要被鼓勵的哦！這樣他們才會有更多的信心和勇氣，可以在跌倒了之後馬上就能爬起來！所以，多多讚美自己的孩子吧！

表達對孩子的愛和關心還可以這樣說！

I love you.
我愛你。
You are the best!
你是最棒的。
You are special!
你是特別的。
You are my boy (girl)!
你是我的好孩子。
Good boy. / Good girl.
好孩子。
You're such a good boy (girl).
你真是個好孩子。
You're being so good.
你做得很好！

孩子聽到爸爸媽媽的稱讚和鼓勵，可別害羞的什麼話都沒有回應爸爸媽媽！要記得跟爸爸媽媽說謝謝！「Thanks, Mom.」或是「Thanks, Dad.」意思是「媽，謝謝你。」或是「爸，謝謝你。」

寬扎節 Kwanzaa

在各種種族和文化相容的美國，除了聖誕節之外，還有其他的冬季節日。寬扎節是來自非洲的人們為了不讓他們的傳統失傳，從 1966 年開始舉辦的節日。從 12 月 26 日到 1 月 1 日的這段時間，跟家人和鄰居彼此分享愛，並且點亮有七個蠟燭的燭台，一起度過穿著漂亮衣服和享用美食的時光。

★常用的會話句子

‧你知道什麼是寬扎節嗎？	Do you know what Kwanzaa is?
‧我不曾聽過，那是什麼？	I've never heard of it. What is it?
‧寬扎節是住在美國的非洲裔美國人，從 12 月 26 日到 1 月 1 日為止，舉行一個禮拜的節日。	It is a festival that lasts for a week from December 26 to January 1. It is a festival for African-Americans living in America.
‧寬扎節要做什麼呢？	What do people do during Kwanzaa?
‧他們會舉行燭光典禮，並交換禮物。	They have a candlelight ceremony and exchange gifts.

光明節 Hanukkah

這是猶太人的冬季節日，根據猶太曆有時是在 11 月底，有時則是在 12 月。作為舊約歷史的重要日子，從光明節的第一天開始將持續八天。這些天吃特定的食物，還有玩遊戲，並且每一天都會在叫做 menorah 的燭台上點上一根蠟燭來紀念。

★ 常用的會話句子

• 在美國，光明節是另一個冬季節日。	Hanukkah is another winter holiday in America.
• 這是猶太人連續八天的節日。	It's a Jewish festival that lasts for eight days.
• 光明節也叫做「光的慶典」。	Hanukkah is also known as the "festival of lights."
• 光明節的八天中一天點一根蠟燭。	For the eight days of Hanukkah candles are lit one by one.
• 他們會使用被稱為 Menorah 的燭台。	They use a special candlestick called Menorah.

和媽媽一起玩
Let's Play！

Chapter 11

孩子們喜歡的基本遊戲

OK! Let's see what we can do.
好啊，我們來看看可以玩什麼。

Mommy, play with me.
媽咪，跟我玩吧！

ch11-01.mp3

要求一起玩的時候

媽，我很無聊。	Mom, I'm bored. ・bored 無聊的
該是玩耍的時間了！	It's play time!
媽，你能和我一起玩嗎？	Mom, can you play with me?
我想知道有什麼好玩的。	I wonder what's fun to play. ・wonder 想知道
你有什麼好玩的嗎？	Do you have anything fun?

現在我要停止看書了。	I'll stop reading now.
我不想再看電視了。	I don't want to watch TV anymore.
我討厭一個人玩。	I hate to play alone.
我需要跟朋友一起玩。	I need friends to play together with.
 要玩點有趣的嗎？	Want to have some fun? 嘗試有趣的事物
你準備好要玩有趣的嗎？	Are you ready to have fun?
我們來找點好玩的吧。	Let's find something fun. ・find 找
 耶！聽起來好棒喔！	Yay! Sounds great! ★ Sounds = It sounds（聽起來像～）的簡略表達。
 好，我的寶貝一定很無聊吧。	Okay. My baby must have been bored. 一定～
當然，你想跟我玩什麼呢，甜心？	Sure. What do you want to do with me, Sweetheart?
我們要玩什麼呢？	What should we play?
玩你想要玩的。	Do whatever you want to do.
 我們隨便玩吧。	Let's do anything.
媽，我們來拼拼圖。	Mom, let's solve a puzzle.
 媽媽今天的狀況很好，可以跟你玩一整天。	Mommy's feeling good today. I can play with you all day long. 一整天
跟我的寶貝玩是最有趣的。	Playing with my baby is the most fun.
我最喜歡媽媽跟我玩遊戲了。	I love it when Mommy plays games with me.

ch11-02.mp3

下次和你玩

下次再玩吧。	Let's play next time.
你沒有看到媽媽很忙嗎？	Can't you see Mom's very busy?
抱歉，媽媽太忙了。	Sorry. Mommy's too busy.
等我洗碗後，再跟你玩。	I'll play with you after I do the dishes.
我在工作，晚一點再跟你玩。	I'm working, so I'll play with you later.
再一會工作結束後，就能跟你玩。	I can play with you in a minute after work.
你能等等嗎？謝謝。	Can you wait? Thanks.
等一下！我們等一下再玩。	Wait! Let's play a little later.
等我五分鐘。	Wait for five minutes.

五分鐘後，你能跟我玩嗎？	Can you play with me in 5 minutes?
現在我就想玩。	I want to play right now.
現在就跟我玩。	Play with me right away.

現在不行。	Not now.
今天沒有時間。	There's no time today. / I have no time today.
太晚了，明天我們再大玩特玩。	It's too late. Let's play a lot tomorrow.
現在有太多事要去做了。	There's too much to do right now.
媽媽也想跟你玩，但是現在不行。	Mommy also wants to play with you, but I can't right now.
去叫爸爸跟你玩。	Ask Daddy to play with you.

爸爸每次都說他很忙。	Dad always says he's busy.
如果我等你的話，你必須要跟我多玩一會。	If I wait, you have to play with me some more.
那麼，你什麼時候有時間呢？	Then when can you find time? / When are you free then?
你可以跟我玩之後再去做吧。	You can do it later after playing with me.

ch11-03.mp3

約定玩的時間

我們要玩多久？	How long should we play?
我們來定個玩的時間吧。	Let's set up a time to play. set up 設立
我把定時器設定 30 分鐘。	I'll set the timer for 30 minutes. • set 設定，設置
定時器一響，我們就停止。	When the timer goes off, we'll stop. goes off （警告等）響起
現在開始，我們玩積木 40 分鐘。	Let's play with blocks for 40 minutes starting now.
我們在遊樂場玩一個小時吧。	Let's play at the playground for an hour.

我要玩兩個小時。	I want to play for 2 hours.

兩個小時太長，我們就玩一個小時。	2 hours is too long. Let's play for only 1 hour.
我們約定好來玩 20 分鐘。	Let's promise to play for 20 minutes.

20 分鐘太短了。	20 minutes is too short.
我需要玩更久。	I need more time to play.

讓我再多玩一回，拜託。 Just one more round, please.
・round （比賽等）一回

就只能再多玩五分鐘。 Only for 5 more minutes.

下次，你要遵守你說的話。 Next time, you should keep your word.

再玩三次後，我們就結束吧。 Let's finish after 3 more rounds.

我們只剩五分鐘了。 We only have 5 minutes left. ・left 剩

時間到了！結束！ Time's up! Done!

鬧鐘響了！ The alarm went off!

我想再多玩一會。 I want to play more.

我在玩的時候，一個小時感覺就像一秒。 When I play, an hour feels like a second.
・second 秒

你答應只玩一個小時，對吧？ You promised to play for an hour, right?

你應該分清楚玩的時間和學習的時間。 You should tell playtime from worktime.
・tell A from B 區分 A 和 B

我是個小孩，我所要做的就是玩。 As a kid, all I do is play.

媽，我會在遊樂場玩到 6 點。 Mom, I'll play on the playground till 6:00.

等這個遊戲結束後，我會整理。 I'll clean up after I finish this game.

ch11-04.mp3

躲貓貓

（藏起來突然出現時）出現了！ Peek-a-boo! ・peek-a-boo 躲貓貓遊戲

寶貝，媽媽在哪裡？ Honey, where's Mommy?

你在這裡啊，媽！ There you are, Mommy!

我抓到你了，媽媽！ I got you, Mommy!

你看不到我，對吧？ You can't see me, can you?

我的小寶貝在哪裡呢？ Where's my little baby?

我聽到你的聲音了。 I can hear you.

我看不到我的寶貝。 I can't see my baby.

他／她去哪裡了？ Where did he / she go?

我要打開門嗎？ Should I open the door?

躲在被子裡面。 Hide under the covers. 被子

喔？是誰在說話？ Huh? Who's talking?

你在這裡呀！ There you are!

噠噠！看到你了！ Ta-da! ★ 兩手張開秀出東西的效果聲。

你在這裡呀。有嚇到嗎？ You were here. Were you surprised?

躲貓貓很好玩嗎？ Isn't peek-a-boo fun?

要再來一次嗎？ Want to do it again?

好好玩喔。可以再來一次嗎？ That was fun. Can you do it again?

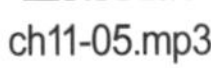

ch11-05.mp3

感官遊戲

我們來玩感官遊戲吧！ Let's play a sensory play.

- sensory play/activity 感官發展遊戲／活動

我把塑膠板分散在地上。 I spread the plastic sheet on the floor.

- plastic sheet 塑膠板

觸摸溼的海草是什麼感覺？ **What does it feel like to touch the wet seaweed?**

試著觸摸這些草莓，然後把它們壓碎！ Try touching the strawberries. Crush them! ・crush 壓碎

感覺如何？ **How does it feel?**

你可以吃這個。 You can eat it.

觸摸米香很好玩，不是嗎？ **It's fun to touch the pop rice, isn't it?**

抓住並擠壓它們。 Grab and squeeze them.

天呀！你身上都是了！ **Oh, my! It's all over you!**

現在該洗澡了。 Now it's bath time.

剪刀石頭布

我們來玩剪刀石頭布吧。 **Let's play rock, paper, scissors.**

剪刀，石頭，布！ Rock, paper, scissors, go!

我來告訴你規則。 **I'll tell you the rules.** ・rule 規則

石頭只要這樣握住拳頭就可以。 You make a fist for rock like this. ・fist 拳頭

石頭看起來真的很像石頭吧？ **Doesn't rock actually look like a stone?**

伸出兩根手指就是剪刀了。 You put two fingers out, and that's scissors.

看起來跟剪紙張的剪刀真的很像，對吧？ **It really looks like a pair of scissors cutting paper, right?** （a pair of：一雙～）

布只要伸出手就是了。 Paper is stretching out your hand. （stretching out：伸出）

布看起來很像一塊布，對吧？ Paper looks like a piece of paper, doesn't it?

石頭贏剪刀。 Rock beats scissors. ‧beat 贏

剪刀贏布。 Scissors beats paper.

布贏石頭。 Paper beats rock.

石頭可以打碎剪刀。 Rock can smash scissors. ‧smash 打碎

剪刀可以剪開布。 Scissors can cut paper.

布可以包住石頭。 Paper can wrap rock. ‧wrap 包

如果雙方都出一樣的話，就是平手。 If you both make the same thing, it's a draw. ‧draw 無勝負，平手

我們都出一樣的了。再來一次。 We both had the same thing. Let's try again.

你們必須要同時出。 You have to make it at the same time. (同時)

如果出了之後，又改變的話，就是犯規。 If you change after throwing one, that's cheating. ‧cheating 作弊行為

如果出太晚就是犯規。 It's cheating if you make it late.

贏的人可以優先。 The winner goes first. ‧winner 勝者

玩剪刀石頭布，我總是贏。 I always win at rock, paper, scissors.

他輸了，可是一直說他贏了。 He lost but keeps saying he won.
‧lose 輸，弄丟 ‧keep -ing 持續

你晚出了。 You made it late.

要遵守規則。 Follow the rules.

我贏了！我先。 I won! I'll go first.

你輸了。 You lost.

ch11-07.mp3

捉迷藏

我們來玩捉迷藏吧。	Let's play **hide and seek.** 捉迷藏
要玩捉迷藏嗎？到這裡來！	Want to play hide and seek? Come here!
我來當鬼，你去躲起來。	**I'll be "it," so you hide.** •it 鬼
要好好躲起來喔。	Hide yourself safely.
好，我要開始數到十。	**Okay. I'll count to ten.**
慢慢地數到十。	Count to ten slowly.
數到十之後，去找出躲起來的人。	**Count to ten and look for the hidden people.**
你不可以偷看。	You shouldn't peek. / No peeking. •peek 偷看，窺視
媽是鬼，我們快點躲起來。	**Mom's "it." Let's hide quickly.**
我們要躲哪裡？	Where should we hide?
不可以躲在危險的地方。	**Don't hide in a dangerous place.**
哎呀，我找不到你。	Whew, I can't find you.
準備好了沒，我來了！	**Ready or not, here I come!** ★ 當鬼的人，開始找人之前說的話。
我看得到你的上衣。	I can see your shirt.
我看到你躲在哪裡了。	**I can see where you hid.** hide（躲藏）的過去式
你躲在椅子後面嗎？	Did you hide behind the chair?
沒有在這裡！甜心，你在哪裡？	**You're not here! Where are you, Sweetie?**
我會找到你，你等著！	I'll find you. Just wait!

我聽到那邊有聲響。 I heard a sound over there.

我知道你躲在被子裡面。 I know you're hiding under the covers.

你在這裡！出來吧。 There you are! Come out.

現在輪到媽媽要躲起來。 Mommy is a hider now. • hider 藏起來的人

你太快找到我了！ You found me too soon!

爸爸，你是鬼，我們是要躲起來的人。 Daddy, you are the seeker, and we're the hiders. • seeker 要去尋找的人

這次輪到你當鬼了。 You'll be "it" this time.

找一個好的隱藏地點。 Find a good hiding spot. • spot 場所，地方

我要躲進書桌下面。 I'll go under the desk.

我要在窗簾後面。 I'll be behind the curtain.

不要動。 Don't move.

彎下你的頭，我能看到你。 Duck your head. I can see you.
• duck 低下頭

噓，安靜！鬼會聽到的。 Hush. Be quiet! The seeker can hear you.

我們就一起躲在這裡。 Let's hide here together.

你真的是玩捉迷藏的高手。 You're a great hide-and-seek player.

找不到，放牛吃草！ Ollie, ollie oxen free!
★ 鬼找不到人時說的話。

ch11-08.mp3

捉人遊戲

有人要玩捉人遊戲嗎？ Who wants to play tag? 玩捉人遊戲

我們來選捉人者。	Let's pick the tagger. / Let's pick "it." • tagger 捉人者（經常用 it 來表達）
誰想要當鬼？	**Who wants to be "it"?**
用剪刀石頭布來決定鬼吧。	Let's pick by playing rock, paper, scissors.
你是鬼。	**You're the tagger. / You're "it."**
我不想當鬼。	I don't want to be "it."
我來當抓人的人。	**I'll be the tagger.**
媽，來捉我吧！	Come and catch me, Mom!
你太快了。媽媽捉不到你。	**You're really fast. Mom can't catch you.**
這次你當鬼。	You're "it" this time.
我先抓到他了。	**I got him first.**
請讓我抓住你！	Let me get you, please!
哎呀，好喘喔！	**It's hard to breathe! / Phew, I'm out of breath. / Eeee, I'm exhausted!** 喘不過氣 • breathe 呼吸 • exhausted 精疲力竭
站在那裡！	Stop there!
媽媽來了。快跑喔。	**Mommy's coming. Run away.** 逃走
不！不要捉我！	No! Don't catch me!
我越來越近了。我快到了。	**I'm getting close. I'm almost there.**
先到家，這樣你就會贏抓人的鬼。	Reach home first. Then, you will win against the tagger.

ch11-09.mp3

扮家家酒

我要玩扮家家酒。	I want to play house. 玩扮家家酒
我們來玩扮家家酒。	Let's have a tea party. 家家酒遊戲
我來當小孩，你當爸爸。	I'll play the role of the baby. You be Dad. • role 角色
我來當媽媽。	I'll play Mom.
我們就用這個當餐桌。	Let's use this for a table.
媽媽，我來為你做沙拉。	I'll make salad for you, Mom.
我來把番茄切成兩半後煮。	I'll cut the tomato in half and cook it. 對半
我把雞蛋放在平底鍋上。	I put the egg in the pan.
媽，我餓了。	Mom, I'm hungry.
寶貝，媽媽來幫你做飯。	Mommy will cook for you, my baby.
甜心，牛奶時間到了喔。	It's time for milk, Sweetie.
嗯嗯，媽媽，好好喝。	Emm... Mommy, it's yummy.
你想用哪種盤子裝？	Which plate do you want it on?
我想用黃色盤子裝。	I want it on the yellow plate.
好，在這裡。	Okay. Here it goes.
你的在那裡。	There you go.
媽媽幫你切。	Mommy will cut it for you.
親愛的，吃晚餐了。	Darling, it's time for dinner.
喔，我的寶貝已經吃完了。	Oh, my baby already finished it.

喔，已經吃完了呀？ Oh, done already, huh?

我們要洗碗。 We should do the dishes.

媽咪給你做更好吃的食物。 Mommy will make more delicious food for you.

湯匙和叉子在這裡。 Here are the spoon and the fork.

我來洗柳橙。 I'll wash the orange.

再等一下，餐點快好了。 Wait a minute. The food's almost done.

你要喝杯茶嗎？ Would you like a cup of tea? / Would you care for some tea?

你想喝什麼茶？綠茶可以嗎？ What kind of tea do you want to drink? Is green tea fine?

green tea 綠茶

醫生遊戲

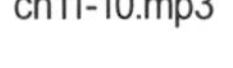
ch11-10.mp3

我們來玩醫生遊戲。 Let's play doctor. / Let's play hospital.

play doctor / play hospital 玩醫生遊戲

媽媽，我來當醫生。 Mom, I want to be the doctor.

好，我來當病人。 Okay, I'll be the patient. • patient 病人

我是幫助醫生的護士。 I'm a nurse to help the doctor.

你哪裡不舒服？ How can I help you? / What's troubling you?

我頭／肚子痛。 My head / stomach hurts.

我耳朵／眼睛／腿痛。 My ears / eyes / legs hurt.

我發燒了，也胃痛。 I have a fever and a stomachache.

• fever 發燒 • stomachache 胃痛

確切是哪一個部位痛呢？ Where exactly do you feel pain? •pain 痛

因為疹子，所以很癢。 It itches because of my rash.
•itch 癢 •rash 疹子

我覺得很癢。 I feel itchy. •itchy 發癢的

張大你的嘴巴，說「啊…」 Open your mouth wide. Say "Ah..."

我來幫你量體溫。 I'm going to take your temperature.
•temperature 體溫

你發高燒了。 You have a high fever.

護士，你能把聽診器給我嗎？ Nurse, can you give me my stethoscope?
•stethoscope 聽診器

深深吸氣，然後吐氣。 Take a deep breath in and out.
•breath 呼吸

我們需要動手術。 We need to do surgery. •surgery 手術

我來幫你開處方箋。 I'll write you a prescription.
•prescription 處方箋

打針

我來幫你打針。 I'm going to give you a shot.

你能讓我打針時不感覺痛嗎？ Can you give me a shot that won't hurt?

會有一點點刺痛。 It will sting a little bit. •sting 刺痛

很好。 Good job.

下一個患者，玩具熊！請進。 The next patient, Teddy Bear! Come in.

醫生，我的孩子很不舒服。 Doctor, my baby's really sick.

請躺在床上。 Lie on the bed, please.

我會塗些藥膏。 I'll put on some ointment. •ointment 藥膏

你需要住院。 You need to stay in the hospital.

護士，你能帶這位患者到診療室嗎？	Nurse, can you take this patient to the treatment room? ・treatment 診療
很疼，不是嗎？	It hurts a lot, doesn't it?
不用擔心，你很快就會好起來。	Don't worry. You will be fine soon.
現在去藥局吧。	Go to the pharmacy now. ・pharmacy 藥局
我是個好醫生吧？	Was I a good doctor?

Chapter 12

美術遊戲

Look at this dinosaur I drew.
看看我畫的這隻恐龍。

Wow, it looks so real!
哇，牠看起來好逼真！

ch12-01.mp3

畫畫

媽，你能畫台車給我嗎？	Mom, can you draw a car for me?

你可以自己畫。	You can draw it by yourself.
試著自己畫畫車輪。	Try drawing the wheels by yourself.
我會畫車。你要上色嗎？	I'll draw the car. Will you color it?

我不太會。	I'm not that good.
我不太會畫畫。	I'm not good at drawing.

媽，看！我畫的圓圈。	Look, Mom! Here's my circle.
看我畫了什麼。	Look what I drew. / Look at my picture.
我畫了這個。	I drew this.
這不是很酷嗎？	Isn't this cool?
媽，我想要畫畫。	Mom, I want to draw.
你想畫什麼呢？	What do you want to draw?
我想要畫海。	I want to draw the sea.
說到海，你想到什麼？	About the sea, what can you think of?
在海裡，我們能看到什麼？	What can we see in the sea?
我想到魚、人魚公主、海浪、船、蚌殼。	I can think of fish, mermaids, waves, ships, and clams. •mermaid 人魚 •clam 蚌
你想先畫什麼？	What do you want to draw first?
畫你想畫的。	Draw whatever you want.
你想用什麼畫呢？	What do you want to draw with?
用蠟筆／顏料／粉蠟筆／色鉛筆畫。	With crayons / paints / pastels / color pencils.
我們打開畫畫本吧。	Let's open the sketchbook.
把圖畫紙拿出來吧。	Get out the drawing paper. 圖畫紙
我們來畫草圖。	Let's make a sketch.
你在這裡畫了什麼？	What did you draw here?
你忘記畫耳朵了。	You forgot to draw the ears.
現在，來上色吧。	Now color the picture.
媽，恐龍要怎麼畫？	Mom, how do you draw dinosaurs?

看我的畫。我不是畫得很好嗎？	Look at my drawing. Didn't I draw it well?
你把樹畫得太小／大了。	You drew the tree too small / large.
沒有畫房子的空間。	There's no room to draw the house.
你要加上幾個臉部表情嗎？	Want to add some facial expressions on it? ・add 添上，增加 facial expressions 臉部表情
 我會用橡皮擦擦掉它。	I'll erase it with an eraser.
 你畫得很好。	You drew it very well.
你是這麼一位優秀的畫家。	You are such a great painter! / We have a great artist here! such a 如此，這麼
哇！看起來真的好像兔子在跑。	Wow! It really looks like a bunny running. ・bunny 兔子
你讓它看起來像真的。	You made it look real. look real 看起來像真的
這部分表現得特別好。	This part is especially expressive. ・expressive 有表現力的
我們把畫展示在這裡吧。	Let's display the picture here. ・display 展出
你要我把畫掛在牆上給爸爸看嗎？	Do you want me to put it on the wall so that Daddy can see it?
等爸爸回家時，我們把這個拿給他看。	Let's show this to Daddy when he comes.

ch12-02.mp3

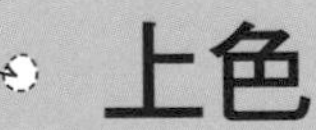

上色

 現在我們來給草圖上色。	Now let's color the sketch.

你要幫你的草圖塗顏料／上色嗎？	Will you paint / color your sketch?
拿出你的蠟筆／色鉛筆。	Get out the crayons / color pencils.
想要用顏料和畫筆嗎？	Want to use paint and a brush?
畫畫時，穿上這件工作服。	Wear this smock when you're drawing. ・smock 工作服，罩衫
你需要什麼顏色？	What color do you need?
這部分，我要塗上黃色。	I'm going to paint this part yellow.
蠟筆斷了。	The crayon is broken. ・broken 折斷的
試著在線內上色就好。	Try to color inside the line.
小心上色。不要留下任何空白部分。	Color it carefully. Don't leave any blank part. ・blank 空白，空格
你想學怎樣上色嗎？	Do you want to learn how to paint?
把需要的顏料擠在調色盤上。	Put the paint you need on the palette. / Squeeze out the paint on the palette.
我們再調多點水吧。	Let's mix some more water.
你要用什麼顏色給花上色呢？	What color do you want to paint the flower? / What color would you paint the flower?
我要把它塗成紫色。	I'm going to paint it purple.
媽，沒有綠色。	Mom, there's no green.
把顏色混合起來用。	Let's use by mixing colors. ・by -ing 透過～
想要混合黃色和藍色嗎？	Want to mix yellow and blue?
哇！ 變成綠色了。	Wow! It's turning green.

大海的顏色看起來好美喔。 The color of the sea looks nice.

我們用了橘色，看起來好漂亮。 It looks nice since we colored it orange.

媽，我手臂疼。你能幫我上色嗎？ Mom, my arm hurts. Can you help me color it?

把畫筆好好洗乾淨。 Clean the brush well.

我的手上都沾滿了顏料。 I got paint all over my hands.

ch12-03.mp3

美術時間

現在，來上美術課了。 Now, it's time for art class.

我們今天來畫圖。 We'll paint a picture today.

準備水彩、畫筆、調色盤、還有洗筆筒。 Prepare the watercolors, brushes, the palette, and the brush washers. 水桶

你想要畫什麼？ What do you want to draw?

今天，我們來畫遊樂場。 Today, we will draw the playground.

我要用蠟筆畫。 I am going to draw with crayons.

輕輕打草稿真的很難。 It is hard to sketch lightly.

我們用黏土來做個人像吧。 Let's make a human figure with clay.

‧figure 畫像；塑像 ‧clay 黏土

在背面塗上一些膠水。 Put some glue on the back side. ‧glue 膠水

用剪刀剪出外形。 Cut out the shape / figure with scissors.

哇，你的草圖看起來很棒！ Wow, your sketch looks great!

小心地幫草圖上色。 Color the sketch carefully.

想一想你要在畫上使用什麼材料。	**Think of what materials you are going to use for your picture.** ・material 材料
你能為你的朋友解釋你的畫嗎？	Can you explain your drawing to your friends? ・explain 說明
這個人的表情很逼真。	**The expression on the face of this person is so real.** ・expression 表情
如果你再上一些顏色，這張畫看起來會更棒。	If you put more colors on it, the picture will look much nicer.
要等畫都乾了。	**Wait till the picture dries up.**
我們來看看你朋友的畫吧。	Let's take a look at your friend's drawing.
說說畫畫的好處吧。	**Let's talk about the good points of the drawing.** 好處
有誰知道是誰畫了這張畫嗎？	Does anyone know who painted this picture?
你現在看的作品名叫做《拾穗》。	**The picture that you are looking at is called *The Gleaners*.**

美術道具及用語

- 彩色筆 color pencil
- 蠟筆 crayon
- 粉蠟筆 pastel
- 水彩顏料 watercolor paint
- 油畫顏料 oil paint
- 素描本 sketchbook
- 美術筆 drawing pencil
- 畫架 easel
- 畫筆 paintbrush
- 調色盤 palette
- 畫畫 draw
- 上色 color
- 塗顏料 paint

欣賞一下梵谷的《向日葵》，並說說看感想。
Take a look at Van Gogh's *Sunflowers* and talk about it.

照你的意思幫這張畫命名吧。
Name the painting as you want. • name 命名

我愛這幅畫。
I love this picture.

這張畫棒極了。
This picture is fantastic.

ch12-04.mp3

貼紙遊戲

我想玩貼紙遊戲。
I want to play with some stickers.

要用貼紙來裝飾這個嗎？
Want to decorate this with stickers?
• decorate 裝飾

你可以拿出貼紙簿嗎？
Can you get out the sticker book?

首先撕下貼紙。
Take off the stickers first.
(Take off：撕下)

你要貼在哪裡？
Where are you going to put it on?

把蘋果貼紙貼上去。
Put the apple sticker on.

媽，貼在這裡對吧？
Mom, is it right to put it on here?
(right to：做～是對的)

媽，這張貼紙撕不下來。
Mom, the sticker won't come off.
(come off：撕下)

媽，我貼錯了。
I put it on wrong, Mom.

這張貼紙撕破了。
The sticker got torn. • torn 撕破 (tear-tore-torn)

我不小心把貼紙撕破了。
I accidentally tore the sticker.

媽，你能幫我撕嗎？
Can you take it off, Mom?

如果你貼錯地方，會很難撕下來的。
It's hard to get it off if you put it in the wrong place.

貼上貼紙後，看起來很酷。 It looks cool with stickers. ・cool 酷的

看圖，然後把貼紙貼在正確的位置。 Look at the picture and put the sticker in the right place.

這個都用完之後，你能買新的給我嗎？ Will you buy me a new one when I use this up? ・use up 用完

這個撕下來後，我可以再用嗎？ Can I use it again after taking it off?

如果有點歪掉，也沒關係。 It's okay if it's a little bit out of place. 不在正確的位置

要撕下來重貼嗎？ Want to take it off and put it on again?

照你的意思裝飾。 Decorate however you want.

這個不夠黏。 It's not sticky enough. ・sticky 黏的

貼紙自己黏在一起了。 It got stuck together by itself. 黏在一起 自己

黏在頭髮上的話，就不容易弄掉了。 If it gets on your hair, it won't come off well.

今天都用完的話，之後就沒得用了。 There's nothing to use later if you use it all today.

ch12-05.mp3

摺紙

我們來摺紙。 Let's do some paper folding. / Let's do origami. ・folding 摺 ・origami 摺紙

跟著說明來摺是很重要的。 It's important to follow the directions. ・directions 說明，指示

你需要像指示說的來摺。 You need to fold it like the directions say. ・fold 摺

把它對半摺。 Fold it in half.

對半

再摺一次。 Fold it again.

斜斜地摺過來。你得到了一個三角形，對吧？ Fold it diagonally. You've got a triangle, right?

• diagonally 斜斜地 • triangle 三角形

準備幾張雙面的色紙。 Prepare some double-sided colored paper. • double-sided 雙面的

色紙

我要用雙面的色紙。 I'm using two-sided colored paper.

• two-sided 雙面的

想要摺隻青蛙嗎？ Want to fold a frog?

要準確地把角對好。 Let the corners meet exactly.

• exactly 準確地

準確地把一個角對準中間的點摺好。 Fold a corner exactly to the middle point.

反過來摺。 Fold the other way.

以點形成的虛線

虛線就是要摺的意思。 The dotted lines mean to fold it.

實線就是要剪掉的意思。 The lines mean to cut it.

往裡／外摺。 Fold it inside / outside.

攤開。 Unfold it. • unfold（把摺好的東西）攤開

倒過來，跟剛剛一樣摺好。 Turn it over and fold it the same way.

倒過來

你必須做階梯摺疊。 You have to do stair folding.

往同一方面摺。 Fold it in the same direction. • direction 方向

用力按下去，做出清楚的摺痕。 Press it firmly to make a good crease.

• firmly 緊緊地 • crease 摺痕

把它摺上去／下去。 Fold it up / down.

媽，這不好摺。 Mom, it doesn't fold well.

媽，還是不行。 Mom, it's not that easy. / I can't do it well.

我好像還是做不好。 I can't seem to get it right.

你摺錯方向了。 You folded it the wrong way.

要對準中間線摺。 Fold it on the center line.

你摺得很好。 You got it exactly.

用麥克筆畫出眼睛。 Draw eyes with a marker.

・marker 麥克筆

噠噠！青蛙完成了。 Ta-da! The frog is done.

ch12-06.mp3

使用剪刀／刀子／膠水

我們用剪刀剪吧。 Let's cut it using scissors. / Let's cut it with scissors.

你有幾把剪刀呢？ How many pairs of scissors do you have?

・a pair of 一雙～，一套～

把你的大拇指放在這裡，食指放這裡。 Put your thumb here and your index finger here. ・thumb 大拇指

(index finger：食指)

試著打開，再合起來。 Try opening and closing it.

你剪得很好。 You're cutting well.

沿著線剪。 Cut along the lines. ・along 沿著～

我不小心剪錯了。 I happened to cut it wrong.

(happened to：碰巧；偶然地)

我不小心把這剪錯了。	I accidentally cut this wrong.
 把雜誌上的圖剪下來。	Cut out the pictures from the magazine.
你要用波浪形剪刀剪嗎？	Want to cut it with the zigzag scissors?
把剪下來的彩紙貼在速寫簿上。	Cut the colored paper and put it on the sketchbook.
你剪好的話，把紙屑都丟掉。	When you're done cutting, throw the shavings away. •shaving 剪掉後剩餘的紙屑
小心！你的手指可能會被剪刀夾住。	Be careful! Your finger might get stuck between the scissors. (get stuck 夾住)
使用美工刀時，你要小心一點。	Be careful when you're using a craft knife. (craft knife 美工刀)
沿著尺來切那條線。	Use the ruler as a guide to cut that line.
你要使用口紅膠，還是膠水？	Do you want to use a glue stick or liquid glue? •glue 膠 •liquid 液體
把膠水塗在背面。	Put the glue on the back.
如果你塗得很均勻的話，會很好黏上去。	It goes on well if you glue it evenly. •evenly 平坦地，均勻地
啊！這裡我塗得太多了。	Oops! There is too much glue on here.
 咦，這個膠水好黏稠喔。	Eeek, the glue's sticky.
它一直掉下來。	It keeps coming off. •keep -ing 持續
 你想把它貼在哪裡？	Where do you want to put it on?
把紙張像這樣捲起來後，再黏起來。	Roll the paper like this and paste it. •roll 捲 •paste 貼，黏
把蓋子緊緊蓋好。	Put the lid on tightly. •lid 蓋子
確實把膠水蓋蓋好。	Make sure you put the lid back on the glue. (Make sure 確實～)

ch12-07.mp3

黏土遊戲

我們來玩黏土吧。	Let's play with clay.
拿出彩色黏土。	Get out the colored clay.
搓揉一段時間，以便讓它混合得更好。	Rub it for a while so it will mix well. ・rub 搓揉　for a while 一段時間
你想做什麼形狀呢？	Which shape do you want to make? / What do you want to make?

我要做個人。	I am going to make a person.
腿一直掉下來／彎掉。	The leg keeps coming off / bending. ・bend 彎曲

用雙手緊緊按下去。	Press it firmly with your hands. ・firmly 緊緊地，確實地
這時候雕刻刀是很好用的。	It's good to use a carving knife for this. carving knife 雕刻刀
這一塊黏土太大了。	The clay lump is too big. ・lump 塊
我們來把它捏成圓形。	Let's make it into a round shape.
放一塊在手掌之間，然後搓揉它。	Put a lump between your palms and roll it. ・palm 手掌
試著把它捏開。	Try stretching it out. stretching it out 伸長，展開
用滾筒把它壓開。	Let's spread it with a roller. ・spread 展開
做好眼睛、鼻子、嘴巴後，把它們貼在臉上。	Make the eyes, nose, and mouth and attach them on the face. ・attach 貼上
你可以使用模型做出不同的形狀。	You can use the molds to have different shapes. ・mold 模子，模型

不要壓得太用力。 Don't press it too hard.

你滿手都是泥。 **Your hands are all muddy.**

小心不要把泥沾到衣服上。 Be careful not to get the mud on your clothes. •mud 泥

已經變硬了。 **It got hardened already.** •hardened 變硬

我們必須把剩餘的黏土裝進密封袋內。 We need to store the leftovers in an airtight bag. •leftover 殘餘物

密封袋

ch12-08.mp3

積木遊戲

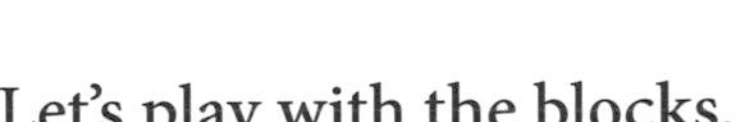

我們來玩積木吧。 **Let's play with the blocks.**

把積木拿出來吧。 Get the blocks out.

哇，形狀和顏色都不一樣！ **Wow, all different shapes and colors!**

媽，我需要一塊藍色的。 Mom, I need a blue piece.

把藍色積木放一起。 **Get the blue blocks together.** •get together 放一起

你能給我一塊正方形的嗎？ Can you get me a square piece?

你想要用積木做什麼？ **What do you want to make with the blocks?**

想要做台火車嗎？ Want to make a train?

這個放不進去。這些不適合。 **This won't go in. These won't fit together.** •fit 適合的

試著對起來看看，讓它們彼此吻合。 Try to match them well. They lock together.

彼此吻合

把藍色積木放在黃色積木上面。 Put the blue block on top of the yellow one.

我們可以疊幾個積木？ How many blocks can we stack? ‧stack 疊

我們來看看誰疊得高吧？ Want to see who can stack them higher?

你蓋了一棟房子！好棒喔！ You built a house! How nice!

把積木排成一條長直線吧。 Let's place them in one long line.

想要用積木來玩骨牌嗎？ Want to play dominos with the blocks?

即使不能照你的想法，也不可以丟積木。 Don't throw the blocks even though it doesn't go your way. 照你的想法

忍住性子，再試一次。 Be patient and try it again.
‧patient 有耐心的

喔，倒了。 Oops, it fell.

車輪形狀的積木不見了。 The wheel-shaped block is gone. 不見
‧wheel-shaped 車輪形狀的

媽，我的塔歪了。 Mom, my tower is tilted. ‧tilted 傾斜的

你想要我幫你蓋什麼嗎？ Do you want me to build something for you?

你可以把它像現在這樣放著嗎？ Can you leave it just the way it is now?

Chapter 13

戶外活動

I want to slide down the slide.
我想從那座溜滑梯溜下來。

Let me hold you, Sweetie.
甜心，讓我抓住你。

ch13-01.mp3

遊樂場

我想去遊樂場。	I want to go to the playground.
媽，我想去遊樂場玩。	Mom, I want to play on the playground.

好！那我們一起去吧。	Okay! Then let's go out together.
今天出門太冷了。	Today is too cold to go out. • too 形容詞 to 動詞 太～，以致不能做～
你不是應該先做功課嗎？	Shouldn't you do your homework first?

我的朋友們在那裡玩。	My friends are playing there.
我們去玩溜滑梯吧。	Let's go down the slide.
我想去溜滑梯。	I want to slide down the slide. •slide 溜滑梯
媽，你能抓住我嗎？	Can you hold me, Mom?
我可以自己玩溜滑梯。	I can slide down by myself.

你不可以從滑梯那裡走上去。	You should not walk up the slide.
不要爬得太高。	Don't climb up too high.
我們去坐翹翹板吧。	Let's get on the seesaw.
媽咪和你一起坐翹翹板。	Mommy will get on the seesaw with you.
你想玩盪鞦韆嗎？	Do you want to swing? •swing 盪鞦韆
當你經過擺動的鞦韆時，要小心一點。	Be careful when you pass around a moving swing.
哇哇！我的寶貝爬下來了。	Wheeeee! My honey's coming down.

更用力／輕輕地推我。	Push me harder / slower.

抓緊了！ 要更高了喔。	Hold on! It's going higher.

媽，你也可以不用推我。	Mom, you don't have to push me.
你可以幫我停住鞦韆嗎？我想下來了。	Can you stop the swing? I want to get off.
看，我飛得這麼高。	Look at me. I'm flying this high.
我感覺像飛在天上。	I feel like flying in the sky. •feel like -ing 感覺像～

我的寶貝到天空上去了！	My baby's going up to the sky!
從鞦韆上跳下來是很危險的。	It's dangerous to jump off the swing.

媽，我害怕爬到攀爬架的頂端上。	Mom, I'm scared to go up the top of the jungle gym.

想要看誰能在單槓上吊更久嗎？	Want to see who can hang on the bar longer? •hang 吊 •bar 單槓
媽咪會坐在板凳上。	Mommy will sit on the bench.

你一定要看著我喔。	You need to be looking at me.

現在我們要回家了。	Now let's go back to the house.

我們再多玩一會吧。	Let's play a little bit more.

寶貝，你看看四周。已經沒有人了。	Look around, Honey. Nobody's here anymore.
其他小孩一定是已經回家了。	The other children must go back home already.

ch13-02.mp3

玩沙

我們去沙池玩沙吧。	Let's go and play in the sandbox.
我們先把袖子捲起來吧。	Let's roll up our sleeves first.
在沙中，我們把鞋子脫掉吧。	Let's take off our shoes in the sand.
你想用沙做什麼呢？	What do you want to do with the sand?

我要用鏟子把沙裝在水桶內。	I'll put some sand in a bucket with a shovel. •bucket 水桶 •shovel 鏟子
媽，在沙子上畫人。	Mom, draw a person in the sand.

你要用外框嗎？噠噠，這是星星。	Want to use a frame? Ta-da~ It's a star. •frame 框架

我們來蓋沙的城堡。	Let's build a sandcastle.
哇，我們蓋了很棒的城堡。	Wow, we made a nice castle. ‧castle 城堡
想把沙子放在你手上嗎？	Want to put some sand on your hands?
沙子輕輕地從指縫中滑落。	The sand is softly slipping through the fingers. ‧slip 滑落
你覺得如何？沙是不是讓你的腳趾癢癢的？	How do you feel? Isn't it tickling your toes? ‧tickling 癢的
哇！你的腳被沙子埋起來了。	Wow! Your feet are in the sand.
 我用濕的沙子做了杯子蛋糕。	I made a cupcake with wet sand.
看！我做了沙子蛋糕。	Look! I made a sand cake.
 把左手放進沙內。	Put your left hand in the sand.
用些沙子蓋住你的左手，並用右手輕拍。	Put some sand over your left hand and pat it with your right hand. ‧pat 輕拍
我的眼睛有沙子跑進來了。	I got sand in my eyes.
我的鞋子內跑進很多沙子。	A lot of sand got in my shoes.
不要用沾有沙子的手揉眼睛。	Don't rub your eyes with a sandy hand.
不要把沙子丟向其他人的臉。	Don't throw sand in other people's faces.
寶貝，不要吃沙子！	No eating sand, Honey!
你的臉都沾滿了沙子。	You got sand all over your face.
把沾在襯衫、手、還有腳上的沙都抖掉。	Shake off the sand on your shirt, hands, and feet. 抖掉
鞋子也要抖一抖。	Shake your shoes, too.
我們回家後把沙子清掉吧。	Let's clean off the sand at home.

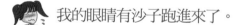

ch13-03.mp3

玩球

	媽咪，我們來玩球。	Let's play ball, Mommy.
	好，我來丟球。	Okay. I will throw the ball. ・throw 丟，投
	甜心，要接住球喔。	Catch the ball, Sweetie. ・catch 接
	好，丟過去了。	Here it goes! / Here we go!
	用力丟給媽媽。	Throw it hard to Mom.
	哇，我沒接到。	Oops, I missed it.
	我不小心掉了。	I happened to drop it.
	球滾走了。	The ball's rolling.
	媽媽來撿球。	Mommy will get the ball.
	去把球撿回來。	Go and get the ball.
	用雙手接球。	Catch the ball with two hands.
	把球夾在兩腿中間。	Put the ball between your legs.
	把球丟高。	Throw the ball up high.
	用手打球試試看。	Hit the ball with your hand.
	像這樣把球彈起來。	Bounce the ball like this. ・bounce 彈起
	從爸爸那接到球，再丟給媽媽。	Catch the ball from Daddy and throw it to Mommy.
	不要丟球了，來滾球吧。	Don't throw the ball. Roll it.
	哇！你真的很會接球耶。	Wow! You can catch the ball very well.
	輪到我丟球了。	It's my turn to throw the ball. ・turn 順序

丟遠一點。 Throw the ball far.

把球丟給我。 **Throw the ball to me.**

傳給我。 Pass it to me.

把球丟回來。 **Throw it back.**

現在輪到我了。 Now it's my turn.

爸，不要丟太遠／太用力。 **Don't throw it too far / hard, Dad.**

我丟球丟得很好。 I throw the ball this well.

看！我很厲害吧。 **See? I'm this good.**

看著你要丟球的地方。 Look at where you're throwing the ball.

丟用力一點。 **Throw it harder.**

ch13-04.mp3

棒球

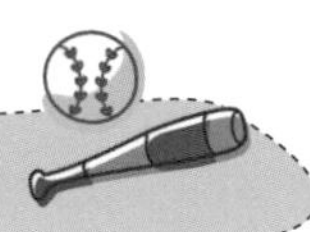

我們來玩棒球。 **Let's play baseball.**

投手是投球的人。 The pitcher throws the ball.

捕手是接球的人。 **The catcher catches the ball.**

打擊手是擊球的人。 The hitter hits the ball.

不可以把球往人的身上丟。 **Don't throw the ball at a person.**
• throw at 瞄準～丟

我們需要手套來打棒球。 We need a glove to play baseball.

我想當打擊手。 **I want to be the batter.**
• batter 打擊手（= hitter）

爸比，你投球吧。 Daddy, you throw the ball.

媽咪，你接球。　Mommy, you catch the ball.

丟輕一點。　Throw it slowly.

我來當裁判。　I'll be the umpire.　• umpire 裁判

好球！／壞球！／出局！　Strike! / Ball! / Out!

一個好球，兩個壞球。　2 balls, 1 strike.

★ 用英文說的話，先說壞球，再說好球。

出界了。　It's a foul.

三個好球，你出局了。　Three strikes and you're out.

哇！安打。　Wow! It's a hit.

跑向一壘。　Run to first base.

捕手沒接到球。　The catcher missed the ball.

奔回本壘。　Come to home plate.

我們得一分。　We scored one run.　• score 得分

我安全上壘了！不是出局。　I was safe! It was not out.　• safe 安全上壘

在被觸殺之前，我先回壘了。　I made it home before I got tagged.（got tagged：觸殺）

我踏上本壘了。我安全上壘了。　I stepped on home plate. I'm safe.

3 比 0。　Three to zero.

如果球超過這條線，我們就會說這是全壘打。　If the ball crosses this line, let's say it's a homerun.　• cross 穿過；越過

把球棒揮向人是很危險的。　It's dangerous to swing the bat toward people.

當有人經過，就停止遊戲。　Stop the game when someone passes by.

把球棒握緊。　Hold the bat tightly.

看好球後再打。	Look at the ball carefully and hit it.
等到最後一刻再揮棒。	Wait until the last minute and swing the bat.
當球來的時候，不要閉上眼睛。	Don't close your eyes when the ball comes.

ch13-05.mp3

足球

有人要踢足球嗎？	Does anybody want to play soccer?
我們把這個當做球門吧。	Let's say this is the goal.
有誰要當守門員嗎？你當守門員吧。	Who wants to be the goalie? You be the goalie. ‧goalie 守門員（= goalkeeper）
 我來當前鋒。	I'll be the striker.
我的球衣號碼是 11 號。	My back number is 11.
傳給我。	Pass to me. / Pass it to me.
爸爸在進攻了，去阻止他。	Daddy's attacking. Go get him. ‧attack 攻擊
 用力踢球。	Kick the ball hard.
盤球，就像是邊跑邊踢一樣。	Dribble the ball. It's like kicking while running. ‧dribble 盤球 (It's like: 像～一樣)
你可以利用好的防守來贏球。	You can win by playing good defense. ‧defense 防禦，防守
好可惜！幾乎要進球了。	That was close! That almost went in.
我們差點得分了。	We almost made it.
試著從爸爸那邊截球。	Try to get the ball from Daddy.

我們來訂作戰計畫。
Let's make a plan.

我們要交換球員。
We need to change players.

踢足球時，你不可用手接球。
You can't catch the ball with your hands in soccer.

只有守門員可以用手碰球。
Only the goalie can use his hands.

如果你抓住某人衣服的話，就是違規。
It's a foul if you grab someone's shirt.
• foul 違規，犯規 • grab 抓住

如果你從後面推人，你會得到一張黃牌。
If you push someone from behind, you'll be given a yellow card.

哇！你踢跟朴智星一樣好。
Wow! You can kick like Park Jisung.

我因為被截球而絆倒了。
I fell because I got tackled.

你為什麼一個人踢球？你應該傳球。
Why are you a ball hog? You should pass the ball.
ball hog：指不傳球而獨自踢球的人

打成平手。我們要以十二碼球來決勝負了。
It's a tie. We are going to a shootout.
• shootout 十二碼球決勝賽

得分！來慶祝一下！
Goal! Celebrate!

跳繩

我們來跳繩！
Let's play jump rope. / Let's jump rope.
jump rope：跳繩

不可以在家中跳繩。
Don't jump rope inside the house.

你要去外面跳繩嗎？
Will you go outside and jump rope?

我要試著跳 10 次。
I'll try to jump ten times.

你能幫我算我能跳多少下嗎？

Can you count how many jumps I can do?

一、二、三，喔！你被繩子纏住了。

One, two, three, oops! You got caught on the rope.

跳繩一直被腳絆到。

It keeps getting caught on my foot.

（getting caught on：絆到～，纏住）

繩子太長了。我來調整一下長度。

The line's too long. I'll adjust the length.

‧adjust 調整　‧length 長度

昨天你跳了三下，今天你跳了五下。

Yesterday you jumped 3 times, and today you did 5 times.

當你跳繩時，你不可以穿拖鞋。

You shouldn't wear slippers when you're jumping rope.

我們試著用單腳跳。

Let's try jumping on one foot.

跟著拍子跳跳看。

Jump to the beat.

（to the beat：跟拍子）

我們跟著節奏跳跳看。

Let's jump rope to the rhythm.

用手腕代替手來旋轉繩子。

Use your wrists instead of your arms to twirl the rope.

‧twirl 旋轉

（instead of：代替～）

交叉跳真的很難。

Jumping crisscross is very difficult.

當繩子在你的上面時，把手臂交叉。

When the rope is above you, cross your arms.

你可以往後跳嗎？

Can you jump rope backward?

我可以一邊跑步一邊跳繩。

I can jump rope while running.

跳完繩後，我肚子好痛喔。

My stomach hurts after jumping rope.

繩子斷了。

The rope broke.

我想我沒辦法通過跳繩考試。

I don't think I can pass the jump rope test.

我們班有人可以做二迴旋。

There's someone in our class who can do a double jump.

使跳繩於跳躍時轉二圈

繩子一直纏在一起。

The rope keeps getting tangled.

• tangled 纏在一起的

我的腿一直在抖。

My legs keep shaking.

爸爸媽媽來轉動繩子，
你們兩個進去跳。

Mom and Dad will turn the rope.
You two go in and jump.

ch13-07.mp3

騎腳踏車

你想要騎腳踏車嗎？

Do you want to ride a bike?

我們來學習怎樣騎兩輪的腳踏車。

Let's learn how to ride a bike with two wheels.

我們把輔助車輪拿掉。

Let's take off the training wheels.

兒童腳踏車兩側的小輪子

你可以抓住腳踏車，
好讓我不會摔倒嗎？

Can you hold the bike so that I won't fall?

答應我你不會放手。

Promise you won't let go of it.

放～

媽咪，不可以放開腳踏車。

Don't let go of my bike, Mommy.

腳踏車一直倒下來。

The bike keeps falling.

不用緊張。

Don't be nervous. • nervous 緊張

抓緊把手。

Grab the handlebars tightly.

• handlebar 把手 (= handle)

確定你戴上了安全帽。

Make sure you put on your helmet.

戴上

把把手往左／右轉。

Turn the handle toward the left / right.

用力踩腳踏板。	Step on the pedal hard. •step 踏
把腳踏板往後轉一點點，再往前踩。	Turn the pedal backward a little and then step forward. •backward 往後 •forward 往前
要注意前面的路。	Keep an eye on the road ahead. （Keep an eye on：注意）
小心車子。	Watch out for cars coming. （Watch out for：小心～）
下坡時要小心。	Be careful going downhill. •downhill 下坡
抓住煞車。	Hold the brakes. •brake 煞車
不可以在車道上騎腳踏車。	Don't ride your bike on the road.
太快了。稍微抓住煞車桿。	It's too fast. Hold down the brake lever slightly. •slightly 稍微
騎很快的時候，不要突然抓煞車桿。你可能會摔倒。	Don't grab the brake levers suddenly while riding fast. You could fall.
 看我騎得多快。	See how fast I'm going.
我們這裡有個很棒的單車騎士。	Here we have a great bike rider! / Wow, you are a great rider.
不要忘記上鎖。	Don't forget to put the lock on. •lock 鎖

ch13-08.mp3

玩直排輪

媽，我們去玩直排輪。	Mom, let's go inline skating.
 你需要穿上防護裝備。	You need to have your protection on. •protection 防物
安全帽一定要戴。	A helmet is a must. •must 必須品

戴上護膝。	Wear your kneepads. •kneepad 護膝
我們試著走走看。	Let's try walking.
右腳、左腳！好，很好！	Right foot, left foot! There you go. Good job!
你要學怎樣停止嗎？	Will you learn how to stop?
抬起你的腳趾，讓溜冰鞋的煞車皮觸碰地板。	Raise your toes to put down the brake pad on the skate.
慢慢地停下來。	Slowly come to a stop.
坐得更低，你可以更快地停下來。	The lower you sit, the more quickly you will stop.
把你的身體放得更低一點。	Lower your body a little more.
不要站太直。你會失去平衡的。	Don't stand up straight. You'll lose your balance. •straight 直地 •lose one's balance 失去平衡
不要害怕摔倒。	Don't be afraid to fall down.
媽咪會抓住你的。一次站起一隻腳。	Mommy will hold you. Get up one foot at a time. 一次
轉向右邊。	Turn to your right.
溜冰鞋合你的腳嗎？	Do the skates fit well on your feet? •fit 合適
你的雙腳要成「V」形。	Your feet should be in a "V" formation.
媽媽，我很害怕。	Mom, I'm scared.
我感覺要摔倒了。	I feel like I am going to fall.
現在，請抓住我。	Please hold me now.
我可以不用戴安全帽嗎？	Can I not put on my helmet? It's stuffy.

這很悶。	• stuffy 悶熱的
 轉圈是這樣做。	This is how to make a turn. 轉圈
身體要傾向你轉圈的方向。	Lean your body in the direction that you want to turn. • lean 傾，彎
同時，內側的溜冰鞋也要小步地邁出去。	Take small steps with your inside skate at the same time. 同時
外側的溜冰鞋要推一下。你看，我剛剛轉了。	Push off with your outside skate. See? I just turned.
擺動你的雙手來保持平衡。	Move your arms to help keep your balance.
今天你也很努力練習了。	You practiced hard today, too.
不要溜太遠。	Don't go riding off too far.
甜心，你溜得很好。	You're doing great, Sweetie.

ch13-09.mp3

做體操

 深呼吸後，慢慢地吐氣。	Take a deep breath and let it out slowly. 深呼吸 吐
吸氣，吐氣。	Breathe in. Breathe out.
把雙手舉高。	Raise your arms up high.
雙手前後擺動。	Shake your arms back and forth.
轉動你的手腕。	Roll your wrists.
逆時針方向轉動你的脖子。	Roll your neck counterclockwise. • counterclockwise 逆時針方向地

背要挺直。	Straighten your back. / Keep your back straight.
低／抬頭。	Drop / Raise your head. / Put your head down / up.
膝蓋彎曲。	Bend your knees.
上半身往下彎，抓住你的腳踝。	Lower your chest and touch your ankle. • chest 胸部 • ankle 腳踝
屁股往後翹。	Keep your hips back.
張開雙腳，與肩膀寬度同寬。	Stand with your feet shoulder width apart.（shoulder width apart 肩膀寬度）
身體要放鬆。	Relax your body. • relax 放鬆
碰到你的腳趾。	Touch your toes.
坐下，雙腳併攏。	Sit down and put your legs together.
雙手放在地上。	Put your hands on the ground.
輕輕地跑。	Jog lightly. • lightly 輕輕地
在原地輕輕地跑。	Jog lightly in place.（in place 原地）
跟著媽媽對拍子。	Follow me to the rhythm.
跟著媽媽做。	Look at me and do as I do.（as I do 根據我做的）
你的小腿痛嗎？	Doesn't your calf hurt? • calf 小腿
轉轉看。	Spin around. • spin 轉
保持上身直立原地跑。	Run while standing still. • still 靜止的

Chapter 14 其他遊戲

Can I use the computer just for a little while?
我可以用一下下電腦嗎？

Only for 30 minutes.
只能 30 分鐘。

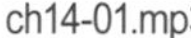
ch14-01.mp3

唱歌

我們要唱什麼歌呢？	What song shall we sing?
你想唱什麼歌呢？	What song would you like to sing?

媽，你能唱《ABC 之歌》給我聽嗎？	Mom, will you sing me *The ABC Song*?
媽，你能再唱一次嗎？	Mom, can you sing it again?
你能唱其他歌給我聽嗎？	Can you sing me something else?

我唱《三隻小熊》給你聽吧？ Want me to sing *Three Bears* to you?

我們一起唱。 Let's sing together.

大聲唱。 Sing out loud. 大聲地

唱慢／快一點。 Sing slowly / fast.

我們好好練習之後，去爸比面前唱。 Let's practice well and sing in front of Daddy.

媽，聽我唱歌。 Mom, listen to me sing.

我的寶貝也許是世界上最厲害的歌手！ My baby may be the greatest singer in the world!

你真的很會唱歌。 You can sing really well.

甜心，你最喜歡的歌是什麼？ What's your favorite song, Sweetheart?

你要不要改變一下歌詞？ Want to change the words?

媽媽唱第一節，你唱第二節。 Mom will sing the first verse. You sing the second.
• verse （歌曲的）節

要跟著拍子唱。 Sing to the beat.

在間奏時，你不用唱歌。 You don't sing in the interlude.
• interlude 間奏

喔，你唱走音了。 Gosh, you're out of tune. 走音

你把歌詞都唱對了。 You can sing without missing a word.

哎唷，你是個音痴。 Ugh, you're tone deaf. 音痴

我忘記歌詞了。 I forgot the words.

我不知道歌詞。 I don't know the lyrics.
• lyric 歌詞

你能幫我寫歌詞嗎？ Can you write the lyrics?

你唱歌的時候，看起來很像天使。 You look like an angel when you sing.

你都記起來了喔？哇，好厲害。 You memorized that? Wow, that's amazing. •memorize 記住 •amazing 驚人的

抱歉，媽媽不知道那首歌。 I'm sorry. Mommy doesn't know that song.

ch14-02.mp3

聽 CD

把你想聽的 CD 拿來。 Bring a CD that you want to listen to.

媽媽來開電源。 Mommy will turn on the power.
turn on 開（電源）

放進／拿出 CD。 Put in / Take out the CD.
Take out 拿出

我們要聽第幾首？ What track should we listen to?

音量太小了。 The volume is too low.

聲音太大了，調小一點。 The sound's too loud. Turn it down.

剛剛好。 That's just right.

媽，聲音太小了。 Mom, the sound's too low.

媽媽可以聽得很清楚。 Mommy can hear it well.

你要用耳機聽嗎？ Want to listen to it with headphones?

甜心，這是你最喜歡的歌。 It's your favorite song, Sweetheart.

按下開始／停止鍵。 Press the start / stop button.

你要先停一下，等一下再聽嗎？ Want to stop and listen later?

你要再聽一次嗎？ Want to listen to it again?

我們從頭開始聽吧。
Let's listen to it from the beginning.
（from the beginning 從頭開始）

像這樣拿著 CD。
Hold the CD like this.

把手指頭放進洞內。
Put your finger through the hole.

用大拇指輕輕地拿著外側。
Gently hold the outer edge with your thumb.

小心不要刮到 CD。
Be careful not to scratch the CD. ‧scratch 刮

把 CD 放進盒子內。
Put the CD in the case.

你要跟著音樂跳舞嗎？
Want to dance to the music?

你能放其他 CD 嗎？
Can you play another CD?

你能再放那首歌嗎？
Can you play the song again?

媽咪很喜歡這首歌。
Mommy loves this song.

ch14-03.mp3

在網路平台上聽音樂

在寫作業的同時，你會聽音樂嗎？
Do you listen to music while doing homework?

我在寫作業的同時，我會聽 Apple Music。
While doing homework, I listen to Apple Music.

我的同學介紹這個音樂平台給我。
My classmate introduced this music platform to me. ‧platform （軟體）平台

媽媽，我可以用你的手機在 Apple Music 上放幾首歌嗎？
Mom, can I use your phone to play some songs on Apple Music?

我最喜歡的歌手剛剛發了新專輯，我想要聽那些歌曲。
My favorite singer just released a new album. I want to listen to those songs.
‧release 發行；發表

你想要用耳機嗎？ Do you want to use earphones?

媽媽跟爸爸想要休息了，你可以把音樂關掉嗎？ Mommy and daddy want to rest. Can you turn off the music?
關掉

好啊，我也想聽點音樂。 Sure, I want to listen to some music, too.

你在聽什麼？ What are you listening to?

我不認為這些歌詞適合給小孩子聽。 I don't think the lyrics are appropriate for children to listen to.
• lyric 歌詞 • appropriate 合適的

我喜歡這首歌，歌手是誰？ I like this song. Who is the singer?

媽媽，我可以訂閱這個音樂平台嗎？ Mom, can I subscribe to this music platform?
訂閱

好啊，我覺得訂閱這個平台是好選擇。 Okay, I think subscribing to this platform is a good choice.

我不喜歡聽音樂的時候被打擾。 I don't like to be disturbed while I listen to music. • disturb 打擾

這個音樂平台有太多廣告了。 There are too many ads on this music platform. • ad = advertisement 廣告

你可以忽略廣告。 You can just ignore the ads.

ch14-04.mp3

看電視

媽，我可以看電視嗎？ Can I watch TV, Mom?

《Pororo》要開始了。 *Pororo*'s going to start.

你能開電視嗎？ Can you turn on the TV?

按下遙控器的綠色按鈕。 Press the green button on the remote.
• remote 遙控器 (= remote control)

啊！ 已經開始了。	 Oops! It's already started.
音量調小一點。	Let's lower the volume. / Please turn it down. •lower 降低
我聽不到，請調大聲一點。	I can't hear. Turn it up, please.
這太大聲了。請把音量調低。	It's too loud. Please turn down the volume.
要媽媽也一起看嗎？	Want Mommy to watch it, too?
《Crong》真的很好笑，不是嗎？	*Crong* is really funny, isn't it?
今天的《Pororo》真好看，對吧？	*Pororo* was really fun today, wasn't it?
寶貝，《Pororo》那麼有趣喔？	Is *Pororo* that fun, Honey?
我們看完《Pororo》就關掉電視。	Let's watch *Pororo* and then turn off the TV.
現在都結束了。	It's over now.
我們不要看了吧。	Let's stop watching.
看太多電視不好。	It's not good to watch too much TV.
媽媽，我想看《Arthur》。	Mom, I want to watch *Arthur*.
你不是答應我不看電視了嗎？	Didn't you promise not to watch TV?
我們只看 30 分鐘。	Let's watch only for 30 minutes.
你不可以吵著只是要看更久。	You shouldn't whine just to watch more. •whine 發牢騷，嘀咕
看多久電視算看很久呢？	How much TV is too much TV?
你在看什麼節目？	What program are you watching?
這個電視劇不是給小孩子看的。	That drama isn't for kids.

現在關掉，你可以明天再看。	Now turn it off. You can watch it again tomorrow.
你看太多電視，媽媽好擔心。	I am worried because you watch too much TV.
電視好像故障了。	The TV seems to be broken. 好像～ • broken 損壞的

玩電腦遊戲

ch14-05.mp3

我要玩一些電腦遊戲。	I'll play a few computer games.
我不可以再多玩一會嗎？	Can't I play it a little bit more?

先做完功課再玩。	Play after you do your homework.
玩完遊戲之後，你一定要做作業。	You have to do your homework after playing games.

我只玩一個小時。	I'll play for just 1 hour.

點一下滑鼠的左鍵。	Click the left button on the mouse.
你可以用方向鍵來控制。	You control with the direction pad. 方向鍵
你可以把喇叭的音量調小嗎？	Can you turn down the speakers?
現在不要玩了。	Stop playing now.
你的視力會變差。	Your eyesight will get bad. • eyesight 視力
你什麼時候開始玩的？	When did you start playing?
你被罰禁止玩遊戲。	You're grounded from playing games. • be grounded from 禁止～（做為處罰）
今天你不可以玩電腦遊戲。	You can't play computer games today.

你不是答應不玩任何遊戲了嗎？	Didn't you promise not to play any games?
我們訂個規定，只能在週末玩。	Let's make it a rule to play only on weekends. 訂規定
我玩的比我的朋友還好。	I'm doing better than my friend.
我必須贏這一局。	I need to win this round.
玩太多遊戲，對你不好。	Playing too many games isn't good for you.
我們應該注意從電腦中散發出的電磁波。	We should beware of the electromagnetic waves from the computer. 注意～ 電磁波
媽媽，這個遊戲不好玩。	Mom, this game isn't fun.
我忍不住想玩遊戲。	I can't stop thinking about playing games. •can't stop -ing 忍不住～
媽媽，我沒辦法連線網路。	Mom, I can't connect to the Internet. •connect 連接
我下載了電腦控制軟體。	I downloaded the PC control software. •control 控制
一旦我幫你設置這個軟體，你才可以用電腦。	You can use it once I set up the software for you. 設置
我可以在手機上看到你在電腦上做什麼。	I can see what you're doing on the computer on my phone.
我想要成為職業玩家。	I want to become a professional gamer.
我擔心你會變得遊戲成癮。	I am worried you'll become a gaming addict. •addict 有癮的人
沒有什麼是好玩的。	Nothing else is fun.

不只有遊戲，還有很多其他好玩的事情。

There are tons of other things that are fun besides games.（tons of：許多～）

ch14-06.mp3

玩平板、遊戲機

我想要玩電玩遊戲。

I want to play video games.（video games：電玩遊戲）

遊戲時間到了，我想玩電玩遊戲。

It's game time. I want to play some video games.

我做完家事可以玩電動嗎？

Can I play video games after I finished the chores?

媽媽，我想要用平板。

Mom, I want to use the tablet.

• tablet 平板電腦

你只能玩一個小時。

You can only play for an hour.

不要離螢幕太近，對你的視力不好。

Don't look too closely at the screen. It's bad for your eyesight.

平板沒電了，不要玩遊戲了。

The tablet has run out of battery. Stop playing games.

這個遊戲手把有點問題，我的角色不能移動。

This game controller has some problems. My character can't move.（game controller：遊戲手把）

我需要一些技巧，你可以教我嗎？

I need some tips. Can you teach me?

耶，我贏了。

Yeah! I won the game.

該睡覺了，關掉平板。

Time to go to bed. Turn off the tablet.

給我遊戲機。

Give me your video game console.（video game console：遊戲機）

我要更長的遊戲時間。

I need more game time.

這是我玩過最棒的遊戲。 This is the best game I've ever played.

ch14-07.mp3

玩手機遊戲

媽媽，我可以用你的手機嗎？ **Can I use your phone, Mom?**

我只要玩一下遊戲。 I'll only play games for a little bit.

我沒有剩下很多行動數據。 **I don't have much cellular data left.**

• cellular data 行動數據

你之前才玩過。 You just played earlier.

完成必須做的事情後，才可以玩。 **Play after you finish the things you have to do.**

我可以下載新遊戲嗎？ Can I download a new game?

我需要新道具，可以請你幫我付錢嗎？ **I need a new item. Can you pay for it please?**

你已經下載很多遊戲了。 You already downloaded a lot.

我可以買一個應用程式嗎？ **Can I buy an app?**

• app = application 應用軟體

不要花錢在應用程式上。 Don't spend money on apps.

如果你一直玩遊戲，你會姿勢不良。 **If you play games all the time, your posture will be ruined.**

• forward head posture 頭部前置姿勢 • posture 姿勢

這是什麼遊戲？ What game is it?

這是現在最流行的遊戲。 **It's the most popular game nowadays.**

這沒有很暴力，對吧？ It's not violent, is it? • violent 暴力的

電池電量很低，不要玩了。 The battery is running low. Stop playing.

我想要設計像這樣的遊戲。 I want to make a game like this.

那就去上編碼課。 Then take a coding class.

哇！我達到等級三了。 Wow! I finished level 3.

我的角色升級到等級六了。 My character levelled up to level 6.
• level up （在電腦遊戲中）升級

ch14-08.mp3

玩棋／牌／拼圖

我們來玩桌遊／牌／拼圖。 Let's play board games / cards / puzzles.

我們來分組。 Let's divide teams.

我們是同一組。 We're a team.

我們用擲骰子來決定。 Let's decide by throwing the dice.
• dice 骰子

我是黑棋，你是白棋。 I'll be the black horse. You be the white horse.

你一定要遵守規則。 You need to obey the rules. • obey 遵守

我們來選懲罰的方式。 Let's choose the punishments.

你必須再移動一格。 You need to go one more block.

看著，好好思考。 Please look and think. • think 思考

媽媽贏了，你要被處罰。 You need to be punished because I won.
（be punished 受罰）

那麼，獎品是什麼？ Then what's the reward? • reward 獎，獎賞

下次，我一定要贏。 I'm going to win next time.

再一次！耶！我拿到積分了。	One more! Yay! I got the bonus.
你作弊！	You cheated!
不要偷看我的牌。	Don't peek at my cards. •peek 偷看
再來一局。	One more round, please.
 這次我不會讓你贏的。	I'm not going to let you win this time. •let A 動詞 讓 A 做~
不可以因為你輸了就發脾氣。	Don't be mad because you lost.
下次你努力贏就好了。	You can try hard and win next time.
快點。我沒有辦法等一整天。	Quickly. I can't wait all day.
不要再催了。我在思考。	Don't urge me. I'm thinking. •urge 催
現在輪到你了。	It's your turn now.
我們把這些拼圖拼在一起吧。	Let's put these pieces together.
從這一塊拼圖開始。	Start with this piece of the puzzle.
這個好像跟這裡很合。	This could go here. / Looks like this fits here.
哇，你真的很會拼圖。	Wow, you're a puzzle king! / You're very good at solving puzzles.

ch14-09.mp3

玩吹泡泡

 你要玩吹泡泡嗎？	Will you play with bubbles? •bubble 泡泡
輕輕地吹氣到吸管。	Lightly blow into the straw. •blow 吹
小心不要把肥皂水濺出來。	Be careful not to spill the soap water. •spill 濺出，溢出

不要吸進去。 Don't breathe in.

不可以喝肥皂水！ Do not drink the soap water!

看這些小小的泡泡。 Look at the small bubbles.

看！這泡泡有彩虹的顏色。 Look! The bubble is a rainbow color.

哇，好大的泡泡。 Wow, it's a huge bubble. • huge 巨大的

你要用手指讓泡泡爆開嗎？ Want to pop it with your finger?
• pop 使爆開

我來幫你吹。 Let me blow it for you.

有兩個黏在一起了。 The two got stuck (黏) together.

用手把它搧上去。 Make it go up by flapping your hands.
• flap 揮動

泡泡飛得好高。 The bubble's flying off high.

媽媽，我要吹。 Mom, I want to blow it.

哇！泡泡在我寶貝的頭上了。 Wow! It's on top of my baby's head.

抓住這個泡泡。 Catch this bubble.

在浴室內吹。 Blow it inside the bathroom.

你要去外面吹嗎？ Want to blow it outside?

不是很好玩嗎？ Isn't it fun?

你吹得真好。 You blow really well.

地板很滑，要小心！ The floor is slippery. Be careful!
• slippery 滑的

ch14-10.mp3

「老師說」遊戲

你知道怎樣玩「老師說」嗎？ Do you know how to play Simon Says?

我忘記怎樣玩了。 I forgot how to play.

媽媽再告訴你一次。聽好了。 Mommy will tell you again. Listen to it.

很簡單。做出老師說的動作就好。 It's simple. Just do what Simon says.

當我說「老師說，閉上眼睛」，你就要照做。 When Simon says, "Close your eyes," you do it.

但是當只是我說的話，就不用聽。 But when I just say, don't listen to me.

開始了。仔細聽好。 Let's start. Listen carefully.

老師說：「拍手。」 Simon says, "Clap your hands."

- clap 拍手

很好。 Good job.

再一次。「抬起你的右腳。」 Let's start again. "Raise your right leg."

喔，命令沒有從「老師說」開始。 Oops, the order didn't start with "Simon says."

那麼，你輸了。 Then you will lose.

輸的人要搖屁股跳舞。 The loser should do the hip roll dance.

- loser 輸的人，敗者
- hip roll dance 搖屁股跳舞

老師說：「轉圈！」 Simon says, "Turn around!"

老師說：「摸耳朵！」 Simon says, "Touch your ears!"

老師說：「張開嘴巴！」 Simon says, "Open your mouth!"

老師說：「舉起左手！」	Simon says, “Put your left hand up!”
老師說：「搖屁股！」	Simon says, “Shake your hips!”
 喔，我搞糊塗了。	Oh, I got mixed up. 搞不清
再一次，再一次。 這次我可以做得很好。	Again, again. I can do well this time.
 集中精神再動作。	集中精神 Pay attention and act.
這次輪到你當老師。	Now you’re it.
老師說：「拍手！」	Simon says, “Clap your hands!”
你以為媽媽會被騙嗎？	Did you think Mommy would get tricked? 被騙
喔，媽咪輸了。	Oops, Mommy lost.
我要用屁股跳舞了。	I have to do the hip dance.
 媽，你好好笑喔。	Mom, you’re funny.

老師說遊戲

這是用英文說出 Simon Says 後，用命令句讓對方做那個動作的遊戲。只有說 Simon Says 的時候，才能動。如果是沒有由 Simon Says 開始的命令句，還跟著做動作的話，就輸了。

試著用英文表達

Chapter 15

心情和情緒

I'm glad you praised me.
我好高興你讚美我。

Mommy's glad that you're happy.
看到你開心，媽媽也很開心。

ch15-01.mp3

高興的時候

	你覺得今天如何？	How do you feel today?
	我覺得很好。	I feel happy / fine / great / good.
	哇！太棒了！	Hurray! Yey!
	我好高興你讚美我。	I'm glad you praised me. / I'm glad you said good things about me. • praise 稱讚

我好高興我考試考得很好。 I'm happy I did a good job on the test.

當你抱著我，我最開心了。 I feel best when you hold me.

當你吃很多我煮的菜時，媽媽真的很開心。 Mom's really happy when you eat a lot of my food.

看到你開心，媽媽也很開心。 Mommy's glad that you're happy.

據說微笑是可以傳播給其他人的。 It is said that（據說～）smiling spreads to other people. •spread 傳播

笑容可以使其他人心情好。 A smiling face makes other people feel good.

如果你高興的話，你就會使其他人高興。 If you're happy, you make other people happy.

寶貝，你讓我今天過得很棒！ You made my day, Honey!

ch15-02.mp3

期待的時候

我等不及要放暑假了。 I can't wait for（迫不急待要～）summer vacation.

我等不及要去旅行了。 I can't wait for the trip.

我等不及禮拜六要開始了 I can't wait for Saturday to begin.

我等不及要開始放假了。 I can't wait for vacation to begin.

我等不及要過生日了。 I can't wait for my birthday.

還剩下多少天呢？ How many more nights are left?

奶奶快來了，我好開心喔。 I'm happy that Grandma will come soon.

我好高興暑假開始了。 I'm happy that vacation has started.

我們到了嗎？我等不及了。	Are we there yet? I can't wait.
 我對今天真的超興奮的。	I'm really excited about today.
等待讓人好興奮。	It's so thrilling to wait.
你想收到什麼禮物？	What present do you want?
我想知道我會收到什麼禮物。	I wonder what present I will get.
我因為太興奮而睡不著覺。	I am so excited that I can't even sleep.

ch15-03.mp3

傷心的時候

 我好難過。	I'm so sad.
我難過到眼淚流不停。	I was so sad that I couldn't stop my tears.
我好難過，所以我一直哭。	I was so sad that I cried a lot.
 抱歉，媽媽讓你傷心了。	I'm sorry that Mommy made you sad.
你看起來很傷心。在學校發生了什麼事呢？	You look sad. What happened at school?
 我難過，因為我的朋友已經轉學了。	I'm sad because my friend has moved to another school.
 你們兩兄弟打架時，媽媽好傷心。	When you two brothers fight, Mommy's very sad.
當我兒子生病時，媽媽的心都碎了。	When my son is sick, Mom's heartbroken. ·heartbroken 心碎的
當我女兒哭泣時，媽媽覺得很難過。	When my girl cries, Mom feels so bad.
不要難過。	Don't be sad.

民肅，不要哭了。	Don't cry, Minsu.
 當你責罵我的時候，我很傷心。	When you scold me, I'm very sad.
當你生氣時，我很難過。	When you get angry, I'm sad.
這是一部悲傷的電影。	This is a very sad movie.
當你的朋友很難過時， 你必須去安慰他／她。	You need to comfort your friend when he's / she's sad. •comfort 安慰

ch15-04.mp3

心煩／失望的時候

我真的很心煩。	I'm really upset. / I feel bad. •upset 苦惱的，心煩的
現在我的朋友必須要走， 我好不捨。	I'm sorry that my friend has to leave now.
媽，為什麼你總是更疼弟弟？ 我好傷心。	Mom, why do you favor my brother over me? I feel bad. •favor A over B 比 B 更偏愛 A
我真的很失望。	I'm really disappointed. / It's really disappointing.
媽，我真的對你很失望。	I'm disappointed in you, Mom. / I feel bad because of you, Mom.
你忘記帶我的禮物，我好失 望喔。	I'm disappointed you forgot to bring any presents.
 你很失望嗎？	Are you disappointed very much?
心煩時，找你的朋友談談。	Talk to your friend when you're upset.
如果你因為媽媽感覺到心煩， 要告訴我。	If you're upset because of Mommy, please tell me.

不要失望。下次你一定會做得更好。

Don't feel so bad. You can do better next time.

請不要讓我失望。

Don't make me disappointed, please.

你等了一整天，看起來相當心煩。

You seem devastated because you were waiting for it all day long.

・devastated 極為震驚的；極為煩亂的

生氣的時候

ch15-05.mp3

我真的生氣了。

I'm really angry.

我越來越生氣了。

I'm getting angrier.

我太憤怒而無法冷靜下來。

I'm so angry that I can't calm down.

發生什麼事了嗎？

What's wrong? / What's the matter? ・matter 問題，事情

表達情緒

中文的「依依不捨、傷心、悶」等等，要用英文直譯是很難的。但是使用 I'm sorry 來表達還是說得過去的。（sorry 在感到後悔，或是同情對方等時使用）比 sorry 再強烈一點的表達是 I'm upset，或是 I feed bad。更加強烈的是 I feel devastated，意思是「心煩」。還有 I feel frustrated 也是更加強烈的表達，意思是「感到挫折」。I feel disappointed 的意思是「失望」，如 I'm disappointed in you 是直接表達對人的失望，也是很嚴重的表達，在使用上要多加小心。

是什麼讓你那麼生氣？ What made you that angry?

寶貝，你為什麼生氣？ Why are you mad, Honey? ・mad 惱火的

雍索一直讓我生氣。 Yongsuo keeps bugging me. / Yongsuo keeps making me mad. / Yongsuo is driving me crazy.

如果你繼續那樣的話，我會生氣的。 If you keep doing it, I'm going to get angry.

停止！媽媽要生氣了。 Stop it! Mom will get angry.

現在我真的生氣了。知道嗎？ I'm really angry now. Okay?

媽，你真的生氣了嗎？ Mom, are you feeling really bad?

媽，我希望你現在氣消了。 I hope you feel fine now, Mom.

媽，不要生氣。 Don't get angry, Mom.

你生氣的時候，我會害怕。 I'm scared when you're angry.

當媽媽生氣時，真的很恐怖。 It's really scary when my mom gets angry.

我被我的朋友激怒了。 I get annoyed (被激怒) by my friend. / One of my friends is really annoying.

因為他聽不懂我的話，我很生氣。 I get angry because he doesn't understand me.

你需要處理你的情緒。 You need to deal with (應付～，處理～) your anger / temper.

鎮定下來。 Calm down. / Get over it!

你很容易生氣。 You're so short-tempered.

你為什麼很容易被激怒？ Why do you get easily bothered?

不要像那樣發脾氣。 Don't lose your temper like that.
• lose one's temper 發脾氣（temper: 情緒，脾氣）

就算生氣，你也不能做出那樣的舉動。 Don't act like that even if you're angry.

當你生氣時，也不可以丟東西。 You shouldn't throw things when you're angry.

生氣並不能解決任何問題。 Getting angry won't solve anything.
• solve 解決

一旦生氣的話，就很難從怒氣當中恢復過來。 Once you are angered, it's not easy to get over it. 從～中恢復過來

你為什麼對我生氣？ Why do you get angry with me?

當你生氣時，看起來很醜。 You look ugly when you get angry. / You look ugly when you're upset.

ch15-06.mp3

驚嚇的時侯

哇！（突然出現大聲嚇人） Peek-a-boo!

天呀！ Oh my gosh! / Oh my goodness!

噠噠～驚喜來了！ Ta-da~! Surprise!

你被嚇到了吧？ Were you surprised?

你嚇到我了。 You scared me! / You surprised me! / You're freaking me out!
★ 朋友之間時才可用 freaking me out。

爸，你嚇到我了。 You made me surprised, Dad.

爸爸突然出來，我被嚇到了。 I am surprised that Dad came.

我驚嚇到差點昏倒。	I was so surprised that I almost passed out. 昏倒
媽，為什麼你沒有被嚇到？	**Mom, how come you're not surprised?**
我對你說出那樣的話感到吃驚。	I'm surprised to hear you say such a thing.

ch15-07.mp3

害怕的時候

我好害怕。	**I'm scared.**
我很怕黑。	I'm scared / afraid of the dark. ★ scared 表達「恐懼的」，afraid 則表達「害怕的，擔心的」。
我害怕一個人去。	**I'm afraid to go alone.**
我害怕一個人。	I'm afraid to be alone.
我害怕一個人睡。	**I'm afraid to sleep alone.**
我害怕打針。	I'm afraid to get a shot.
我害怕去看牙醫。	**I'm afraid to go to the dentist.**
我怕得直發抖。	I'm trembling in fear. 恐懼，害怕 ・tremble 發抖
我起雞皮疙瘩了。	**I'm getting goosebumps.** ・goosebump 雞皮疙瘩
令人毛骨悚然。	It's creepy. ・creepy 毛骨悚然的，不寒而慄的
我在發抖。	**I'm shivering.** ・shiver 顫抖
寶貝，不用害怕。	Don't be scared, Honey.

你不需要害怕。

You don't need to be afraid. / There is no need to be afraid.

你害怕嗎？

Are you scared?

我一點也不害怕。

I'm not scared at all.

兒子，你很勇敢。

You are very brave, my son!

你在害怕什麼？

What are you scared / afraid of?

幽靈和怪物都很可怕。

Ghosts and monsters are scary.

世界上沒有幽靈。

There are no ghosts in the world.

沒有幽靈和怪物這種東西。

There are no such things as ghosts or monsters.

抱住我，我就不會害怕了。

Hold me so that I don't get scared.

拿出勇氣來！

Get brave!

堅強點！

Be strong!

家人都在後面支持你。

You have a family behind you.

爸爸媽媽都會在你身旁。

Mom and Dad will be beside you.

• beside 在～旁邊

爸爸媽媽會保護你的。

Mom and Dad will protect you.

ch15-08.mp3

擔心／後悔

我擔心會下雨。

I'm worried it might rain. / I'm afraid that it will rain.

我擔心會犯錯。

I'm afraid to make mistakes.

我擔心媽媽不會很快好起來。 **I'm afraid Mom won't get better soon.**

我擔心考試會考砸。 I'm worried that I messed up the exam.

我擔心敏希不再跟我說話。 **I'm worried because Minxi wouldn't talk to me.**

不要擔心太多。 Don't worry too much. / Don't be too anxious.
• anxious 焦慮的

你不需要擔心。 **You don't need to worry.**

我當時應該用功讀書的。 I should have studied hard.
• should have + 過去分詞
應該～（對過去發生的事情後悔）

我當時應該聽媽媽的話。 **I should have listened to Mom.**

我當時不應該買這個玩具的。 I shouldn't have bought this toy.

媽，我很抱歉沒有聽你的話。 **I'm so sorry that I didn't listen to you, Mom.**

現在後悔也沒用了。 It's no use being sorry now.

現在要用功讀書，不然你以後會後悔的。 **Study hard now, or you will feel sorry later.**

ch15-09.mp3

疲勞／壓力

我累了。 **I'm tired. / I'm tired out.**

我好累喔，好想休息。 I'm so tired that I want to take a rest.

我好像要昏倒了。 **I feel faint. / I feel like I'm going to collapse.**
• faint 昏厥 • collapse 累倒

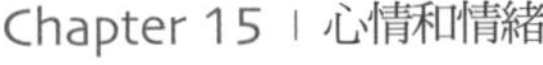

我感覺到有壓力。	I'm stressed out.
不要給我壓力。	**Don't stress me out. / Don't bother me.**
這個作業真的讓我好有壓力。	The homework is really stressful.
不要覺得有壓力。	**Don't get stressed out. / Don't let things stress you.**
我們做些什麼來解除壓力吧。	Let's do something to ease our stress.
我們應該即時抒解緊張。	**We have to get rid of our tension instantly.**

• tension 緊張　• instantly 立即

Chapter 16

描述個性

Andy is a little shy.
安迪有一點害羞

Oh, really? I didn't know it.
噢！真的嗎？我都不知道。

ch16-01.mp3

性格好

蘇洪人很好。	Suhong is nice / generous. / Suhong is a good person.
蘇洪很親切。	Suhong is kind.
蘇洪對每個人都很好。	Suhong is nice to everyone.
蘇洪很有禮貌。	Suhong has good manners.
蘇洪很為他人著想。	Suhong is caring / thoughtful.

蘇洪很能理解他人。 Suhong is very understanding.

蘇洪很正面。 **Suhong is very positive.**

蘇洪很友善。 Suhong is friendly.

蘇洪跟朋友們相處得很好。 **Suhong gets along well with his friends.**

蘇洪很真誠。 Suhong is sincere.

蘇洪很有責任感。 **Suhong is responsible.**

性格不好

ch16-02.mp3

蘇吉表現得好像她什麼都知道。 **Suji acts as if she knows everything.** (as if：好像～)

蘇吉只是在炫耀。 Suji is just showing off. (showing off：炫耀)

蘇吉總是在吹噓。 **Suji is bragging all the time.**
・brag 吹噓

蘇吉喜歡引人注目。 Suji likes to stand out. (stand out：引人注目)

蘇吉很傲慢。 **Suji is arrogant.** ・arrogant 傲慢的

蘇吉喜歡控制一切。 Suji tries to control everything. / Suji likes to boss people around.
・boss around 高傲地指揮～

蘇吉非常自私。 **Suji is very selfish.**

蘇吉不知道要替他人著想。 Suji doesn't care about others.

蘇吉只想到自己。 **Suji only thinks about herself.**

蘇吉對每件事都很挑剔。 Suji is picky about everything.

蘇吉很貪心。 **Suji is greedy.**

蘇吉態度惡劣。	Suji is ill-mannered.
蘇吉會說髒話。	**Suji uses bad words.**
蘇吉會欺負其他人。	Suji bullies others. / Suji picks on others. 找碴
蘇吉把自己的錯推給別人。	**Suji blames others for her own faults.** • blame 歸咎於～
蘇吉只會模仿別人。	Suji is a copycat.

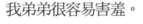

ch16-03.mp3

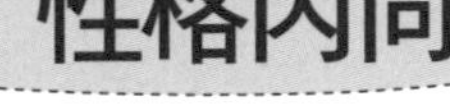

性格內向

我弟弟很容易害羞。	**My brother is very shy.**
我弟弟有一點內向。	My brother is a bit introverted. • introverted 內向的
我弟弟很膽小。	**My brother is timid.**
我弟弟很沉默寡言。	My brother is reserved. • reserved 寡言的
我妹妹有點安靜。	**My sister is kind of quiet.** 有點
我妹妹很溫和安靜。	My sister is gentle and quiet.
我妹妹有點遲鈍。	**My sister is a bit blunt.** • blunt 遲鈍的
我妹妹不喜歡引人注目。	My sister doesn't like to stand out.
真叫人難為情。	**It's embarrassing.** • embarrassing 令人尷尬的

有自信點。	Be more confident. • confident 自信的
不要躲在我後面。	**Don't hide behind my back.**
不要竊竊私語。	Don't whisper. • whisper 耳語

說大聲點。	**Say it louder.**
你必須把你想要的東西清楚地說出來。	You need to say what you want clearly.
你應該好好地跟大人們打招呼。	**You need to say "Hi" to adults clearly.**

ch16-04.mp3

性格外向／活潑

我哥哥很活潑。	**My brother is really active.**
我哥哥很擅長交際。	My brother is really sociable. • sociable 擅長交際的
我哥哥是很外向的人。	**My brother is an outgoing person.** • outgoing 外向的
我哥哥對每件事都很積極。	My brother is very active in everything.
我哥哥做每件事都很有自信。	**My brother does everything with confidence.**
我哥哥一直都在主導別人。	My brother always leads others. / My brother is a good leader.
我想像姊姊一樣活潑。	**I want to be active like my sister.**
我姊姊一點也不害怕說出自己的想法。	My sister is not afraid to speak her mind. • speak one's mind 坦白說內心話
蘇敏在朋友之中很受歡迎。	**Sumin is popular among her friends.**
民肅很健談。	Minsu talks a lot. / Minsu is very talkative. • talkative 健談的
民肅是有說服力的人。	**Minsu is a very eloquent person.** • eloquent 有說服力的

ch16-05.mp3

性格文靜／急躁

敏基很謹慎。	Minji is very calm. / Minji is careful.
敏基很鎮定。	Minji is calm. / Minji is not hasty.
敏基很有耐心。	Minji is very patient.
敏基是一個很隨和的人。	Minji is such an easygoing person. / Minji has a laid-back nature. • laid-back 悠閒的 • nature 本質
敏基做什麼事都很慢。	Minji is slow in everything.
民肅性格很急躁。	Minsu is impatient. / Minsu is hasty.
民肅很容易生氣。	Minsu is hot-tempered. / Minsu is short-tempered.
民肅有些敏感。	Minsu is kind of sensitive.
民肅很容易注意力不集中。	Minsu is easily distracted.

ch16-06.mp3

性格固執

伍尚很頑固。	Wushang is stubborn. • stubborn 頑固的
伍尚固執得跟騾一樣。	Wushang is as stubborn as a mule. • mule 騾；固執的人
如果事情沒有照著伍尚的意思，他就會失去控制。	Wushang is out of control (失去控制) if he does not get his way (按照他的意思).
伍尚希望每件事都要順著自己的心意。	Wushang wants everything to go his own way.

伍尚總是遵守規定。	Wushang always follows the rules.
伍尚的思考模式沒有變通。	Wushang is not flexible in his way of thinking. / Wushang does not easily change the way he thinks. • flexible 有變通的
伍尚對某些事情超級著迷。	Wushang gets strongly obsessed by some things. • obsessed 著迷的
不要那麼不聽話。	Stop being so stubborn.
不要太倔強。	Don't be too stubborn.
你到底是像誰才會這麼倔強？	I wonder who you're like by being so stubborn.

ch16-07.mp3

意志薄弱

敏基對每件事都不是很積極。	Minji is not very active in everything.
敏基有點優柔寡斷。	Minji is somewhat wishy washy. 優柔寡斷的
敏基無法自己做決定。	Minji can't decide anything. / Minji is indecisive.
敏基的意志很不堅定。	Minji is very weak-minded.
敏基很容易被他人主導。	Minji is likely to do as she is told by others. / Minji is easily led by others.

表示性格的表達

- active 活躍的，積極的（↔ passive：被動的）
- aggressive 進取的
- arrogant 傲慢的，自大的，自負的
- bad-tempered 易怒的，惡劣的
- blunt 遲鈍的
- brave 勇敢的（↔ cowardly：膽小的）
- bossy 愛指揮他人的
- brutal 殘酷的，惡毒的
- calm 鎮定的，冷靜的
- careless 草率的，不細心的
- clever 聰明的
- cold-blooded 冷酷的（↔ warm-hearted）
- competitive 好競爭的
- conservative 保守的（↔ liberal）
- considerate 深思熟慮的，關懷的（= thoughtful）
- courageous 有勇氣的 （= brave）
- creative 創造性的，有創意的
- critical 批判的，刁難的
- cruel 殘忍的
- cunning 狡猾的
- diligent 勤奮的（= industrious）
- dishonest 不誠實的（↔ honest）
- disorganized 沒有規畫的（↔ organized：有系統的）
- easygoing 隨和的，悠閒的（= lazy）
- foolish 笨的，跟傻瓜一樣的
- frank 真誠的，坦白的
- funny 好笑的，滑稽的，奇異的
- generous 寬厚的，慷慨的
- good-natured 溫和的，溫順的
- gentle 文雅的，溫和的
- greedy 貪心的，欲望很多的
- hardworking 勤勞的
- honest 正直的，誠實的，單純的（↔ dishonest）
- hot-tempered 性急的，易怒的
- humane 有人情味的，仁慈的
- humorous 幽默的
- impatient 不耐煩的（↔ patient：有耐心的）
- impolite 無禮的，粗魯的（↔ polite）
- imprudent 魯莽的（↔ prudent）
- jealous 忌妒的，猜忌的

- kind 親切的，和藹的（↔ unkind）
- lazy 懶惰的，慵懶的
- mean 卑鄙的，吝嗇的
- merciful 慈悲的
- modest 謙虛的，審慎的，端莊的
- moody 情緒化的（=capricious）
- naughty 頑皮的，淘氣的
- negligent 隨便的，粗心的
- notorious 惡名昭彰的
- outgoing 外向的，善交際的（= sociable）
- polite 客氣的，有禮貌的
- practical 實際的，踏實的
- liberal 開放的（↔ conservative）
- prudent 慎重的
- punctual 準時的
- reliable 可信賴的（= dependable, trustworthy）
- reserved 寡言的，含蓄的
- right 正確的，準確的，公正的
- rude 無禮的，低俗的（= impolite）
- ruthless 無情的，殘忍的
- selfish 自私的
- sensible 明智的，懂情理的
- shy 羞怯的
- silly 愚蠢的，糊塗的
- simple 單純的
- sincere 真誠的（↔ insincere：不真誠的）
- sociable 善交際的（↔ unsociable：不善交際的）
- stingy（特別是指錢）小氣的
- strict 嚴格的
- stubborn 頑固的，固執的，倔強的
- stupid 愚蠢的，笨的
- sweet 逗人喜愛的
- sympathetic 有同情心的
- talented 有能力的（= able）
- talkative 健談的
- thoughtful 深思熟慮的，有同理心的
- thoughtless 欠考慮的，不顧他人的
- timid 膽小的，沒有勇氣的
- ungrateful 不知感恩的，忘恩負義的（↔ grateful：感恩的）
- unkind 刻薄的，不親切的（↔ kind）
- warm-blooded 熱情的（=ardent）
- warm-hearted 有同情心的，熱心的（↔ cold-blooded）
- wise 賢明的，有智慧的

Chapter 17 喜歡的／討厭的

What's your favorite food?
你最喜歡的食物是什麼？

I like pizza the best.
我最喜歡披薩。

ch17-01.mp3

喜歡／討厭的食物

你最喜歡的食物是什麼？	What's your favorite food?
你最不喜歡的食物是什麼？	What's your least favorite food? •least 最不

我最喜歡韓式烤肉。	I like bulgogi the best. / My favorite food is bulgogi.
我最喜歡炸醬麵。	I love Zhajangmian the most.
我喜歡中華料理。	I like Chinese food.

媽，你煮的菜都很好吃。 All of your food is delicious, Mommy.

我不太喜歡日本料理。 I don't like Japanese food very much.

我不太喜歡咖哩飯。 I don't like curry and rice very much.

我不想吃蔬菜。 I don't want to eat any vegetables.

我討厭磨菇。 I hate mushrooms.

我從沒吃過鴨肉。 I've never tried duck.

我沒辦法吃咖哩，因為它太辣了。 I can't eat curry because it's too spicy.

我還不太能吃辣的食物。 I can't eat spicy food very well yet.

看你吃，媽咪就覺得很幸福。 Mommy's happy when I watch you eat.

我很開心，因為你吃得很好。 I'm happy since you ate well.

你會幫我訂披薩嗎？ Will you order me a pizza? ・order 訂購

媽，我想吃日式炸豬排。我們去外面吃吧。 I want to eat pork cutlet, Mom. Let's eat out.
（pork cutlet 日式炸豬排；eat out 在外用餐）

我可以再多吃一塊／湯匙嗎？ Can I have one more piece / spoonful?

很好吃。 It's very delicious.

好甜。 It's sweet.

正好合我的胃口。 This is my kind of food.

ch17-02.mp3

喜歡／討厭的衣服

我想穿紅色洋裝。 I want to wear a red dress.

我很喜歡洋裝。 I really like the dress.

這件T恤很合身。 This T-shirt fits me well. ‧fit 合（身）

這件襯衫真的很美。 This shirt is really pretty.

這件裙子和襯衫真的很搭。 The skirt and shirt match really well.

哇！我喜歡你的帽子！ Wow! I like your hat!

這真的很適合你。 It looks really good on you. 真的很適合～

這件毛衣的顏色很適合你。 The color of the sweater looks good on you.

我喜歡有條紋的衣服。 I like stripes on clothes. ‧stripe 條紋

我要穿有蕾絲的襪子。 I want to wear socks with lace on them.

比起褲子，我更喜歡裙子。 I like skirts more than pants.

我的朋友們說這衣服很好看。 My friends say that this is pretty.

公主洋裝很受歡迎。 Princess dresses are popular.

媽，你能買件公主洋裝給我嗎？ Mom, will you buy me a princess dress?

買件有小熊維尼的襯衫給我。 Buy me a shirt with *Winnie the Pooh* on it.

你每天都要穿那件嗎？ Are you going to wear that every day?

你昨天不是穿了那件嗎？ Didn't you wear that yesterday?

你真的很喜歡那些衣服，對吧？ You really like those clothes, don't you?

我不想把這件脫下來。 I don't want to take this off.

我最喜歡這件了。 I like this the most.

我不喜歡穿裙子。 I don't like to wear skirts.

我討厭這條褲子。它穿起來不舒服。 I hate these pants. They are not comfortable.

ch17-03.mp3

喜歡／討厭的人

在班上，誰是你最好的朋友？ Who is your best friend in class?

吉娜是我最好的朋友。 Jina is my best friend.

我想和憫宿成為朋友。 I want to be friends with Minsuo.

我喜歡我的同桌夥伴。 I like my partner / deskmate.

跟我談談你最好的朋友。 Tell me about your best friend.

我喜歡她，因為她漂亮又友善。 I like her because she's pretty and nice.

因為他很親切又帥氣，所以我喜歡他。 I like him because he's kind and handsome.

我長大後，想跟吉娜結婚。 I want to marry Jina when I grow up.

我們非常適合彼此。 We are perfect for each other.

宋錦很了解我的感受。 Songjin understands my feelings.

我以我的朋友為榮。 I'm proud of my friend.

從第一次見面開始，我就很喜歡她。 I liked her from the moment we met first.

- from the moment 主詞 + 動詞　從～瞬間開始

我想跟我朋友一樣很會寫字。 I want to write well like my friend.

我可以邀請她到我們家嗎？ Can I invite her to my house?

你的老師對你好嗎？ Is your teacher nice to you?

你為什麼喜歡這位老師？ Why do you like the teacher?

誰是你的學習對象？ Who's your role model?

模範，模仿的對像

我尊敬居里夫人。 I respect Marie Curie.

我想成為跟居里夫人一樣的科學家。
I want to be a scientist like Marie Curie.

我喜歡的歌手是 Rain。
My favorite singer is Rain.

Shiny 的唱歌跳舞都很酷。
Shiny's dancing and singing is cool.

我想像那位歌手一樣很會唱歌。
I want to sing well like that singer.

我不想跟蘇吉玩。
I don't want to play with Suji.

我不喜歡那位英文老師，因為她很可怕。
I don't like the English teacher because she is very scary.

我不喜歡那位老師，因為他太嚴格了。
I don't like the teacher because he is too strict.

我討厭任何人對我嘮叨。
I don't like anyone who nags me.

我不喜歡在那邊的那個女孩。她對我很不好。
I don't like the girl over there. She is mean to me.

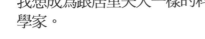

ch17-04.mp3

討厭做的事

我沒心情吃飯。
I don't feel like eating. •feel like -ing 想做～

我為什麼要費心去做那件事？
Why should I bother to do that?
•bother 煩惱

那個太無趣了，我不想做。
I don't want to do it because it's boring.

媽，你能幫我做嗎？
Can you do it for me, Mom?

你不能讓健民代替我去做嗎？
Can't you let Jianmin do it instead of me? 代替～

我不想刷牙。
I don't want to brush my teeth.

我為什麼一定要刷牙呢？
Why do I have to brush my teeth?

不要叫我做這做那的。	Don't ask me to do this and that.
我不想去。	**I don't want to go.**
我可以不做作業嗎？	Can I not do my homework?
我可以不做我不想做的嗎？	**Can I not do what I don't want to do?**
即使我不想做，也一定要做嗎？	I still have to do it even if I don't want to?
我等一下再做。	**I'll do it later.**
不要只是說「不！」	Don't just say "No!"
即使你不想做，你也一定要做。	**You need to do it even if you don't want to.**
如果你討厭的話，你不一定要做。	You don't have to do it if you hate it.
我希望你不會因此而後悔。	**I hope you won't feel sorry (後悔) for this.**
如果你現在不做這件事的話，你以後會手忙腳亂。	If you don't do this now, you'll be in a rush.

Chapter 18

外貌

Thanks, Dad!
謝了，老爸！

How pretty my daughter is!
我的女兒多可愛啊！

ch18-01.mp3

帥氣／美麗的外表

他很帥氣。	**He is very handsome. / He is a good-looking boy.**
他是秀氣的男孩。	**He is a beautiful boy.**
他長得很像貴公子。	**He is a boy of noble appearance.** • noble 高貴的，貴族的　• appearance 外貌

他好可愛。	**He is so cute. / He is such a cute-looking boy.**

她很漂亮。 She is pretty.

他是俊男。／她是美女。 He is a handsome boy. / She is a pretty girl.

他／她長得很像電影明星。 He / She looks like a movie star.

他／她是位很時尚的人。 He / She is a very stylish person.

我的兒子比他更帥。 My son is more handsome than him.

我覺得我女兒比她更漂亮。 I think my daughter is prettier than her.

我女兒好漂亮喔！你長得像誰呢？ My girl is this pretty! Who do you look like?

媽，我長得像你。 I just look like you, Mom.

ch18-02.mp3

平凡的外表

他長得不是很帥。 He is not really handsome.

她長得不是很漂亮。 She is not really pretty.

他／她長得很平凡。 He / She just has a common look.

他／她看起來有點醜。 He / She looks kind of ugly.

我有黑眼睛。 I have dark eyes.

我有黑頭髮。 I have black hair.

ch18-03.mp3

身材

我媽很苗條。 My mom is slender. ‧slender 苗條 (= slim)

我媽的身材維持得很好。	My mother stays in good shape.
我媽有 S 曲線的身材。	My mom has a curvy shape. / My mom has an hourglass figure. • curvy 曲線美的 • hourglass 沙漏
我媽很胖。	My mom is overweight. / My mom is big. ★ 千萬不要使用 fat 這個單字。
我媽有點豐滿。	My mom is a bit plump.
我爸是肌肉男。	My dad looks jacked. / My dad is a muscleman.
我爸的肚子很大。	My dad has a big belly.
我爸太瘦了。	My dad is too skinny.

ch18-04.mp3

臉部長相

他的眼睛很大／小。	He has big / small eyes.
他有雙眼皮。	His eyes have creases. • crease 皺褶
她的鼻子很挺。	She has a high nose.
她有個塌鼻子。	She has a flat nose. • flat 平坦的
她的鼻子有點塌。	Her nose is a little flat.
他的鼻子很大。	His nose is big.
他的嘴巴很大／小。	His mouth is big / small.
他／她是鵝蛋臉。	Her face is egg shaped. / She has an oval face. • oval 橢圓型的
她的臉很長。	Her face is long.

她的臉很圓。 Her face is round.

她的頭很小。 Her head is small.

他有個大頭。 He has a big head.

他有深色的眉毛。 He has dark eyebrows.

他有酒窩。 He has dimples. ・dimple 酒窩

她的臉很蒼白。 Her face is white.

她的皮膚很白皙。 Her skin is fair.

她的皮膚很黑。 Her face is dark.

她的皮膚很嫩。 Her skin is very soft.

她的皮膚不好。 Her skin is not healthy. / Her skin is not clean.

ch18-05.mp3

有特色的外表

他有突出的的額頭。 He's got a pointed forehead. ・pointed 突出

他有個長下巴。 He has a long jaw.

他的耳朵非常長。 His ears are extremely long.
・extremely 非常，極端地

他有青春痘。 He has pimples. ・pimple 青春痘

他有雀斑。 He has freckles. ・freckle 雀斑

她的嘴巴旁邊有一顆痣。 She has a dot next to her mouth. ・dot 痣

她的外表輪廓鮮明。 She has a sharp look. / She looks sharp.

她看起來人很友善熱忱。 She looks nice and warm.

她有吸引人的微笑。 She has an attractive smile.

and unfriendly.

不樂的

/ a little curly.

ht.

ir.

short.

and smooth. • silky 如絲綢般的

rmed.

in length. • length 長度

t short.

ng and straight.

hort.

a crew cut. 平頭

t of gray hair.

的頭髮」，而一般我們講的「帶灰色

air。

我爺爺是禿頭。 My grandpa is bald.

爸，我幫你把白頭髮拔起來，好嗎？

Can I pull out your gray hairs, Dad?
拔出

個頭／身高

ch18-07.mp3

他很高／矮。	**He is tall / short.**
他有 130 公分高。	He is 130cm tall. • cm = centimeters（非縮寫時要注意使用複數）
他的身高超過 140 公分。	**He's taller than 140cm. / He's over 140cm tall.**
她的身高還不到 120 公分。	She is shorter than 120cm. / She is not even 120cm tall.
她比同年紀的更高／矮。	**She is taller / shorter than her peers.** • peer 同年齡的人
她又矮又瘦。	She's short and skinny. • skinny 極瘦的

我們來看看你有多高。	**Let's see how tall you are.**
你在很短的時間內長高很多。	You grew more in such a short time.（in such a short time：在很短的時間內）
哇…你已經長了好多喔！	**Wow... you have grown quite a bit!**
你長高了 1 公分。	You grew 1cm.
你比吉娜高／矮一點。	**You're a little taller / shorter than Jina.**

我想再高一點。 — I want to be taller.

在你的班上，誰最高？ — **Who's the tallest in your class?**

民肅是我們班上最高的。	Minsu is the tallest in our class.
我想長得跟爸爸一樣高。	**I want to be tall like Dad.**

我希望我再高一點就好了。	I wish I could be taller. • I wish 主詞 + 過去動詞 ～就好了
我忌妒高的人。	**I'm jealous of tall people.** • jealous of 忌妒
你的身高剛剛好。	Your height is perfect. • height 身高
如果你好好吃飯的話，你會長得更快。	**You'll grow more if you eat well.**
你要多喝牛奶，才能長得更高。	You need to drink milk to grow taller.
你要早點睡覺，才能長得更高。	**You need to go to sleep early to grow taller.**
也有些人長得比較慢。	There are people who grow late.
媽媽也是後來才長高的。	**Mom also began to get taller late. / Mom also had a late growth spurt.** growth spurt：快速長高的時期

ch18-08.mp3

體重／減肥

我過重。	**I am overweight.**
我的體重是 20 公斤。	I weigh 20kg. • kg = kilograms（非縮寫要注意複數）
我們來量一下你的體重。	**Let's measure your weight.**
站到體重機上。	Step on the scale. • scale 體重計
你體重減少／增加了。	**You've lost / gained weight.**
看起來你好像增重了。	It looks like you've gained weight.
你很／不怎麼重。	**You weigh a lot / a little.**

因為你很苗條，看起來很不錯。 You look good because you're slim.

你胖得很好看。 **You are pleasingly plump.** ‧plump 豐滿

我喜歡保持健康的體態。 I like to stay in good shape.

我想減肥。 **I want to lose weight.**

你一點都不胖。 You are not overweight at all.

你應該透過運動來減輕體重。 **You should lose weight by exercising.**

你需要運動來減肥。 You need some workouts to lose weight.
‧workout 運動

你應該節食。 **You should go on a diet.** 節食

現在開始，試著少吃一點。 Try to eat less from now on.

現在不要吃太多點心。 **Don't eat too many snacks now.**
‧snack 點心

你應該增加一些體重。 You need to gain weight.

你不需要減重。 **You don't need to lose weight.**

透過挨餓來減重很不好。 It's bad to starve to lose weight.
‧starve 挨餓

我甚至喝水也會變胖。 **I can get fat even from drinking water.**

我的朋友們都叫我胖子。 My friends call me a fatty. ‧fatty 胖子

取笑別人的外表是不好的。 **It's bad to make fun of people for their looks.** 取笑～

過胖對健康是有害的。 Obesity is bad for your health. /
Being overweight is bad for your health.
‧obesity 過胖

ch18-09.mp3

煩惱外表

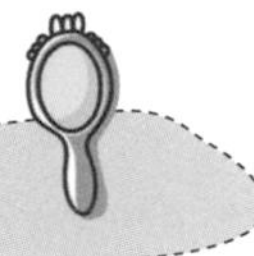

我想要長更高。 I want to be taller.

我希望我的皮膚可以更白。 I want my skin to be whiter.

我希望我的頭髮可以更長。 I want my hair to be longer.

我想變得更漂亮。 I want to be prettier.

我希望我的眼睛可以更大。 I wish my eyes were bigger.

媽，我很醜嗎？ Am I ugly, Mom?

你已經夠漂亮了。 You're pretty enough.

你這樣就很可愛了。 You're adorable the way you are.

• adorable 可愛的

我忌妒長得漂亮的朋友。 I'm jealous of my pretty friends.

內在比外表更重要。 What's inside you is more important than what's outside.

不可以只透過外表來評斷一個人。 Don't judge people by their looks. / Don't judge a book by its cover.

★ 第二句為俗語「不要以貌取人」。

我好像遺傳了爸媽的缺點。 It seems like I have Mom's and Dad's bad traits. • trait 特徵

你有你自己的魅力。 You have your own charm. • charm 魅力

我想穿好看的衣服。 I want to wear pretty clothes.

衣服只要乾淨就可以了。 Clothes have to be clean.

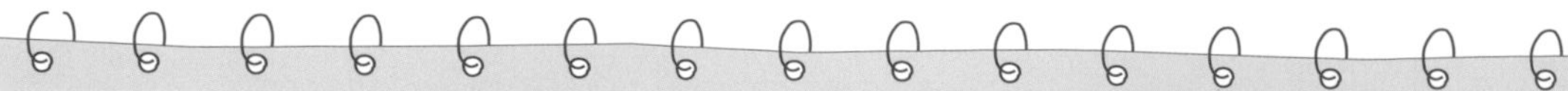

美國的重要紀念日

母親節 Mother's Day

在美國，五月的第二個星期日是Mother's Day。這一天，孩子們會為媽媽準備卡片或禮物來表達感謝之情。跟台灣不同的是，美國的母親節不只是跟自己的親生媽媽表達感謝，對奶奶、阿姨、姑姑、朋友、鄰居等等只要是當媽媽的人們，都可以獻上禮物、卡片、花來表達感謝。而六月的第三個星期日是Father's Day，跟台灣取「爸爸」諧音而將父親節訂在八月八日的情況不同。

★ 常用的會話句子

・母親節快樂！	**Happy Mother's Day!**
・母親節是什麼時候？	**When is Mother's Day?**
・那是五月的第二個星期日。	**It's on the second Sunday in May.**
・媽，這是我為您準備的禮物。	**Mom, this is my gift for you.**
・媽，我寫了這張卡片給您。	**I wrote this card for you, Mom.**

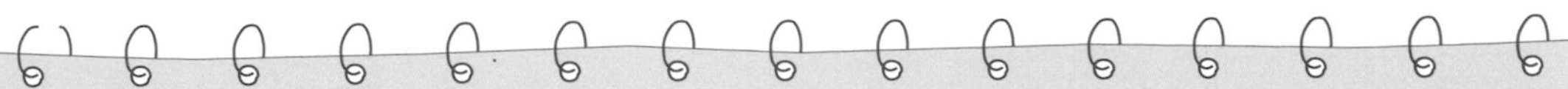

陣亡將士紀念日 Memorial Day

美國這個節日針對「陣亡的」美軍官兵，並將此日訂在五月最後一個星期日。這一天是為了追思為國家參加戰爭而失去生命的人們。在日常生活中也表示這天之後就是夏天的開始。美國的夏天有超過十週的暑假，也是家族旅行的時期。

★ 常用的會話句子

・陣亡將士紀念日是五月的最後一個星期天。	Memorial Day is celebrated on the last Monday of May.
・美國人在這一天對為國捐軀的人們表達感謝。	Americans are thankful for the people who died for their nation on this day.
・這節日意味著夏天的開始。	It marks the beginning of summer.
・暑假開始的日子通常跟陣亡將士紀念日很近。	Summer vacation usually starts around Memorial Day.

不同情況的生活會話

Chapter 19

打招呼／感謝／道歉

Hello, Andy!
哈囉！安迪

Hello!
哈囉！

ch19-01.mp3

見面時的打招呼

民肅，你好！	Hello, Minsu!
哈囉！	Hello!
早安！／午安！／晚安！	Good morning! / Good afternoon! / Good evening!
你好嗎？	How are you?
一切順利嗎？	How's everything going?

吉娜，很高興認識你。 Nice to meet you, Jina.

好久不見！ **Long time no see!**

很高興再次見到你。 Good to see you again.

你的父母好嗎？ **Are your parents fine?**

你的父母近況如何？ How are your parents?

你的兄弟／姊妹好嗎？ **Is your brother / sister well?**

很高興見到你。 Nice to see you.

你好嗎？ **How do you do?**

我聽說了很多有關你的事情。 I've heard a lot about you.

很高興在這裡見到你。 **Fancy meeting you here.**

是什麼風把你吹來的？ What brings you here?

我沒想到會在這裡遇到你。 **I didn't expect I would see you here.**

我們來握手吧。 Let's shake hands.

從上次見面已經有一段時間了。 **It's been quite a while since we met.**

我很想你。 I missed you.

為什麼你沒有保持聯絡？ **Why didn't you keep in touch?**

保持聯絡

ch19-02.mp3

分開時的打招呼

掰掰。 **Goodbye.**

下次見。 See you again.

晚點見。 **See you later.**

晚安。明天早上見。	Good night. See you in the morning.
掰。到時見。	Bye. See you then.
週一見。	See you on Monday.
保重。	Take care.
祝你週末愉快。	Have a good weekend.
下週見。	See you next week.
祝你有個愉快的一天。	Have a good day.
我會想念你的。	I'm going to miss you. •miss 思念
幫我跟你媽媽問好。	Say hi to your Mom for me.
我們保持聯絡吧。	Let's keep in touch.
你到家後，打電話給我。	Call me when you get home.
當你到家後，傳給簡訊給我。	Text me when you get home. / Give me a text message when you get home.
寫 Email 給我。	Email me. / Write me.
我不想說再見。	I don't want to say goodbye.
我很開心有你的陪伴。	I've enjoyed your company. •company 陪伴
我不會忘記你。	I won't forget you.

ch19-03.mp3

感謝的表達

謝謝。	Thank you.

非常謝謝你。	Thank you very much.
我真的很感謝那件事。	I'm so grateful for that. ・grateful 感謝的
謝謝你的稱讚。	Thank you for the compliment. ・compliment 稱讚，表揚
謝謝。我會回報你的。	Thank you. I'll pay you back.
沒關係。	It's fine.
這沒什麼。	No problem. / It was not a big deal.
不客氣。	You're welcome.
謝謝你幫了我。	Thank you for helping me.
媽，謝謝你的一切。	Mom, thank you for everything.
謝謝你為我做的一切。	Thank you for everything you've done for me.
我才是要說謝謝的人。	I'm the one who should say thanks.
我不知道該怎麼謝謝你。	I don't know how to thank you.
這裡有個小禮物。	Here's a little present.
我想表達我的感謝之情。	I want to express my thanks. ・express 表達
這是感謝信。	It's a thank-you note.
這禮物太棒了。	It's a great present.
跟你弟弟說謝謝。	Say thank you to your brother.
你應該學習說謝謝。	You should learn to say thanks.

ch19-04.mp3

道歉

	媽，對不起。	I'm sorry, Mom.
	我真的很抱歉。	I'm really sorry.
	沒關係。	It's okay. / No problem.
	別擔心。	Don't worry.
	不好意思，我遲到了。	I'm sorry I'm late.
	對不起，是我的錯。	I'm sorry. It was my fault. ・fault 錯誤
	不用在意。	Never mind.
	就忘記它吧。	Just forget it.
	媽，請你原諒我。	Mom, forgive me please. ・forgive 原諒
	我很抱歉造成這樣的麻煩。	I'm sorry for the trouble I've caused.
	那不是個問題。	That's not a problem.
	我不是故意那樣做的。	I didn't mean to do that.
	這是個失誤。	It was a mistake.
	我會原諒你的。	I'll forgive you.
	我會賠償的。	I'll pay for it.
	跟你妹妹說對不起。	Say sorry to your sister.
	道歉不是丟臉的事情。	Apologizing isn't something to be shy of. ・apologize 道歉
	只是說抱歉是不夠的。	Just saying sorry isn't enough.
	大人也是會犯錯的。	Adults also make mistakes. (make mistakes 犯錯)

Chapter 20 自我介紹／家族介紹

What school do you go to?
你在哪所學校上學？

I go to Taipei Elementary School.
我在台北國小讀書。

ch20-01.mp3

自我介紹

我來自我介紹。	Let me introduce myself.	• introduce 介紹
我的名字是吉娜。	My name is Jina.	

很高興認識你。我是李民肅。	Nice to meet you. I'm Minsu Lee.
很高興認識你。我是 Matthew。	Glad to meet you. I'm Matthew.

你在哪所學校上學？	What school do you go to? / Where do you go to school?

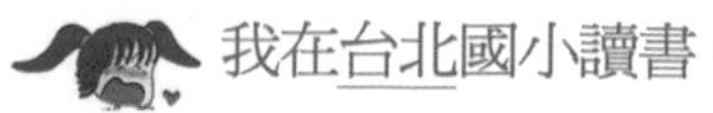
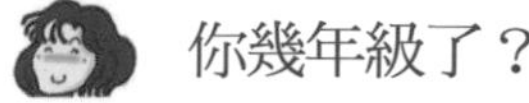

我在台北國小讀書。	I go to Taipei Elementary School.
你幾年級了？	What grade are you in? •grade 年級
我是一年級。	I'm in first grade. / I'm a first grader.
你幾歲了？	How old are you?
我八歲了。	I'm 8 years old.
你的嗜好是什麼？	What's your hobby?
我喜歡彈鋼琴。	I like playing the piano.
你在哪裡出生？	Where were you born?
我在高雄出生。	I was born in Kaohsiung.
你來自哪裡？	Where are you from? •from 來自
我來自台灣。	I'm from Taiwan.
我是台北的當地人。	I'm a native of Taipei. •native 本地人
你喜歡做什麼？	What do you like to do?
我喜歡跟我的朋友們玩。	I like to play with my friends.
我喜歡畫畫。	I like to draw.
你將來想當什麼？	What do you want to be in the future? (in the future 將來，未來)
我想當鋼琴家。	I want to be a pianist.
長大後，我想當鋼琴家。	I want to be a pianist when I grow up.

介紹家人

ch20-02.mp3

你家裡有幾個人？	How many people are there in your family? / How many people do you have in your family?

我家有四個人。	There are four people in my family.
四個。媽媽、爸爸、姊姊，還有我。	Four. My mom, dad, sister, and me.
我家有爸爸、媽媽、哥哥，還有我。	My dad, mom, brother, and I are in my family.
我和媽媽、爸爸、姊姊住一起。	I live with my mom, dad, and sister.
我們是小家庭。	We are a small family.
我們是大家庭。	We are a big family.
我家有很多人。	We have a lot of people in our family.
你有其他兄弟姊妹嗎？	Do you have any siblings? • sibling 兄弟姊妹
你有任何兄弟姊妹嗎？	Do you have any brothers or sisters?

是的，我有兩個姊姊。	Yes, I have two sisters.
我有一個弟弟，但是沒有妹妹。	I have a brother but not a sister.
沒有，我是獨生子。	No, I'm an only child.
我是家裡的老么。	I'm the youngest in the family.
我是家中最大的小孩。	I'm the oldest in the family.

ch20-03.mp3

介紹父母／祖父母

你爸爸在做什麼？	What does your father do?

他在某家公司上班。	He works in some company.
他在電腦公司上班。	He works for a computer company.
他為華碩電腦工作。	He works for ASUS.
他為政府工作。	He works for the government.
我媽媽在學校教書。	My mom teaches at a school.
我媽媽是家庭主婦。	My mom is a homemaker.
我爸媽都有工作。	My parents both work.
我爸很嚴厲。	My dad is very strict. ·strict 嚴厲的
爸爸太忙了，不能常跟我玩。	Daddy's too busy to play with me often.
爸爸在週末跟我們玩。	Daddy plays with us on weekends.
爸爸會幫忙打掃家裡。	Daddy helps clean the house.

職業名稱

在表示職業的單字後面常會出現以 -man 結尾的單字。man 不只可以指男性（male），還有人類（human）的意思。因此，使用在表示職業或地位的單字後面時，其意思是「做～的人」。不過，最近因為 man 無法準確傳達女性從事相同的職業，所以開始使用其他單字。

policeman – police officer（警察官）
chairman – chairperson（主席）
postman – mail carrier（郵差）
fireman – firefighter（消防人員）
spokesman – spokesperson（發言人）
statesman – politician（政治家）

我媽很會做飯。	My mom's a good cook.
因為媽媽必須照顧我們，所以很忙。	Mommy's busy because she has to take care of us.
我長得跟媽媽很像。	I look a lot like my mom.
我媽和我爸的感情很好。	My mom and dad are in a good relationship. ・relationship 關係
我尊敬我的爸媽。	I respect my parents. ・respect 尊重，尊敬
我爸媽離婚了。	My parents got divorced.
 你的祖父母好嗎？	How are your grandparents?
 他們都很健康。	They're both healthy.
我爺爺已經過世了。	My grandfather passed away. 過世
我奶奶在我很小的時候就去世了。	My grandmother died when I was young.
 你外公幾歲了？	How old is your grandfather?
 他有 66 歲了。	He's 66 years old.
外公跟我們住在一起。	My grandfather lives with us.
我外婆不是很健康。	My grandmother isn't very healthy.
我的外公外婆真的很愛我。	My grandparents really love me.
外公外婆對我很好。	My grandparents are nice to me.
我最愛我的外公外婆了。	I love my grandparents the most.

ch20-04.mp3

介紹兄弟姊妹

 你妹妹幾歲？	How old is your younger sister?

她五歲了。	She's 5 years old.
你比你弟弟大幾歲？	How much older than your brother are you?

我們差三歲。	We are 3 years apart. ・apart 相隔
我弟弟比我小三歲。	My brother is 3 years younger than me.
我姊姊比我大三歲。	My sister is 3 years older than me.

你跟弟弟處得好嗎？	Are you and your brother nice to each other? / Do you get along well with your brother?

我總是跟弟弟打架。	I always get in fights with my brother. （get in fights：打架，爭吵）
我和弟弟有很多共同點。	My brother and I have a lot in common. （in common：共同）
我和弟弟很不一樣。	My brother and I are very different.
我們是雙胞胎。	We are twins.
我們是同卵雙胞胎。	We are identical twins. （identical twins：同卵雙胞胎）
我們是異卵雙胞胎。	We are different-looking twins. ★ 異卵雙胞胎也叫做 fraternal twins。

弟弟不在這時，我會很想他。	I miss my brother when he's not here.
我弟弟是個小搗蛋鬼。	My brother is a little troublemaker.
我弟弟總是到處搗蛋。	My brother is always monkeying around. （monkeying around：調皮搗蛋）
我妹妹在上幼稚園。	My sister is in kindergarten. / My sister goes to kindergarten.
我姊姊在上大學。	My sister is in college. / My sister goes to college.
我哥哥對我很好。	My brother is very nice to me.

ch20-05.mp3

介紹親戚

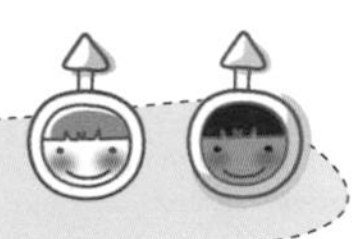

我有很多親戚。	I have a lot of relatives. ‧relative 親戚
我的親戚不多。	I don't have many relatives.
我有很多阿姨和叔叔。	I have many aunts and uncles. ‧aunt 阿姨，姑姑，嬸嬸 ‧uncle 叔（伯）父，姨丈，姑丈
我有一位姑姑和一位伯伯。	I have one aunt and one uncle.
我阿姨住在首爾。	My aunt lives in Seoul.
學校放假的時候，我會去親戚家玩。	I go to my relative's house during school break. ‧break 放假，休假
過節的時候，我們會聚在一起。	We all get together during holidays.
我有很多表兄弟姊妹。	I have a lot of cousins. ‧cousin 表（堂）兄弟，表（堂）姊妹
我跟我的堂兄弟姊妹相處得很好。	I get along well with my cousins. / My cousins and I are friends with each other.

親戚的稱呼

中文在表達親戚關係時區分得很細，英文就相對單純多了。

- uncle 伯父，叔叔，舅舅，姨丈，姑丈
- aunt 伯母，嬸嬸，舅媽，阿姨，姑姑
- cousin 堂兄弟姊妹，表兄弟姊妹

我和堂哥們在我祖父母家玩。
My cousins and I play at my grandparents' house.

我經常跟嬸嬸們見面。
I meet my aunts often.

伯伯有時會來我們家。
My uncle sometimes comes to our house.

我有一位叔叔住在美國。
One of my uncles lives in America.
（One of：其中一位～）

ch20-06.mp3

介紹寵物

我有一隻狗。
I have a dog.

牠的名字是 Happy。
His name is Happy.

當我放學回來時，牠會搖尾巴。
He shakes his tail when I get back from school.
（get back from：從～回來）

牠被訓練得很好。
He is trained well.

我們養牠養了兩年。
We've had him for 2 years.

牠五歲了。
He's 5 years old.

Happy 不喜歡泡澡。
Happy doesn't like to take baths.
（take baths：泡澡）

Happy 總是跟著我跑來跑去。
Happy always follows me around.

Happy 是我們家的一員。
Happy is a member of our family.

Happy 喜歡跟我去散步。
Happy likes to take a walk with me.

Happy 會做一些特技。
Happy knows how to do some tricks. / Happy can do some tricks.
・trick 特技

Happy 會跳躍和翻滾。
Happy can jump and roll.

當我請牠吃東西時，它就會跳。	He's jumpy when I give him treats. • treat 請客
Happy 最喜歡狗狗潔牙骨。	Happy likes dog gum best.
Happy 是母／公的。	Happy is a female / male. • female 雌性　• male 雄性
我媽不喜歡狗，因為牠們有很多毛。	My mom doesn't like dogs because they have fur. • fur 毛
我餵魚。	I feed the fish. • feed 餵
你必須換魚缸的水。	You need to change the water in the fish tank. 魚缸
你必須在鳥籠裡面放些水。	You need to put water into the birdcage.
我討厭清大便和小便。	I hate cleaning up poo and pee. • poo〈幼兒用語〉大便　• pee 小便
蜥蜴是很奇特的寵物。	Lizards are weird pets. • lizard 蜥蜴　• weird 奇特的；怪異的
豪豬生了個小寶寶。	The porcupine had a baby. • porcupine 豪豬（刺蝟類的動物）
我給牠注射了預防針。	I got him / her a shot. • give a shot 注射

ch20-07.mp3

介紹玩具

你最喜歡的玩具是什麼？	What's your favorite toy?
我最喜歡這個娃娃。	I like this doll the most.
這是爸比送我的禮物。	It was a present from my daddy.

這是我三歲時就有的。	I've had it since I was 3.　•since 自從～
 你在哪裡買的？	Where did you buy it?
 這是我收到的生日禮物。	I got it as a birthday gift.
這是聖誕老公公給我的禮物。	I got it from Santa Claus.
我出門時，一定帶著這個娃娃。	I take this doll whenever I go out.
我也會跟娃娃一起睡覺。	I go to sleep with it, too.
我沒有它會睡不著。	I can't sleep without it.
這是我最喜歡的玩具。	It's my favorite toy.
要像這樣玩。	This is how you play with it.
 讓你的朋友也玩一次。	Let your friend use it once.
 我不要。這是我最喜歡的。	I don't want to. It's my favorite.
它的名字叫 Nana。我幫它取的名字。	Its name is Nana. I named it.
我在收集這一個系列。	I'm collecting this series.
我組裝時，它就會變身。	It transforms when I build it. •transform 變形，變身
這是無線遙控車。	It's a wireless car.　•wireless 無線的
你可以在文具店買到。	You can buy it at the stationery store. 文具店
因為它壞了，現在動不了。	It won't move because it's broken.

ch20-08.mp3

介紹住的地方

 你住哪裡？ Where do you live?

 我住在彩虹公寓。 I live in Rainbow Apartments.

 彩虹公寓在哪裡？ Where is Rainbow Apartments?

 它在賈梅爾小學附近。 It's next to Gamel Elementary School.

我家在七樓。 My house is on the 7th floor.

 離這裡有多遠？ How far is it from here? •far 遙遠的

 搭公車大約需要 30 分鐘。 It takes about 30 minutes by bus.
It takes：花～（時間）

 你在那裡住多久了？ How long have you lived there?

 我在那裡住四年了。 I've lived there for about 4 years.

我從幼稚園開始就住那裡。 I've lived there since kindergarten.

 你家地址是什麼？ What is your address?

你的電話幾號？ What's your phone number?

你家電話幾號？ What's your home phone number?

你知道媽媽的手機號碼嗎？ Do you know Mom's cell phone number?

 2022-1114。區碼是 02。 It's 2022-1114. The city code is 02.

02-2022-1114。 It's 02-2022-1114.

 不要忘記你的電話號碼。 Don't forget your phone number.

Chapter 21

天氣

How's the weather today?
今天的天氣如何？

It's sunny.
是晴天。

ch21-01.mp3

風和日麗

今天天氣如何？ What's the weather like today? / How's the weather today?

今天是個大晴天。 It's a bright, sunny day.

天氣很好。 It's beautiful.

天氣會變晴。 It's going to be fine.

天氣會越來越溫暖。 It's getting warmer and warmer.

• get + 比較級 越來越～

太陽很大，要擦防曬乳霜。	Put sunscreen on because the sun is hot. •sunscreen 防曬乳霜
如果你不擦的話，你的臉會被曬傷。	Your face will get sunburned if you don't put it on. •sunburned 曬傷
戴上遮陽帽來遮太陽。	Cover yourself from the sun with a sun cap.
盡可能走有陰影的地方	Try to walk on the shady side. •shady 陰影的
跟我一起撐陽傘走吧。	Walk with me under my parasol.

ch21-02.mp3

陰天

CLOUD

天好陰。	It's cloudy.
今天的天空有很多雲。	A lot of clouds are in the sky today.
是個陰天。	It's a very cloudy day.
霧真的很濃。	It's really foggy. •foggy 有霧的
有很多烏雲。	There are a lot of dark clouds.
天氣昏暗又多雲。	It's dark and cloudy.
天空被雲覆蓋住了。	The sky is covered with clouds. (is covered with：被～蓋住)
快要下雨了。	It's going to rain soon.
很可能馬上要下雨了。	It's likely to rain soon. •likely 很可能
霧太濃了，我幾乎看不見任何東西。	It's so foggy that I can barely see anything. •barely 幾乎沒有～
天氣陰森森的。	The weather's creepy. •creepy 陰森森的

部分陰天，部分晴天。	It's partly cloudy and partly sunny. • partly 部分地
即使是白天，還是太暗了。	It's too dark even during the day. • day 白天
之前是晴天，但現在轉陰了。	It's been sunny, but it is turning cloudy now.
陰天似乎會持續更久。	Cloudy days seem to last longer. • last 持續
不要再陰天了！	No more cloudy days! / I wish we had no more cloudy days.

ch21-03.mp3

下雨天

下雨了。	It's raining.
開始下雨了。	It's starting to rain.
下毛毛雨了。	It's drizzling. • drizzle 下毛毛雨
外面正下著大雨。	There is a heavy rain shower outside.
雨傾盆而下。	It's pouring rain. • pour 傾瀉
雨停了。	The rain has stopped.
從昨天開始就一直下雨。	It's been raining since yesterday.
一整天雨都在下下停停。	It's been raining off and on all day.
今天已經下了整天的雨。	It's been raining the whole day today.
雨應該不會下那麼大。	It's not going to rain that much.
又打雷又閃電的。	There are thunder and lightning. • thunder 雷 • lightning 閃電

下傾盆大雨了。
It's raining cats and dogs. 下傾盆大雨

我擔心會淹水。
I'm afraid it's going to flood.
• flood 洪水泛濫，淹水

因為下雨，空氣很潮濕。
It's too humid because of the rain.
• humid 潮濕的

現在是雨季。
It's the rainy season. 雨季

八月是一年的雨季。
August is a rainy time of the year. 雨季

我們把窗戶關上吧。
Let's close the windows.

穿上雨衣怎麼樣？
How about wearing a rain jacket?

我不喜歡下雨天，
我都不能去外面玩。
I don't like rainy days. I can't play outside.

今天蠻悶熱的。
It's kind of muggy today. • muggy 悶熱的

我們需要開除濕機。
We need to turn on the dehumidifier.
• dehumidifier 除濕機

天氣放晴了。
The weather has cleared up. （天氣）放晴

ch21-04.mp3

下雪天

外面下雪了。
It's snowing outside.

哇，這是今年的初雪！
Wow, the first snow of the year!

下好多雪。
It's snowing a lot.

雪下了 10 公分。
It snowed 10cm.

地上積了很多雪。
There's a lot of snow on the ground.

下了整週的雪。 It snowed all week.

世界被雪覆蓋住了。 The world is covered in snow.

世界都變成白色的了。 The world is all white.

雨雪正夾雜著下。 It's sleeting. ‧sleet 雨雪夾雜著下

我想知道暴風雪是不是要來了。 I wonder if a snowstorm is coming.
‧snowstorm 暴風雪

路上都結冰了。 The road is frozen. ‧frozen 結冰的

因為這些雪，我們動彈不得。 We can't even move because of all the snow.

爸爸，我們來打雪仗吧。 Let's have a snow fight, Dad. (snow fight: 雪仗)

我想要滑雪橇。 I want to go sledding. (go sledding: 滑雪橇)

我要堆雪人。 I want to make a snowman.

我們去溜冰吧。 Let's go ice-skating.

我希望雪不會融化。 I don't want the snow to melt. ‧melt 融化

小心不要滑倒。 Be careful not to slip. ‧slip 打滑，滑倒

我們把積在車上的雪清掉吧。 Let's get the snow off the car.
‧get off 去除，掃掉

ch21-05.mp3

冷天

今天好冷。 It's so cold today.

天氣變冷了。 The weather's gotten cold.

相當冷。 It's pretty cold. / It's freezing. ‧pretty 相當

今天氣溫降了很多。	The temperature fell a lot today. • temperature 氣溫
好糟糕的天氣。	**It's awful weather.** • awful 糟糕的
暴風雨要來了。	There's a storm coming.
我還以為我要凍死了。	**I thought I was going to freeze to death.** (to death ～死了) • freeze 凍結
我要凍死了。	I'm freezing to death.
今天真的感覺很像冬天。	**It really feels like winter today.**
我在外面時，都冷到骨頭裡了。	I was chilled to the bone outside.
風好大。	**It's really windy.**
風大到連走路都很難。	It's hard to walk through the wind.
我的帽子要飛掉了。	**My hat's going to fly off.**
我的手被凍僵了。	My hands are freezing.
 今天冷颼颼的，穿多一點衣服。	**It's chilly today. Wear a lot of clothes.** • chilly 冷颼颼的
戴上圍巾。	Put a scarf on.
戴上手套。	**Wear gloves.**
你的臉真的很冷。	Your face is really cold.

ch21-06.mp3

熱天

今天好熱。	 **It's hot today.**
真的很熱。	It's really hot.

熱極了。 It's extremely hot. ·extremely 極度地

又熱又潮濕。 It's hot and humid.

今天真的很像夏天。 It really feels like summer today.

今天一點風都沒有。 There isn't any wind blowing today.

過去幾天都很熱。 It's been hot for the past few days.

我的汗像發瘋似地一直流。 I'm sweating like crazy. 像發瘋似地

我的背一直流汗。 My back keeps sweating. ·sweat 流汗

我的疹子很癢。 My rash is itchy. ·rash 疹子 ·itchy 癢

你可以開一下冷氣／電風扇嗎？ Can you turn on the air conditioner / fan? ·fan 電風扇；扇子 冷氣

你在流汗，你最好沖個澡。 You're sweating. You'd better shower.

如果你去沖個澡，會比較好。 It will be better if you shower.

在陰影處坐一下。 Sit in the shade for a little while. ·shade 陰影

我希望能下雨就好了。 I wish it would rain.

ch21-07.mp3

沙塵暴

沙塵暴的季節要來了。 The yellow dust season has come. 黃沙

已經發出沙塵暴的警報了。 There's a yellow dust warning. ·warning 警報

最強的沙塵暴襲擊全國。 The worst yellow dust storm hit the country.

看看這些黃沙。 Look at the yellow dust.

外面都是灰塵。 It's very dusty outside.

我們在春天有沙塵暴。 We get sandy yellow dust in the spring. 沙塵暴

什麼是沙塵暴？ What is the yellow dust?

是指沙塵隨風吹來。 It's dust winds blowing.

灰塵和沙子從中國飛來這裡。 Dust and sand from China fly over here.

現在車子變成黃色的了。 The car is yellow now.

你帶了口罩嗎？ Did you get your mask?

今天要戴上口罩。 Wear your mask today.

不可以揉眼睛。 Don't rub your eyes. •rub 揉搓

因為沙塵暴，我們必須把窗戶關起來。 We need to close the windows because of the yellow dust.

今天就待在室內吧。 Just stay inside today.

因為沙塵暴很嚴重，不要去戶外。 Don't go outside since the yellow dust is blowing hard.

ch21-08.mp3

用智慧語音助理查天氣

我們來問 Siri 天氣。 Let's ask Siri about the weather.
•Siri 蘋果系統中的人工智慧助理

問 Friends 明天在高雄的天氣。 Ask Friends what the weather in Kaohsiung is like tomorrow.

Genie，台北的天氣如何？ Genie, what's the weather in Taipei like?

今天是多雲、最高溫度是 33℃。 Today is cloudy and the high is 33°C.

飛塵的程度非常嚴重，請待在室內。 The level of fine dust is very bad. Please stay indoors. ·fine dust 飛塵

天氣晴朗，低溫將會是 10℃。 It will be clear and the low will be 10°C.

人工智慧（Artificial Intelligence）

隨著智慧裝置的發展，除了鍵盤或觸控操作之外，還出現了透過辨識人的語音進行操作的設備。Siri 和 S Voice 為手機內建的語音辨識（voice recognition）功能，是日常生活中廣泛使用的人工智慧語音，人工智慧的英文為 artificial intelligence，簡稱 AI。 這種擁有 Alexa、Genie、Tinker Bell、Friends 等多種名稱的 AI 音響，英文簡稱為 smart speaker，也被稱為智慧個人助理，因為人們可以將它當成個人助理一樣，並用它確認行程、查詢天氣、播放音樂和播放電視。據說，人工智慧機器人將很快成為人們日常生活的一部分。

Chapter 22

健康的生活

What's wrong?
有什麼問題嗎？

My stomach hurts.
我肚子痛。

ch22-01.mp3

表示健康

我很健康。	I'm very healthy. / I'm very healthy and strong. / I'm doing great.
我一點病也沒有。	I'm not sick at all.
我沒有健康的問題。	I have no health problems.
我一點也不累。	I'm not tired at all.

我覺得我很強壯。 I feel strong. / I feel energetic inside.

媽，我吃了還想再吃。 Mom, I can't stop eating.

我希望你一直很健康。 I hope you are always healthy.

ch22-02.mp3

表示疼痛

媽，我生病了。 I am sick, Mom.

我覺得不舒服。 I don't feel well. / I'm not feeling well.

我一整天都想躺著。 I want to lie down all day. (lie down 躺下)

我不想吃。 I don't want to eat.

我沒有胃口。 I've lost my appetite. ‧appetite 胃口

你生病了嗎？ Are you sick?

你哪裡不舒服？ Where do you feel bad?

我痛到受不了了。 I can't stand the pain. ‧stand 忍受 ‧pain 疼痛

我覺得頭暈。 I feel dizzy. ‧dizzy 頭暈的

我覺得要吐了。 I feel like throwing up. (throwing up 嘔吐)

我一動就會痛。 It hurts whenever I move.

我覺得有什麼東西在刺我。 It feels like something's poking me. ‧poke 戳，刺

這裡覺得痛。 It feels sore here. ‧sore 痛的

是擠壓的那種痛。 It is kind of a squeezing pain. ‧squeezing 擠壓的

如果你碰那裡，會很痛。	If you touch there, it hurts.
我覺得我的肌肉抽筋了。	I feel my muscles cramping up.（cramping up：抽筋，抽搐）
 這很痛嗎？	Does it hurt a lot?
這從什麼時候開始痛的？	When did it start hurting? / When did your pain start?
你要媽咪看一下嗎？	Want Mommy to take a look?

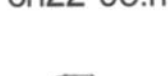

ch22-03.mp3

累的時候

 我累了。	I'm tired.
我覺得虛弱。	I feel weak.
我越來越累了。	I keep getting tired.
我不想做任何事。	I don't want to do anything.
我甚至沒辦法自己洗澡。	I can't even wash myself.
我甚至連手指頭都動不了。	I can't even move a finger.
我的眼皮都要蓋下來了。	My eyes are getting drowsy. •drowsy 睏
 你有黑眼圈。	There are dark circles under your eyes. / You have dark circles under your eyes.
你為什麼看起來那麼沒精神？	Why do you look so down? •down 提不起精神的
你看起來精疲力盡了。	You look exhausted. •exhausted 精疲力竭的（比 tired 更強烈的表達）
想要小睡一下嗎？	Want to take a nap?（take a nap：小睡一下）

ch22-04.mp3

摔倒／撞倒的時候

媽，我摔倒了。	Mom, I fell down.
我在地板上滑倒了。	I slipped on the floor.
我在跑的時候摔倒了。	I fell down while running.
我被石頭絆倒了。	I tripped over a rock. 被～絆倒
我失去重心後摔倒了。	I lost my balance and fell. • lose one's balance 失去重心

你還好嗎？有受傷嗎？	Are you okay? Did you get hurt?
你的褲子破了個洞。	You got a hole in your pants. • hole 洞
你的膝蓋流血了。	Your knee is bleeding. • bleed 流血
你膝蓋瘀青了。	You bruised your knees. • bruise 使瘀青
你的手掌瘀青了。	Your palm got bruised. • bruised 瘀青的，挫傷的
快點站起來。	Get up quickly.
把灰塵拍掉。	Get it off. / Shake the dust off.
這條路崎嶇不平的。	The streets are very bumpy. • bumpy 凹凸不平的
我們要小心注意地面。	Let's watch the ground carefully.
哇！你並沒有像寶寶一樣哭泣。	Wow! You're not crying like a baby.
沒事了，不要哭。	It's okay. Don't cry.

撞到頭了！	Bonk!

你撞到頭了嗎？	Did you bump your head? • bump 撞，碰

你的眼睛好像瘀青了。 Looks like you're going to get a black eye.
（Looks like：看起來像～(= It looks like)；black eye：眼睛瘀青）

你應該小心看前面的。 You should have looked ahead carefully.
• ahead 向前

我們手牽手再繼續走吧。 Let's hold hands and walk again.

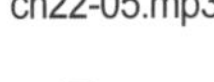
ch22-05.mp3

割到／流血的時候

我流血了。 I'm bleeding.

我被割到了。 I got a cut.

我被刀子割到自己了。 I cut myself with a knife.

我被紙張割到了。 I got a paper cut.

我被針扎到了。 I got poked by a needle.

我被一片玻璃割傷了。 I got cut by a piece of glass.

因為流血了，我很害怕。 I'm scared because I'm bleeding.

沒關係，很快就會止血的。 It's fine. It's going to stop soon.

我們必須清潔傷口。 We need to clean the wound. • wound 傷口

你怎麼被割到的？ How did you get cut?

我告訴過你要小心尖銳的東西。 I told you to watch out for sharp things.
（watch out：小心）

哎喲！消毒藥好痛。 Ouch! The sterilizer hurt.
• ouch（痛苦時發出的聲音）哎喲 • sterilizer 消毒藥

我來幫你塗藥膏。 Let me put the ointment on.
• ointment 藥膏

我們把 OK 繃貼在傷口上。
Let's cover the wound with a band-aid. •band-aid OK 繃

讓繃帶包住傷口一段時間。
Keep the bandage on the wound for a while. •bandage 繃帶

它有助於防止病菌跑到裡面去。
This helps prevent germs from getting inside. •germ 病菌

為了保護傷口，這裡將會長出結痂。
A scab will form to protect the wound. •scab 結痂

不要摳你的結痂。
Don't pick your scabs.

ch22-06.mp3

流鼻血的時候

媽，我流鼻血了。
My nose is bleeding, Mom.

低著頭。
Tilt your head down. •tilt 傾斜

我們先用面紙蓋住你的鼻子。
Let's put a tissue on your nose first.

我們用棉花球堵住你流血的鼻子。
Let's put a cotton ball up your bloody nose. •cotton ball 棉花球 •bloody 流血的

不要把血吞下去。
Don't swallow the blood. •swallow 吞下

用你的嘴巴呼吸。
Breathe with your mouth.

我的襯衫也沾到血了。
I have blood on my shirt.

沒關係，不用擔心其他事情。
It's okay. Don't worry about anything.

ch22-07.mp3

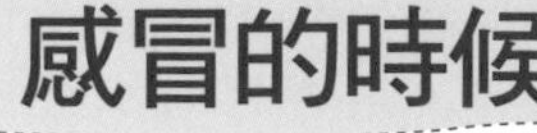

媽，我感冒了。	**Mom, I caught a cold.**
媽，我覺得冷到發抖。	I feel cold and shaky, Mom. / Mom, I feel cold and am shivering. • shaky 發抖的 • shiver 發抖
我的喉嚨很痛。	**I have a sore throat.** 喉嚨痛，喉嚨發炎
我流鼻水了。	I have a runny nose. 流鼻水，流鼻涕
我鼻塞了。	**I have a stuffy nose.** • stuffy （鼻子）塞住的
我吞東西時，我的喉嚨很痛。	My throat hurts when I swallow. • swallow 吞下
我喉嚨很痛，我不想吃東西。	**I don't want to eat because my throat hurts.**
我一直咳嗽。	I have a bad cough. / I am coughing a lot.
我的喉嚨內有痰。	**I have some phlegm in my throat.** • phlegm 痰
你咳得很嚴重。	You're coughing too hard. • cough 咳嗽
你的鼻涕是黃色的。	**Your snot is yellow.** • snot 鼻涕
我覺得你感冒了。	I think you have a cold. / You seem to have caught a cold.
你好像得了流行性感冒。	**You seem to have caught the flu.**
這是很嚴重的感冒。	It is such a severe cold. • severe 嚴重的
你可能是從雍索那傳染過來的。	**You might have caught a cold from Yongsuo.**
你需要去看醫生。	You need to see a doctor. / Let's go to see a doctor.

今天不要洗澡了。	Don't take a shower today.
不要到外面吹冷風。	Don't go out in the cold air.
醫生叫你不要吃冷的食物，對吧？	The doctor told you not to eat cold things, right?
我們把毛巾圍在你的脖子上吧。	Let's put a towel around your neck.
喉嚨痛的話，不要說太多話。	Don't talk too much since your throat hurts.
用力擤鼻涕。	Blow your nose hard. ‧blow one's nose 擤鼻涕
你必須把痰吐出來，不要吞下去。	You need to spit out the phlegm and not swallow it. (spit out 吐出)
當你要咳嗽時，用你的手遮住嘴巴。	Cover your mouth with your hand when you cough.
試著不要對著人咳嗽。	Try not to cough on people.

ch22-08.mp3

發燒的時候

媽，我覺得很熱。	Mom, I feel very hot.
我發燒了，所以我的身體真的很燙。	I have a fever, so my body feels really hot.
我感覺頭很暈。	I feel dizzy.

讓我看看你是否發燒了。	Let me see if you have a fever. (Let me see if 讓我看是不是～)
我們來量一下體溫。	Let's check your temperature. ‧temperature 溫度
我來摸一下你的額頭。	Let me feel your forehead.

你發燒了。	You have a fever.
你發高燒了。	You have a high fever.
你的額頭真的很燙。	Your forehead's really hot.
來吃點退燒藥吧。	Let's take a fever reducer. 退燒藥
你需要多喝水。	You need to drink a lot of water.
你需要把衣服脫掉。	You need to take off your clothes.
我用濕毛巾來幫你降溫。	I'll cool you down with a wet towel.
拿著這個冰袋。	Hold this ice pack.
我想你的身體正在跟細菌戰鬥。	I guess your body's fighting the germs right now.

ch22-09.mp3

頭／肚子痛的時候

媽，我頭很疼。	I have a headache, Mom.
我有很嚴重的頭痛。	I have a terrible headache.
我看看。我可以摸一下你的額頭嗎？	Let me see. Can I touch your forehead?
你很痛嗎？	Do you feel a lot of pain? / Are you sick very much?
我拿藥給你。試試看。	I'll give you some medicine. Let's see. • medicine 藥
媽，我肚子痛。	I have a stomachache, Mom.
我想我要吐了。	I think I'm going to throw up.

我拉肚子了。	I have diarrhea. ・diarrhea 拉肚子
我的便便像水一樣流出來。	My poop's coming out like water.
 看起來你鬧肚子了。	It looks like you got stomach upset.
我給你些助消化的糖漿。	I'll give you some digestive syrup. ・digestive 助消化的
你之前吃了什麼？	What did you eat before?
你好像吃太多冰的東西了。	Looks like you ate too many cold things.
你需要去大便嗎？	Do you need to poop? ・poop 大便
你應該躺下休息。	You should lie down and rest. ・rest 休息
我來按摩你的肚子。你很快就會好起來。	Let me rub your tummy. You'll be fine soon.
你要放個熱水袋在你的肚子上嗎？	Want to put a hot pack on your tummy?

ch22-10.mp3

牙齒晃動／疼痛的時候

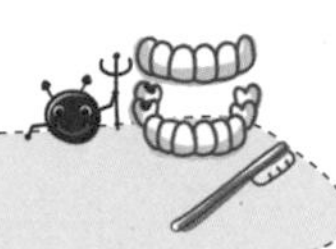

 媽，我有一顆牙齒在搖了。	I've got a loose tooth, Mom. （a loose tooth：晃動的牙齒 (= wiggly tooth)）
我的臼齒很痛。	My inner tooth hurts. （inner tooth：裡面的牙齒）
我的牙齒痛到不能咀嚼了。	I can't chew it because my tooth hurts. ・chew 咀嚼
張開你的嘴巴，說「啊～」。	Open your mouth. Say "Ah~."
哪一顆牙齒痛？	Which tooth hurts?
看起來你的牙齒要掉了。	It looks like your tooth's going to fall off. （fall off：脫落）

你需要去看牙醫。	You need to see the dentist. •dentist 牙醫
我們明天去看牙醫，把這顆牙拔掉。	Let's go to see a dentist tomorrow to take the tooth out.
媽媽用線來把它拔掉。	Mommy will pull it out with a thread.
把牙齒放在枕頭下吧。	Place your tooth underneath your pillow.
你睡覺的時候，牙仙會來把它拿走。	The tooth fairy will come while you sleep and take your tooth. ★tooth fairy 是牙仙，在西方國家傳說中，把拔下來的牙齒放在枕頭下面睡的話，牙仙就會把牙齒拿走，並留下錢。
她會放禮物／錢來作為回報。	She will leave you a present / money in return.
牙仙會給我什麼禮物呢？	What present will the tooth fairy give me?
我不確定。快點去睡吧，這樣牙仙才能來。	I don't know for sure. Go to sleep early so that the tooth fairy can come.
看起來你有蛀洞了。	It looks like you have got a cavity. •cavity 蛀洞
看起來你吃太多甜的東西了。	It looks like you ate too much sweet stuff. 甜的東西
用你不痛的牙齒來咀嚼。	Chew with your teeth that don't hurt.
我害怕去牙科。	I'm scared to go to the dentist.
不用擔心。醫生會很溫柔地幫你治療。	It's okay. The doctor will treat you gently. •gently 溫柔地
媽，晃動的牙齒掉了。	Mom, the wiggly tooth fell out.
奇怪。一點也不痛。	That's strange. It didn't hurt at all.
我第一次掉牙齒。	My tooth fell out for the first time.

我都不知道我牙齒掉了。 I didn't know my tooth fell out.

吉娜還沒有掉過牙齒。 Jina still has not lost any teeth.

因為一些牙齒掉了，咀嚼起來很困難。 It's hard to chew because some of my teeth are missing.

再等等吧。你的新牙很快就會長出來。 Wait for a while. Your new teeth will grow soon.

張開你的嘴巴。我們看看你掉了幾顆牙齒。 Open your mouth. Let's see how many teeth have fallen out.

ch22-11.mp3

得傳染病的時候

我想我把自己的身體搞壞了。 I think I broke something in my body.

我全身突然長出什麼了。 I broke out all over my body.

broke out （皮膚上）突然長出～

你好像得了水痘。 It seems like you have chicken pox.

你今天不可以去學校。 You shouldn't go to school today.

今天待在家裡。 Stay home today.

你的朋友們也有可以被你感染。 Your friends could also catch it from you.

・catch 染上（疾病）

不要跟你弟弟一起用這個杯子。 Don't use the cup together with your brother.

我們來用不同的毛巾和湯匙吧。 Let's use different towels and spoons.

你不希望全家人都被傳染，對吧？ You don't want the entire family to get sick, do you?

・entire 全部的

我希望你快點康復。 I hope you get well soon.

get well 痊癒

我不可以跟弟弟玩嗎？ Can't I play with my brother?

等一陣子，等你康復再來玩。 Wait a little and play when you get better.

我什麼時候會康復？ When can I get better?

也許一個禮拜多一點。 Maybe in a week or so.

你為什麼把妹妹送去奶奶家？ Why did you send my sister to Grandma's?

我擔心你妹妹也傳染到。 I was afraid that your sister might catch it, too.

I was afraid that 我擔心～

ch22-12.mp3

被蟲咬／發癢的時候

媽，我想我這裡被蟲咬了。 I think I got a bug bite here, Mom.

bug bite 被蟲咬

又腫又紅。 It's swollen and red. •swollen 腫脹的

很癢。 It's ticklish. / It's itchy. •ticklish 怕癢的

我癢到睡不著了。 I can't sleep because it itches.

我想知道你被什麼咬了。 I wonder what bit you.

bit bite（咬）的過去式

不要去抓它。 Don't scratch it. •scratch 抓

如果你抓它的話，會更嚴重的。 It can get worse if you scratch it.

即使很癢，也不可以抓。 Don't scratch it even if it's ticklish.

如果你抓的話，細菌就會跑進去。那會讓你更癢。 If you scratch it, germs will get in. It'll get more itchy.

我忍不住了。 I can't hold it. / I can't stand it.

這個止癢藥會有幫助。	This itch relief will help. 止癢藥
我幫你擦些治療蚊蟲咬的藥。	I'll put on some bug bite remedy for you. • remedy 治療藥物
把這個冰袋敷上去。	Put this ice pack on it.
如果你不去抓的話，它就會好起來。	It will get better if you don't scratch it.
看。你抓了之後，就流血了。	Look. It's bleeding after you scratched it.

ch22-13.mp3

去醫院

我們去醫院。	Let's go to the hospital. / Let's go to see a doctor.
 我一定要打針嗎？	Do I have to get a shot? 打針
 不，你只是要讓醫生檢查一下。	No, you'll just check with the doctor.
這只是定期的體檢。	It is just a regular checkup. • checkup 體檢
跟醫生打招呼。	Say hello to the doctor.
深呼吸。	Take a deep breath.
他要看你的耳朵和鼻子。	He's going to look at your ears and nose.
我們來量身高和體重吧。	Let's measure your height and weight. • measure 測量 • height 身高 • weight 體重
你有 135 公分，25 公斤。	You are 135cm tall and weigh 25kg.
你需要打流感疫苗。	You need to get a flu shot. 流感疫苗
會有一點刺痛。不用害怕。	It will sting a little. Don't be scared.

哇，你沒哭，表現得很好。 Wow, you're doing well by not crying.

我們拿處方箋就可以走了。 Let's get the prescription and go.

現在都結束了。 It's all over now. / Everything's done now.

我們去領藥處吧。 Let's go to the pharmacy. ·pharmacy 領藥處

ch22-14.mp3

吃藥

 來吃藥了。 Let's take some medicine. ·take medicine 吃藥

 我不想吃任何藥。 I don't want to take any medicine.

 那麼，你不會康復。 Then you won't get better. 痊癒；康復

你能吃嗎？ Can you take it?

飯後 30 分鐘後，吃掉它。 Take it 30 minutes after meal.

你一天必須吃兩次。 You need to take it twice a day. 一天兩次

這些是抗生素，你一定要吃。 These are antibiotics, so you need to take them. ·antibiotic 抗生素

這是治咳嗽的，這是治鼻涕的。 This is for your cough, and this is for your runny nose. ·cough 咳嗽

你吃了這些藥後就會好起來。 You'll get better after taking this medicine.

真厲害，你把藥吃了。 Good job taking your medicine. 做得好

把它都喝掉。 Drink all of it.

如果你把藥吐掉，你必須再吃一次。 You need to take it again if you spit it out.

這裡有水和糖果。
Here's some water and candy.

吃完這個之後，把糖果放進嘴巴內。
Put the candy in your mouth right after taking this.

我還想再吃藥。
I want to take the medicine again.

不行！你必須根據指示來吃藥。
No way! You should take your medicine like you are told. 照你所被告知地

好苦。
It's very bitter.

吃了藥之後，我覺得很睏。
I feel sleepy since I took the medicine.

ch22-15.mp3

吃對身體好的食物

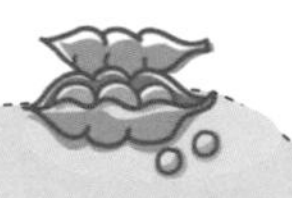

如果你喝牛奶，你會長更高。
You'll get taller if you drink milk.

魚乾可以讓你的骨骼更強壯。
This dry fish will help your bones get stronger.

海帶可以讓你的血更乾淨。
Seaweed makes your blood cleaner.
• seaweed 海菜類

如果你吃蔬菜的話，你的皮膚就會變得更光滑。
Your skin will get smoother if you eat vegetables. • smooth 光滑的

我們來吃菠菜，變得跟大力水手卜派一樣強壯吧。
Let's eat spinach and be strong like Popeye. • spinach 菠菜

媽媽為你做了愛心料理。
Mom cooked with love for you.

雜糧米比一般的白米更好。
Multigrain rice is better than plain rice.
• multigrain 雜糧

豆類可以讓你更強壯，而且讓你長肌肉。
Beans make you stronger and give you muscles. • bean 豆

開心地吃的話，你會消化得更好。	Eat happily so you'll digest your food better. ‧digest 消化
即使它不好吃，但是對健康很好。	It's good for you even though it tastes bad. (even though 即使)
當季的食物總是最新鮮的。	Seasonal food is always fresh. ‧seasonal 季節性的
把它完全煮熟就會很安全。	It's safe to cook it fully. ‧cook 煮
均衡飲食是很重要的。	It's important to eat everything.
不要那麼挑食。	Don't be so picky about food. ‧picky 挑剔
媽媽因為不吃胡蘿蔔，所以視力才會不好。	Mom's eyesight is bad because I didn't eat carrots. ‧eyesight 視力 ‧carrot 胡蘿蔔
 我喜歡吃蔬菜。	I love to eat vegetables.

ch22-16.mp3

注意有害的食物

 糖果會讓你的牙齒變糟。	Candy will make your teeth bad.
吃太多冰淇淋的話，你的肚子會痛的。	Too much ice cream will give you a stomachache.
你不應該吃太多太鹹的食物。	You shouldn't eat much too salty food. ‧salty 鹹的
不要吃聞起來很怪的食物。	Don't eat food that smells weird.
速食對你的健康不好。	Instant food is bad for your health. (is bad for 對～不好)
這些飲料滿滿的都是色素。	This drink is full of coloring. (is full of 充滿～)
路邊的食物不乾淨。	Street food isn't clean.

我擔心街頭食物不安全。	I'm afraid that street food is not safe.
如果你沒有吃每種食物，你就不會長大。	You won't grow if you don't eat everything.
如果你只吃肉，不吃蔬菜的話，你的血液就不能好好運作。	Your blood won't work well if you eat just meat but no vegetables.
如果你吃太多油膩的食物，你會變胖的。	You'll get fat if you eat too much fatty food. ・fatty 油膩的，脂肪的
如果你吃太多辣的食物，你的胃會壞掉。	If you eat too much spicy food, your stomach will hurt. ・stomach 肚子，胃
如果你不把水果洗乾淨，你根本就是把農藥都吃進去了。	If you don't clean the fruit, you are basically eating all the pesticides. ・pesticide 殺蟲劑，農藥
這食物已經過期了。我們把它丟掉吧。	The food has expired. Let's throw it away. ・expired 過了有效期限
不可以！不要吃掉到地上的東西。	Nope! Don't eat it after you drop it on the ground.
 媽，不要喝太多的咖啡。	Don't drink too much coffee, Mom.
爸，不要喝太多啤酒。	Don't drink too much beer, Dad.

Chapter 23 生理現象

I want to pee, Mom.
媽～我想尿尿

OK, I'll be right out!
好，我馬上出來。

ch23-01.mp3

尿尿

你要尿尿嗎？	Do you want to pee? / Do you want to go to the bathroom? ・pee〈幼兒用語〉尿尿
 我不用。	I don't need to go.
我要尿尿。	I need to pee.
 現在？	Right now?
 我忍不住了。我要尿出來了。	I can't hold it. I need to pee really bad.

忍一下！忍住！ Hold it! Hold it!

把馬桶座掀起來後，再尿。 Pee after holding the toilet seat up. 馬桶座

尿完之後，用衛生紙擦乾淨。 Use toilet paper after you pee. 衛生紙

把裙子拉起來尿。 Hold your skirt up and pee.

確定尿尿不會濺到馬桶座上。 Make sure the pee doesn't get on the seat.

盡可能尿到馬桶中間。 Try to pee in the center of the toilet.

你沖水了嗎？ Did you flush?

如果你憋尿太久的話，對身體不好。 If you hold your pee for too long, it's not good for you.

我尿了一點。 I peed a little.

喔！我尿在衣服上了。 Oops! I peed on my clothes.

媽，對不起。我尿床了。 Sorry, I wet the bed, Mom. 尿床

看吧，我告訴你要去廁所的。 See? I told you to go to the bathroom.

你出門前，先去廁所。 Go to the bathroom before you leave.

睡覺之前，要先去廁所。 Go to the bathroom before you go to sleep.

ch23-02.mp3

大便

媽，我要大便。 I have to poop, Mom. ·poop〈幼兒用語〉大便

我肚子痛。我要去大便。 My tummy aches. I have to poop.

關上門，便便很臭。 Close the door. It smells.

你都上完之後，告訴媽咪。	Call Mommy when you're done. • done 完成，結束
我的便便看起來像蕃薯。	My poop looks like a sweet potato.
我孩子的大便好像山羊大便。	My baby's poop is like goat poop. • goat 山羊
你好好地擦屁股了嗎？	Did you clean your bottom well? • bottom 屁股
你都上完之後，要沖水。	Flush when you're done.
要洗手。	Wash your hands.
媽，你能幫我擦嗎？	Will you wipe it, Mom? • wipe 擦
媽，我大了好多。	I pooped a lot, Mom.
啊！好臭！	Eeek! It stinks! • stink 發出惡臭
我們不要再談大便了。	Let's stop talking about pooping.
如果我不大便的話，會怎樣？	What happens if I don't poop? （What happens if：～的話，會怎樣？）
如果沒有每天大便的話，會不健康嗎？	Is it unhealthy if you don't poop every day? • unhealthy 不健康的
那麼，大便就會留在肚臍下面。	Then the poop sits here below your belly button. （belly button：肚臍）
我今天早上大便了。為什麼又要出來了？	I pooped this morning. Why is it coming out again?
看起來似乎食物被消化得很好。	It looks like the food got digested well.

ch23-03.mp3

便祕

媽，我大不出來。 I can't poop, Mom.

用力點。 Try to push.

我肚子很痛，但是我大不出來。 My stomach hurts, but I can't poop.

你應該喝很多水。 You should drink a lot of water.

因為你不吃蔬菜才會這樣。 The reason is that you haven't eaten any vegetables.

我想你便祕了。 I think you're constipated.

• constipated 患便祕的

先從廁所出來，等一下再試試。 Come out of the bathroom and try it later.

等一下再試。 Try again later.

要我幫你按摩肚子嗎？ Want me to rub your tummy?

如果很嚴重的話，我會給你一些藥。 I'll give you some medicine if it's really bad.

我等一下上。 I'll poop later.

不要把書帶進廁所。 Don't take your book into the bathroom.

那不是個好的廁所習慣。 That's not a good bathroom habit.

ch23-04.mp3

放屁

喔，這是什麼味道？ Gosh, what's this smell?

	你放屁了，這傢伙！	You farted, dude! • fart 放屁 • dude（對男性的俚語稱呼）傢伙
	我剛剛放屁了，真的好臭。	I just farted, and it stinks really bad.
	我都不能呼吸了。	I can't even breathe.
	爸比的屁聞起來好像大便。	Dad's fart smells like poo.
	爸，你是放屁精。	You're such a farty pants, Dad.
	誰放屁了？	Who farted? / Who cut the cheese?
	不是我，是你嗎？	It wasn't me. Was it you?
	不是我。為什麼一直看我？	It wasn't me. Why do you keep looking at me?
	哇，你放得好大聲。	Wow, you've got a loud sound. • loud 大聲的
	媽，我無法停止放屁。	I can't stop farting, Mom.
	這太糟了。你怎麼可以在我臉上放屁？	It's terrible. How come you farted in my face?
	你要在地板上弄個洞了。	You're going to make a hole in the ground.
	不要再取笑我了。 已經沒有臭味了。	Stop making fun of me. The smell's gone now. • be gone 消失，沒有
	我們需要打開窗戶。	We need to open the window.
	我需要讓臭味消失。	I need to get rid of the smell.
	無聲屁比響屁更臭。	Quiet farts smell worse than loud ones.
	噠噠！爸比要放屁了！摀住鼻子！	Ta-da! Dad's going to fart! Hold your nose!

ch23-05.mp3

鼻屎

敏基，看我的鼻屎。 Look at my booger, Minji. ・booger 鼻屎

天呀！好噁！ Oh my! It's gross! ・gross 噁心的，令人討厭的

清掉它！ Get it off!

你是挖鼻屎大王！ You booger digger! ・digger 挖～的人

不要再挖鼻子了。 Stop picking your nose.
・pick one's nose 挖鼻子

不要吃鼻屎。 Don't eat your boogers.

我應該如何處理這個鼻屎？ What should I do with this booger?

用面紙擦掉。 Clean it off with a tissue.

你為什麼把那個給媽媽？ Why are you giving that to Mommy?

媽，鼻屎挖不出來。 The booger would not come out, Mom. (come out 出來)

不要在他人面前挖鼻孔。 Don't pick your nose in front of people.

如果你一直挖，你會流鼻血。 If you pick too much, your nose can bleed.

是誰把鼻屎沾在這裡的？ Who put this booger here?

ch23-06.mp3

打嗝

媽，我打嗝了！ I have the hiccups, Mom! ・hiccup 打嗝

我要怎樣才能停止打嗝？ How can I stop hiccups?

把口水吞下去。 Swallow your spit. ·swallow 吞 ·spit 口水

屏住呼吸，並數到三。 Hold your breath and count to three.
·breath 呼吸，氣息

你要喝點溫水嗎？ Will you drink some warm water?

讓我嚇一跳。或許可以把打嗝治好。 Scare me. It might cure the hiccups.
·scare 使驚嚇 ·cure 治癒

呀！你現在好一點了嗎？ Peek-a-boo! Are you okay now?
·Peek-a-boo! 呀！（嚇人時發出的聲音）

嗯，我現在好一點了。 Yeah, I seem fine now.

不，我還是持續打嗝。 No, I still have them.

ch23-07.mp3

打噴嚏

媽，我打噴嚏了。 I'm sneezing, Mom. ·sneeze 打噴嚏

我的鼻子很癢。 My nose is ticklish. ·ticklish 癢的

這也許是因為花粉的關係。 It's probably because of the pollen.
·pollen 花粉

打噴嚏時的禮儀

在英國、美國等國家，看到有人打噴嚏時，我們會說 Bless you！它的意思是「願上帝保佑你不會感冒」。若你打噴嚏的時候，有人跟你說 Bless you 的話，只要回答 Thank you 就可以。

用手摀住你的嘴。 Cover your mouth with your hand.

不可以對著人打噴嚏。 Don't sneeze on other people.

小心！ 口水噴得到處都是。 Watch out! There's spit going everywhere.

哈啾！抱歉！ Achoo! Excuse me.

ch23-08.mp3

呵欠

媽，我在打呵欠。 I'm yawning, Mom. ·yawn 呵欠

你累了嗎？要我打開窗戶嗎？ Are you tired? Want me to open the windows?

你的呵欠讓其他人也跟著打起來了。 Your yawn made others yawn, too.

你打呵欠後，我也好像要打呵欠了。 I feel like yawning after you yawned.

打呵欠是會傳染的。 Yawning is contagious. ·contagious 有傳染性的

請試著不要在課堂上打呵欠。 Please try not to yawn during class.

ch23-09.mp3

打飽嗝

媽，民肅打飽嗝了。嘿嘿。 Minsu burped, Mom. Hehe. ·burp 打飽嗝

那很沒禮貌。 That's impolite. ·impolite 不禮貌的

在餐桌上打飽嗝很沒禮貌。 It's not polite to burp at the table.

不要像那樣打飽嗝。很丟臉。 Don't burp like that. It's embarrassing.
·embarrassing 令人尷尬的

打飽嗝很好玩。 Burping is fun.

剪手指甲／腳趾甲

ch23-10.mp3

天呀！你的手指甲怎麼這麼長呢？ Oh my! Why are your fingernails this long? •fingernail 手指甲

太長了。你應該修剪一下指甲。 They're too long. You should trim your nails. •trim 修剪

你能幫我剪嗎？ Will you cut them?

把指甲剪拿來。 Get the nail clippers. 指甲剪

不要動。你會受傷的。 Don't move. You can get hurt.

你會用這個抓傷別人的。 You can scratch someone with this.

在指甲下面有髒髒的東西。 There's dirt under your fingernails. •dirt 塵垢

不要咬指甲。 Don't bite your fingernails.

如果你的指甲很長，會很難握住鉛筆的。 It's hard to grab a pencil if your fingernails are long.

如果你的指甲很長，要叫我幫你剪。 Ask me to cut your fingernails if they are long.

現在把另一隻手給我。 Now give me the other hand.

我們也來剪你的腳趾甲吧？ Let's cut your toenails, too.

如果你的腳趾甲很長，你的襪子會被戳破洞。 You can get a hole in your socks if your toenails are long. •toenail 腳趾甲

我可以自己剪嗎？ Can I cut them by myself? •by oneself 自己

因為你剪得太短了，我很痛。 It hurts because you cut them too short.

Chapter 24

電話用語

Daddy's calling you, Mom!
媽，爹地打電話給你。

Will you answer it for me?
你可以幫我接嗎？

ch24-01.mp3

接電話

喂！ 這是吉娜的家。	Hello! This is Jina's residence.
請問哪裡找？	Who's calling, please?
您要找哪位？	Who are you calling, please?
不好意思。你打錯電話了。	Sorry. You've got the wrong number.

媽，這是要找你的。	It's for you, Mom.

 問問看是誰打來的。	Ask who's calling.
 請等一下。	Hold on, please.
好，我請她來接。	Okay. I'll get her.
媽媽說等一下回電話給你。	Mom said she'll call you back. • call back 回電
你可以留下你的電話嗎？	Will you leave your number? • leave 留下
 電話在響了。	The bell's ringing.
你能幫我接一下電話嗎？	Will you pick up (接（電話）) the phone for me? / Will you answer the phone for me?
你能把電話給我嗎？	Will you get the phone to me?
掛斷電話。	Hang up (掛斷) the phone. / Put down the phone.
 我來接。	I'll pick it up. / Let me answer it. / I'll get it. • answer 接，應答（電話，電鈴等）
誰打來的電話？	Who is calling?
是我不知道的號碼。	I don't know this number.
如果是不認識的人的話， 讓我來聽。	Put me on the phone if it's a stranger.
再見。很高興聽到你的消息。	Goodbye. It was nice hearing from you.
抱歉。我要掛斷電話了。	Sorry. I have to put the phone down.
你沒有看到我正在講電話嗎？	Can't you see I'm talking on the phone?

ch24-02.mp3

打電話

要打電話給爸爸嗎？ Want to call Dad?

我自己可以打。 I can call myself.

你要仔細撥電話。 You need to dial carefully.
• dial 撥號

你記得爸爸的電話號碼嗎？ Can you remember Dad's number?

電話被切斷了。 The phone got cut off.

電話中。 The line is busy. • busy （電話）佔線的

沒有人接電話。 No one's picking up the phone.

晚點再打。 Let's call later.

喂。民肅在那嗎？ Hello. Is Minsu there?

這裡是金宏，是民肅的朋友。我可以跟民肅通話嗎？ This is Jinhong, Minsu's friend. Can I talk to Minsu?

你可以請民肅聽電話嗎？ Will you put Minsu on the phone?

我可以留言給他嗎？ Can I leave a message for him?

我好像打錯電話了。對不起。 I think I called the wrong number. I'm sorry.

它說沒有這個電話號碼。 It says the number is not listed.
• listed 在名單上的，登記的

你好像打錯電話了。 It looks like you dialed incorrectly.

媽，你能告訴我吉娜的電話號碼嗎？ Can you tell me Jina's number, Mom?

ch24-03.mp3

使用手機

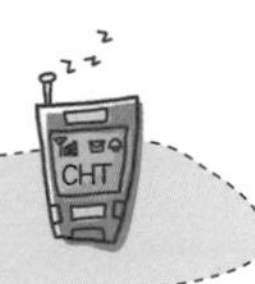

 不要玩媽媽的手機。	Don't play with Mom's cell phone.
那是每個月有限額的。 不要打太多。	There is a monthly limit. Don't use it too much. • monthly 每月一次的　• limit 限制
在家的話，打家用電話。	Use the home phone at home.
在學校，要把手機關掉。	Turn off your cell phone at school.
電池沒電了。	The battery's dead.
把你的手機充電。	Recharge your cell phone.　• recharge 充電
 我可以換支新手機嗎？	Can I have a new cell phone?
 小孩子不應該用昂貴的手機。	Kids shouldn't use expensive cell phones.
容易弄壞，也容易弄丟。	It's easy to break and easy to lose.
把號碼存起來。	Save the number.　• save 存
不要讓你的手機靠近水。	Keep your cell phone away from water. • keep away from 遠離～，不要靠近～
不要在路上邊走邊看手機。	Don't walk on the street while looking at your cell phone.
在公共場所時，把你的手機轉震動。	Leave your phone on vibrate in public places.　• vibrate 震動　公共場所
我討厭人們用手機大聲講話。	I hate people talking too loudly on their cell phones.
 爸，不要在開車時用手機。	Don't use your cell phone while driving, Dad.

ch24-04.mp3

確認簡訊

有簡訊來了。 | Here's a message.

是誰寄簡訊給你呢？ | Who sent the text message to you? 文字簡訊

爸爸傳來的簡訊。 | The message is from Dad.

這是垃圾簡訊。 | It's spam.

我要刪掉它。 | I need to delete it. ‧delete 刪掉，刪除

我要回簡訊。 | I need to reply. ‧reply 回覆

你到的時候，請傳簡訊給我。 | Please text me when you get there.
‧text 傳簡訊

傳給簡訊給媽媽。 | Send Mom a text message.

在公共場所使用簡訊比較好。 | It's better to use text messages in public places.

媽，你打錯字了。 | Mom, you typed it wrong. ‧type 打字

媽，我回簡訊了。 | I sent a reply, Mom.

媽，你確認簡訊了嗎？ | Did you check the text message, Mom?

這是哪國的語言呢？ | What kind of language is this?

它們是表情符號。 | They are emoticons.

ch24-05.mp3

使用智慧型手機

媽媽，我想要智慧型手機。 | Mom, I want a smartphone.

我會在你上國中時買給你。 | I'll buy you one when you're in middle school.

我所有朋友都有智慧型手機。 | All my friends have smartphones.

我很不高興，因為你一直看手機。 | I'm upset because you keep looking at your phone.

一旦你長大，我會買手機給你。 | I'll buy you a phone once you're ready for one. •be ready for 準備做～

你知道在上課期間要把手機關機，對嗎？ | You know to turn off your phone during class, right?

我才剛下載一個新應用程式。 | I just downloaded a new application.

這個英文教育的應用程式很好玩。 | This English education app is fun.

你在看另一部影片嗎？長度多長？ | Are you watching another video? How long is it?

看完這個後，我就不會看了。 | I'll stop watching after this.

我在投票給我最喜歡的偶像團體。 | I'm voting for my favorite idol group. (voting for：投票～)

媽媽，我想要創一個 Instagram 帳號。 | Mom, I want to make an Instagram account. •Instagram 一種社群網路平台

賢宇在臉書上面有很多朋友。 | Hyunwoo has a lot of Facebook friends. •Facebook 一種社群網路平台

我必須按讚元英的臉書狀態。 | I have to like Wonyong's Facebook status.

為什麼你一直看你的手機？ | Why do you keep looking at your phone?

我希望大家在吃飯時，不要看手機。 | I wish you wouldn't look at your phone while you're eating.

我收到來自娜妍的 LINE 訊息。 I got a LINE message from Nayeon.

我們四個在一個群組聊天室。 The four of us are in a group chat.

與很多人共用的聊天室

太大聲了，把群組聊天室的通知關掉。

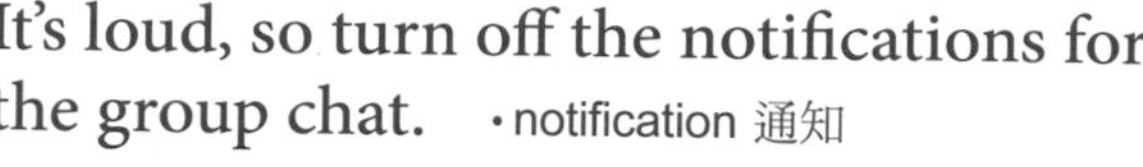

It's loud, so turn off the notifications for the group chat. ‧notification 通知

你們在講什麼？ What are you talking about?

我們在講下週的作業。 We're talking about next week's homework assignment.

不要在群組裡背著別人講壞話。 Don't talk behind someone's back in the group chat.

背著～說壞話

你必須退出群組聊天室。 You need to leave the group chat.

我們來用 Google 查詢方向。 Let's look up directions on Google.

‧directions 方向 ‧Google 一個搜尋引擎

用地鐵的應用程式查查看，搭到台北車站要花多久的時間。 Check how long it takes to get to Taipei Station on the subway app.

我們來用 Google 查查看台中車站好吃的餐廳。 Let's look up good places to eat at Taichung Station on Google.

媽媽，迦納的首都是什麼？ Mom, what is the capital of Ghana?

在 Google 上查詢。 Look it up on Google.

來這裡！我們來拍幾張照片。 Come here! Let's take some pictures.

好的，對相機微笑！ Okay, smile for the camera!

一、二、三，Cheese！ One, two, three, cheese!

看著相機說「Cheese」！ Look at the camera and say "Cheese".

你要不要跟我拍張自拍？ Why don't you take a selfie with me?

‧selfie 自拍照

我現在在錄影。 I'm taking a video now.

媽媽，我幫你拍照。 I'll take a picture of you, mom.

我們來跟爸爸視訊。 Let's video chat with dad. • video chat 視訊

奶奶想要跟你視訊，說嗨！ Grandma wants to video chat with you. Say hi!

Chapter 25 料理

Let's make cake for dinner.
我們晚餐做個蛋糕吧！

Let me mix the dough.
讓我來混合麵糰吧。

ch25-01.mp3

洗菜

我們來洗小黃瓜吧。	Let's wash the cucumbers.
你要好好把蔬菜洗乾淨。	You need to clean the vegetables well.
萵苣的菜葉要一片一片洗。	Clean the lettuce leaves (萵苣的菜葉) one by one.
可能會有農藥留在上面。	There can be pesticides on it.

• pesticide 殺蟲劑，農藥

要用一些洗潔劑嗎？	**Want to use some detergent?** • detergent 洗潔劑
不可以有洗潔劑留在上面。	There shouldn't be any detergent on it.
要多洗幾次。	**Wash it several times.**
用流動的水來洗會比較好。	It's better to clean it in flowing water.
先泡在水中，之後再洗。	**Soak them in water and clean them later.** • soak 浸泡
輕輕地搓洗。	Scrub it gently. • scrub 搓洗
如果你太用力搓洗，營養成分會被洗掉的。	**The nutrients will get washed away if you scrub it too hard.** • nutrient 營養成分
蔬菜用冷水洗的話，會保持新鮮。	Vegetables stay fresh when you wash them with cold water.
我們把這些煮過的蔬菜用冷水沖一沖吧。	**Let's rinse these cooked vegetables with cold water.** • rinse 沖洗
你要切蔬菜之前，要先洗一洗。	You need to wash vegetables before you cut them.
你煮魚之前，要先洗一洗。	**You need to wash fish before you cook it.**

ch25-02.mp3

剪／切

我要把這切成小方塊。	**I need to dice this.** • dice 將切成小方塊
我們把肉切碎吧。	Let's chop the meat. • chop 切碎；剁碎
我幫你把火腿切成薄片。	**Let me slice the ham for you.** • slice 切薄片
我們把胡蘿蔔切成絲。	Let's shred this carrot. • shred 切絲

我們把它切成長度 1 公分的小方塊。	Let's cut it into cubes 1cm long. ・cube 方塊
我們要切得更小／大一些。	Let's cut it a little smaller / bigger.
我們把大蒜切碎。	Let's mince the garlic. ・mince 切碎
我們來削馬鈴薯。	Let's peel the potatoes. ・peel 削皮
我們把它切成適當的大小。	Let's cut it into the right size.
這樣就很容易吃進嘴巴裡。	So it will go into your mouth easily.
你最好用剪刀剪它。	You'd better cut it with scissors.
 媽，小心用刀。	Be careful with the knife, Mom.
小心！你可能會傷到你的手。	Watch out! You might hurt your hand.
媽，我能切它嗎？	Can I cut it, Mom?
 你要用麵包刀切麵包嗎？	Want to cut the bread with a bread knife?
如果你切太厚的話，會煮不熟。	It won't cook well if you cut it too thick. ・thick 厚的

切的表達

- 切 cut
- 切成小方塊 dice
- 削皮 peel
- 切碎 mince
- 切碎；剁碎 chop
- 切薄片 slice
- 切絲 shred

把叉子壓下去然後將它切斷。 Cut it by pressing with a fork.

把它切成相同大小。 Cut it into equal pieces. • equal 相同的

刀子變鈍了，要磨利才行。 The knife gets dull and has to be sharpened. • dull 鈍的 • sharpen 磨利

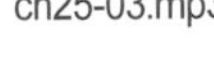

ch25-03.mp3

加熱

我們來煮水。 Let's boil some water.

我們來熱湯。 Let's heat up the soup. (heat up 把～加熱)

蓋子在震動了。 The lid is shaking.

出現水蒸氣了。 There's steam coming up. • steam 蒸氣，水蒸氣

這很燙，看著就好。 Just look at it since it's hot.

我們需要再煮滾一下。 We need to boil it a little more. • boil 煮

按順序把材料放進去。 Add the ingredients in order. • ingredient 材料，食材

我們等到食物煮熟吧。 Let's wait till it gets cooked.

油會濺出來，離遠一點。 Stay away since the oil splatters. • splatter 濺

媽，我聞到燒焦的味道了。 I smell something burned, Mom.

熱度太高了嗎？ Is the heat too hot?

把火轉小來煮。 Reduce the heat to low and cook. (to low 到低點)

用大火煮一小段時間。 Use high heat and cook for a short period of time. (a short period of time 短時間)

好好攪拌，這樣它才不會黏在鍋底。	Stir well so that it does not get stuck to the bottom. ‧stir 攪拌 ‧bottom 底部 黏到
因為手把很燙，要戴上手套。	Put gloves on because the grip is hot. ‧grip 手把
要小心，因為如果你打開蓋子，會有蒸氣跑出來。	Be careful since hot steam will come out if you open the top.

ch25-04.mp3

塗抹

你要在吐司上塗什麼？	How do you like your toast? / What do you spread on your toast? ‧spread 塗
你要塗果醬還是奶油？	Do you want jam or butter?
我要在麵包上塗些果醬。	I want some jam for my bread.
要均勻地塗。	Spread it evenly. ‧evenly 均勻地
每種果醬用不同的湯匙。	Use different spoons for each one.
我要自己塗。	Let me spread it myself.
我來試試看。	Let me try.
媽，它一直流出來。	It keeps coming out, Mom.
媽，它一直滴出來。	It keeps dripping, Mom. ‧drip 滴下
那太多了。用適當的量。	That's too much. Use the right amount. ‧amount 量
一定要確實蓋上蓋子。	Be sure to close the top.
這樣可以嗎？	Is this about right?

我把它挖出來的時候，掉下來了。	I dropped it while getting it out.

盛在盤子內

你能幫我把盤子拿來嗎？	Will you get a plate for me?
我們需要更大的盤子。	We need a bigger plate.
我們需要較深的盤子。	We need a hollow plate. •hollow 凹陷的
你能把湯碗拿給我嗎？	Can you bring me the soup bowls? •bowl 碗
不要盛太多東西在碗內。	Don't put too much in the bowl.
我們把它盛在中間。	Let's put it in the middle.
你要盛更多在盤子上嗎？	Will you put some more on the plate?
媽，把它放在我的碗內。	Put it in my own bowl, Mom.
請盛很多在我的盤子內。	Put a lot on my plate, please.
我們把盤子的邊緣擦乾淨。	Let's clean the rim of the plate. •rim 邊緣
我們拿一些出來。	Let's take out a little bit.
我們還需要幾個盤子？	How many more plates do we need?
把這些盤子擺在餐桌上。	Place these plates on the table. •place 放置
那些盤子很容易破，要小心點。	Watch out because the plate can break easily.

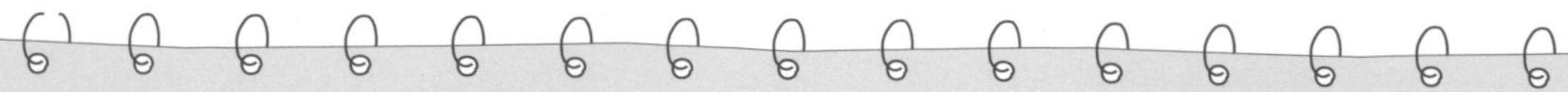

美國感恩節的習俗

感恩節 Thanksgiving

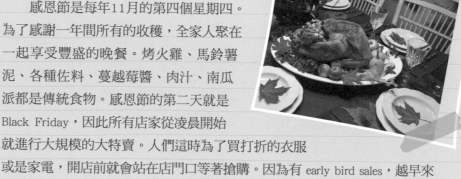

感恩節是每年11月的第四個星期四。為了感謝一年間所有的收穫，全家人聚在一起享受豐盛的晚餐。烤火雞、馬鈴薯泥、各種佐料、蔓越莓醬、肉汁、南瓜派都是傳統食物。感恩節的第二天就是Black Friday，因此所有店家從凌晨開始就進行大規模的大特賣。人們這時為了買打折的衣服或是家電，開店前就會站在店門口等著搶購。因為有 early bird sales，越早來排隊就越能搶到便宜。

★ 常用的會話句子

- 感恩節是我們收成作物，並因此對神表示感謝的時候。 **Thanksgiving is when we harvest crops and give thanks to God for it.**
- 它在美國是非常重要的節日。 **It is such an important holiday in the US.**
- 他們吃什麼樣的食物？ **What kind of food do they eat?**
- 吃烤火雞、馬鈴薯泥、肉汁、南瓜派。 **Roasted turkey, mashed potatoes, gravy, and pumpkin pie.**
- 在感恩節，所有的家人聚在一起享用晚餐。 **On Thanksgiving, all the family members gather and eat dinner together.**

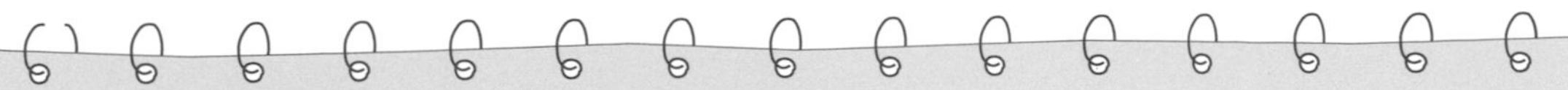

美國小孩的特別日

去朋友家睡 Sleepover

小學生之間的 sleepover 是很特別的日子。因為那天可以去好朋友的家過一夜，還可以一直玩有趣的遊戲玩到很晚。父母親之間經過邀請、允許之後，小孩子就可以去邀請朋友到家裡玩到第二天才回去。發出邀請的父母要把行程和是否招待晚餐等事項告訴其他小孩的父母，並且不可以只把小孩子放在家中。因為可以穿睡衣玩和睡，所以也叫做 slumber 或 pajama party。

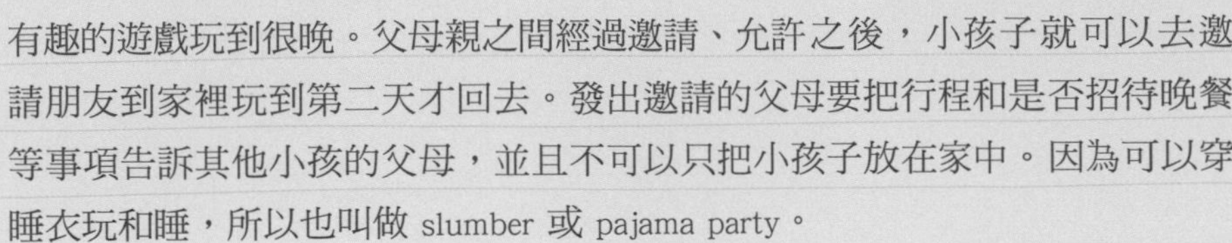

★ 常用的會話句子

媽，你上次說今天我可以在吉娜家睡，對吧？	Mom, last time you told me that I could sleep over at Jina's house, right?
是的，沒錯。所以她媽媽允許你去嗎了？	Yes, I did. So did you get her parent's permission?
是的，她說好。	Yes. She said it's fine.
好。那麼，你為什麼還不準備一下要帶的東西？不要忘記牙刷。	Okay, then. Why don't you pack the things that you will need? Don't forget your toothbrush.
在吉娜家的時候，一定要乖。不要太吵。不要在她家裡亂跑。好嗎？	Behave well at Jina's home. Don't be too noisy. Do not run around inside her house. Okay?
要聽吉娜父母的話。	Listen to Jina's parents.
媽咪不在也要好好睡。祝你在朋友家有個美好有趣的夜晚。	Sleep well without Mommy. Have a very nice and fun sleepover!

週末和紀念日

Chapter 26

享受週末假期

Mom, what day is it today?
媽，今天是星期幾？

Today is Saturday. You can sleep more.
今天是星期六。你可以多睡一點。

ch26-01.mp3

享受週末

我等不及週末開始了。	I can't wait for the weekend to begin.
這是令人期待的週末。	It's an exciting weekend.
假日實在太好玩了。	Holidays are fun.
這個週末我不用去學校。我喜歡。	I don't have to go to school this weekend. I love it.

從明天開始就是週末了。	It's going to be the weekend tomorrow.

你六、日都不用去上學。	You don't have to go to school on Saturdays and Sundays.
你的週末要跟家人一起渡過。	You spend the weekends with your family.
跟你的朋友們說週末愉快。	Tell your friends to have a good weekend.
週末愉快！	Have a good weekend!
我希望每天都跟這個週末一樣。	I wish every day were like the weekend.
我不用去學校，對吧？	I don't have to go to school, do I?
如果你不去學校的話，你就見不到你的朋友了。	You can't meet your friends if you don't go to school.
這個週末，我們要去哪裡嗎？	Are we going somewhere this weekend?
我們會去博物館。	We will go to a museum.
我想要去美術博物館。	I want to go to an art museum.
我們要不要有一個週末農場，這樣就可以種蔬菜了？	Cant' we own a weekend farm so that we can grow vegetables? ·own 擁有
媽，這個週末我們去遊樂園吧。	Mom, let's go to the amusement park this weekend.
週末我們可以去旅行嗎？	Can we go on a trip during the weekend?
這個週末，你有課要補上。	You have a makeup lesson on the weekend. ·makeup 補足
已經週日了。	It's already Sunday.
這個週末要結束了。	The weekend is coming to an end.
明天，新的一週就要開始了！	A new week is going to start tomorrow.

連休就要開始了！ The long holiday is going to start!

（週末加上國定假日有三天以上的）連休

這次的國定假日剛好在週末。 The holiday falls on a weekend.

正逢（某日）

我浪費了週末，什麼都沒做。 I wasted my weekend doing nothing.

ch26-02.mp3

叫爸爸起床

爸，起床了！ Get up, Dad!

張開眼睛。 Open your eyes.

爸比太累了。 Daddy's too tired.

我要多睡一會。 I'm going to sleep a little more.

你答應我要去公園的。 You promised to go to the park.

甜心，饒了我吧。 Give me a break, Sweetie.

你不能跟媽咪去嗎？ Can't you go with Mom?

不要，我想跟爸比去。 No, I want to go with Daddy.

你應該要在週末陪我玩。 You need to play with me on weekends.

他不要起床。 He won't get up.

我會等到他起床。 I'll wait until he gets up.

你能叫爸爸起來吃午餐嗎？ Can you wake Daddy up for lunch?

去給爸爸搔癢直到他起床。 Go tickle Dad till he wakes up.

• tickle 搔癢

爸，起床了。我們去運動。 Dad, wake up. Let's go to exercise.

我希望我可以跟爸爸玩。	I wish I could play with Dad.
我忌妒跟爸爸玩足球的小孩。	I'm jealous of the kids who play soccer with their dads. 忌妒～
我想跟爸比玩。快起床跟我玩。	I want to be with Dad. Get up, and then let's play.
 爸比看起來真的很累。	Daddy looks really tired.
別吵他。讓他多睡一會。	Just leave him. Let him sleep more.
爸比因為昨天晚上工作到很晚，所以很累。	Daddy's tired because he worked late last night.
爸爸看起來根本連眼睛都張不開。	It looks like Dad can't even open his eyes.
 週末／假日的時候，爸爸總是在睡覺。	Dad always sleeps on weekends / holidays.
為什麼爸爸在中午才起床？	How come Dad got out of bed at midday? 為什麼～？ •midday 正午

ch26-03.mp3

無所事事

 這個週末，我們就好好來休息，重振一下精神。	We'll rest and refresh ourselves this weekend. •refresh 使～恢復精神
我不想做任何事情。	I don't want to do anything.
 好吧。我可以看電視嗎？	Fine. Can I watch TV?
媽，不要打攪我。	Don't bother me, Mom. •bother 打擾
 我們去外面吃午餐。	Let's eat out for lunch.

你們都一起躺著，什麼都不做嗎？
Are you all lying down together doing nothing?

你們今天就只想懶懶地過嗎？
Are you just going to be lazy today?

做任何你想做的事。
Do whatever you want.
• whatever 任何～事情

有點無聊。
It's kind of boring.

時間過得好慢。
Time goes by so slowly.
（時間）過去

已經晚上了，我們還是什麼都沒做。
It's already evening, and we haven't done anything.

總之在家是最好的。
Being at home is best anyway.

我們不要再無所事事了。
Let's stop being lazy.

現在，真的要做點什麼了嗎？
Want to actually do something now?

ch26-04.mp3

去購物

媽媽要去百貨公司。
Mommy's going to the department store.

你可以帶我去購物中心嗎？
Can you take me to the mall?
• mall 購物中心

爸爸要買禮物給我。
Daddy's going to buy me a gift.

今天是爸爸的生日，所以我要在購物中心買禮物給他。
It's dad's birthday so I got him a gift at the mall.

媽媽，我們什麼時候可以去美食廣場？
Mom, when can we go to the food court?

週末去購物，並且在那裡吃午餐吧。
Let's go shopping on weekend and eat lunch there.

 爸爸，我們去購物中心吧。

Let's go to the mall, Dad.

 這個週末去暢貨中心。

Let's go to the outlet mall this weekend.

在暢貨中心買冬天的外套吧。

Let's buy a winter jacket at the outlet mall.

 媽媽，我想要買一雙鞋子。

Mom, there are a pair of shoes I want to buy.

 找那間店在哪裡。

Find out where that store is.

我通常會透過家庭購物頻道買東西。

I usually buy things through the home shopping channel.

 那就是送貨人員每天都來的原因。

That's why a delivery person comes every day.

 我應該從超市買食品雜貨的。

I should get groceries from the supermarket. • groceries 食品雜貨

 在大超市有很多物品可以買。

There are a lot of things to buy at the big grocery store.

 媽媽，這個買一送一。

Mom, this is buy one get one free.

• buy one get one free 買一送一

 我花很多錢在大超市。

I spend a lot of money at the big grocery store.

 但是，購物還是很好玩。

Nonetheless, shopping is still fun.

• nonetheless 但是；仍是

ch26-05.mp3

訂週末計畫

 這個週末，你想做什麼？

What do you want to do this weekend?

這個週末，你想去水上樂園嗎？ Want to go to the water park this weekend?

這個週末，你要去動物園嗎？ Want to go to the zoo this weekend?

這個週末，你要去博物館嗎？ Want to go to the museum this weekend?

你這個週末要去看電影嗎？ Want to go to watch a movie this weekend?
watch a movie 看電影

請帶我去看電影。 Please take me to movies.

這個週末，我們去哪玩玩吧。 Let's go somewhere this weekend.

我的朋友去了農村體驗。 My friend went on a farm stay.

我們這個週末要去爺爺家。 We're going to Grandpa's this weekend.

這是個讓人興奮的週末。 It will be an exciting weekend.

我們來訂假日計畫吧。 Let's work out our vacation plan.
work out 制訂（計畫等）

你最想看的是什麼？ What do you want to see the most?

我一直很想去那裡。 I've always wanted to go there.

ch26-06.mp3

訂休假計畫

暑假來臨了。 Summer break is coming up.
coming up 來臨
• break 休息時間；假期

這次的假期有多久？ How long is this vacation?

五天四夜。 It's 4 nights and 5 days.

我想我們可以好好度過這個假期。 I think we can spend this vacation well.

這個假期，我們要去海邊。 We're going to the beach this vacation.

去參加歷史活動也很好。 It will be nice to go to a historic event.

‧historic 歷史性的 ‧event 活動

爸爸在休息日上班

ch26-07.mp3

爸爸已經去上班了嗎？ Did Dad go to work yet?

爸爸去上班了，因為他有很多工作要做。 He went to work because he had a lot to do.

他會在下午回來。 He'll be back in the afternoon.

打電話叫爸比趕快回家。 Call and ask Daddy to come home soon.

爸，你去哪裡了？ Where are you going, Dad?

我必須回去工作。 I have to go to work.

我以為你說過要跟我玩。 I thought you said you would play with me.

抱歉。或許下一次吧。 I'm sorry. Maybe next time.

爸爸到公司要晚了。 Dad's late for work.

我不得不去。 I need to go.

我可以跟你去嗎？ Can I go with you?

不，不行。你跟媽媽一起等我。 No, you can't. Stay with Mommy and wait for me.

不過我答應你會快點回來。 I promise to hurry back, though.

‧though 可是，不過

為什麼爸比連週末也要去上班？ Why does Daddy have to go to work on weekends?

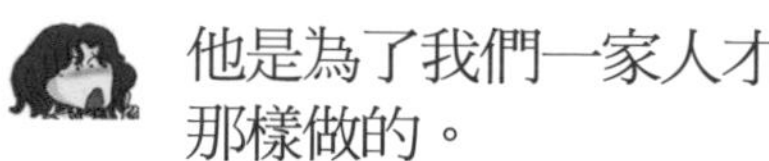

他是為了我們一家人才那樣做的。 He's doing it for our family.

ch26-08.mp3

陽曆假日

1 月 1 日是假日。	January 1 is a holiday.
1 月 1 日是陽曆的新年。	January 1 is New Year's Day on the solar calendar. • New Year 新年
2 月 28 日是和平紀念日。	February 28 is Peace Memorial Day.
過去，在台灣，有許多人因為誤解而彼此爭鬥，造成了許多悲劇。	In the past, many people fought with each other because of misunderstandings and caused lots of tragedies. • misunderstanding 誤解 • tragedy 悲劇
不可以忘記我們曾經有過的悲傷歷史。	Don't forget the sad history that we had before.
4 月 1 日是愚人節。	April 1 is April Fools' Day.
在愚人節開點玩笑是很好玩的。	Just some jokes are fine on April Fools' Day.
但是太過取笑他人的話，就會是個問題。	But making fun of others too much is a problem. 取笑～
清明節是在 4 月 5 日。	Tomb Sweeping Day is on April 5.
很多台灣人在那天清掃墳墓。	A lot of Taiwanese sweep tombs on that day. • tomb 墳墓
4 月 4 日是兒童節。	April 4 is Children's Day.

對所有小孩來說，這是最幸福的一天了。	It's the happiest day for all of the children.
5 月 1 日是勞動節。	May 1 is Labor Day.
8 月 8 日是父親節。	August 8 is Father's Day.
9 月 3 日是軍人節。	September 3 is Armed Forces Day.
我們應該記得那些為國家犧牲的軍人。	We should remember those soldiers' sacrifices for our nation. • soldier 士兵，軍人　• sacrifice 犧牲
9 月 28 日是教師節。	September 28 is Teacher's Day.
給老師送個小禮物和感謝卡。	Give your teacher a little present and a thank-you note. 感謝信，感謝卡
在某些假日，你不用去學校。	You don't have to go to school on some holidays.

陽曆假日的英文名稱

- 愚人節 April Fools' Day
- 植樹節 Arbor Day
- 兒童節 Children's Day
- 母親節 Mother's Day
- 教師節 Teacher's Day
- 父親節 Father's Day
- 和平紀念日 Peace Memorial Day
- 清明節 Tomb Sweeping Day
- 勞動節 Labor Day
- 軍人節 Armed Forces Day
- 國慶日 National Celebration Day
- 青年節 Youth Day

教會

ch26-09.mp3

我們是基督徒。	We are Christians.
我們週六及週日去教會。	We go to church on Saturdays and Sundays.
我們去作禮拜。	Let's go to the service. •service 禮拜
我們作禮拜要遲到了。	We're going to be late for the service.
作禮拜的時候，不可以講話。	Don't talk during the service.
我們來祈禱吧。	Let's pray. •pray 祈禱
我們來說主的祈禱文吧。	Let's say the Lord's Prayer.
你奉獻的錢準備好了嗎？	Did you get the offering? •offering 捐款，奉獻
我們應該奉獻十分之一。	We should tithe. •tithe 十一奉獻
跟牧師打招呼。	Say hello to our pastor. •pastor 牧師
耶穌被釘在十字架上而死去。	Jesus was nailed to the cross and died. •nail 將~釘牢 •cross 十字架

我要去教會的週日學校。	I'll go to Sunday school.

教堂

ch26-10.mp3

我們是天主教。	We are Catholics.
我們去大教堂吧。	Let's go to the cathedral. •cathedral 大教堂
我們去做彌撒。	Let's go to Mass. •Mass 彌撒

做彌撒不要晚到。	Don't be late for Mass.
戴上你的彌撒頭巾。	Wear your veil to Mass.
安靜！神父在佈道。	Be quiet! The priest is preaching. • priest （天主教）神父　• preach 佈道
我們來唸玫瑰經。	Let's do a rosary.　• rosary 唸玫瑰經
我們的修女們人都很好。	Our Sisters are all very nice.　• sister 修女
請主原諒你的過錯。	Ask God for forgiveness for your wrongdoings. • forgiveness 原諒　• wrongdoing 做壞事
現在去懺悔吧。	Go to confession now.　• confession 懺悔
主啊，請賜福給我們！	May the Lord bless us!　• bless 賜福

ch26-11.mp3

寺廟

我們是佛教徒。	We are Buddhists.
今天是佛陀誕生日。	Today is Buddha's Birthday.
和媽媽一起去寺廟。	Let's go to the temple with Mom. • temple 寺廟
像這樣跟僧人打招呼。	Greet the monks like this. • monk 僧人，師父
雙手合起來，深深地鞠躬。	Put your hands together and bow low.
在佛像面前，你必須安靜。	You need to be quiet in front of the Buddhist statue.　• statue 像，雕像
不要在寺廟內亂跑。	Don't run inside the temple.

Chapter 27

今天是特別的日子

Today is my birthday.
今天是我生日。

Guess what day it is today.
猜猜看今天是什麼日子。

ch27-01.mp3

生日邀約

你的生日快到了。	Your birthday is coming up.
邀請朋友們來家裡開派對吧。	Let's invite some friends and have a party.
你想邀請多少人？	How many do you want to invite?
你想邀請多少就邀請多少吧。	Invite as many as you want.

大約 10 個人。	About 10.

我想邀請全班。	I want to invite all of my classmates.
我們先來製作邀請函。	Let's make some invitations first. • invitation 邀請函，邀請
我要製作邀請函。	I want to make an invitation. • invitation 邀請函
我要在邀請函上寫什麼呢？	What should I write on the invitation?
我要告訴他們幾點來？	What time should I tell them to come?
告訴他們放學後直接過來。	Tell them to come right after school.
把邀請函拿給你的朋友們。	Give your friends the invitations.
問問朋友們他們是否能來。	Ask your friends if they can come.
我什麼時候要把邀請函送出去。	When should I give out the invitations?
明天我去上學，就拿給他們。	I will give them tomorrow when I go to school.
我要在哪裡辦生日派對？	Where should I have my birthday party?
就請你的朋友們來家裡吧。	Let's just have your friends over to our house.
我想在家裡的話會太擠了。	I think it will be too crowded in the house. • crowded 擁擠的
我會訂餐廳。	I'll make a reservation (預訂～) at a restaurant.
媽咪需要計畫一下你的生日派對。	Mommy needs to plan the birthday party for you.
把你想要邀請的朋友名字寫下來。	Write down the names of your friends you want to invite.
你想收到什麼生日禮物？	What do you want for your birthday?
我想要玩具車作為生日禮物。	I want a toy car for my birthday.

ch27-02.mp3

參加生日派對

	我受邀參加朋友的生日了。	I got invited (受到邀請) to my friend's birthday.
	我從朋友那收到了邀請函。	I got an invitation from my friend.
	放學後，我會去吉娜的生日派對。	I'm going to Jina's birthday party after school.
	媽，吉娜邀請我去參加她的生日派對。	Mom, Jina invited me to her birthday party.
	喔，那聽起來很棒！	Oh, that sounds good!
	我應該送她什麼禮物呢？	What should I give her for a present?
	那，想想她喜歡什麼。	Well, think of something that she likes.
	派對是什麼時候？	When is the party?
	這週六下午兩點。	At 2 o'clock on this coming Saturday.
	她的生日其實是 12 號，但是她提早慶祝。	Her birthday is actually on the 12th, but she is celebrating it ahead of time (提前，提早). • celebrate 慶祝
	她要在哪裡開派對？	Where is she going to have the party?
	在她家／餐廳。	At her house / a restaurant.
	週四嗎？但是那天你有補課耶。	On Thursday? But you have a make up lesson on that day.
	我只有那天不去上課可以嗎？	Can I just miss class on that day only?
	因為她是我最好的朋友，我應該要去。	I should go because she is my best friend.

媽，我想要有像她一樣的生日派對。

Mom, I want to have a birthday party like her.

不要忘記帶你預先買好的禮物。

Don't forget to bring the present you bought before.

派對結束後，打電話給我。我會去接你的。

Call me when the party is over. I will pick you up.

ch27-03.mp3

生日派對

我要來準備派對了。

I'll get ready for the party.

你的朋友們都到了。

Your friends are here.

我們需要幾根蠟燭？

How many candles do we need?

我們來唱「生日快樂歌」。

Let's sing "Happy Birthday".

許願吧。

Make a wish.

把蠟燭吹滅。

（用嘴）吹熄

Blow out the candles.

你要來切蛋糕分給朋友們嗎？

Will you cut the cake and give it to your friends?

ch27-04.mp3

送生日禮物

謝謝你們來參加我的派對。

Thanks for coming to my party.

生日快樂！

Happy birthday!

這是我送你的禮物。

Here's my present. / This is my present for you.

這是我帶來給你的。 I brought this for you.

打開禮物吧。 Open your presents.

哇！我真的很想要這個。 Wow! I really wanted this.

我真的很喜歡這禮物。 I really like the presents.

好好玩喔。 Have fun. / Have a good time.

哇，這玩具車真的很酷。 Wow, this toy car is awesome / fantastic.

這是我從爸爸那收到的。 I got this from my dad.

我爸買這個給我。 My dad bought this for me.

你的阿姨透過社群網路給你禮金。 Your aunt has sent you some gift money via SNS.

你的叔叔寄給你蛋糕的禮券。 Your uncle has sent you a cake coupon for your birthday.

ch27-05.mp3

長輩的生日

這週三是你爺爺的生日。 Your grandpa's birthday is coming up this Wednesday.

我們來為爺爺選禮物吧。 Let's choose a gift for Grandpa.

爺爺會喜歡什麼禮物呢？ What gift would Grandpa like?

我來寫卡片。 I'm going to write a card.

禮物是我畫的畫。 The gift is something that I drew.

爺爺會很喜歡那個的。 Grandpa would like that.

我來做爺爺喜歡的食物。 I'll make Grandpa's favorite food.

插上跟爺爺歲數一樣的蠟燭。	Put on the same number of candles as Grandpa's age.
爺爺，祝您生日快樂！	Happy birthday, Grandpa!
謝謝，甜心。	Thanks, Sweetheart.
幫爺爺唱「生日快樂歌」。	Sing "Happy Birthday" for Grandpa.
爺爺，祝您健康長壽！	Be healthy, Grandpa!
請打開禮物。	Open your gift, please.
爺爺，你喜歡你的禮物嗎？	Grandpa, do you like your gift?
我花了很多天為您選禮物。	It took me days to choose your gift.
甜心，謝謝！我非常喜歡。	Thank you, Sweetie! I like this very much.

ch27-06.mp3

過年

1 月 1 日是陽曆的新年。	January 1 is New Year's Day on the solar calendar.
我們還有一個陰曆的新年。	We have another New Year's Day on the lunar calendar.
陰曆的新年又是華人的新年。	The lunar January 1 is also the Chinese New Year.
我們祭拜祖先。這是很重要的傳統。	We worship our ancestors. That is an important tradition. • worship 祭拜 • tradition 傳統
我們在過年時吃團圓飯。	We eat a family reunion dinner on New Year's Day.

當你吃了團圓飯，你就長了一歲。	You get one year older when you eat the family reunion dinner.
過年跟中秋節都是台灣很重要的節日。	New Year's Day is an important Taiwanese holiday along with Moon Festival.
過年時，我們要去位於台南的爺爺家。	We'll be visiting Grandpa's place in Tainan on Chinese New Year.
我們穿上新衣服去奶奶家給她拜年吧！	Let's go to Grandma's place with our new clothes on to give a big bow to her. • bow 鞠躬
穿上新衣服後，你看起來更美了！	You look prettier with your new clothes on!
該給大人們拜年了。	Time to give a big bow to the adults!
新年快樂！	Have a happy new year!
希望你有個幸運的一年！	I wish you good luck this year!
這是新年紅包。	Here's your red envelop. / Here's your New Year's money.
爺爺，謝謝您！	Thanks, Grandpa!
我收到 1 千元的紅包。	I got 1,000 NT from the red envelop.

ch27-07.mp3

清明節

現在是四月份，清明節快到了。	It's April. Tomb Sweeping Day is coming. 清明節
清明節是在四月五日。	Tomb Sweeping Day is on April 5.
這是向祖先表示敬意的日子。	It's a day for showing respect to ancestors. • ancestor 祖先

清明節是假日。
Tomb Sweeping Day is a holiday.

我們在清明節要做些什麼呢？
What do we do on Tomb Sweeping Day?

清明節有些必做的活動。
There are some must-do activities on Tomb Sweeping Day.
must-do 必須做的

我們會花時間整理墳墓和墓碑。
We spend time tidying up the graves and tombstones.
tidying up 整理

• grave 墳墓 • tombstone 墓碑

我們會除墳墓上的雜草。
We will remove weeds from the tomb.
remove weeds 除草

我們會燒紙錢、燒香，並為祖先準備食物。
We will burn spirit money and incense sticks and offer food to our ancestors.
spirit money 紙錢　incense sticks 香

這是傳統節日。
It's a traditional festival.
• traditional 傳統的

我們會帶你和弟弟去體驗這個節日。
We'll take you and your brother to experience it.

在清明節，我想和你們一起去掃墓。
I want to join you and clean the graves on Tomb Sweeping Day.

ch27-08.mp3

端午節

媽媽，請告訴我關於端午節的事。
Mom, please tell me something about Dragon Boat Festival.
Dragon Boat Festival 端午節

這是其中一個最重要的傳統節日。
It's one of the most important traditional festivals.

它在農曆五月初五時慶祝。
It is celebrated on May 5 of the lunar calendar.

一般會落在五月或六月。
It generally falls in May or June.
falls in 落在

• generally 通常地

端午節時人們會做些什麼呢？

What will people do on Dragon Boat Festival?

端午節會舉辦傳統划龍舟比賽。

There are some traditional boat rowing (划船) competitions on Dragon Boat Festival.

• competition 競爭

人們在端午節會吃什麼？

What do people eat on Dragon Boat Festival?

節日的指標性食物是粽子。

The iconic festival food is Zongzi.

• iconic 非常出名的 • Zongzi 粽

粽子包含很多食材，像是豬肉、米飯、蔬菜、香菇、雞蛋和花生。

Zongzi has various ingredients such as meat, rice, vegetables, mushrooms, eggs and peanuts.

• various 各種不同的 • ingredient （食品）材料

我們可以透過網路訂購不同種類的粽子。

We can order different types of Zongzi online.

ch27-09.mp3

中秋節

下週就是中秋節了嗎？

Is it already Mid-Autumn Festival next week?

中秋節在農曆的 8 月 15 日。

Mid-Autumn Festival is on August 15 on the lunar calendar.

中秋節、端午節和過年是三大重要的傳統節日。

Mid-Autumn Festival, Dragon Boat Festival and Chinese New Year are the three most important traditional holidays.

月亮在當天會很圓。

The moon will be round on that day.

希望晚上的天氣很好。

Hope the weather will be fine at night.

這顆文旦很大顆。 This pomelo is so big. ·pomelo 文旦，柚子

我等不及要吃月餅了！ I can't wait to eat mooncakes!（can't wait to：好想～）

我們到外面去吃烤肉大餐吧。 Let's go outside to have a barbecue party.

ch27-10.mp3

情人節／白色情人節

2 月 14 日是情人節。 February 14 is Valentine's Day.

女生會送巧克力給喜歡的男生。 A lady gives candy to a man she likes.
★ 巧克力也算 candy（糖果）的一種。

我們來為爸爸準備巧克力吧。 Let's prepare some chocolate for Dad.

我要買些巧克力送給我的朋友們。 I'll buy some chocolate to give to my friends.

這是要給金宏的巧克力。 This chocolate is for Jinhong.

我從朋友們那收到巧克力。 I received some candy from my friends.

情人節

在西洋的情人節，父母、朋友、戀人之間都會互相贈送禮物。跟一般認知只是女生對喜歡的男生表示情感的情人節是不同的。如果是平時就景仰的人的話，也會邊告白邊在卡片上寫 a secret admirer 來開玩笑。家中有小孩子的父母則會為小孩準備要送給同班同學的糖果，小孩子則在卡片上寫上 Happy Valentine！

3月14日是白色情人節。 March 14 is White Day.

男生會送糖果給喜歡的女生。 Boys give candy to girls they like.

在韓國、日本和台灣有慶祝這個節日。 It's celebrated in Korea, Japan, and Taiwan.

ch27-11.mp3

兒童節

耶！兒童節要到了。 Yay! Children's Day is coming soon!

在兒童節，你想收到什麼禮物？ What present do you want on Children's Day?

我想要新的樂高組合玩具／芭比娃娃。 I want a new Lego set / a Barbie doll.

我想去遊樂園。 I want to go to an amusement park (遊樂園).

爺爺給你寄了大禮物。 Grandpa sent you a big present.

你的阿姨和叔叔寄了些錢給你。 Your aunt and uncle sent some money to you.

打電話給爺爺說謝謝。 Call Grandpa and say thank you.

媽，我們有什麼特別計畫嗎？ Do we have any special plans, Mom?

嗯，我們去吃些好吃的，玩些好玩的。 Well, let's just eat some good food and have fun.

兒童節快樂！ Happy Children's Day!

我希望天天都是兒童節。 I wish every day were Children's Day.

ch27-12.mp3

聖誕節

 聖誕節快到了。 It's almost Christmas.

萬歲！是聖誕節耶。 Hooray! It's Christmas.

 還沒，寶貝！那是 12 月 25 日。 Not yet, Honey. It's December 25.

 我希望是個白色聖誕節。 I wish for a white Christmas.

我們來唱聖誕歌。 Let's sing a Christmas carol.

我最喜歡聖誕節。 I love Christmas the most.

 我們來把聖誕樹架起來。 Let's put up our Christmas tree.

立起，架

我們也要裝飾聖誕樹吧？ Shall we decorate the Christmas tree, too? • decorate 裝飾

我們在頂端放一顆星星吧。 Let's put a star on the top.

今年我們也做了一棵很好看的聖誕樹。 That's a great-looking tree we made this year! / We made a wonderful tree for Christmas this year, too.

• great-looking 很好看的

 你讀了我寫的聖誕卡了嗎？ Did you read my Christmas card?

 你的聖誕卡很讓人很感動。謝謝你，寶貝。 Your Christmas card is very touching. Thank you, Honey. • touching 感人的

明天是聖誕節。早點去睡。 It's Christmas tomorrow. Go to sleep early.

 啊，我忘記掛襪子了。 Oops, I forgot to put up the stockings.

 把它們掛在聖誕樹旁邊。 Put them next to the Christmas tree.

你這一年都是乖小孩嗎？聖誕老公公只拜訪乖小孩。	Have you been (到現在為止) a good child for the entire year? Santa only visits good kids.
 看！聖誕老公公把禮物放在樹下了。	Look! Santa put a present under the tree!
我要打開我的禮物。	I want to open my present.
聖誕老公公給了我想要的禮物。	Santa gave me the gift I wanted.
 媽，真的有聖誕老公公嗎？	Mom, does Santa really exist? •exist 存在
 當然。因此，你才收到禮物。	Of course. That's how you got his present.

Chapter 28

和家人在社區散步

Do you all want to take a walk?
你們都想要散步嗎？

Can I ride in-line skates?
我可以溜直排輪嗎？

Sounds great!
聽起來很棒！

ch28-01.mp3

去公園散步

我們去散步。	Let's go for a walk.
要去散步運動一下嗎？	Want to go for a walk to exercise?
我們去公園玩吧。	Let's go out to play in the park.
要去公園騎腳踏車嗎？	Want to ride our bikes at the park?

哇！公園有好多人。	Wow! There are a lot of people at the park.

跟鄰居打招呼。 Say “hi” to our neighbors.

要手牽手嗎？ Want to hold hands? ·hold 牽

寶貝，你要確實跟著我。 Make sure you follow me, Honey.

不可以把垃圾丟在地上。 Don’t throw trash on the ground. ·trash 垃圾

不可以摘花。 Don’t pick the flowers.

不可以折樹枝。 Don’t break the branches.

不可以踩草地。 Don’t step on the grass.

這天氣很適合散步。 It’s great weather for a walk.

微風真的很棒。 The breeze is really nice. ·breeze 微風

媽，我們休息一下。 Mom, let’s rest for a little.

媽，我的腿好痛。 Mom, my legs hurt.

我想我們走太遠了。 I think we came too far.

現在要回去了嗎？ Want to go back now?

我想再待更久。 I want to stay longer.

我知道，但是越來越晚了。 I know, but it’s getting late.

媽，我要上廁所。哪裡有廁所？ Mom, I have to go to the restroom. Where is it? ·restroom 廁所

廁所在那裡。 The restroom is over there.

要使用這個運動器材嗎？ Want to use this exercise machine?

媽，我也要騎。 I want to ride it, too, Mom.

你去試試那個。那邊沒有人用。 Try the one over there. Nobody is using it.

公廁

我們來排隊。	Let's wait in line.
進廁所前要敲門。	Knock on the door before going into the restroom.
不要隨意吐痰。	Don't spit. •spit 吐痰
不要在廁所的牆壁亂畫。	Don't draw on the wall of the restroom.
你上完之後要沖水。	Flush the toilet after you're done. •flush 沖水
好好地洗手。	Wash your hands well.

超市

媽咪要去買菜。	Mommy needs to go grocery shopping. (買菜)
去拉一台推車過來。	Go get a cart.
我們來看需要購買物品的清單。	Let's see the grocery list.
我們先去農產品區。	Let's go to the produce corner first. •produce 農產品
我們買些水果。	Let's buy some fruit.
這個多少錢？	How much is this?
給我 1 公斤。	Give me 1kg of it.
我要這個。	I'll take this.
把它放進推車。	Put it in the cart.

你知道魚在哪裡嗎？　Do you know where I can find the fish?

這肉真的很便宜／貴。　The meat's really cheap / expensive.

整袋裝的拉麵在打折。　The pack of ramen is on sale.（on sale 在打折）

我們晚餐吃魚吧。　Let's have fish for dinner.

今天晚餐的菜單是炒章魚。　Tonight's dinner is sautéed octopus.

• sautéed 炒的

確認一下我們有沒有忘了什麼。　Check if we forgot anything.

推車都滿了。　The cart is full.

我們可以買零食嗎？　Can we get some snacks?

我想吃肉。媽，買些肉。　I want some meat. Buy some meat, Mom!

我可以在試吃區試吃麵包嗎？　Can I try some bread in the tasting corner?（tasting corner 試吃區）

我們去結帳吧。　Let's go to the checkout counter.（checkout counter 結帳處，收銀台）

把食物都放在櫃台上。　Get the groceries on the counter.

我可以要一個袋子嗎？　Can I get a bag?

我們把它放進袋子裡。　Let's put it in the bag.

ch28-04.mp3

餐廳用餐

可以給我們菜單嗎？　Can we get a menu?

選你想吃的。　Choose what you want to eat.

你選好你想要吃的了嗎？　Did you choose what you want?

我想吃炸醬麵和糖醋肉。 I want zajangmian and sweet and sour pork.

你好。現在我可以點餐了嗎？ Hello. May I order now? •order 點餐

請給我些水。 Get me some water, please.

你可以快點供餐嗎？ Can you get it quickly?

我還要等多久，菜才會出來？ How long do I have to wait till the dishes come out?

你能擺一下湯匙和筷子嗎？ Can you set the spoons and chopsticks?

不可以在餐廳閒晃。 Don't goof around in the restaurant.

你的嘴巴上沾到食物了。媽媽幫你擦掉。 You have food on your lips. Mom will clean it off for you. •lip 嘴唇

還要多吃一點嗎？ Want some more?

我的也很好吃。你要嚐一些嗎？ Mine's good, too. Want to try some?

剩下的食物給媽媽吃。 Mommy will eat the leftovers. •leftover 剩飯菜

媽，我的水濺出來了。 Mom, I spilled my water.

請把剩餘的打包起來。 Can you pack the rest, please? •pack 打包

請給我結帳單。 Can we get the check, please? •check 帳單

這食物太鹹／清淡了。 The dish was too salty / bland. •bland 淡而無味的

ch28-05.mp3

美容室

● 在家

我現在就想弄頭髮！ | I want my hair done now!

你的頭髮太長了。我們去美容室吧。 | Your hair's too long. Let's go to a beauty shop. 美容室(= beauty salon)

上次剪髮之後，已經有好一點時間了。你的頭髮長很長了。 | It's been a while since your last trim, and your hair is getting long. 一段時間

・since 從～以後　・trim 修剪

我不想去理髮廳。 | I don't want to go to the hair shop.

如果你的頭髮很雜亂，你的朋友們會取笑你的。 | Your friends will make fun of you if your hair's messy. ・messy 雜亂的

由於天氣很熱，你要剪短嗎？ | Since it's hot, do you want your hair short?

你想燙頭髮嗎？ | Want to get a perm?

● 在美容室

你想要怎樣做你的頭髮？ | How do you want your hair done?

我要怎樣幫你呢？ | How can I help you?

我想剪頭髮。 | I want my hair cut.

我想燙捲。 | I want my hair permed.

我想燙直。 | I want my hair straight.

你想怎樣剪？ | How do you want it cut?

我想剪短。 | I want it short.

只要稍微修剪一下就好。	**Just trim it a little.**
不要剪得太短。	Don't cut it too short.
只要修剪瀏海就好。	**Just trim my bangs.** ‧bangs 瀏海
我想要染髮。	I want my hair dyed. ‧dye 染髮
請挑染這一塊。	**Please highlight this part.** ‧highlight 挑染頭髮
乖乖坐好，我們才能剪得好看。	Sit still so we can cut it nice.
不要動！	**Don't move!**
你能低一下頭嗎？	Will you tilt your head down? ‧tilt 傾斜
如果你說話的話，頭髮會跑進你的嘴巴。	**Hair will get in your mouth if you talk.**
你喜歡剪的這個髮型嗎？	Do you like your haircut?
你剪髮後，看起來很像王子／公主。	**You look like a prince / princess after your haircut.**
我兒子看起來很不一樣了。	My son looks different.
看起來好酷！真可惜我們沒有早點來剪。	**You look cool! Sorry we didn't cut it earlier.**
今天有很多客人。	There are a lot of people today.
下次要再來嗎？	**Want to come next time?**

ch28-06.mp3

桑拿浴

我們去桑拿浴吧。	**Let's go to the sauna.**

先洗乾淨，再進去桑拿浴。 Clean up first and then go into the sauna.

你是大男孩了，跟爸比一起去。 Go with Daddy since you're a big boy.

穿上桑拿浴的衣服。 Put on your sweatsuit.

• sweatsuit 桑拿浴的衣服；運動套裝

要去那裡嗎？ Want to go in there?

媽，我不能呼吸。 I can't breathe, Mom.

我要出去外面一會。 I'll go outside for a little.

我們來冷卻一會吧。 Let's cool down for a few minutes.

cool down 冷卻

你流了很多汗。 You're sweating a lot. • sweat 出汗

一定要喝大量的水。 Make sure to drink plenty of water.

plenty of 大量的～

我想要喝些水。 I want to drink some water.

你可以買些水煮蛋和飲料給我嗎？ Can you buy me some boiled eggs and a drink?

boiled eggs 水煮蛋

我要躺在這裡。 I'm going to lie down here.

待太久也不好。 It's not good to stay for too long.

我們要待多久呢？ How long will we stay?

我們什麼時候回家？ When do we go home?

感覺相當好！ That feels good!

我們把澡洗好然後回家。 Let's clean up and go home.

ch28-07.mp3

電影院

 我們去看電影。	Let's go to watch a movie.
 你想看什麼？	What do you want to see?
有什麼電影正在上映？	What movies are on?
 我想看 3D 電影。	I want to watch a 3D movie.
我們要看幾點的？	What time should we watch the movie?
我們看下午場。	Let's watch a matinee. • matinee（電影等的）下午場
我來提前訂票。	Let me buy the tickets beforehand. / Let me reserve the movie tickets. • reserve 預訂
我去買票。	I'll get the tickets.
已經都賣完了。	It's already sold out.
離電影開始，我們還有十分鐘。	We have about 10 minutes till the movie starts.
電影開始前，先去上廁所。	Go to the bathroom before the movie starts.
我可以買爆米花和飲料嗎？	Can I get popcorn and a drink?
媽，你訂了電影票了嗎？	Did you reserve the tickets, Mom? / Did you buy the tickets ahead of time, Mom?
你在售票處拿到票了嗎？	Did you receive the tickets from the box office?
在這裡排隊進去。	Wait in line here and go in.

你能找到我們的座位嗎？ Can you find our seats?

裡面很暗，小心你的腳步。 **It's dark inside. Watch your steps.**

媽，你把手機轉震動了嗎？ Mom, did you set your phone to vibrate?

• set 使處於 • vibrate 震動

我等不及了。 **I can't wait.**

我看不到，因為那對情侶擋住我的視野。 I can't see because that couple is blocking my view. • block 擋住 • view 視野

不要踢你前面的椅子。 **Don't kick the seat in front of you.**

噓！在電影院內要安靜。 Hush! Be quiet in the theater.

這部電影有趣嗎？ **Was the movie fun?**

媽，我們下次再來看電影。 Let's watch another movie later, Mom!

ch28-08.mp3

書店

要去書店嗎？ **Want to go to the bookstore?**

有任何你想讀的書嗎？ Are there any books you wanted to read?

這裡有很多有趣的書。 **There are a lot of interesting books here.**

看這些科學雜誌。 Look at all the science magazines.

選你想要讀的。 **Pick what you want to read.** • pick 挑選

這些都是新書。 These are all new books.

哪一本看起來很有趣？ **Which one looks fun to you?**

要去那邊嗎？ Want to go over there?

這些是你想要的書！ **Here are the books you wanted!**

想要讀讀這本嗎？ Want to read this?

恐龍的書在哪裡呢？ Where are the dinosaur books?

你能幫我找出那本書嗎？ Can you find me the book?

我可以在這裡看嗎？ Can I read this book here?

這是這個系列的第 4 本。 This is the 4th book in the series.

我可以買這本嗎？ Can I get this book?

你又要買漫畫書嗎？ Do you want a cartoon book again?

我們買些英文故事書吧。 Let's buy a few English storybooks.

ch28-09.mp3

圖書館

今天是我們要去圖書館的日子。 Today's the day we go to the library.

我們來申請借書證吧。 Let's apply for a library card.

要用電腦找書嗎？ Want to find some books with a computer?

我可以借多少本書？ How many books can I borrow?

我們只能借 4 本。 We can only get 4 books.

不用急，慢慢來。 Don't rush. Take your time. • rush 著急

媽，讀這本書給我聽。 Mom, read me this book.

我可以坐在這裡讀嗎？ Can I sit here and read?

不可以在圖書館喧嘩。 Don't be loud in the library.

在圖書館要安靜。 Be quiet in the library.

你不能大聲地把書唸出來。 You should not read the books out loud.（大聲地）

你不可以在圖書館吃東西。 You should not eat in the library.

你不可以把書撕破。 You should not tear the books. •tear 撕破

你都選好全部的書了嗎？ Did you choose all the books?

我發現了一本不錯的書。 I found a good book.

我馬上就想讀。 I want to read it immediately.
•immediately 馬上，立刻

我們把它們借出去吧。 Let's check them out. •check out 借出

先把卡片給圖書館員。 Give the librarian the card first.
•librarian 圖書館員

在這裡讀書，直到媽媽選好書。 Read here until Mom chooses a book.

我們要還的書，你都準備好了嗎？ Did you get all the books we need to return? •return 送回，歸還

這些書在星期三就會逾期。 The books are due on Wednesday.
•due 過期

圖書館今天閉館。 The library is closed today.

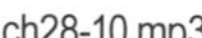

ch28-10.mp3

銀行

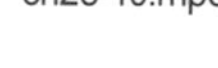

銀行是做什麼的地方？ What is a bank for? / What does a bank do for us?

你在銀行做什麼？ What do you do at the bank?

我們把錢保管在銀行。 We keep money in the bank.
•keep 保管

我們來幫你開個帳戶。 | Let's open an account for you.
• account （銀行）帳戶

抽號碼牌。 | Get a number.

我們要填好表格。 | We need to fill out the form. • form 表格

我想要存一萬元到銀行。 | I want to save 10,000 to the bank.

我要在這裡提領一萬元。 | I want to take out 10,000 here. / I will withdraw 10,000 here.
• withdraw 提領

你帶了存摺和印章嗎？ | Did you bring your account book and seal? • seal 印章
存摺

銀行幾點開門？ | What time does the bank open?

早上九點開門。 | It opens at 9:00 AM.

等我裝滿撲滿，我就拿去銀行。 | After I fill my piggy bank, I'll bring it to the bank.
撲滿

ch28-11.mp3

消防局

當發生火災要打 119。 | Call 119 when there is a fire.

消防員會幫忙滅火。 | Firefighters help put out fires.
滅火

絕對不可以打惡作劇電話給消防局。 | Don't ever prank call the fire department.
惡作劇電話

當消防車來的時候，車子一定要讓路。 | Cars need to move out of the way when a fire truck is coming.

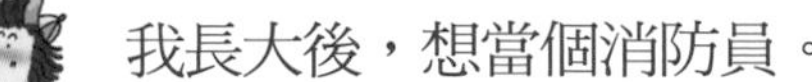
我長大後，想當個消防員。 | I want to be a firefighter when I grow up.

在消防局，我們可以看到消防員和消防車。
We can see firefighters and fire trucks at the fire department.

ch28-12.mp3

警察局

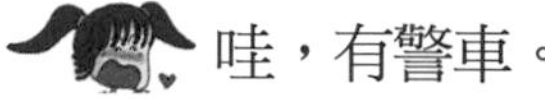
哇，有警車。
Wow, there's a police car.

警察制服很帥氣。
The police uniform is cool.

因為我們鎮上有警察局，我感到很安心。
I feel safe because we have a police station in town. ・safe 安全的

我長大後，我要當個警察。
I want to be a police officer when I grow up.

如果你想當警察，你必須很勇敢。
You need to be brave if you want to be a police officer.

你知道警察局的電話嗎？
Do you know the number of the police station?

是 110。
It's 110.

警察保護人民的生命和財產。
The police protect people's lives and property. ・property 財產

Chapter 29

去旅行

We're finally at the top.
我們終於在山頂了。

Hooray!
萬歲！

ch29-01.mp3

爬山

	我們去健行吧。	Let's go hiking.
	空氣很新鮮。	The air is fresh.
	去爬山很好。	It's great to go up to a mountain.
	山太高了！	The mountain is too high!
	小心上去／下來。	Go up / down carefully.

我的腿很痛。 My legs hurt.

我們休息一下吧。 Let's rest for a little bit.

要去飲水機那喝點水嗎？ Want to drink some water from the fountain? ·fountain 噴泉式飲水器

我們終於到達山頂了。 We're finally at the top.

我們從大老遠來到這裡。 We came all the way up here.

來吶喊一下萬歲！ Shout hooray!

剛開始很累，但是來到山頂後，感覺很棒。 It was hard at first, but it feels good here at the top. （at first：剛開始）

ch29-02.mp3

海邊旅行

我們去海邊旅行吧。 Let's go on a trip to the sea.

哇，是海耶！ Wow, it's the sea!

海灘好乾淨。 The beach is very clean.

海浪太高了！ The waves are too high!

沙子一直跑進鞋子內。 The sand keeps getting in my shoes.

脫掉鞋子，去海裡吧。 Take off your shoes and go into the sea.

水好冰／鹹。 The water's too cold / salty.

要在這裡搭帳篷嗎？ Want to set up the tent here? （set up：搭起，設立）

我們來生營火。 Let's set a fire!

去帳篷裡面睡。 Go sleep in the tent.

ch29-03.mp3

游泳池

進泳池前，要先沖一下身體。
Shower before you go in the pool.

洗乾淨之後，換上泳裝。
Clean up and change into your swimming suit. ·swimming suit 泳裝

也不要忘記你的泳帽和蛙鏡。
Don't forget your swim cap and goggles, either. ·goggles 蛙鏡

進泳池前，先去上廁所。
Go to the restroom before getting into the pool.

你做伸展操了嗎？
Did you stretch? ·stretch 做伸展操

我會幫你的游泳圈灌氣。
I'll inflate your inner tube. ·inflate 充氣

地板很滑，要小心。
Be careful since the floor is slippery.

不要去泳池深處的一端。
Don't go into the deep end of the pool.

請不要跳水。
Please don't dive.

試著不要讓水濺到其他人。
Try not to splash water on others. ·splash 潑（水）

不要在泳池內閒晃。
Don't goof around in the pool. (goof around: 閒晃)

不要在泳池內製造噪音。
Don't make loud noises in the pool. (make loud noises: 製造噪音)

剛吃完，不可以馬上游泳。
Don't swim right after you eat.

等一下再進去。
Go in a little later.

不要在水裡待太久。
Don't stay in the water for too long.

你的嘴唇變藍了。先暖一下身體。
Your lips are blue. Stay warm for a minute.

我用毛巾幫你擦乾。
Let me dry you off with a towel.

媽媽會在泳池附近。
Mom will stick around in the pool area. 停留於～

這太陽光太強了。擦些防曬乳吧。
The sun's rays are very strong. Put some sunscreen on. 太陽光

我一定要擦防曬乳嗎？
Do I have to put on sunscreen?

我不想擦防曬乳。
I don't want to put any sunscreen on.

這黏黏的。
It's sticky. • sticky 黏黏的

我們把游泳圈內的氣漏掉吧。
Let's remove the air from your inner tube. • remove 去掉，消除

你進更衣室之前，要先擦乾身體。
Dry yourself off before you go into the changing room.

ch29-04.mp3

遊樂園

我們去遊樂圈吧。
Let's go to the amusement park.

我們去買自由使用所有遊樂設備的票。
Let's buy tickets for all of the rides.
• ride 遊樂設備

我去拿票。在這裡等。
I'll get the tickets. Wait here.

排隊等。
Wait in line. 排隊

要搭這個嗎？
Want to ride this?

媽，我想要搭這個。
I want to ride this, Mom.

那看起來太可怕了。
That looks too scary.

你太矮了，不能搭這個。
You're too short to ride this.
• too 形容詞 to 動詞 太～而不能～

我們去參觀遊行。 Let's go and watch the parade.
・parade 遊行，行列

隊伍太長了。我們去搭其他的好嗎？ The line's too long. Shall we ride something else?

我想要坐旋轉木馬。 I want to ride the merry-go-round.

我們坐摩天輪吧。 Let's ride the Ferris wheel.

我要去坐雲霄飛車。 I'm going to ride the roller coaster.

海盜船最好玩了。 I like the Viking Ride the most. / The Viking Ride is the most fun.

我頭暈了。我想我要吐了。 I'm dizzy. I think I'm going to throw up.
嘔吐

我們在陰影下休息吧。 Let's rest in the shade. ・shade 陰影

我還想要搭。 I want to ride it again.

跟遊樂園相關的表達

「遊樂園」的英文是 amusement park，也可以說成 theme park。amusement park 特別是指具備各種遊樂設施的公園，而 theme park 是指設計成海、電影等特定主題的公園。其他的話，如水上樂園或海洋世界也可以叫做 water park。

遊樂設備（ride）的種類：

- 旋轉木馬 merry-go-round
- 雲霄飛車 roller coaster
- 旋轉鞦韆 swing ride
- 海盜船 pirate ship
- 摩天輪 Ferris wheel
- 自由落體 drop tower
- 水上遊樂設施 water ride

我還可以再搭嗎？ Can I ride it again?

我不想一個人搭。 I don't want to ride alone.

要跟媽咪一起坐嗎？ Want to ride with Mom?

關門的時間到了。 It's time to close.

所有的遊樂設施都很好玩。 All of the rides are so fun.

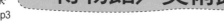

ch29-05.mp3

博物館／美術館

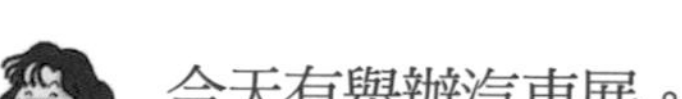
今天有舉辦汽車展。 There's a motor show going on today.

我聽說下個月會有史努比的展覽會。 I heard the Snoopy Exhibition is coming up next month.
• exhibition 展覽會

我們今天去恐龍博物館吧。 Let's go to the dinosaur museum today.

博物館是展出有歷史意義物品的地方。 A museum is a place where historic things are displayed.
• historic 歷史性的 • display 展出

今天我們去美術館吧。 Let's go to the art museum today.

美術館是展出各種美術品的地方。 An art museum displays many works of art. 美術作品

這是誰的作品？ Whose work of art is this? • whose 誰的

你覺得這個作品如何？ What do you think of this work?

我也想畫出這麼棒的畫。 I want to draw something this cool.

閱讀這裡的說明。 Read the descriptions here.
• description 說明，描述

好好聽導遊的說明。 Listen to what the guide says.

不要碰。用看的就好。	Don't touch that. Just look at it.
在博物館內是禁止照相的。	You are not allowed to take photos in the museum. 不被允許
你在展示廳要保持安靜。	You should be quiet in the showrooms. • showroom 展示廳

ch29-06.mp3

照相

我們在這裡拍張照。	Let's take a picture here. 拍照
要跟你的朋友一起照嗎？	Want to take a picture with your friend?
站在你朋友的旁邊。	Stand next to your friend.
往後退一點。	Move back a bit.
往前站一點。	Step ahead a little.
往左／右邊移一點。	Move to the left / right a little.
各位，靠在一起。	Everyone, squeeze together.
說 cheese！	Say cheese!
請對著相機微笑。	Smile for the camera.
請給我一個大大的微笑。	Make a big smile, please.
你看起來很緊張。	You look nervous.
擺出帥氣的樣子。	Try to look good.
你可以為我的相機擺個姿勢嗎？	Will you pose for my camera? • pose 擺姿勢

媽，幫我跟吉娜照張相。	Mom, take a picture of Jina and me.

這次我來拍照。	I'll take it this time.
媽，我不想照相。	I don't want to take a picture of myself, Mom. / I don't want my picture taken, Mom.
相機晃到了。我們再拍一張。	The camera was shaking. Let's take another picture.
哇，這張看起來很棒。	Wow, it looks great.
我女兒很上相。	My daughter is photogenic. / My girl looks great in a photo. • photogenic 很上相的
給我看照片。	Show me the picture.
這照片拍得很好／不好。	The picture looks good / bad.
我不太會照相。	I'm not much of a photographer.
我們來拍全家福。	Let's take a family photo.
我們去請其他人幫我們拍。	Let's ask someone to take a picture of us.
不好意思，可以請您幫我們拍照嗎？	Excuse me, but could you take a picture of us?
用我手機的相機。	Use the camera on my phone.
把手機轉向旁邊。	Turn the cellphone sideways. • sideways 向旁邊
請刪掉這張照片。	Delete this picture, please.
 我會編輯這張照片。	I will edit this photo. • edit 編輯

Chapter 30

交通工具

Take a bus today.
今天搭公車吧。

Let's take a taxi!
我們搭計程車啦！

ch30-01.mp3

走路

今天你要走路去圖書館嗎？ Will you walk to the library today?

走路的話，要花多久的時間？ How long does it take by walking? (多久～？)

20 分鐘左右。 About 20 minutes.

今天我走路去。 I'm going to walk today.

走路太遠了。 It's too far to walk.

牽著我的手走。 Hold my hand and walk.

不可以在街上閒晃。 Don't goof around on the street.

我們晚了。走快點。 We're late. Let's walk faster.

我很喘。 I'm breathless. ·breathless 氣喘吁吁的

我們走太多了。休息一下吧。 We walked too much. Let's rest for a little.

我腿很痛。 My legs hurt.

走路很好，不是嗎？ It's nice to walk, isn't it?

我們也遛狗吧。 Let's walk our dog, too. ·walk 遛狗

如果我們走路，會更健康。 We can be healthy if we walk.

我們好像走到相當遠的地方。 It seems like we came pretty far. ·pretty 相當

想要邊走邊唱歌嗎？ Want to sing while we walk?

好熱喔，要喝點什麼嗎？ Want to drink something since it's hot? ·since 因為，因此

ch30-02.mp3

過馬路

過馬路時，要小心車子。 Always be careful of cars when crossing.

你應該穿越斑馬線。 You should cross at the crosswalk. ·crosswalk 斑馬線

要停在斑馬線的前面。 Stop in front of the crosswalk.

不可以在斑馬線上奔跑。 Don't run in the crosswalk.

媽，綠燈了。我們走吧。 Mom, the light is green. Let's go.

當變綠燈時，也要看一下左右兩側再走。 Look to both sides and walk when the light turns green. 兩側

當你過馬路時，要舉起你的手。 Hold your hand up when you cross.

當綠燈在閃的時候，要停下來。 Stop when the green light is flickering.
• flicker 閃爍

我們等下一個燈號吧。 Let's wait for the next light.

不可隨便穿越馬路。 Don't jaywalk! • jaywalk 隨便穿越馬路

這裡沒有燈號。 There are no lights here.

沒有燈號的地方一定要小心看路。 Look carefully where there aren't any lights.

有地下道。 There is an underpass. • underpass 地下道

我們過天橋吧。 Let's cross on the overpass. • overpass 天橋

媽，那輛車闖紅燈。 Mom, that car's running the red light.

因為他沒有遵守規則，警察會逮捕他。 The police will arrest the driver since he didn't follow the rules.
• arrest 逮捕 • rule 規則

ch30-03.mp3

坐車

我們上車。 Let's get in the car. 上（車）

誰要先上車？ Who wants to get in first?

開門前先確認一下。 Check before opening the door.

看看是否有其他車過來。 See if there are any cars coming.

繫上安全帶。

Fasten your seatbelt.

‧fasten 繫 ‧seatbelt 安全帶

你繫好了嗎？

Did you buckle up? 扣上（安全帶等）

我不想繫。

I don't want to buckle up.

當你坐車的時候，一定要繫。

You need to buckle up when you're in a car.

我不想坐兒童座椅。

I don't want to ride in the car seat.

這讓我看起來像個小孩。

It makes me look like a baby.

不過，坐在裡面更安全。

It's safer to sit in it, though. ‧though 不過

這門打不開。請幫我開門。

The door's not opening. Please open it for me.

我可以坐前座嗎？

Can I ride in the front seat? ‧front 前面的

前座很危險，所以小孩子不可以坐。

The front seat's dangerous, so kids shouldn't sit there.

把你鞋子上的泥土弄掉後，再上車。

Get the dirt off your shoes and get in the car. ‧dirt 泥土

屁股往後坐。

Sit back on your bottom. 向後靠著坐

在車內要乖乖坐好。好嗎？

Sit still in the car. Okay? 乖乖坐好

出發前確認一下有沒有什麼沒拿的。

Check if you left anything before we move.

說「出發！」

Say "Go!"

出發！

Go! / Move!

ch30-04.mp3

在車內

安靜。你讓爸爸的注意力分散了。	Be quiet. You're distracting Dad. •distract 使分心
不可以把手伸出車窗外。	Don't put your hand out the window.
太熱了。把窗戶降下來吧。	It's too hot. Roll down the window.
我可以玩我的隨身遊戲機吧？	Can I play my portable video game? •portable 便於攜帶的

只能玩 30 分鐘。	For only 30 minutes.
如果你在車內打遊戲的話，你的視力會變差。	Your eyesight will get bad if you play the game in the car. •eyesight 視力
在車內讀書對你的眼睛不好。	Reading books in a car is bad for your eyes.
唱首歌讓爸爸保持清醒吧。	Sing a song for Daddy to keep him awake. •awake 清醒的

爸，你超速了。	Dad, you're speeding. •speed 超速行駛
我想去廁所。	I want to go to the restroom.
我們在休息站停一下。	Let's stop at the rest area. 休息站

要放 CD 嗎？	Want me to play a CD?
如果你累了，就睡一下吧。	If you're tired, sleep a little.
到了的話，我會叫醒你的。	I'll wake you up when we get there.

我們已經到了嗎？	Are we there yet?
我們要開多遠？	How far should we go?

我們還要開多久？ How much more do we have to go?

我覺得我暈車了。 I feel like I'm getting carsick. ・carsick 暈車

的

ch30-05.mp3

公車

今天我們搭公車吧。 Let's take a bus today.

公車站在那裡。 The bus stop is over there.

我們來看一下路線圖。 Let's check the route. ・route 路線

我們要搭幾號公車？ What number bus do we need to take?

我們可以搭 5538 或 571 公車。 We can take the number 5538 or 571 bus.

我們要過馬路去搭公車。 We should cross the street to take the bus.

公車為什麼還沒來？ How come the bus isn't coming?

那輛公車是幾號？ What number bus is that?

公車來了。我們上車吧。 The bus is here. Let's get in.

抓住把手。 Grab the handle. ・grab 抓住

去坐在空位上。 Go sit in an empty seat. ・empty 空的

請把位子讓給這位女士。 Please give your seat to this lady.

爺爺／奶奶，請坐這裡。 Sit here, ma'am / sir.

★ 在英語系國家，不會稱陌生的老人為爺爺、奶奶。

說話小聲點，乖乖坐好。 Keep your voice down and behave.

不要玩你的腳。 Don't play with your feet.

你不可以在公車內大聲說話。 You should not be loud inside the bus.

ch30-06.mp3

計程車

我們去搭計程車吧。	Let's take a taxi.
因為我們很趕，搭計程車吧。	Let's just take a cab since we're in a rush (急忙地). •cab 計程車
只會被收取基本車資。	Just the base fare will be charged. •fare 車資 •charge 索價
計程車費是根據行車的距離來算。	Taxi fares depend on (根據~) the distance traveled. •distance 距離
結果車資很貴。	The fare turned out to be expensive.

ch30-07.mp3

地鐵

我們坐地鐵去你阿姨家。 Let's take the subway to visit your aunt.

我們要坐幾號線？ Which subway line do we need to take?

我們要坐一號線。 We need to take the number one line.

媽，電車來了。 Mom, the train is coming.

那是我們要搭的電車嗎？ Is that the train we need to take?

對。退到安全線後。 Right. Step behind the safety line (安全線).

等人們都下車後，我們再上車。	Get on the subway train after people get off.
快！上車！	Hurry! Get in! 上車
上車時，要小心腳。	Watch your step when you get on. 上車
媽，有個空位。	Mom, there's an empty seat. • empty 空的
把包包給我，我來拿。	Hand me the bag. I'll hold it. • hand 交給
還剩幾站？	How many more stops are left?
 還有三站。	Three stops from here.
不可以在電車內跳。	Don't jump around in the subway train.

教孩子英文時所需要的英文表達

Chapter 31

教授的基本表現

What color is this?
這是什麼顏色？

It's blue.
這是藍色。

ch31-01.mp3

顏色

我們來用英文說顏色吧。 Let's say the name of colors in English.

消防車是什麼顏色？ What color is the fire truck?

這件襯衫是什麼顏色？ What color is this shirt?

這件襯衫的顏色是藍色。 The color of the shirt is blue.

你最喜歡的顏色是什麼？ What is your favorite color?

我最喜歡紅色。 My favorite color is red.

媽媽，這是什麼顏色？ Mom, what color is this?

這是深／淺褐色。 That is dark / light brown.

• dark 深色的 • light 淺色的

如果我們把黃色和藍色混合的話，會出現什麼顏色？ What color will we get when we mix yellow and blue?

對！當我們混合黃色和藍色就會變成綠色。 Right! It turns green when we mix yellow and blue. • turn 變成

什麼顏色是暖色／冷色？ What color feels warm / cold?

白色、黑色和灰色都不鮮豔。 White, black, and gray are not colorful. / White, black, and gray have no hue.

• hue 顏色，色彩

媽，我喜歡彩虹的顏色。 Mom, I like the colors of the rainbow.

紅色，黃色和藍色是三原色。 Red, yellow, and blue are the three primary colors. (原色)

你能在家中找出紫色的東西嗎？ Can you find something purple in our house?

你想要把這個塗成什麼顏色？ What color do you want this to be? / What color do you want for this?

我想把這個塗成粉紅色。 I want to color this pink.

ch31-02.mp3

數字

我們來用英文學習數字。 Let's learn numbers in English.

我們從一讀到十吧。 Let's read up to ten. (到～)

你可以從一數到十嗎？
Can you count from one to ten?

你可以數十以上的數字嗎？
Can you count after / more than 10?

我們以十為單位來數。
Let's count by tens.

哇，你知道怎麼用英文說「100」？
Wow, you know how to say "100" in English?

媽媽有幾隻眼睛？
How many eyes does Mom have?

你有兩隻眼睛。
You have two eyes.

盤子上有幾顆蘋果？
How many apples are on the plate?

有五顆蘋果。
There are five apples.

我們來看看誰的彈珠多。
Let's see who has more marbles.
• marble 彈珠

我的更多。
I have more. / I'm the one who has more.

我有七顆彈珠，吉娜有五顆。
I have seven marbles, and Jina has five.

當我們數順序時，數字的形式是不一樣的。
The numbers are different when counting the order. • order 順序

當我們看是哪個先的時候，使用序數。
We use ordinal numbers to see which comes first.
序數（例如，first, second, third等）

這張桌子有五個抽屜，對吧？
The desk has five drawers, right?

打開矮衣櫃的第三個抽屜。
Open the third drawer of the dresser.
• dresser 化妝台；矮衣櫃

ch31-03.mp3

圖形

書是什麼形狀？
What shape is a book?

 是長方形。 It's a rectangle.

 大衣衣架是什麼形狀？ **What shape is a coat hanger?**

 是三角形。 It's a triangle.

 彩色紙是什麼形狀？ **What shape is colored paper?**

 是正方形。 It's a square.

 鈕扣是什麼形狀？ **What shape is a button?**

 是圓形。 It's a circle.

 圓形沒有端點，也沒有邊。 **A circle has no points and no sides.**
- point 尖端

你能在房間內看到圓形的東西嗎？ Can you see something round in the room?

 時鐘是圓形的。 **The clock is round.**

 罐頭是圓柱體的形狀。 A can is in the shape of a cylinder.
- cylinder 圓柱體

球是球體。 **A ball is a sphere.**

圖形的名稱

- 圓形 circle
- 正方形 square
- 長方形 rectangle
- 三角形 triangle
- 圓錐體 cone
- 立方體 cube
- 圓柱體 cylinder
- 角錐體 pyramid
- 平面圖形 plane figure
- 立體圖形 solid figure

冰淇淋是什麼形狀？ What shape is an ice cream cone?

這是圓錐體。 It's a cone.

骰子是立方體。 A dice is a cube. ‧cube 立方體

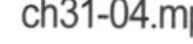

大小

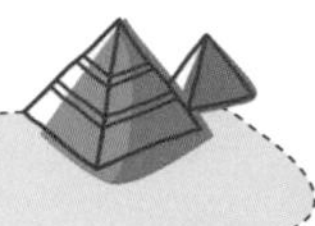

ch31-04.mp3

大象很大隻，兔子很小隻。 The elephant is big, but the bunny is little. ‧bunny〈兒童用語〉兔子

爸爸很大，但你很小。 Dad is big, but you are small.

鉛筆很長，但橡皮擦很短。 The pencil is long, but the eraser is short.

大樓很高，但平房很矮。 The building is high, but the house is low.

你和爸比，誰比較高？ Who is taller, you or Daddy?

我的甜心寶貝比爸爸矮。 My sweet baby is smaller than his dad.

媽媽的手比你的大。 Mom's hand is bigger than yours.

我的書桌比你的大。 My desk is larger than your desk.

這條街比那條更窄／寬。 This street is narrower / wider than that one.

我們來看看這有多長。用這把尺量。 Let's see how long this is. Use this ruler.

身體

ch31-05.mp3

你知道身體部位的英文嗎？ Do you know the body parts in English?

這是頭，這是臉。	This is the head, and this is the face.
我們的臉上有什麼？	**What do we have on our faces?**
有鼻子、嘴巴、眼睛和耳朵。	We have a nose, mouth, eyes, and ears.
我們也有眉毛、眼睫毛、下巴和臉頰。	**We also have eyebrows, eyelashes, a chin, and cheeks.** ·eyebrow 眉毛 ·eyelash 眼睫毛
讓我看你的手臂和腿。	Show me your arms and legs.
媽，看我的手指和腳趾頭。	**Mom, look at my fingers and toes.**
肚子和肚臍在哪裡？	Where's your tummy and belly button? (belly button: 肚臍) ·tummy〈兒童用語〉肚子 (= belly)
轉動一下你的手臂。	**Turn your arms around.**
你的手肘在哪裡？	Where is your elbow?
伸出你的雙腿。	**Stretch out your legs.**
彎曲膝蓋坐在地板上。	Bend your knees and sit on the floor.
像這樣跺腳。	**Stomp your foot like this.** ·stomp 跺腳
寶貝，搖動你的屁股。	Shake your hips, Honey.
媽的屁股很大！	**Mom's hips are huge!**

屁股的英文是什麼？

在日常生活中，會把「屁股」稱作 bottom。關係較親密的也可以說 butt，但是一不小心很容易變成辱罵，所以還是使用 bottom 比較方便。

ch31-06.mp3

動物／植物

動物分為兩種：草食性和肉食性。

There are two kinds of animals: plant eaters and meat eaters.

人類也是動物。

Human beings are animals, too.

老虎、兔子和狗是哺乳動物。

Tigers, rabbits, and dogs are mammals.
• mammal 哺乳動物

牠們生出小孩，並且給寶寶餵奶。

They give birth to (生（孩子）) babies and breast-feed them. • breast-feed 母乳餵養

鳥有翅膀，還會生蛋。

Birds have wings and lay eggs (生蛋，產卵).
• wing 翅膀

魚有魚鰓，在水裡。

Fish have gills and live in the water.
• gills 鰓

爬蟲類如短吻鱷全身覆蓋著鱗片，也會生蛋。

Reptiles like alligators are covered with scales and lay eggs.
• reptile 爬行類 • scale 鱗

青蛙和蟾蜍是屬於兩棲類。

Frogs and toads are amphibians.
• amphibian 兩棲動物

牠們可以住在水裡及陸地。

They live both in water and on land.

有翅膀，還有六隻腳的動物叫作昆蟲。

Animals with wings and six legs are called insects.

甲蟲、蒼蠅和蟬等昆蟲也是動物。

Insects like beetles, flies, and cicadas are animals, too. • beetle 甲蟲 • cicada 蟬

動物和植物的差別是什麼？

What is the difference between an animal and a plant? • difference 差別

動物會移動，但植物不會。

Animals move, but plants do not move.

是的，對喔。動物可以自己移動，但是植物卻不行。

Yes, that's right. Animals can move by themselves, but plants can't do that.

動物和植物都是生物。

Animals and plants are living things. 生物

媽媽，寄生蟲呢？牠們也是動物嗎？

Mom, what about worms? Are they animals, too? •worm 蠕蟲，寄生蟲

寄生蟲也可以動，所以牠們也是動物。

Worms also move, so they are animals.

樹和花叫做植物。

Trees and flowers are called plants.

植物有根、莖和葉三部分。

Plants have three parts: roots, stems, and leaves. •root 根 •stem 樹幹 •leaf 葉子

根在土裡牢固地抓住植物。

The roots hold the plant strongly in the soil.

植物用它們的葉子製造養分。

Plants make food in their leaves.

植物需要陽光和水才能成長。

Plants need sunlight and water to grow.

日期

日曆顯示日期。

The calendar shows the date.

一年有 12 個月。

There are 12 months in a year.

一個月有 30 天或 31 天。

A month has 30 or 31 days.

今天是 8 月 6 日。

Today is the sixth of August.

那麼，昨天是幾號？

Then what was the date yesterday?

8 月 5 日。

It was August fifth.

那麼，明天是幾號？

Then what will be the date tomorrow?

8月7日。	It will be August seventh.
五天後是幾號？	**What date will it be five days from today?**
前天你做了什麼？	What did you do the day before yesterday? 前天
後天我們有晚餐的計畫。	**We have dinner plans the day after tomorrow.** 後天
日曆有兩種形態：陰曆以及西曆（即陽曆）。	There are two types of calendars: the lunar calendar and the western calendar. • lunar 陰曆的
2月7日是你的陽曆生日。	**February 7 is your birthday on the western calendar.**

說說日期

月（month）

· 一月 January	· 二月 February	· 三月 March	· 四月 April
· 五月 May	· 六月 June	· 七月 July	· 八月 August
· 九月 September	· 十月 October	· 十一月 November	· 十二月 December

〈年度的讀法〉1994：nineteen ninety-four
2011：two thousand eleven
〈日期的讀法〉3月3日：March third / the third of March

ch31-08.mp3

星期

一星期有七天。

There are 7 days in a week.

從星期一到星期五是平日。

From Monday to Friday are the weekdays.

我們把星期六和星期日叫做週末。

We call Saturday and Sunday the weekend.

今天是星期幾？

What day is it today?

今天是星期四。

Today is Thursday.

昨天是星期三。

Yesterday was Wednesday.

明天是星期五。

Tomorrow will be Friday.

星期一之後是星期幾？

What day comes after Monday?

是星期二。

It's Tuesday.

我最喜歡星期五，因為隔天我可以休息。

I like Friday the most because I can rest the next day.

星期一是最忙的一天。

Monday is the busiest day.

ch31-09.mp3

時間

一天有 24 小時。

There are 24 hours in a day.

時鐘只顯示 12 個小時。

The clock shows only 12 hours.

因此，時針一天跑兩圈。

So the hour hand (時針) goes around two times a day.

時鐘的短針告訴你幾點。
The short hand tells you the hour on the clock.

長針告訴你幾分。
The long hand tells you the minute.

當時針指在 1，而分針指在 12 的時候，就是 1 點。
When the hour hand points to 1 and the minute hand points to 12, it's 1 o'clock.
指～

一個小時有 60 分鐘。
1 hour is 60 minutes.

1 代表 5 分鐘，而 2 代表 10 分鐘。
1 represents 5 minutes, and 2 represents 10 minutes.
・represent 代表

這好像以每五分鐘來簡略計算。
It's like skip counting by 5s.

一秒跟眼睛眨一下的時間差不多。
One second is equal to one blink of an eye.
・blink 眨眼
等於～

60 秒就是 1 分鐘。
60 seconds are equal to 1 minute.

AM 是早上，PM 是下午和晚上。
AM is the morning, and PM is the midday and evening.

現在幾點？
What time is it now?

4 點 45 分。
It's four forty-five.

還有 15 分，就 3 點了。
It's fifteen to three.

季節

你最喜歡哪一個季節？
Which season do you like the most?

我最喜歡春天。
I love spring the most.

我們一年有四個季節。
We have four seasons in a year.

春天花會開，苗會發芽。	In spring, the flowers bloom, and the green sprouts bud. • bloom 開花　• sprout 苗；新芽　• bud 發芽
夏天很熱，樹的葉子很茂密。	Summer is hot, and the trees are thick with leaves.
暴風和雨季在夏天來臨。	Storms and the rainy season come during summer.
在秋天的期間，樹木的顏色會變換成紅色、黃色和橙色。	During fall, trees change their colors to red, yellow, and orange.
冬天很冷，偶爾還會下雪。	Winter is cold, and sometimes snow falls.
現在是八月。我們在哪個季節？	It's August. What season are we in?
現在的季節是夏天。	The season is summer.
不是所有的國家都有四季。	Not all countries have four seasons.
學校在春天開學。	School starts in the spring.
我們都會在夏天放假。	We all go on vacation in the summer.
我的學校在秋天舉辦運動會。	My school has a sports day in the fall.

美國的運動會

美國的運動會叫做 Sports Day 或 Track and Field Day，因此只進行賽跑。有個人的長跑、短跑，套袋賽跑（sack race），接力賽跑（relay），兩人三腳（three-legged race）等等。最後，會發給選手印有名次的帶子。這是增強體力並兼具趣味性的活動。

我喜歡冬天的長假。 I love the long vacation in the winter.

ch31-11.mp3

位置

桌子的下面有球。 There is a ball under the table.

書桌的上面有杯子。 There is a cup on the desk.

鉛筆盒裡面有橡皮擦。 There is an eraser inside the pencil case.

狗屋在房子外面。 The doghouse is outside the house.

你的手機在你的包包前面。 Your cell phone is in front of your bag.

你的手機在書的下面。 Your cell phone is under the book.

看一下書的右下角。 Look at the bottom right of the book.

看一下畫面的左上角。 Look at the top left on the screen.

對街有一家大型百貨公司。 There is a big department store across the street.

我們學校附近有文具店。 There is a stationery store near our school.

超市在美容院旁邊。 The supermarket is next to the hair salon.

超市在銀行和書店之間。 The supermarket is between the bank and the bookstore.

圖書館的右邊是警察局。 There is the police station to the right of the library.

學校門口的左邊是麵包店。 There is a bakery to the left of the school entrance.

ch31-12.mp3

職業

先生，你是做什麼的？	What do you do, sir?

我是個消防員。	I'm a firefighter.
我是醫生。	I'm a doctor.
我是牙科醫生。	I'm a dentist.
我是警察。	I'm a policeman.
我是郵差，所以我要送信。	I'm a mail carrier, so I deliver letters. • deliver 遞送

你的爺爺是漁夫。	Your grandfather was a fisherman.
你叔叔是農夫。	Your uncle is a farmer.
世界上有許多不一樣的職業。	There are a lot of different jobs in the world.
所有的職業都很重要。	Every job is important.

職業的種類

- 銀行員 bank teller
- 店主 store owner
- 獸醫 vet（=veterinarian）
- 祕書 secretary
- 攝影師 photographer
- 學生 student
- 老師 teacher
- 計程車司機 taxi driver
- 科學家 scientist
- 歌手 singer
- 畫家 painter
- 校長 principal
- 店員 clerk
- 護士 nurse
- 飛機駕駛員 pilot
- 演員 actor / actress
- 太空人 astronaut
- 公務員 public servant

Chapter 32

各科目的基礎表現

What is 10 plus 3?
10 加 3 等於什麼？

10+3=?

The sum is 13.
總和是 13

ch32-01.mp3

英文發音

看這些英文字母！	Look at all these letters of the alphabet! ★ 英文字母的總稱是 alphabet，指單個字母是 letter。
我們一起來唱英文字母歌。	Let's sing the alphabet song together.
每個字母都有不同的發音。	Each letter has a different sound.
當我們把某些字母放在一起，就會變成單字。	When we put some letters together, we can make words. ‧put together 組合

看？我有 c，a，t。這是什麼？ See? I have a “c”, “a”, and “t”. What is this?

這是「CAT，貓。」 It's “CAT.”

t，t，t，字母 t 的發音是ㄊ。 t, t, t... The letter “t” sounds like / t / .

字母 a 的發音是什麼？ How does the letter “a” sound?

我們聽聽看短音的 a。 Let's listen to a short “a” sound.

我發出 a 的長音後，你跟著我唸唸看。 I'll say a long “a,” and you say it after me.

c 和 t 之間要出來什麼字母，才會變成 cat？ What letter should come between “c” and “t” to make “cat”?

如果我們把 c 變成 b，那我們會得到什麼單字？ If we change the “c” to “b”, what word do we have?

這是「BAT，蝙蝠。」 It's “BAT.”

我們唸一下卡片後面的單字。 Let's read the word on the back of the card.

我們找找看卡片中有哪個字發 / æ / 的音。 Let's find the word with the / æ / sound from the cards.

有些時候，兩個字母會只發一個音。 Sometimes two letters make just one sound.

s 和 h 放一起時，發 / ʃ /。就像「SHIP，船。」 The “s” and “h” make a / ʃ / sound like in “ship.”

不過，這個單一字母有兩種不同的發音。 But this single letter has two different sounds.

字母 g 在 go 的發音是 / g /，在 gel 中則發 / ʒ / 。 The letter “g” sounds like the / g / in “go” or the / ʒ / in “gel.”

k 在 n 的前面時，不發音。 When “k” comes before “n,” it is silent.

• silent 不發音的

找找看開頭是同樣發音的單字。	Look for the words that begin with the same sound. 尋找～
我們來找以 / e / 音開頭的單字。	Let's look for the word that starts with an / e / sound.
找出彼此互相押韻的單字吧？	Why don't you look for some words that rhyme with each other? ‧rhyme 押韻

ch32-02.mp3

數學

● 加法

3 加 2 是多少？ — What's 3 plus 2?

3 加 2 等於 5。 — 3 plus 2 equals 5. ‧equal 等於 (= be equal to)

看！多來了 2 隻鳥。一共有多少隻鳥？ — Look! 2 more birds came. How many birds are there in all? 總共

已經有 3 隻，所以總共有 5 隻。 — There were 3 birds already. So there are 5 birds all together.

如果我們寫成數學算式的話，就是 3+2=5。 — If we write it in a number sentence, it's 3+2=5. 數學公式

5 是 2 加上 3。 — 5 is 2 more than 3.

● 減法

5 減去 2 是多少？ — What's 5 minus 2?

5 減去 2 等於 3。 — 5 minus 2 equals 3.

這裡有 5 隻鳥，不過飛走了 3 隻。還剩多少隻鳥呢？ — There were 5 birds, but 3 birds flew away. How many birds are left?

從 5 那裡拿掉 3，現在還剩 2 隻鳥。

I'll take away 3 from 5. 2 birds are left now. 拿走，帶走

我們把它寫成算式吧。這就是 5-3=2。

Let's write it in a number sentence. It's 5-3=2.

我從 5 個蘋果中拿走 2 個。那還剩下多少個？

I took away 2 apples from 5 apples. How many are left?

我再多給你 3 個蘋果。那你現在有多少個？

I will give you three more apples. How many do you have now?

2 比 5 小多少？

By what number is 2 smaller than 5?

3 比 5 少多少？

What is 3 less than 5?

2 比 5 少 3。

2 is 3 less than 5.

● 乘法

3 乘 2 是多少？

What's 3 times 2?

讀讀這個乘法算式。

Read this multiplication sentence.

• multiplication 乘法

3 乘 2 等於 6。

3 times 2 equals 6.

我有兩組三支鉛筆的組合。我有多少鉛筆？

I have 2 sets of 3 pencils. How many pencils do I have?

有 6 支鉛筆。這和 3 加 3 是一樣的。

Six pencils. It's the same as 3 plus 3.

● 除法

6 除以 2 是多少？

What's 6 divided by 2? • divided 除

讀讀這個除法算式。

Read this division sentence. • division 除法

6 除以 2 等於 3。

6 divided by 2 equals 3.

把六支鉛筆平均分給兩個小孩。每個人可以有幾支？

Two kids will share 6 pencils equally. How many pencils can each have?

• share 分配　• equally 平均地　• each 每個

因為 6 除以 2，每個小孩可以有 3 支鉛筆。

Each kid can have 3 pencils because 6 is divided by 2.

● 分數

如果把 1 平均地分成 3 塊的話，每塊就叫做 3 分之 1。

If 1 is equally divided by 3, each part is called one third.

這個讀做 4 分之 1。

It's read one fourth.

這比 1 小嗎？

Is it smaller than 1?

我們把麵包切成 3 塊。一塊叫做什麼呢？

Let's cut this bread into 3 pieces. What do you call one piece?

• cut A into 3 pieces 把 A 切成三等分

一塊是 3 分之 1。

One part is one third.

分數的算式看起來像這樣。

The fraction sentence looks like this.

分數的唸法

用英文讀分數時，跟中文是不一樣的。要先讀分子，再讀分母。分子用基數讀，分母用序數讀。分子大於 1 的時候，分母的後面要加上 -s。例如，$\frac{3}{5}$ 讀作 three fifths。5 等分後，有 3 個，所以要加上表示複數的 -s。

這是 $\frac{3}{5}$。 It's three fifths.

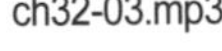

ch32-03.mp3

科學

天體

	現在是正午。你怎麼知道呢？	It's midday. How do you know that?
	因為天空中有太陽。	Because the sun is in the sky.
	太陽帶給我們光和熱。	The sun gives us light and heat.
	沒有太陽，就沒有生命能夠存活。	Without the sun, no living things could live.
	晚上很暗。你在天空上看到什麼？	It's dark at night. What do you see in the sky?
	我們在夜空上看到月亮。	We can see the moon in the night sky.
	我們看看月亮怎樣變化形狀。	Let's see how the moon changes its shape.
	有滿月、半月和新月。	There are a full moon (滿月), a half moon, and a crescent moon (新月).
	我們在夜空中還能看到什麼？	What else can we see in the night sky?
	我們能看到很多星星。	We can see lots of stars.
	來找找北斗七星吧？	Why don't we try finding the Big Dipper (北斗七星)?

環境

	媽，什麼是回收？	Mom, what's recycling? • recycling 回收利用
	回收是我們試著再使用舊東西。	It's when we try to use old things again.

我們可以回收玻璃瓶後，再次使用。

We can recycle glass bottles to use them again. ·recycle 回收利用

不要用太多洗髮精。

Don't use too much shampoo.

據說乾淨的水快被我們消耗光了。

It is said that we're running out of clean water.
～用完，耗盡

你浪費太多水了。

You're wasting too much water.
·waste 浪費

我們應該試著少用點水來節省水資源。

We should save water by trying to use less. ·save 節省

在城市連呼吸都不容易。

It's not easy to breathe in the city.

汽車排放的黑煙汙染了空氣。

Smoke from cars is polluting the air.
·pollute 汙染

腳踏車不會汙染空氣。

Bikes don't pollute the air.

我們騎腳踏車的話，可以減少碳足跡。

When we ride our bikes, we can reduce our carbon footprint.
碳足跡（二氧化碳的排出量）

現在地球生病了。我們需要保護它。

The Earth is sick now. We need to protect it.

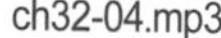

ch32-04.mp3

社會

我們來談談我們的城鎮吧。

Let's talk about our town.

這裡有房子、街道和很多建築物。

There are houses, streets, and lots of buildings.

我們來畫我們鎮上的地圖。

Let's draw a map of our town.

跟別人說說我們鎮上的優點。

Tell the others something nice about our town.

我們的城鎮還需要些什麼呢？ **What do we need more of for our town?**

城市跟鄉村的不同之處是什麼？ What are some differences between the city and the country?

城市裡住著很多人。 **There are many people living in the city.**

住在鄉下／城市的話，有什麼好處？ What is nice about living in the country / city?

住在城市／鄉下的話，會有什麼問題呢？ **What are some problems with living in the city / countryside?**

你記得什麼時候去過鄉下嗎？ Can you remember when you went to the countryside?

在城市裡可以找到哪些工作？ **What are some jobs that are found in the city?**

我叔叔是住在鄉下的農夫。 My uncle is a farmer who lives in the countryside.

漁夫捕到魚後，把牠們送到城市。 **A fisherman catches fish and then sends them to the city.**

礦工的人數越來越少。 Miners are getting smaller in number. (in number：在數字上)

• miner 礦工

ch32-05.mp3

體育

我們現在來上體育課吧。 **Let's have our PE class now.**

• PE 體育（= physical education）

上體育課的時候，你最好穿上體育服。 You'd better wear your gym clothes in PE class. (gym clothes：體育服)

• 'd (= had) better 最好做～

我也想穿我的跑步鞋。 **I also want to wear my running shoes.**

太棒了！大家都去運動場吧！ Cool! Everyone, come out to the field!

我們從暖身運動開始。 **We will start with some warmup exercises.** • warmup 暖身運動，熱身

像這樣伸展你的手臂跟腿。 Stretch your arms and legs like this.

我們分成兩隊進行比賽。 **We will divide into two teams and play a game.** divide into 分成～

我們來賽跑吧。 Let's have a race.

請在起跑線上排好隊。 **Line up at the starting line.**

跑運動場一圈。 Run around the field one time.

我會記錄你跑的時間。 **I will record your running time.** • record 記錄

盡力跑。 Try your best.

體育時間結束時，我們來做緩和運動。 **We do cool-down exercises at the end of PE.** cool-down exercises （使身體冷卻的）緩和運動

Chapter 33 要不要讀英文故事書？

Do you want me to read you a book?
你希望我唸一本書給你聽嗎？

Sure. This book looks fun.
好啊，這本看起來有趣。

ch33-01.mp3

選英文童話書

好，今天我們要讀什麼書？ Okay, so what are we going to read today?

我想要自己選。 I want to choose it by myself.

媽，我想要你幫我選。 I want you to pick for me, Mommy.

把你任何想讀的書拿過來。 Bring any book that you want to read.

我們要讀幾本書？ How many books are we going to read?

媽，今晚你唸書給我聽。
Mom, I want you to read to me tonight.

我們何不輪流讀呢？
Why don't we take turns? 輪流
為什麼不～（= Let's～）

我讀一本給你聽，你也讀一本給我聽。
I will read one book to you, and you read one book to me.

我可以讀這本書代替讀英文書嗎？
Can I read this book instead of an English one?
代替～

那麼，我唸一本英文書和兩本書給你聽。
Then I will read you one English book and two books.

媽，我喜歡這本書的圖畫。
Mom, I like the drawings in this book.

我很喜歡這位作者寫的書。
I like books by this author very much.
• by 根據～，寫～（= written by）

這本書的字太多了。
There are too many words in this book.

這本書再怎麼讀都不會膩。
I never get tired of reading this book.
厭煩～

那本書你已經讀太多次了。
You have read that book too many times.

為什麼你不試著也讀一些其他的書呢？
Why don't you try to read some other books, too?

每次讀，我都覺得很有趣。
It's fun every time I read it.

這本書看起來很有趣。
This book looks fun.

哇，封面很漂亮。這本書怎麼樣？
Wow, the cover looks pretty. How about this book? • cover 封面

又是那本書？
That book again?

這本書有那麼有趣嗎？
Is this book that much fun?

你選了一本媽咪真的很喜歡的書。
You chose a book that Mommy really likes.

這本書太難了。
This book is too hard / difficult.

嗯，這是給小嬰兒讀的書。你為什麼不選其他本呢？	Hmm, this book is for babies. Why don't you choose another one?
看你拿了這麼多的書！。	Look at all the books that you brought!
我快沒有聲音了。	I'm going to lose my voice. • lose one's voice 失去聲音

ch33-02.mp3

講故事

現在，我要跟你講這本書的故事了。	Now I am going to tell you the story of this book.

書名是什麼？	What is the title?

這本書的書名是《小精靈和鞋匠》。	This book's title is *The Elves and the Shoemaker*.
作者是格林兄弟，插畫家是漢娜。	The authors are the brothers Grimm, and the illustrator is Hannah. • author 作者 • illustrator 插畫家
我們先看封面。你看到什麼？	Let's look at the cover first. What do you see?

我看到一個老人、一些鞋子和精靈。	I see an old man, some shoes, and elves, too.

那麼，你覺得會發生什麼故事呢？我們來找出來吧！	So what do you think will happen in the story? Let's find out!
把圖看得更仔細一點。	Look more closely at the pictures.

我知道那個故事。	I know that story.

我們來確定一下這個是不是你已經知道的故事。	Let's check if this story is one you already know.

下一頁會發生什麼事呢？	What will happen on the next page?
看這張圖。你覺得正在發生什麼事情呢？	Look at the picture. What do you think is happening?
 我想那隻鳥要飛走了。	I think the bird will fly away.
 真的嗎？我來讀讀看你的猜測對不對。	Really? I'll read and see if your guess is correct. ・guess 猜測 ・correct 正確的
賓果！你說的是正確的。	Bingo! What you said was actually right.
現在，我們讀完這本書了。你們喜歡嗎？	Now, we are done reading the book. Did you guys like it? (you guys：大家（指很多人）)
 是的。請再讀一次！	Yes. Read it again, please!
 哪一個部分最有趣呢？	Which part was the most interesting?
 太有趣／傷感／無聊了。	It was so fun / sad / boring.
我喜歡紙袋公主踹王子的那一段。	I like when the Paper Bag Princess kicked the prince.

ch33-03.mp3

大聲朗讀

 我們大聲唸出來吧。	Let's try reading it out loud. (out loud：發出大的聲音)
你可以慢慢地唸。	You can read it slowly.
我唸這一頁，你唸它的另一頁。	I will read this page, and you read the other side.
 我唸完之後，覺得喉嚨痛。	I think I have a sore throat from reading. (sore throat：喉嚨痛)
 你的聲音不需要太大聲。	Your voice does not have to be very loud.
只要你自己能聽得到就好。	As long as you can hear yourself, it's fine. (As long as：只要)

我根本就聽不到你唸的聲音。	I can't hear you at all. 根本
錯了也沒關係。我會幫你。	It's okay if you get it wrong. I will help you.
當我一行一行的唸，我希望你跟著複誦。	I want you to repeat after me as I read line by line.
我不知道這個單字怎麼唸。	I don't know how to read this word.
我發不出這個音。	I can't really pronounce it. • pronounce 發音
你試著發音看看。從「l」開始。	Try to sound it out. It starts with an "l."
我幫你錄起來給你聽。	I will record it and let you listen to it.
如果你持續練習的話，你一定會唸得更好。	If you keep on practicing, you will get better for sure. / Practice makes perfect. 更好 肯定
 如果我唸不出來，請幫我。	If I can't read, I want you to help me.

ch33-04.mp3

安靜閱讀

 我不想要大聲朗讀這本書。	I don't want to read the book out loud.
 那麼，今天你就靜靜地讀吧。	Well, then today you can read silently.
不過你還是必須把它讀完。	But you still have to read it thoroughly. • thoroughly 完全地
 媽，我希望房間保持安靜。	Mom, I want the house to be quiet.
媽，我已經讀完一本了。	Mom, I finished reading one book already.
 哇，你讀得那麼快？	Wow, you read that fast?

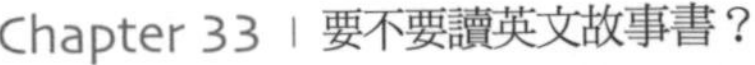

你讀的時候，有什麼不懂的地方嗎？	Is there anything that you didn't understand while you were reading?
你隨時都可以問我。	You can always ask me.
就算有些字你不懂，也要繼續讀下去。	Even if you don't know some words, just keep on reading.
剛開始，你或許會發現很難安靜地讀書。	At the beginning, you might find it hard to read books silently.
你很快就會習慣。	You will get used to it very soon. (get used to 習慣～)
你也要好好看圖。它們看起來都很有趣。	Pay attention to the pictures, too. They all look interesting. (Pay attention to 注意～，集中)
你一邊讀的時候，要一邊想這是關於什麼的故事。	Think about what the story is about as you are reading the book. • what A is about A 跟什麼有關
你好像沒有集中精神。	It seems like you're not paying attention.

ch33-05.mp3

用點讀筆閱讀

	你想要用點讀筆嗎？	Would you like to use the reading pen? • reading pen 點讀筆
	按下電源紐。	Press the power button.
	試著用點讀筆掃描句子。	Try scanning a sentence with the reading pen. • scan 掃描
	這支筆會讀句子。	This pen reads the scanned sentences.
	這支筆非常聰明！	This pen is very smart!
	聽這支筆播出的內容，並跟著複誦一次。	Listen to what the pen says and repeat after it.

這支筆會幫你閱讀得更好。 This pen will help you read well.

我喜歡用點讀筆。 I love using the reading pen.

很像是這本書在說話。 It's like the book is talking.

只要按一下，就可以閱讀任何單字。 With a simple touch, it can read any word.

我要輸入另一份音檔到這支筆上。 I am going to load another audio file onto the pen. • load 把資訊輸入電腦

媽媽，請把這本書的檔案放到筆上。 Mom, please put this book's file on the pen, too.

這支筆的聲音太大／小聲了。 The pen's sound is too loud/quiet.

我在這個貼紙上加了音檔。 I added audio to this sticker.

觸碰貼紙就可以聽了。 You can tap the sticker to listen.

你也可以自己錄音。 You can record yourself, too.
• record 錄音

按下錄音按鈕。 Press the record button.

燈光閃爍時，你可以開始錄音。 When the light blinks, you can start recording. • blink 閃亮，閃爍

我把整個系列的音檔一起放到一張聲音貼紙上。 I put the sound files of the whole series together into one sound sticker sheet.
• sound sticker sheet 聲音貼紙

用點讀筆輕點任何你想要的書本貼紙。 Tap any book sticker you want with the sound pen.

你想要用耳機嗎？ Do you want to use the headphones?

媽媽，電池要沒電了。 Mom, the battery ran out.

我來幫你充電。 Let me charge it for you.

我們出門時，你要我幫你帶著點讀筆嗎？	Do you want me to bring your sound pen with us when we go out?
 媽媽，可以請你幫我帶點讀筆嗎？	Mom, can you please bring my reading pen?

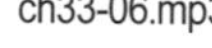

ch33-06.mp3

理解單字的意思

 在這一頁，你有不懂的單字嗎？	Is there any word that you don't know on this page?
你記得這個單字嗎？	Do you remember this word?
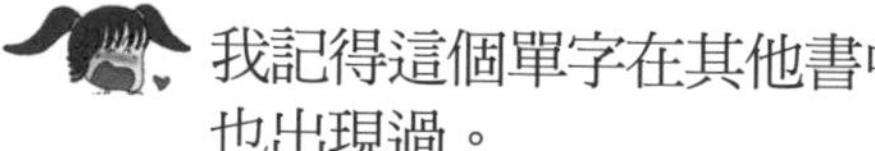 我記得這個單字在其他書中也出現過。	I remember seeing this word in another book.
喔！我知道那個單字！我曾經聽過。	Oh! I know that word! I've heard it.
 這是你第一次看到這個字嗎？	Is this your first time to see this word?
我們再看一次新的單字。	Let's take a look at the new words once more.

點讀筆

孩子看書時經常用的點讀筆，英文稱為 talking pen、reading pen，或是 sound pen。正式名稱是點讀筆，但又被稱為智慧筆，因為它是為智慧時代量身打造的學習工具。

我們要標記一下你今天學到的單字嗎？	Should we mark the words that you learned today?
媽媽會在黑板上寫下這些單字。	Mommy will write the words on the blackboard.
 媽，它在故事裡面是什麼意思？	What does it mean in the story, Mom?
 試著猜測它的意思。	Try to guess its meaning. •guess 猜測
透過這個單字的前後文猜猜它的意思。	Try to guess its meaning by looking before and after the word. •by -ing 透過～
我們用字典查一下。	Let's look it up in the dictionary. （在字典等）查
你想要用字典查嗎？	Do you want to look it up in the dictionary?
那單字的意思是「強壯的」。	That word means "strong."
再想一想這個單字可能是什麼意思。	Try to think about what the word might mean one more time.
 媽，那個意思跟我之前學的不一樣。	Mom, its meaning is different from what I learned before.
 這個單字有幾種意思。	The word has several meanings. •several 幾個

ch33-07.mp3

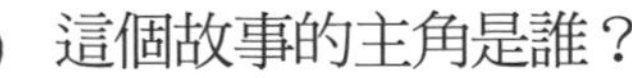

描述故事情節

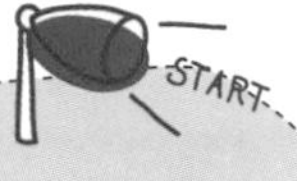

 這個故事的主角是誰？	Who is the main character of the story? 主要人物
主角是 Hansel 和 Gretel。	The main characters are Hansel and Gretel.
 那個小孩在做什麼，他是在	What is the kid doing, and where is he

哪裡做的？	doing it?
為什麼他那樣做？	Why did he act that way? ‧act 行動
在剛開始發生了什麼事？	What happened in the beginning?
為什麼會發生那樣的事？	Why did that happen?
故事的中間發生了什麼事？	What happened in the middle of the story? ～的中間，中途
現在，我們來看看那樣做的結果。	Now let's see the results of that action. ‧result 結果
這個情況下，他的心情如何？	How would he have felt in this situation?
如果是你的話，你會怎麼做？	What would you have done if that were you?
如果我是他的話，我想我不會那樣做。	I don't think I would have done that if I were him.
在那之後，發生了什麼？	After that, what happened?
你覺得最後會怎樣發展？	What do you think will happen in the end?
故事的最後發生了什麼事？	What happened at the end of the story?
你希望故事怎樣結束？	How would you like the story to end?
問題是如何解決的？	How is the problem solved? ‧solve 解決
主角克服了困難／挑戰。	The main character overcame the difficulty / challenge. ‧overcome 克服
當他們找到遺失的鑰匙，問題就解決了。	The problem was solved when they found the lost key.
我很欣慰是個幸福的結局。	I'm so relieved that the story ended happily. ‧relieved 欣慰的，感到放心的

ch33-08.mp3

談談登場人物

我們看看這本書有什麼角色。	Let's see what characters are in this book.
動物是這本書的主角。	An animal is the main character of this book.
那個女孩在做什麼？	What is the girl doing?
這一段，為什麼男孩生氣了？	Why was the boy mad in this part?
他是個怎麼樣的人？	What kind of person is he?
你最喜歡誰？	Who do you like the most? / Who is your favorite character?
 我最喜歡 Kipper。	I like Kipper the most.
Arthur 幾歲了？	How old is Arthur?
媽，Nate 總是吃薄煎餅。	Mom, Nate always eats pancakes.
蒼蠅為何能說話？	How come the fly talk?
 嗯，在書中動物可以和彼此交談。	Well, in books, animals can talk with one another.
 媽，我覺得這男孩真傻。	Mom, I think this boy is really silly. • silly 愚蠢的
媽，這孩子的媽媽在哪裡？	Mom, where is this child's mother?
他／她一個人生活嗎？	Does he / she live alone?
公主怎麼會那麼醜呢？	How come the princess is so ugly?
 這本書中有好幾位主角。	There are several main characters in this book.

我想 DW 比 Arthur 更像主角。	I think DW is more like the main character than Arthur.

主角看起來像什麼？	What does the main character look like?
主角做了什麼？	What did the main character do?
主角在哪裡，和誰住在一起？	Where, and with whom, does the main character live?
隨著故事的發展，他的心情是怎麼改變的？	How did his feelings change throughout the book? ·throughout 遍及

ch33-09.mp3

聽 CD

請仔細聽。	Please listen carefully.
集中精神聽故事。	Concentrate and listen to the story.
你會從 CD 中聽到故事。	You will hear a story from the CD.
一邊聽一邊看著這些字。	Look at the words as you are listening to it.
你可以邊聽邊用手指頭指著這些字。	You can point to the words with your finger while listening. （用手指頭）指～
好，那麼我播放 CD 囉。	Okay, I'll play the CD then.
邊聽邊想想看這是什麼故事。	Think about the story while you are listening.

我想再聽一次。	I want to listen to it one more time.
你能把最後的那幾秒再播放一遍嗎？	Can you play the last few seconds again? / Can you play that last minute again?
你能回去播放上一節嗎？	Can you go back and play the last track?

媽，你能暫停一下 CD 嗎？ Mom, can you stop the CD for a minute?

那個人讀得太快，我不知道該看哪裡了。 I don't know where to read because the person is speaking too fast.

翻到這一頁。在中間的部分。 Turn the page. It's on the middle part.

從下面／上面算來第五行。 It's the 5th line from the bottom / top.

那個聲音真的很好笑。哈哈！ The voice sounds really funny. Haha!

這太難了。我想聽不同的。 It's too difficult. I want to listen to a different one.

我想要你唸這本書給我聽。 I want you to read the book to me.

你想要我幫你戴耳機嗎？ Do you want me to put the headphones on you?

你在好好聽故事嗎？ Are you doing fine listening to the story?

媽咪也覺得這部分最有趣了。 Mommy finds this part to be the most fun, too.

你錯過了那個部分囉。 You missed that part. •miss 錯失

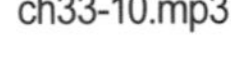

ch33-10.mp3

掃描音檔 QR 碼

媽媽，這本故事書有 QR 碼。 Mom, this storybook has QR Codes.
•QR Code = quick response code

要如何使用這個 QR 碼？ How do I use the QR Coeds?

媽媽，你可以掃描這個 QR 碼嗎？我想要聽這則故事。 Mom, can you scan this QR code? I want to listen to this story. •scan 掃描

我去拿手機。 Let me get my phone.

我的手機在這，我來教你怎麼使用。 Here is my phone. Let me teach you how to use it.

你可以用智慧型手機掃描QR碼，並打開音檔的網站。 You can use a smartphone to scan the QR Codes and open the audio website.

要怎麼掃描 QR 碼？ How can I scan QR Codes?

我可以借你的手機來掃描 QR 碼嗎？ Can I borrow your phone to scan the QR Code?

只要打開 QR 碼應用程式並對準 QR 碼，接著按播放。 Just open the QR Code App and aim at the QR Codes. Then press play.

- aim at 瞄準；對準
- press 按

你現在可以聽故事了。 You can listen to the story now.

那真是方便。 That is so convenient.

我不需要用 CD 播放器了。 I don't have to use a CD player.

ch33-11.mp3

閱讀後的活動

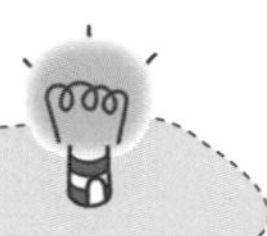

這本書如何？ How was the book?

很感動／有趣／一般。 It was moving / fun / just okay.

- moving 感動的

對你來說，太難了嗎？ Was it too difficult for you?

我大部分都能懂。 I understood most of it.

我不知道故事內容是什麼。 I don't know what the story is about.

你想跟媽咪講講這個故事嗎？ Do you want to talk about the story with Mommy?

我們一起來總結這個故事。 Let's summarize the story together.

- summarize 總結

媽，我來跟你說這個故事在講什麼。	Mom, let me tell you what the story is about.

你要試著寫讀書心得嗎？	Do you want to try writing a book report? 讀書心得
我們寫封信給主角吧。	Let's write a letter to the main character.
你要不要和我一起玩角色扮演？	Why don't you and I do the role-playing activity together? 角色扮演活動
既然你都讀完了，就寫在閱讀記錄表上。	Write in your reading log since you're done reading it. 閱讀記錄表

到目前為止，我讀了 200 本書。	I've read 200 books so far. 到目前為止

Chapter 34

觀賞英文影片

What DVD do you want to watch today?
你今天想看什麼 DVD？

Please play *Shrek*.
麻煩請放《史瑞克》。

ch34-01.mp3

選英文影片

媽，是看 DVD 的時間了！	Mom, it's time to watch a DVD!
媽，我可以看 DVD 嗎？	Mom, can I watch a DVD?
今天你要看什麼 DVD？	What DVD do you want to watch today?
你要看最近我們新買的那片嗎？	Want to watch the new one that we recently bought? •recently 最近
自己選一片，如何？	Why don't you pick one by yourself? （Why don't you ～，如何？）

請播放《Caillou》。 — Please play *Caillou*.

我要看《Magic School Bus》。 — I want to watch the *Magic School Bus*.

你要我幫你選嗎？ — Do you want me to choose it for you?

那個你已經看過很多次了。 — You have watched it too many times.

試著選其他的看，如何？ — Why don't you try to choose another one?

今天我可以看兩片 DVD 嗎？ — Can I see two DVDs today?

嗯，你知道看太多電視對你不好。 — Well, you know that watching too much TV is not good for you.

我可以再看一次嗎？ — Can I watch it again?

我想看我昨天看的那一片。 — I want to watch the one that I saw yesterday.

因為昨天民肅選了他喜歡的，這次輪到我選 DVD 了。 — It's my turn to choose the DVD because Minsu picked his favorite yesterday.

我們只會看 30 分鐘的 DVD，知道嗎？ — We'll watch the DVD for 30 minutes only. Okay?

我最喜歡迪士尼的卡通了。 — I like the Disney animations the most.
‧animation 卡通，動畫

我要有英文字幕的。 — I want the English subtitles. ‧subtitle 字幕

我可以打開字幕看嗎？ — Can I watch it with the subtitles on?

我們來看沒有任何字幕的。 — Let's watch it without any subtitles.

你只能看這一次。 — You can watch it this time only.

嗯，我們今天就播到這吧。 — Well, let's stop here today.

ch34-02.mp3

播放 DVD

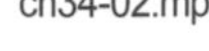

媽，我要怎麼播放 DVD？ Mom, how do I play the DVD?

我示範給你看，仔細看好。 I will show you how, so watch carefully.

我們試著用遙控器來操作。 Let's try to control it with the remote control. 遙控器（簡稱 remote）

把 DVD 放進播放器內。 Place the DVD into the player.

把你的食指放入中間的洞來拿著。 Handle it by inserting your index finger into the center hole.
• handle 拿 • insert 插入

如果 DVD 被刮傷了，它們會被弄壞。 If DVDs get scratched, they can be broken. • broken 損壞的
被刮傷

媽，我想要自己播放 DVD。 Mom, I want to play the DVD by myself.

好，可以。你試試！ Okay, sure. Give it a try!

蓋上蓋子後，按下播放鍵。 Put the lid back and push the play button. • lid 蓋子

把電視轉到「外部輸入」的模式。 Change the TV into "outside input" mode.

媽，它沒有運作耶。 Mom, it does not work. / it's not working.

我已經看過這個部分了。請跳到下個部分。 I saw this part already. Please skip the movie to the next part. • skip 跳過，躍過

聲音太大了。請轉小聲。 It's too loud. Please turn it down.
• turn down（聲音）轉小

你不覺得聲音已經太大了嗎？ Don't you think the sound is already too loud?

我想這剛剛好。 I think this will be just right.

你能把音量調大一點嗎？ Can you please turn the volume up a little? ‧turn up（聲音）調大

你要我把音量調大一點嗎？ Do you want me to turn up the volume a little bit?

如果你聽得那麼大聲，你的耳朵會受傷的。 If you listen to it that loud, your ears will get hurt. 受傷

按下停止鍵。 Press the stop button.

當光碟停止轉動，我們就把它拿出來。 When the disc stops spinning, we'll take it out. ‧spin 轉動 ‧take out 取出

當你看完時，一定要把電視和音響關掉。 When you are finished, be sure to turn the TV and audio off.

把 DVD 小心地放入盒子內。 Put the DVD back into the case carefully.

ch34-03.mp3

看 YouTube 影片

我可以在你的手機上看 YouTube 嗎？ Can I watch YouTube on your phone? ‧YouTube 影音搜尋平台

媽媽，你可以打開《Super Simple Songs》嗎？ Mom, can you turn on Super Simple Songs?

在 YouTube 上看。 Watch it on YouTube.

你只能看 YouTube 一個小時。 You can only watch YouTube for an hour.

在 YouTube 上面有很多有趣的影片。 There are a lot of fun videos on YouTube.

我想要拍影片並上傳到 YouTube。

I want to film a video and upload it on YouTube.

來上傳奕蓉大聲唸英文書的一些影片吧。

Let's upload some videos of Yeryung reading English books aloud.

哇，觀看次數在上升。

Wow, the number of views is going up.

如果你一直看 YouTube，視力會變差的。

Your eyesight will get bad if you constantly watch YouTube.

• eyesight 視力 • constantly 不斷地

我們今天先暫停，週末在繼續看。

Let's stop watching today and continue this weekend. • continue 繼續

我只會看一集《Peppa Pig》。

I'll just watch one episode of Peppa Pig.

YouTube 上有這麼多廣告好討厭。

It's annoying that there are so many ads on Youtube. • ads = advertisements 廣告

你可以跳過就好了。

You can just skip it. • skip 跳過

有很多影片是免費觀看的。

There are lots of things to watch for free.

• for free 免費的

在 YouTube 上看一些有教育意義的影片！

Watch something educational on YouTube!

有些影片含有暴力內容，所以記得要先問過我的許可。

There are some videos with violent content, so remember to ask for my permission first. • permission 許可

ch34-04.mp3

討論遊戲實況主

你最喜歡的遊戲實況主是誰？

Who is your favorite game streamer?

• streamer 實況主

你在看什麼？ What are you watching?

這個實況主好好笑。 This streamer is so funny.

他為這個遊戲展示了好多技巧。 He shows so many tips for the game.

這些技巧在玩遊戲的時候很好用。 These tips are useful while playing games. • useful 有用的

這個實況主介紹了一款新遊戲，我可以買嗎，媽媽？ The streamer introduced a new game. Mom, can I have it?

ch34-05.mp3

選英文卡通

你想要看卡通嗎？ Do you want to watch the cartoon?

看英文卡通可以增進英文聽力。 Watching English cartoon can improve your listening.

你在看什麼卡通？ What cartoon are you watching?

媽，我現在可以看卡通嗎？ Mom, can I watch the cartoon now?

在晚上六點有我想看的卡通。 There is a cartoon I want to watch at 6:00 P.M.

這是我最喜歡的卡通。 This is my favorite cartoon.

這集非常好笑。 This episode is so funny.

這個角色好酷。 The character is so cool.

這些角色好可愛。 The characters are cute

你最喜歡的卡通是什麼？ What's your favorite cartoon?

《Peppa Pig》是我其中一個最喜歡的卡通。 *Peppa Pig* is one of my favorite cartoons.

這是一部最受歡迎的卡通。 It's one of the most popular cartoons.

主角是誰呢？ Who are the main characters?

主角是一隻叫做 Peppa 的小豬。 The main character is a piggy called Peppa.

媽媽，你可以跟我一起看這部卡通嗎？ Mom, can you watch this cartoon with me?

我們一起看這部卡通吧。 Let's watch this cartoon together.

ch34-06.mp3

用影音平台看英文影片

哪一個影片串流平台適合小孩？ Which video streaming platform is suitable for children?

（video streaming platform：影片串流平台）

我認為 Disney+ 很適合小孩。 I think Disney+ is suitable for children.

（suitable for：適合～）

Disney+ 串流平台可以選擇很廣泛的卡通。 The Disney+ Streaming Service has a wide range of cartoons to choose from.

（a wide range of：範圍廣泛的～）

你喜歡在影片串流平台看卡通或電影嗎？ Do you like to watch cartoons or movies on this video streaming platform?

媽媽，我們可以訂閱這個影音平台嗎？ Mom, can we subscribe this video platform?

這個影片平台有所有我有興趣的電視節目。 This video platform has all the TV shows that I'm interested in.

我想要看在 Netflix 上《Paw Petrol》。 I want to watch *Paw petrol* on Netflix.

《Inside Out》在 Disney+ 上映了。 *Inside Out* was released on Disney+.

我們可以在 Netflix 上看最流行的電視節目。

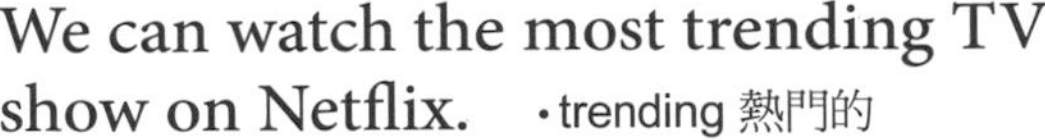

We can watch the most trending TV show on Netflix. • trending 熱門的

爸爸和我想要看 Netflix 上的新戲劇。

Daddy and I want to watch a new drama on Netflix.

這個影音平台對使用者很友善。

This video platform is so user-friendly.
• user-friendly 容易使用的

我喜歡在 Netflix／Disney+ 追劇。

I like to binge-watch TV shows on Netflix / Disney+. • binge-watch 狂看影片

Chapter 35

英文日記／讀書心得

What should I write in my diary?
我應該在日記裡寫什麼呢？

Try to think what you did today.
試著想想看你今天做了什麼。

ch35-01.mp3

英文讀書心得

這本書的書名是《Thank You, Mr. Falker》。	The title of the book is *Thank You, Mr. Falker.*
這本書的作者是 Patricia Polacco。	The author of the book is Patricia Polacco.
插畫家是 Amanda Smith。	The illustrator is Amanda Smith.
故事的主角是 Trisha。	The main character of the story is Trisha.

主角是 Trisha 和 Falker 先生。	The main characters are Trisha and Mr. Falker.
故事的背景是 1950 年代。	The setting of the story is the 1950s.
我喜歡這則故事，因為 Falker 先生是很優秀的老師。	I like the story because Mr. Falker is a great teacher.
我最喜歡的部分是 Trisha 跟 Falker 先生學習如何閱讀。	My favorite part is when Trisha learns how to read with Mr. Falker.

ch35-02.mp3

英文日記

● 好心情

我將要用英文寫日記。	I will write a journal in English.
今天我很興奮。	I was so excited today.
玩鬼抓人真的很有趣。	Playing tag was really fun. ‧tag 捉人遊戲
今天是這麼棒的一天！	Today is such a fantastic day!
我希望每天都可以像今天這樣。	I hope every day will be like today.
我媽買了新的褲子給我，我好開心。	I am so happy my mom bought me new pants.
我太開心了，所以我蹦蹦跳跳地。	I was so happy that I jumped up and down.
我絕對忘不了今天。	I will never forget today.
因為我考試考了滿分，所以我很開心。	I'm very happy because I got a perfect score on my test. ‧perfect 完美的 ‧score 分數
我笑死了。	I was laughing to death. 極度的，非常

這次我第一次搭火車，我感到很驚奇。	It was my first time to ride on a train, and I felt amazing. ·amazing 驚奇的

● 壞心情

我心情很差。	I feel terrible.
我真的很苦惱。	I'm really distressed. ·distressed 苦惱的
我和朋友打架了。	I fought with my friend.
我把錢弄不見了。	I lost my money.
我對每件事情都感到惱怒。	I got annoyed at everything. (got annoyed 感到惱怒)
我最喜歡的玩具壞了。	The toy that I like the most is broken.
我擔心我可能無法把它修好。	I am worried that I might not be able to get it fixed. ·get A fixed 把 A 修好
在學校有個高大的小孩打我的背。	A big kid hit me in the back at school.
我必須強迫自己不要哭。／我試著不要哭太大聲。	I had to force myself not to cry. / I tried not to cry very hard. ·force oneself to 強迫～
我對我弟弟感到很抱歉，因為我對他發脾氣了。	I feel sorry for my brother because I got mad at him. (got mad at 對～發脾氣)
我非常沮喪，因為我被媽媽責備了。	I am very depressed because I got scolded by Mom. (got scolded 責備) ·depressed 沮喪的
因為我朋友搬家了，所以我很傷心。	I was very sad because my friend moved away. (moved away 離開，搬家)
我對於沒有得獎感到又傷心又難受。	I feel bad and sad about not winning the prize. (winning the prize 得獎)
我真的很想打我姐姐。	I wanted to hit my sister so much.

因為下雨，我今天不能出門。	I could not go out today because of the rain.
今天一直發生很多壞事。	So many bad things kept happening today.
我的心很痛，因為我的魚死了。	My heart was aching so much because my fish died. ·aching 疼痛的

年齡別英文表現：從出生到小學

Chapter 36

孩子即將出生

Wow, it's great!
哇！太棒了！

Mom is having a baby!
媽媽懷了小寶寶了。

ch36-01.mp3

宣布懷孕的消息

我有個好消息要告訴你。	I have some really good news for you.
媽媽有小寶寶了！	Mom is having a baby!
媽咪這裡有小寶寶。	Mommy has a baby here.
你很快就會有個弟弟或妹妹了。	You will have a baby brother or sister soon.
你要當姐姐了。	You're going to be a big sister.

小孩就會長得跟你很像。
The baby will look exactly like you.
‧look like 和～像 ‧exactly 確切地

哇，我現在要當姐姐了嗎？
Wow, am I going to be a big sister now?

現在，我也有弟弟了！
Now I have a baby brother!

現在，我也有妹妹了！
Now I have a baby sister!

我一直很羨慕有弟弟／妹妹的朋友。
I have always envied my friends who have younger brothers / sisters. ‧envy 羨慕

你會跟你的弟弟或妹妹好好玩吧？
Are you going to play well with your baby brother or sister?

我會對小寶寶很好的。
I will be nice to the baby.

我會把我的玩具分給弟弟或妹妹玩。
I will share my toys with my brother or sister.

我們給奶奶打電話，告訴她這個好消息吧。
Let's call Grandma and tell her the good news!

ch36-02.mp3

是妹妹？還是弟弟？

小寶寶的名字是什麼？
What's the baby's name?

我們還沒有決定。現在，我們先叫他「兔兔」吧。
We haven't decided yet. Let's just call it Rabbit for now. ‧decide 決定

小寶寶的胎名是「鈕扣」。
The baby's pre-birth name is Button.
胎名 (= fetal name)

你想要妹妹，還是弟弟？
Do you want a baby sister or brother?

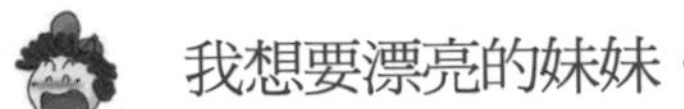

我想要漂亮的妹妹。
I want a pretty baby sister.

你想要你的弟弟叫什麼名字？
What do you like for your baby brother's name?

我想文宿會是個好名字。

I think Wensu will be a good name.

我想叫他文宿。

I want to call him Wensu.

你保證不可以只疼小寶寶。好嗎？

Make sure you don't only love the new baby. Okay?

你們兩個都是我們的小孩，所以你們兩個我都一樣愛。

Both of you are our children, so I will love both of you equally. 兩個都～

當然！媽媽最愛宋錦了，然後才是小寶寶。

Of course! Mom loves Songjin the most. The baby is the next.

媽咪的肚子裡面有小寶寶嗎？

Is there a baby inside Mommy's tummy?

接下來的十個月小寶寶會在媽媽的肚子裡長大。

The baby will be growing in my tummy for the next ten months.

所以，從現在起我需要你的幫忙。

So I need help from you from now on. 從現在開始

媽咪，不用擔心。我會幫你做所有辛苦的事情。

Don't worry, Mom. I will help you out with all the hard work.

ch36-03.mp3

談預產期

今天我要去看醫生做定期檢查。

I have to see my doctor for a regular checkup today. 定期檢查

小寶寶何時出來？

When is the baby due? ・due 預定的

離預產日還有多少天？

How many days are left till the due date? 預產期

為什麼小寶寶還沒出來？

Why isn't the baby coming out yet?

是呀，還久呢。

Well, it's still far away. 離很遠

你還要等一段時間。

You have to wait a long time.

看起來，他／她還沒準備好看這個世界。	It seems like he's / she's not ready to see the world.
小寶寶會在一個月後出生。	The baby will be born in a month.
離預產日，還有 15 天。	Fifteen days are left till the baby's due date.
大約再一週，小寶寶就要出來了。	In a week or so, the baby will come out.
小寶寶出生的時間快到了。	It's almost time for the baby to come.
再過幾天，你就會看到你的弟弟了。	In a few days, you will meet your baby brother.
明天就是寶寶的預產期了。	Tomorrow is the due date for the baby.
唉呀，預產期都已經過了，但是小寶寶還是沒有出來。	Well, the due date has passed, but the baby is still not coming out.
 我等不及跟我的弟弟見面了。	I can't wait to see my baby brother.

ch36-04.mp3

對肚子內的小寶寶說話

 嗨，小寶寶。我是媽咪。	Hi, baby. This is your Mommy.
甜心，你聽到媽媽的聲音了嗎？	Sweetie, do you hear Mommy's voice?
媽咪和爸比都很開心有了你。	Mommy and Daddy are so happy to have you.
每當我想起你的時候，我都感到很幸福。	Whenever I think of you, I feel so happy.
你是媽媽和爸爸的禮物和喜悅。	You are Mommy and Daddy's gift and joy.

媽咪和爸比都很想快點見到你。	Mommy and Daddy can't wait to see you.
你也等不及想見到媽咪和爸比嗎？	You can't also wait to see Mommy and Daddy? •can't wait to 等不及～
媽媽唱歌給你聽。	Mommy is going to sing you a song.
這是媽媽最喜歡的歌。 好好聽喔。	This is Mommy's favorite song. Listen to it.
媽媽讀故事給你聽。	Mommy will read you a story.
媽媽告訴你一個故事。	Mommy will tell you a story.
喔，甜心，你現在在踢耶！ 哇，看看你多強壯啊！	Oh, Sweetie, you're kicking now! Wow, look at how strong you are!
媽媽為了你在吃好吃的草莓。 很好吃不是嗎？	Mommy is eating the delicious strawberries for you. Aren't they delicious?
媽咪正在聽幾首好聽的歌。 你能聽到嗎？	Mommy is listening to some beautiful songs now. Can you hear them?
親愛的弟弟，我也迫不及待地想見你。	My dear baby brother, I can't wait to see you, too.
當我們見面後，我們一起踢足球和玩遊戲吧。	When we meet, let's play soccer and some games together.
我會好好照顧你的。我發誓。	I will take good care of (好好照顧～) you. I promise.
你出生後，我會每天陪你玩。	When you come out, I will play with you every day.
不要讓媽媽太辛苦，好嗎？	Don't give Mommy a hard time. Okay?
要好好地對媽咪，親愛的弟弟！	Be nice to Mommy, dear brother!
我非常期待見到你！	I look forward to seeing you very much! •look forward to -ing 期待～

ch36-05.mp3

小寶寶的出生

今天我要去生小寶寶了。
I'm going to have our baby today. / I'm going to give birth today.

你好，我的寶寶。我是媽咪。
Hi, my baby. I'm your mommy.

你為了來看這個世界很辛苦吧？
Did you have a hard time coming to see the world? •have a hard time -ing 做～很辛苦

你真的、真的做得很好。
You really, really did a good job.

甜心，媽媽非常以你為榮。
Mommy is very proud of you, Sweetie.

你比媽媽想像得漂亮多了。
You look so much prettier than Mommy imagined. •imagine 想像

你不知道我們等了多久才見到你。
You have no idea how much we were waiting to see you.

媽咪和爸比很高興你是個健康的寶寶。
Mommy and Daddy are so happy that you are a healthy baby.

我的弟弟，我真的很想見到你。
I really wanted to see you, my baby brother.

我是你的姐姐。
I'm your big sister.

ch36-06.mp3

雙胞胎

寶寶們是同卵雙胞胎。
The babies are identical twins.
•identical 完全相同的

寶寶們是異卵雙胞胎。
The babies are fraternal twins. / The twins look different from each other.
•fraternal 兄弟的

他們的眼睛、鼻子、嘴巴都看起來一模一樣。	Their eyes, noses, and lips all look the same.
兩個都很可愛。	Both of them are so adorable! • adorable 可愛的
我不能辨別他們誰是誰。	I can't tell who's who. • tell 辨別
你覺得誰是弟弟？	Who do you think the younger one is?
先出生的寶寶是哥哥／姐姐。	The baby who was born first is the older brother / sister.
每一樣東西，我們都需要兩份。	We will need two of everything.
媽咪要照顧雙胞胎，會加倍地辛苦。	Mommy will have twice as hard a time taking care of the twins.
如果吉娜能幫助媽媽，那就真的太好了。	It will be really nice if Jina can help Mommy.

我有個朋友也是雙胞胎。	One of my friends is a twin, too.

我們來慶祝雙胞胎的出生吧！	Let's celebrate the birth of the twins!
現在，我們是一家人了。	We are now one family.

產後護理中心

產後護理中心不是醫院內的設施，由此可知這是特別給產婦、嬰兒的照護機構。產後護理服務的英文是 after-birth care services，如果要表達場所，則是用 a maternity care center。

Chapter 37

孩子，有你真好（0~12個月）

Mom, Baby is crying.
媽，小寶寶在哭耶

Okay, okay. Mommy will feed you very soon.
好啦，好啦，媽咪很快就會來餵你了。

ch37-01.mp3

餵牛奶

該喝牛奶了。	It's time for some milk.
你餓了嗎？甜心，你想要喝牛奶嗎？	Are you hungry? Do you want some milk, Sweetie?
好，好。媽咪馬上餵你。	Okay, okay. Mommy will feed you very soon. •feed 餵，給～食物
媽媽這就調牛奶。稍等一下，知道嗎？	Mommy will mix a bottle. Just wait for a second. Okay? •bottle 奶瓶

媽媽馬上給你餵奶。	Mommy will nurse you soon. • nurse 餵奶；照顧
看起來，比起用奶瓶餵，你更喜歡媽咪親餵。	It looks like you prefer the breast to the bottle. • breast 乳房
你餓了嗎？喝奶快快長大喔。	Were you hungry? Drink the milk and grow well.
啊，好痛。不要咬媽媽！	Oh, that hurts. Don't bite Mommy! • bite 咬
吸母乳很難吧？	Is it too hard to suck Mom's breast? • suck 吸
好，我們休息一下。	Okay. We'll take a break for a second.
看看你！你很會吃喔！	Look at you! You are eating very well!
為什麼你不再多吃一點呢？	Why don't you have a little bit more?
喔，你不吃了嗎？你飽了嗎？	Oh, you want to stop? Are you full now?
太多母乳出來嗎？你在咳嗽！	Is too much milk coming out? You are coughing! • cough 咳嗽
母乳出來得不順嗎？抱歉，我的母乳不太夠。	The milk won't come out well? Sorry. My breast milk is not enough.
看媽媽怎樣餵寶寶。	See how Mommy nurses our baby.
幾年前，你也是這樣。	You were just like this years ago.
好，寶寶。現在你需要打嗝。	Okay, baby, now you need to burp.
我來幫你打嗝。	Let me help you burp.
媽媽會輕輕拍你的背。	Mommy will gently pat your back. • pat 輕拍，拍打
哇，你做到了！	Wow, you did it!

哎呀，你吐了！	Gosh, you threw up! 吐

換尿布

喔！你的尿布濕了。	Oops! Your diaper is wet. •diaper 尿布
你在尿布上尿尿了嗎？	Did you wet your diaper?
好，寶貝。我們該換尿布了。	Okay, baby, it's time to change your diaper.
讓我們看看。嗯…濕了嗎？	Let's see. Hmm... Is it wet?
喔，尿布還好。	Oh, the diaper is still okay.
哇，你大了很多便便。	Wow, you pooed a lot. •poo 〈幼兒用語〉便便，大便（= poop）
喔，你還便便了。好臭喔！	Oh, you even made some poo-poo. It stinks! •stink 臭的
你的便便看起來水水的。你肚子痛嗎？	Your poop looks too watery. Was your tummy sick? •watery 濕的，像水的
媽咪不知道你尿尿／便便了。	Mommy didn't know you peed / pooed.
啊！讓我把髒的尿布拿掉。	Eeek! Let me take off the dirty diaper.
好，不要動。	Okay, stay still. •still 靜止的
我們用濕紙巾擦屁屁。輕輕地擦。	Let's clean your hips with baby wipes. Wishy-washy! 嬰兒用濕紙巾（成人用濕紙巾是wet tissue）
我們撲點粉在上面。	We also have to put some powder on.
好，甜心，現在你感覺如何？有沒有感覺很乾淨清爽？	So, how do you feel now, Sweetie? Feel dry and fresh?

好，現在把你的漂亮屁股抬高。	Okay, now put your pretty hips upward. ・upward 向上
寶貝，你要媽咪幫你按摩腿嗎？	You want Mommy to massage your legs, Honey?
把腳伸開！媽咪幫你馬殺雞。	Stretch~ stretch! Mommy will give you a massage.
好，現在彎下膝蓋。然後，把腳伸開！	Okay, now bend your knees. Then, stretch them up!
現在，我們把你漂亮的雙腿往天空抬高！	Now let's put your pretty legs up toward the sky!
現在，我們來穿新的尿布。	Now, let's put on a new diaper. （put on：穿上，穿著）
耶！尿布換好了。感覺很棒吧？	Yay! Your diaper has been changed. Feel great?

洗澡

ch37-03.mp3

嘿，甜心，要洗澡了喔。	Hey, Sweetie, it's time for a bath.
現在，我們把衣服和尿布都脫下來。	Now, let's get rid of your clothes and your diaper, too. （get rid of：去除～）
我們進浴缸裡吧。	Let's get into the tub.
這水是不是又棒又溫暖呢？還是不夠熱？	Doesn't the water feel nice and warm? Or is it not warm enough?
我們跟鴨子玩具一起玩吧。呱呱！	Let's play with the toy duck. Quack, quack!
你要不要用腳划水呢？划呀，划呀！	Why don't you paddle your feet? Splash! Splash! ・paddle （用手腳）划水

我們先洗頭髮吧。	**Let's wash your hair first.**
媽媽把洗髮精搓成泡泡。	Mommy will make some bubbles with the shampoo. ・bubble 泡泡
我們用些乾淨的水來洗。	**Let's wash it with some clean water.**
這個滑滑的東西叫做肥皂。	This slippery thing is called soap.
現在，我們來洗臉和搓身體。	**Now, let's wash your face and rub your body.** ・rub 揉搓
眼睛很刺痛嗎？	Do your eyes hurt?
媽媽很快沖掉它。	**Mommy will rinse it off quickly.** ・rinse 沖洗
好，現在我們來把肥皂洗掉。	Okay, now let's wash off all the soap.
都洗好了。我來用毛巾把你擦乾。	**It's all done. Let me dry you off with a towel.**
洗完澡後，你變得更漂亮／帥了。	You are even prettier / more handsome after a bath. ・even（放在比較級前面）更加
寶貝，你覺得乾淨嗎？	**Do you feel clean, baby?**
現在我們洗完澡了，你覺得如何？	Now that we have taken a bath, how do you feel?

ch37-04.mp3

抱／背

你要媽媽抱嗎？	**Do you want me to hold you?**
你要媽媽背嗎？	Do you want me to give you a piggy-back ride? 背著走

甜心，過來。媽媽背你。	Come here, Sweetie. Let me give you a piggy-back ride.
媽咪去拿嬰兒背帶。	Mommy will bring the baby strap. • strap 帶子
媽咪用嬰兒背帶抱你。	Mommy will hold you with the baby carrier. 嬰兒背帶
怎麼樣？你覺得舒服嗎？	How is it? Are you comfortable? • comfortable 舒適的
有什麼東西讓你不舒服嗎？	Is there anything that's bothering you?
靠著媽媽就好。	Just lean on Mommy. 依靠在～上
甜心，你喜歡讓媽媽背嗎？	Sweetie, do you like riding on Mommy's back?
在媽媽的背上睡覺，好嗎？	Why don't you sleep on Mommy's back?
你能聽到媽媽的心跳嗎？	Can you hear Mommy's heartbeat? • heartbeat 心跳

嬰兒用品的名稱

- baby carrier 我們經常使用的嬰兒背帶，可以把嬰兒固定在前面或後面
- baby sling 西式的嬰兒背巾
- baby car seat 嬰兒汽車安全座椅，有些有手把，可以將嬰兒提著走
- crib 嬰兒床
- baby stroller 嬰兒推車
- baby swing seat 嬰兒用的搖搖椅

你現在想下來了嗎？	Do you want to come down now?
你何不下來呢？。媽媽的手臂疼了。	Why don't you get down? Mommy's arms hurt.
你要在媽媽的背上多待一會嗎？	Want to stay on Mommy's back for a little longer?
好，現在讓你下來。	Okay, let me put you down now.

哄寶寶睡覺

ch37-05.mp3

該睡午覺了。	It's time for a nap. ·nap 小睡
你為什麼哭？你想睡了嗎？	Why are you crying? Are you sleepy?
你開始哀哀叫了。	You are starting to whine. ·whine 哀哀叫
你累了嗎？我想你該睡覺了。	Are you tired? I think it's time to sleep.
來這裡。媽咪哄你睡覺。	Come here. Mommy will put you to sleep. ·put A to sleep 讓 A 入睡
你想躺在媽媽旁邊一起睡嗎？	Do you want to lie beside Mom and sleep together?
你想趴在媽媽的背上睡嗎？	Want to ride piggy-back while you try to sleep?
你想坐在嬰兒推車上睡嗎？	Do you want to ride in the stroller as you try to sleep? ·stroller 嬰兒推車
甜心，睡個好覺。	Sleep tight for a while, Sweetie.
你想聽我唱搖籃曲嗎？	Do you want me to sing you a lullaby?
邊聽媽媽的搖籃曲，邊進入夢鄉吧。	Go to dreamland as you listen to Mommy's lullaby.

乖小孩在睡覺前，都不會生氣哦。	A good girl / boy never gets peevish before sleeping. ‧peevish 抱怨的，易怒的
你今晚脾氣很糟糕。	You're so cranky tonight. ‧cranky 脾氣壞的
你的奶嘴在這裡。	Here's your pacifier. ‧pacifier 奶嘴
你一定要睡覺，才能長大。	You have to sleep so that you can grow.
甜心，現在閉上你的眼睛，好好睡吧。	Sweetie, close your eyes now and sleep tight.
你睡越多，就會長越大。	The more you sleep, the more you grow. ‧the 比較級, the 比較級 越～越～
甜心，你會在夢裡見到媽媽。	You can meet Mommy in your dreams, Sweetie.
哇，你睡覺的樣子像個天使。	Wow, you sleep like an angel.

ch37-06.mp3

牙牙學語

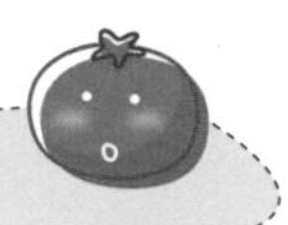

嘿，你開始學說話了！	Hey, you started babbling! ‧babbling 牙牙學語
你一整天都在小聲說話。	You've been cooing all day long. ‧coo 嬰兒、鴿子等發出小的咯咯聲
你一直發出咯咯聲。你的心情很好嗎？	You keep gurgling. Are you feeling good? ‧gurgle 嬰兒發咯咯聲；水發汩汩聲
對，那樣就對了。	Right. That's right.
喔，甜心，你想要說話嗎？	Oh, sweet baby, do you want to talk?
你很快就會說話了。	You will be able to talk soon.

看著媽咪，繼續說話。	Look at Mommy and keep talking.
你在說什麼？／那是什麼意思？	What are you saying? / What do you mean?
我們有個多話寶寶。	Here we have a chatty baby. ・chatty 多話的
喔，現在不要再咿咿呀呀了。	Oh my, stop cooing now.
甜心，不要再咿咿呀呀了，吃點東西。	Stop cooing and eat, Sweetie.
耶！你看起來心情很好喔。	Yay! It seems like you're feeling great.
手搖腳晃。你那麼開心嗎？	Arms waving. Legs kicking. Are you that happy?
你看起來很興奮。我看著也跟興奮起來了。	You look so excited. I'm excited to see you.

ch37-07.mp3

哄在哭的小孩

你為什麼一直哭？什麼在煩你呢？	Why do you keep on crying? What's bothering you? ・keep on -ing 持續～
寶貝，怎麼了呢？	What's wrong, Honey?
我想知道發生什麼事了。	I wonder what's going on.
好，好，甜心。媽咪在這裡。	Okay, okay, Sweetie. Mommy's here.
停！不要哭了，甜心。	Stop! Stop crying, Sweetie.
尿布濕了嗎？	Is your diaper wet?
你生病了嗎？我確認你有沒有發燒。	Are you sick? Let me check if you have a fever. （check if 確認～）

你睏了嗎？你想睡個午覺嗎？

Are you sleepy? Do you want to take a nap?

你餓了嗎？那是你為什麼哭嗎？

Are you hungry? Is that why you are crying?

你想要喝些奶嗎？

Do you want some milk?

你要我幫你泡一瓶牛奶嗎？

Do you want me to give you a bottle?

寶貝，請不要再哀嚎了。

Please stop whining, baby. ・whine 哀鳴

你真是個難搞的寶貝。

You're such a demanding baby.
・demanding 要求很多的，不容易滿足的

如果你還一直哭的話，可怕的怪物就會來把你抓走！

If you keep on crying, a scary monster will come and get you!
・scary 可怕的 ・monster 怪物

ch37-08.mp3

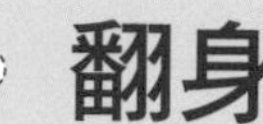

翻身

你不想要仰睡嗎？

You don't want to lie on your back?
・lie on one's back 仰臥

你想要翻身嗎？

Do you want to roll over?

你要翻身四處移動一下嗎？

Are you going to turn over and move around?

看看你！你正努力翻身呢！

Look at you! You are trying to turn yourself over!

好，你幾乎快做到了。再努力一點點。

Okay, you are almost there. Try a little bit harder.

哇，你終於靠自己翻身了！

Wow, you finally turned over by yourself!

哇，寶貝，你做到了！	Wow, you made it, baby! (made it：成功)
甜心，這很辛苦，不是嗎？	It was pretty tough, wasn't it, Sweetie? • pretty 相當，很
喔，不！我在幫你換尿布時，不可以翻身。	Oh, no! Don't turn over while I am changing your diaper.

坐

ch37-09.mp3

你想坐起來嗎？	Do you want to sit up? (坐起來，站著坐下去則叫做 sit down)
喔，你會摔倒的。小心！	Oh, you might fall down. Be careful!
現在，挺直你的背，用力撐住。	Now straighten your back and hold it strongly. • straighten（姿勢）挺直
坐起來，坐起來…坐起來…	You are sitting, sitting... sitting...
喔，你幾乎要做到了。	Ah, you were almost there!
哇，你終於坐起來了！	Wow, finally, you sat up!
你現在累了嗎？你想再躺下來嗎？	Are you tired now? Do you want to lie down again?
你要不要坐學步車？	Will you sit in the baby walker? (學步車)

爬行

ch37-10.mp3

該趴著一下了。	It's time for tummy time.
喔，天呀！你能趴著用手把自己撐起來了。	Oh my! You can push yourself up on your tummy.

現在你學會了爬行！	Now you have learned how to crawl! • crawl 爬行
你想爬嗎？	Do you want to crawl?
你想要往前／後爬嗎？	Want to crawl to the front / back?
再努力一點，就是那樣。	Put a little more effort into it. There you go! • effort 努力
你在用你的膝蓋爬。	You are using your knees to crawl.
你在抬起膝蓋爬耶。	You are crawling with your knees up.
爬向媽媽。	Crawl over to Mommy.
好，再努力一點。爬向媽媽。	Okay, put more effort into it. Come to Mommy. • effort 努力
你爬得很好。	You are crawling so well.
你滿屋子爬。	You're crawling all over the house.
喔，不！這個爬來爬去的小搗蛋到處亂摸。	Oh no! This crawling baby touches everything.

Tummy Time

tummy time 是指讓醒著的嬰兒趴著的時間。這樣做的話，孩子就可以在地板上玩玩具，還可以練習抬脖子，也是開始翻身的第一步。因此可以邊說 It's your tummy time 邊讓小孩趴一會兒。注意嬰兒趴著的時候，大人一定要看著。

ch37-11.mp3

長牙齒的時候

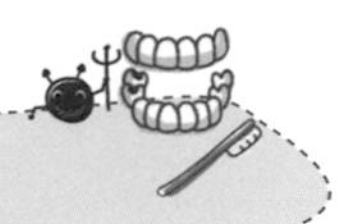

讓我看看你的嘴巴裡面。	Let me look in your mouth.
你的牙床不會癢癢的嗎？／ 你的牙床一定很癢。	Don't your gums feel itchy? / Your gums must be itching. • gum 牙床 • itchy 癢癢的
這是給你咬的玩具哦。	Here's your teether. • teether 小孩長牙齒時咬的玩具
看起來你的乳牙要長出來了。	It seems like your baby teeth will come out. 乳牙
恭喜！你的第一顆牙齒要長 出來了。	Congratulations! You're about to get your first teeth. • be about to 正要~
終於，你的乳牙長出來了。	Finally, your baby teeth are coming out!
嘿，寶貝，你現在有牙齒了！	Hey, baby, you have teeth now!
我看到在下面有兩顆門牙。	I see two front teeth on the bottom. • bottom 底部
我想你很快就會有兩顆在 上面的門牙。	I think you will have two front upper teeth soon.
甜心，媽咪幫你刷牙。	Mommy will brush your teeth, Sweetie.
媽媽幫你按摩牙床。	Mommy will massage your gums.
喔！寶貝，你流太多口水了。	Oh my! You drool too much, Honey. • drool 流口水
你流這麼多的口水，長疹子 了。	You've gotten a rash from all that drooling. • rash 疹子

ch37-12.mp3

抓著走路

我們試著站起來。	Let's try standing up.
寶貝，你想你現在能站得起來嗎？	Do you think you can stand up now, baby?
抓住媽媽的手。	Hold on to Mommy's hands. Hold on to：抓著～
好，現在我們站起來了。	Okay, now we're standing up.
不要放棄。你快做到了。	Don't give up. You are almost there! give up：放棄
對。你做得很好！	That's right. You are doing great!
不要放開媽媽的手。	Don't let go of Mommy's hands. let go of：放開
小心。你可能會摔倒。	Be careful. You might fall down.
喔，你摔倒了。	Oops, you fell down.
不痛嗎？你還好嗎？	Doesn't it hurt? Are you okay?
不要哭。沒事的。我們再試一次。	Don't cry. It's all right. We'll try one more time.
現在你站起來了！	Now you are standing up!

ch37-13.mp3

餵副食品

甜心，該吃你的飯飯了。	It's time for your meal, Sweetie.
你一定很餓了。我們現在就來吃吧。	You must be hungry. Let's eat now.
我們今天要吃什麼呢？	What will we have to eat today?

這是很美味的蔬菜粥。	It is very delicious vegetable porridge. • porridge 粥
嗯，聞起來很棒，對吧？	Hmm. It smells nice, right?
看！顏色很漂亮吧？	Look! Isn't the color so pretty?
說「啊」。很好吃，不是嗎？	Say "Ah." Delicious, isn't it?
寶貝，好好享受你的飯飯。	Enjoy your meal, Honey.
在你吞下去之前，不要忘記咬一咬。	Don't forget to chew before you swallow. • chew 咀嚼 • swallow 吞下
哇，你能咀嚼得很好。	Wow, you can chew really well.
你流出一些了。	You spilled some. • spill 流出
你滿臉都是食物。我幫你擦掉。	You got food all over your face. Let me wipe it off for you. • wipe off 擦掉
不，不！不要吃掉在地上的食物。	No, no! Don't eat food that has fallen on the floor.
來，吐出來。	Come on. Spit it out.
你要不要多吃一口？	Why don't you have one more bite? • bite 一口
你想再多吃一些嗎？	You want some more?
你不想再吃了嗎？現在你覺得飽了嗎？	You don't want to eat anymore? Are you full now?
你流掉的食物比你吃的食物還要多。	You've spilled more food than you've actually eaten.
我可愛的寶貝吃得很好。	My lovely baby is such a good eater!
看起來你已經吃夠了。	It seems like you've eaten enough.

Chapter 38

一天一天地長大（13~36個月）

Sweetie, let's try walking now.
甜心，我們現在試著走路。

Look, Daddy! Peter is walking!
爹地！你看，彼得在走路！

ch38-01.mp3

學走路

好，甜心，我們現在試著走路。	Okay, Sweetie, let's try walking now.
抓住媽媽的手。	Hold Mommy's hands.
好，現在跨出第一步。	Okay, now take one step.
一腳，再一腳。	Now one foot. Now the other.
好！你真的做得很好！	Good! You are doing really well!

現在，媽媽要放開你的手了。 Now Mommy will let go of your hands.
放開～

你覺得你可以自己走嗎？ Do you think you can walk by yourself?

摔倒也沒關係。 It's okay to fall down.

媽咪會抓住你的。 Mommy will hold you.

你能一直走到媽媽這邊嗎？ Can you walk all the way up to Mommy?
一直　到～

慢一點！慢慢來！ Easy! Easy does it.

哎呀，你摔倒了。 Oops, you fell down.

不要哭。沒關係。我們可以再試一次。 Don't cry. It's all right. We can try one more time.

只要你再多練習一點，你就會走得很好。 You will walk very well if you practice a little bit more.

今天我們就到這裡結束吧。 Let's stop here for today.

耶！我的憫所終於走路了！ Yay! My Minsuo is finally walking!

ch38-02.mp3

排便訓練

你想要尿尿／便便嗎？ Do you want to pee / poop?
• pee 尿尿　• poop 排便（= poo）

你想要去廁所嗎？ Do you want to go to the bathroom?

你想要尿尿嗎？ Don't you feel like peeing? • feel like -ing 想要～

該跟媽媽去尿尿了。 It's time to go pee with Mom.

拉下你的內褲，坐到馬桶上。 Pull down your underpants and sit on the potty. • underpants 內褲　• potty 幼兒用馬桶

因為你是男生，所以你要站著尿尿。	Since you are a boy, you have to stand when you pee.
你尿在褲子上了嗎？	**Did you pee on your pants?**
你有需要那樣急嗎？	Did you need to go that badly?
你不應該忍著。你應該去上馬桶。	**You should not hold it. You should go to the potty.** ・hold 忍
如果你到處尿的話，媽媽會很辛苦的。	If you pee anywhere, Mom will have a very hard time.
沒關係。下次你會做得更好。	**It's all right. You will do better next time.**
當你想尿尿時，叫我一下。	When you feel like peeing, just call me.
你尿在馬桶內了。非常好！	**You peed in the potty. Very good!**
你從現在開始一定要在這個馬桶裡便便。	You'll have to poop in this potty from now on. 從現在開始
便便時必須坐在這裡便便。	**You have to sit here when you poo.**
你好了嗎？	Are you finished?
我來把它擦掉。把你的屁屁轉向媽咪。	**Let me wipe it off. Turn your butt toward Mommy.** ・butt 屁股
先穿上你的內褲後，再穿上你的褲子。	Pull up (向上拉) your underwear first. Then, pull up your pants. ・underwear 內衣
好！你真的做得很好。	**Good! You did really well.**
甜心，你戒掉尿布了。	You're done with diapers, Sweetie!
不用再使用尿布了。	**No more diapers anymore.**

ch38-03.mp3

戒掉奶瓶

從現在開始，你一定要吃飯來代替喝奶。 From now on, you have to eat meals instead of drinking milk. ·meal 吃飯，一餐

哭也沒有用。 Crying won't do anything.

奶瓶是給躺在床上的嬰兒用的。 Bottles are for babies lying in bed.

媽咪已經把所有的奶瓶都丟掉了。 Mommy already got rid of all the baby bottles. 去除～，消除～

因為你是個大男孩了，奶瓶都不見囉。 The bottles are all gone since you're a big boy. ·be gone 消失，沒有 ·since 因為

我們現在跟奶瓶說再見吧。 Let's say bye to the baby bottles now.

我們用杯子喝牛奶吧。 Let's drink milk from a cup.

這真的是個很漂亮的杯子。 This is a really pretty cup.

我會把牛奶倒入有吸管的杯子內。 I will pour the milk into a cup with a straw. ·pour 倒入

試著像媽媽一樣喝牛奶。 Try drinking milk like Mom.

你必須吃飯才能長大。 You need meals to grow.

我給你買了盤子和湯匙。 I bought a plate and a spoon for you.

你想在這放些美味的食物嗎？ Do you want some delicious food here?

我的寶貝跟爸爸媽媽一樣用湯匙耶。 My baby uses a spoon like Mom and Dad.

ch38-04.mp3

舔手指頭的習慣

不，不。你不應該把手指頭放進嘴巴裡。 No, no. You should not put your finger into your mouth.

現在把手指頭拿出來。	Take out your finger now.
手指頭上有很多髒東西。	There's a lot of dirt on your finger. • dirt 灰塵，汙物
如果你舔手指頭的話，你會肚子痛的。	If you lick it, your tummy will hurt. • lick 舔
你的手指頭也會變醜。	Your finger will get ugly, too.
看看你在做什麼。	Look at what you are doing.
你又把手指頭放進口中了。	Your finger is in your mouth again.
那是好吃的東西嗎？	Does it even taste good?
現在你滿手都是口水。	Your hand is now all covered with your saliva. • saliva 口水
媽咪幫你擦掉。	Mommy will wipe it off for you.
我不知道怎麼做才能讓你不吸手指頭。	I don't know how to (～的方法) stop you from sucking your fingers.
媽咪真的希望你不要再吸手指頭了。	Mommy really wants you to stop sucking your fingers.

ch38-05.mp3

帶嬰兒出門

● 嬰兒推車

現在，我們要坐嬰兒推車了。	Let's get into the stroller now.
把你的腿穿過這裡。	Put your legs through here. • through 穿過
怎麼樣？舒服嗎？	How is it? Is it comfortable?
我們也把遮陽罩戴上。	Let's put on the sunshade, too.

你一定要繫上安全帶。 You have to fasten the seatbelt / safety belt. • fasten 繫上 • seatbelt 安全帶

這安全帶太鬆／緊了。 The belt is too loose / tight.

嗚嗚。我們走吧！ Vroom, vroom. Here we go!

抓緊手把。 Hold on tightly to the handle.

這邊有點不平，一定要抓緊。 It will rattle, so hold on tightly. • rattle 咯咯作響

把你的身體往後靠。 Lean your body backwards. • backwards 向後

● 嬰兒安全坐椅

從現在起，這裡就是你的座位。 This is your seat from now on.

甜心，我來幫你坐進嬰兒座椅。 Sweetie, let me help you to sit in the car seat.

怎麼了？你不想坐那裡嗎？ Why? Don't you want to sit there?

把你的背緊緊靠在椅背上。 Place your back all the way to the backrest. • backrest 椅背

你覺得那裡像在家一樣嗎？ Do you feel at home there?

坐在嬰兒座椅內才安全。 It is safe to sit in the car seat.

你從嬰兒座椅可以更容易地看到窗外。 You can look out the window better from the car seat.

好，我們出發！ Okay, we are going!

各位，請讓路！ Everyone, get out of the way!

你又在嬰兒座椅上鬧脾氣了。 You are getting cranky again in the car seat. • cranky 脾氣壞的

再忍一下。我們快到了。

Hold on for a second. We are almost there.

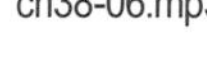

拒絕給點心

你又想要點心了嗎？
Do you want a snack again?

都沒有了。你已經都吃完了。
They are all gone. You already ate them up.

這是今天最後的點心了。
This is the last snack of the day.

你再怎樣找點心也是沒用的。
Your searching for snacks won't help.
• search 尋找

不在那裡。你找不到的。
It's not there. You won't find it.

你在哪裡都找不到的。
You can't find it anywhere.

我說過不能再吃，知道嗎？
I said no more. Okay?

先吃你的飯。
Eat your meal first.

你應該先吃飯，才能吃點心。
You should eat a snack after your meal.

一旦你吃完飯，我會給你一些。
Once you are done with the meal, I will give you something.

如果你先吃點心的話，會沒有胃口吃飯的。
If you eat a snack first, you will lose your appetite for the meal.
• appetite 食慾

如果你還持續哭鬧，我就不告訴你糖果在哪裡。
If you keep on whining, I won't tell you where the candy is.
• whine 哭喊

寶貝，哭是沒用的。
It's no use crying, Honey.
• It's no use -ing 做～沒用

我們已經吃完點心了。等到明天吧。	We've eaten all the snacks already. Let's wait till tomorrow.

性別的疑惑

ch38-07.mp3

	為什麼只有女生穿裙子？	Why do only girls wear skirts?
	男生跟女生是不一樣的。	Men and women are different.
	媽，為什麼你的胸部很大？	Mom, why are your breasts big?
	這是因為我是女生。	It's because I'm a woman.
	媽媽的乳房內有牛奶吧？	Is there milk inside your breasts?
	嗯，以前有餵你的母乳。	Yes. There used to be milk to feed you. used to：過去曾～
	女生坐著尿尿，因為我們沒有小雞雞。	Women pee sitting down because we don't have peanuts. • peanut〈幼兒用語〉小雞雞
	媽，為什麼我有小雞雞？	Mom, why do I have a peanut?
	為什麼女生沒有呢？	Why doesn't a girl have one?

「小雞雞」的各種稱呼

男人的性器官是 penis，小孩子的則會說 willie。在說小孩子的性器官時，也有人很可愛地稱之為 peanut。不過，用 peanut 來表達的話，難免會有些俗氣，因此也有人直接稱之為 penis。

男生跟女生的身體不一樣。	Men and women have different bodies.
男生有小雞雞，女生則沒有。	Men have willies while women don't have them. ・willie〈幼兒用語〉小雞雞
男生塊頭大，相反地女生的則小。	Men are big while women are small. ・while 相反地～

我想變得跟爸比一樣強壯。	I want to be strong like my dad.

ch38-08.mp3

去寶寶課程

今天我們要去媽咪寶寶課。	Today we are going to Mommy and Baby Class.
來去這間百貨公司的寶寶課程。	Let's go to the baby class in the department store.
在寶寶課之後去餐廳吧。	Let's go to a restaurant after the baby class.
你喜歡這裡的遊戲時間嗎？	Do you like the play time here?
你可以想怎麼跑就怎麼跑。	You can run as much as you want.

寶寶課程

寶寶課程的英文是 preschool age program，也可以稱為 mom and baby classes 或是 toddler classes。

我喜歡這個社區中心的冬季課程。	I love the winter programs in the community center. ・community center 社區中心
看著你的老師。	Look at your teacher.
跟我一起做。	Do it with me.
你好像非常喜歡寶寶課程。	You seem to enjoy the baby class a lot.
你從課程回來時很累嗎？	Are you tired when you come back from the class?

Chapter 39

有弟弟妹妹了

I wish he were not here!
真希望他不在這裡就好了！

You are a big sister. Let him have it.
妳是姊姊，讓他玩玩具。

ch39-01.mp3

疼弟弟妹妹的時候

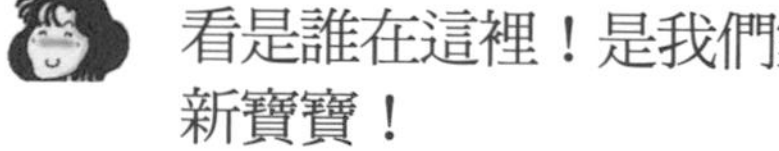

看是誰在這裡！是我們家的新寶寶！

Look at who's here! This is our new baby!

哇，現在我是大姐姐了！

Wow, I'm a big sister now!

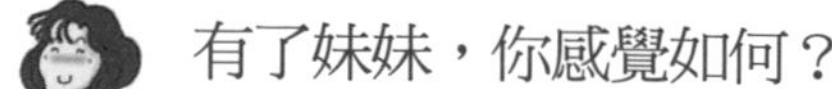

有了妹妹，你感覺如何？

How do you feel about having a baby sister?

• How do you feel about -ing 對～感覺如何？

我真的很高興有她。 I'm really happy to have her.

她好可愛！ She is so cute!

她的手好小好可愛。 Her hands are so small and cute.

她長得比我好看。 She is better looking than me.

當她這樣笑的時候，最好看了。 She looks the best when she smiles like this.

她是世界上最可愛的寶寶！ She is the cutest baby in the world!

你也很可愛！ You are very cute, too!

他比民肅的弟弟還可愛。 He is cuter than Minsu's brother.

因為他太可愛，我很想捏他！ I want to pinch him because he is so adorable! ・pinch 捏 ・adorable 可愛的

她看起來像漂亮的娃娃。 She looks like a pretty doll.

我很高興你很愛你弟弟。 I'm so glad you love your brother so much.

你的弟弟就跟你愛他一樣愛你。 Your brother likes you just as much as you like him.

ch39-02.mp3

討厭弟弟妹妹的時候

我討厭我弟弟。 I don't like my brother.

你為什麼不喜歡他？ Why do you not like him?

他太會煩我了。 He bothers me too much.

他是個搗蛋鬼。 He is a troublemaker. ・troublemaker 搗蛋鬼

他太調皮了。	He is too mischievous. ・mischievous 調皮的
他總是把我的事情弄得很糟。	He keeps messing up my work. (弄糟)
他舔我的玩具。真讓人討厭！	He licks my toys. It's gross! ・gross 讓人討厭的
我希望你把他送去別人家裡。	I want you to give him away to another family.
我希望他不在了。	I wish that he was gone.
你不應該那樣說。	You should not say that.
如果你弟弟聽到的話，他會很傷心的。	Your brother will be sad if he hears that.
你應該愛你的弟弟。	You should love your brother.
你不知道謹宿有多愛你。	You do not know how much Jinsu loves you.
他只是一直大聲地哭鬧。	He just keeps crying very loudly.
嗯，當你是個嬰兒時，你也跟他一樣。	Well, you were just like him when you were a baby.
我告訴他不可以碰我的東西，但是他就是不聽。	I tell him to stop touching my things, but he does not listen.
好，那麼我把他送走。	Okay, then I'm going to give him away.
想一想，他可能會很傷心。	Come to think of it, he might be very sad. (想一想～)
我會跟寶寶好好相處的。	I'll get along well with the baby. (和睦相處)

ch39-03.mp3

吃醋的時候

為什麼媽媽只喜歡憫所呢？ Why do you like only Minsuo?

那是什麼意思？我愛你跟愛他一樣多。 What do you mean? I love you just as much as I love him.

你和你弟弟對我來說都很重要。 You and your brother are both important to me.

但是你只抱憫所。 But you only hold Minsuo.

嗯，憫所是個嬰兒。所以我才會經常抱他。 Well, Minsuo is a baby. That's why I'm holding him often.

我也想要你抱我。 I want you to hold me, too.

請跟餵寶寶一樣餵我。 Please feed me like you feed the baby.

給我背背。我腳痛。 Give me a piggy-back ride. My legs hurt.

讓我去你的床上跟你一起睡。 Let me sleep with you in your bed.

嗯，當你是個嬰兒時，媽媽也經常抱你。 Well, I held you a lot when you were a baby.

過來，我給你抱抱。 Come here, and I'll give you a hug.

• give a hug 擁抱

你不知道媽咪有多麼愛你。 You don't know how much Mommy loves you.

但是你只稱讚憫所。 But you only praise Minsuo. • praise 稱讚

還有，你總是責罵我。 And you always scold me.

因為你做錯事情，我才責罵你。 I scolded you because you did something wrong.

憫所還只是個嬰兒。
他還什麼都不知道。

Minsuo is only a baby. He still does not know anything.

所以，你認為媽媽只愛憫所嗎？

So you think that Mommy only loves Minsuo?

那就是你為什麼傷心。

That's why you were sad.

我幫他更多，因為他是個嬰兒。

I'm just helping him more because he is a baby.

你們兩個對媽媽來說都很重要。

Both of you mean a lot to Mommy. / You are both so precious to me.

• precious 珍貴的

我對你們兩個的愛是一樣的。

I love you both the same.

你是神給我們的第一個禮物。

You are the first present from God to us.

在這個世界上，我比任何人都還愛你。

I love you more than anyone else in the whole world.

Chapter 40

上幼稚園

It's Sunlight kindergarten.
是「陽光幼稚園」。

Peter, what's the name of your kindergarten?
彼得，你幼稚園的名字是什麼？

ch40-01.mp3

幼稚園入學

終於，你要去上幼稚園了。	Finally, you are going to kindergarten. • kindergarten 幼稚園
我不敢相信你已經要上幼稚園了。	I can't believe that you are already in kindergarten.
這個書包不是很漂亮嗎？	Doesn't this book bag look nice?
你去學校時，就可以背著這個書包。	You will carry this backpack when you go to school.

媽咪，我不想要去。

Mommy, I don't want to go.

為什麼不去？幼稚園是個那麼好玩的地方。

Why not? Kindergarten is such a fun place.

如果你去那裡，你就會有很好的老師和許多朋友。

If you go there, you will have a great teacher and a lot of friends.

媽媽，我在學校要做什麼？

Mom, what do I do at school?

嗯，你會跟朋友一起玩，一起學習。

Well, you play and study with your friends.

那裡有很大的遊樂場。

There is a big playground there.

你會看到很多家裡沒有的玩具和遊戲。

You'll see many toys and games that you don't have at home.

學校還會每天提供好吃的午餐。

The school will serve a wonderful lunch every day. ‧serve lunch 提供午餐

這裡就是你要去的幼稚園。

This is the kindergarten that you will be going to.

我很高興有了老師和新朋友。

I'm so glad to have a teacher and new friends.

美國的幼稚園

幼稚園雖然叫做 kindergarten，其實是以滿 5 歲為對象的公立學校。更小的小孩子去的教育場所是 preschool，那些都是家庭式的教育。進 kindergarten 之前沒有另外的入學典禮，只是花一週的時間，每天把 4-5 名的學生召集在一起，進行一天的學校生活訓練。 一週之後，所有的學生就正式開始上學。preschool 則是只要有空缺，隨時都可以入學。

ch40-02.mp3

班級／老師的分配

你是黃色班。 You are in the class called Yellow.

黃色班有 12 名學生。 There are 12 students in Class Yellow.

這是黃色班的教室。 This is the classroom for Yellow.

但是我不喜歡黃色。我可以去粉紅色班嗎？ But I don't like yellow. Can I be in Class Pink?

我想轉去粉紅色班。 I want to transfer to Class Pink.

• transfer 移動，轉動

我想跟葉久同班。 I want to be in the same class with Yejiu.

我很高興葉久在我們班。 I'm glad Yejiu is in our class.

嗯，粉紅色班是七歲上的喔。 Well, Class Pink is for 7 year olds.

你是六歲，六歲都要去黃色班。 You are six, and six year olds go to Class Yellow.

我的老師是誰？ Who is my teacher?

黃色班的老師是吳老師。 Miss Wu is the teacher of Class Yellow.

老師的稱呼

在西方國家，不會對老師稱 teacher，而是以 Ms. Kay, Mr. Brown 這樣的方式稱呼。

哇，我的老師真漂亮。 Wow, my teacher is really pretty.

我最喜歡我的老師了。 I like my teacher the most.

老師看起來很可怕／嚴格。 The teacher looks scary / strict.

我們應該去跟老師打招呼吧？ Shall we go and say hello to your teacher?

你在學校的時候，你的老師就像是你的媽媽。 Your teacher is like your mother when you are at school.

ch40-03.mp3

伙食

媽，今天的午餐是什麼？ Mom, what's for lunch today?

老師給了我學校午餐的菜單。 The teacher gave me the menu for the school lunch.

嗯，我不知道。但是，一定跟平常一樣好吃。 Well, I don't know, but it must be good as usual.

as usual 跟平常一樣

嗯，我想我必須要看一下菜單。 Well, I guess I have to take a look at the menu.

take a look at 看一下～

看起來你會有很多好吃的食物。 It seems like you will have a lot of delicious food.

我很高興你在學校不挑食。 I'm glad you're not picky about food at school. ‧picky 挑剔的

因為今天有派對，所以會提供特別的午餐。 A special lunch will be served because there is a party today.

be served 被提供

耶！我也會吃到炸雞和蛋糕！ Yay! I will eat chicken and cakes, too!

你今天的午餐吃了什麼？ What did you have for lunch today?

午餐好吃嗎？	Was your lunch delicious?
我吃了我最喜歡的炸馬鈴薯。	**I had my favorite food—fried potatoes.**
真的很好吃。	It was really good.
今天的麵很糟糕。	**The noodles were terrible today.** • noodle 麵
你吃了很多泡菜嗎？	Did you eat a lot of kimchi?
你一點都不剩地吃完了嗎？	**Did you eat everything without leaving anything left over?** • leave 剩
我太飽了，剩了一些在盤子內。	I left some food on my plate because I was too full.
試著把食物都吃光， 那樣你才會更健康。	**Try to finish all of your food so that you can be healthier.**
如果我沒有吃完午餐， 老師會責備我。	My teacher will scold me if I don't finish my lunch.

ch40-04.mp3

收集貼紙

今天老師給我一張貼紙。	**The teacher gave me a sticker today.**
 你要怎麼做才能得到一張 嘉獎貼紙呢？	How can you receive a praise sticker? • receive 得到 • praise 稱讚
 每當我們做了好事，她就會 給一張。	**She gives one whenever we do something nice / good.** • whenever 每當～的時候
當你正確地說出答案時， 就可以得到一張。	You can get one when you answer a question correctly.
如果你遵守規則，你可以	**If you follow the rules, you can get**

得到貼紙。

stickers.

如果你幫助生病的朋友，
你可以得到三張貼紙。

If you help a friend who is sick, you can get three stickers.

哇，那真的是漂亮的貼紙。

Wow, that is a really pretty sticker!

我們把它貼在貼紙簿上吧。

Let's stick it in the sticker book. • stick 貼

看所有我得到的貼紙。

Look at all the stickers I've got!

哇，你已經收集了很多貼紙！

Wow, you have collected a lot of stickers!
• collect 收集

收集最多貼紙的人可以得到獎賞。

The person with the most stickers will be rewarded. • reward 獎賞，獎勵

如果我收集 20 張貼紙，
老師會給我一個大禮物。

If I collect 20 stickers, the teacher will give me a big present.

喔，真的嗎？那麼，你一定要努力收集。

Oh, really? Then you should try hard to get the stickers.

那麼，誰收集的貼紙最多？

So, who has the most stickers?

是吉娜。

Jina does.

我到現在只收集了 10 張貼紙。

I've got only 10 stickers so far.

當你收集了 100 張貼紙，
我會給你很棒的禮物。

When you collect 100 stickers, I'll give you a good present.

如果你一天讀三本書，
我會給你五張貼紙。

If you read 3 books a day, I'll give you 5 stickers.

ch40-05.mp3

放假／升級

	你的假期從今天開始！	Your vacation begins today!
	媽，放假是什麼？	Mom, what is a vacation?
	放假的意思是不用去上學。	Vacation means no school.
	不用早起床！太好了！	No waking up early! Hooray!
	那麼我不想放假。我想去幼稚園。	I don't want vacation then. I want to go to kindergarten.
	假期太長了。	The vacation is too long.
	我想快點回去幼稚園。	I can't wait to go back to kindergarten.
	媽咪，我不喜歡放假。	I don't like vacation, Mommy.
	我想我的老師和朋友。	I miss my teacher and my friends.
	距離我回去學校，還有幾天呢？	How many days are left until I go back to school? ・left 剩餘
	你還要等十天。	You have to wait for ten more days.
	放假結束後，我不要回幼稚園了。	I won't go back to kindergarten after the vacation.
	我喜歡跟媽媽待在家裡。	I like staying home with you.
	放假後，你將會去高年級的班。	You'll go to the older kids' class after vacation.
	那麼，我很快就會在粉紅色班。	Well, then I'll be in Class Pink soon.
	你的教室和老師也都會換喔。	Your classroom and teacher will change, too.

我的同學呢？

What about my classmates?

會有些舊面孔，不過，
也會有些新同學。

There will be some old faces, but there will also be some new students.

我不想跟慖所不同班。

I don't want to be in a different class than Minsuo's.

ch40-06.mp3

才藝表演／畢業典禮

我們下週會有一個才藝表演。

We are going to have a talent show next week.

我們班會表演木偶舞蹈。

Our class will do a puppet dance.
• puppet 木偶

我們班會表演戲劇。

Our class will do a play.

我們班會表演合唱。

Our class will form a choir. /
Our class will sing as a choir at the show.
• choir 合唱

明天是你的畢業典禮。

Tomorrow is your graduation day.
• graduation 畢業

我不敢相信你已經要畢業了！

I can't believe that you are already graduating! • graduate 畢業

你將要變成一個小學生了。

You will become an elementary school student.

你在學校真的表現得很好。甜心，我為你感到驕傲。

You've been really good at school. I'm so proud of you, Sweetie.

我不想要畢業。

I don't want to graduate.

我想繼續上幼稚園。

I want to keep going to kindergarten.

如果我畢業的話，還能見到我的老師嗎？	Will I be able to see my teacher if I graduate?
嗯，只要你想，任何時候都可以去拜訪。	Well, you can always visit when you want to.
畢業典禮時，你要乖乖坐好。	Sit still during the graduation ceremony.
媽媽會站在教室後面。	Mom will be standing at the back of the classroom.
恭喜你！	Congratulations!
 我得到了模範獎。	I got a good behavior award. ‧award 獎
 我們跟你的老師、朋友們一起照相吧。	Let's take some pictures with your friends and teacher.
我們去跟老師說謝謝。	Let's go and say thank you to your teacher.
 我會非常想念我的朋友和老師。	I will miss my friends and teacher so much.
 這是媽咪給你的畢業禮物。	This is your graduation gift from Mommy.
畢業照拍得很好看。	The graduation photos came out really well.

Chapter 41

當上小學生

Now you are going to elementary school.
現在你要上小學了。

Yeah, I'm not a baby anymore.
耶，我已經不再是小寶寶了。

ch41-01.mp3

入學／去上學

我不敢相信你已經是個學生了！	I can't believe that you're a student already!
你從現在開始要去上小學了。	You'll go to an elementary school from now on.
快一點。我們要去參加開學典禮。	Hurry up. We need to go to the opening ceremony.

恭喜你開始上小學！

Congratulations for starting elementary school!

現在你是大哥哥／大姐姐，再也不是小孩子了。

Now you're a big boy / girl and not a baby anymore.

要去學校了，你會興奮嗎？

Are you excited about going to school?

嗯，我很興奮，但是我也有點害怕。

Well, I'm excited, but I'm kind of scared, too. 有一點

兒子你要去第幾班？

What class should my son go to?

我是在一年四班。

I'm in Class 4 in the 1st grade.

在教室內，你一定要穿室內鞋。

You have to wear indoor shoes in the classroom. •indoor 室內的

把你的鞋袋放在鞋架上。

Put your shoe bag on the shoe shelf.

媽媽會帶你去學校。

Mommy will take you to school.

我們早上 8:30 之前要到學校。

We have to be at school by 8:30 AM.

不過，老師說我們要在早上 8:30 的前 10 分到。

But the teacher said that we have to be there by 10 minutes before 8:30 AM.

我的書包很重，因為我們今天有很多課。

My bag is very heavy because we have a lot of classes today.

你可以把你的教科書放在置物櫃裡。

You can leave your textbooks in your cubby. •cubby（沒有上鎖，類似書架的）置物櫃

如果都是在學校使用的物品，就放進你的置物櫃內。

Put the things inside your locker if you always use them at school. •locker 置物櫃

我們班的午餐時間是 12 點。

Lunchtime for our class is 12 o'clock.

媽，你洗了我的教室用鞋嗎？

Mom, did you wash my classroom shoes?

你在學校要仔細聽老師的話。	Listen carefully to the teacher at school.
你需要好好聽老師的話。	You need to listen carefully to your teacher.
跟你的朋友們好好相處。	Get along well with your friends.
祝你有個美好一天！	Have a good day!
今天學校幾點放學？	At what time will your school be over today? ・over 結束
我會在學校正門口等你。	I'll be waiting for you at the school gate.

ch41-02.mp3

自我介紹

我來自我介紹一下。	Let me introduce myself. ・introduce 介紹
我的名字是是季吉娜。	My name is Jina Ji.
我八歲。	I'm 8 years old.
我住在 ABC 公寓。	I live in ABC Apartment.
我家有四個人：爸爸、媽媽、弟弟和我。	There are four people in my family: my dad, mom, my younger brother, and me.
我身高有 130 公分，體重是 25 公斤。	My height is 130cm, and my weight is 25kg.
我最喜歡的食物是巧克力。	My favorite food is chocolate.
我非常喜歡閱讀。	I like reading books very much.
我養了一隻狗當寵物。	I have a pet dog. ・pet 寵物

我是李民肅。我是一年三班的學生。	I'm Minsu Li. I'm in the first grade in class 3.

因為我跑很快，所以我的綽號是飛毛腿。	My nickname is Lightfoot because I'm a fast runner. •nickname 綽號
雖然我不太擅長運動，但是我很喜歡。	I like sports although I'm not really good at them. •be good at 擅長～
我希望跟大家都成為好朋友。	I want to be good friends with all of you.
我長大後，想當一個足球選手。	I want to be a soccer player when I grow up.
我的夢想是長大後當一名醫生。	My dream is to be a doctor when I grow up.
我想成為科學家，創造出世界上最棒的機器人。	I want to be a scientist and create the best robot in the world.
我會努力學習來成為偉大的人。	I will study hard to be a great person.

ch41-03.mp3

換座位

我們一週會換一次座位。	We change seats once a week.
我們用抽籤來決定誰跟誰坐在一起。	Let's decide on seatmates by drawing lots. •lot 抽籤

敏基，這次你跟我坐同桌。	Minji, you are my seatmate this time.
你又跟我坐同桌了。	You are my seatmate again.
我很高興成為你的同桌伙伴！	I'm really happy to be your seatmate!
我們很合得來。	We are made for each other! / We are just meant to be!
老師，請幫我們換座位。	Sir, please change our seats.

我們可以待在原位嗎？
我們不想換座位。

Can we stay in our seats? We don't want to change seats.

誰是你的同桌伙伴？

Who is your seatmate?

你喜歡跟女生同桌，還是跟男生同桌？

Would you prefer a girl seatmate or a boy seatmate? ・prefer 較喜歡

我都喜歡。

I like both.

我想跟憫所坐在一起。

I want to sit with Minsuo.

這次你的座位在哪？

Where is your seat this time?

我坐在第一排的第三個位置。

I'm sitting in the 3rd row of the first column. ・row 列，橫排 ・column 行，直排

★ 英語的習慣為先橫再直。

你喜歡你的同桌同學嗎？

Do you like your seatmate?

嗯，沒有很喜歡。

Well, not really.

我還不知道。

I don't know yet.

老師，我想坐到前面，
因為我看不太清楚。

Sir, I want to sit at the front because I cannot see clearly. (at the front：前面)

因為你很高，所以你必須坐在後面。

You need to sit in the back because you are very tall. (in the back：後面)

ch41-04.mp3

課程

你今天有多少堂課？

How many classes do you have today?

我今天有五堂課。

I have five classes today.

今天學校提早放學了。

School ends early today.

今天學校的時間縮短了。
The school hours are shortened today.
• shortened 縮短，變短

你最喜歡的課程是什麼？
What is your favorite class / subject?

我最喜歡體育課。
I like PE class the most.

每堂課有多久？
How long does each class last? • last 持續

有 40 分鐘。
It lasts for 40 minutes.

休息時間的時候，你做什麼？
What do you do during your break time?
休息時間

休息時間的時候，我跟朋友們玩卡片遊戲。
I play picture card games with my friends during recess. • recess 休息時間

今天你在學校學了什麼？
What did you learn at school today?

老師跟我們講了一個非常有趣的故事。
The teacher told us a very funny story.

老師問了什麼問題？
What did your teacher ask?

你大聲地回答老師的問題了嗎？
Did you answer the question with a loud voice?

你今天好好上課了嗎？
Did you participate in class today?
• participate 參加

今天你做了很棒的報告嗎？
Did you make a good presentation today? • presentation 報告；演講

上課的時候，我不斷舉手，但是都沒有機會回答。
I constantly raised my hand during the class, but I didn't get a chance to answer.
• constantly 不斷地

今天所有的課都是我最喜歡的。
All of today's classes are my favorite ones.

今天的課一點都不有趣。
Today's class was not fun at all.

我在學校覺得很累。	I was very tired at school.
上課時，我一直打瞌睡。	I kept on falling asleep during my classes.
我們在實驗室／音樂教室／美術教室上課。	We had a class in the lab / music room / art room.

ch41-05.mp3

作業／準備物品／提醒單

	你何不先完成你的家庭作業呢？	Why don't you finish your homework first?
	我們今天沒有家庭作業。	We don't have any homework today.
	我想不起來今天的作業。	I can't remember today's homework.
	去看一下你的作業提醒單。	Check your homework reminders.
	到習題本的第 23 頁，我都必須完成。	I have to finish up to page 23 in my workbook. 完成
	你的作業都做好了嗎？	Are you done with your homework?
	我還在做。	I'm still working on it.
	我還沒有做完。	I'm not done yet.
	我把作業簿放在學校了。	I left my assignment notebook at school.
	你明天的課程需要什麼？	What do you need for tomorrow's class?
	水彩、調色盤還有畫筆。	Watercolors, a palette, and brushes.
	媽，我需要買些上課用的材料。	Mom, I need to buy some materials for my class. ‧material 材料，原料

我會去文具店買些學校用品。	I will go to the stationery store to buy some school supplies. 學校用品
不要忘記帶明天上課要用的材料。	Don't forget to bring the materials for tomorrow's class!
仔細看有沒有任何漏掉的。	Carefully see if there is anything missing. 看是不是～ • missing 缺掉的
打電話給你的朋友，問他明天要帶什麼去學校。	Call your friend to ask him about what you need to bring tomorrow.

媽，今天有兩張通知單。	Mom, there are two handouts today. • handout 傳單，通知單
媽，請讀學校的通知信。	Mom, read the announcement letter from the school. • announcement 通知，公告
媽媽，可以請你在我的學校計畫簿上簽名嗎？	Mom, can you please sign my school planner?

好，把你的學校計畫簿拿來。	Okay, bring me your school planner then.
當你在計畫簿上寫東西的時候，要寫得更整齊一點。	Write more neatly when you write on your agenda. • neatly 整齊地

提醒單

在英文系國家中，是沒有「提醒單」這個概念的。小學高年級的老師會讓學生在 school planner 或 agenda 中記下每天要做的事情，還有作業等注意事項。父母也藉此知道孩子的學校生活。同時，老師也會透過寄家庭通知信給父母親來通知主要作業和準備物品。

ch41-06.mp3

做作業

	你今天有任何作業嗎？	Do you have any homework today?
	有。我要用一些日常用語做一個口頭報告。	Yes. I have to do an oral report on some daily sentences.
	這個作業明天就要交。	The homework is due tomorrow.
	跟我一起做功課吧。	Do your homework together with me.
	那麼，我來幫你。	I'll help you then.
	試著自己做功課看看。	Try to do your homework by yourself.
	把你的語言筆記本拿來練習。	Bring your language notebook to practice it.
	你還在做作業嗎？	Are you still working on your homework?
	媽，這作業對我來說太難了。	Mom, the homework is too hard for me.
	今天我有太多的功課了。	I've got too much homework today.
	看你把家庭作業做得多好！	Look at how well you do your homework!
	我喜歡我的作業。這很有趣！	I like my homework. It's so fun!
	老師跟我們說不要忘記作業。	My teacher told us not to forget about the homework.
	如果我做功課的話，老師會給我貼紙。	If I do my homework, my teacher will give me a sticker.
	我在星期四要把作業帶去。	I have to bring my homework on Thursdays.

我在學校已經做得夠多了。為什麼我還要在家做呢？

I've worked enough at school. Why should I do work at home?

你的作業可以幫助你複習學過的東西。

Your homework helps you review what you learned. ・review 複習

沒有作業，你可能會忘記學過的東西。

Without homework, you could forget what you learned.

ch41-07.mp3

遲到／早退／缺席

你上學要遲到了！

You will be late for school!

我再也不要上學遲到了。

I will never be late for school again.

我想我可能上學會遲到。你能載我去嗎？

I think I might be late for school. Can you give me a ride? ・give a ride 開車送～

如果你再遲到一次的話，你會挨罵的。

If you're late one more time, you will be in trouble. 挨罵

呼，我沒有遲到地到學校了！

Phew, I made it without being late! 及時趕到

因為我不舒服，我想我今天不能去學校了。

I don't think I can go to school today because I'm sick.

我想你今天就不要去上學了。

I think you should just skip school today.
・skip 不出席

在家休息吧。

Take a rest at home.

我打電話給你的老師，跟她說你會缺席。

Let me call your teacher and tell her you'll miss school. 學校缺席

嗯，試著儘可能不要缺課。

Well, try not to miss school as much as possible. ・as 形容詞 as possible 儘可能

如果待在學校覺得很不舒服的話，跟你的老師報告。 | If it's too hard for you to stay in school, just tell your teacher.

老師，我今天可以早點回家嗎？ | Can I go home early today, Sir?

你今天可以早退。在家裡好好休息吧。 | You can leave early today. Just stay home and take a rest.

吉娜因為身體不舒服缺席了。 | Jina is absent because she is sick.

ch41-08.mp3

課後活動

下課後，你想學什麼？ | What do you want to study after school?

我想學小提琴。 | I want to learn the violin.

漢字課應該很有趣。 | The Chinese character lesson should be fun.

芭蕾課排定一週兩堂。 | The ballet lessons are scheduled for twice a week. (are scheduled 排定)

機器人課是最熱門的放學後課程。 | The robot class is the most popular after-school program.

這是課後課程的介紹小冊。 | Here's the brochure for the after-school lessons. • brochure 小冊子

根據這張課程表，美術課和鋼琴課的時間重疊了。 | The art lesson overlaps with the piano lesson according to the schedule. • overlap 重疊

你不可能做所有你想做的，所以只能挑兩個。 | You can't do everything that you want to do, so just choose two.

你想要學摺紙嗎？ | Do you want to learn origami?

你在哪裡上小提琴課？ | Where do you take your violin lesson?

在 2 年級 3 班的教室。 It's in classroom 3 of the 2nd grade.

那些課程結束後，你要馬上回家。 You have to come home straight after those lessons. • straight 馬上

你所有的放學後課程都結束了。 All of your after-school programs are over.

ch41-09.mp3

管理零用錢

媽媽，我想要零用錢。 Mom, I want an allowance.
• allowance 零用錢

你要給我多少？ How much are you going to give me?

你想要多少？ How much do you want?

嗯，我一週給你 100 元。 Well, I will give you 100 a week.

那太少了。 That's too little.

我想那應該剛剛好。 I think that is just about right.

反正你沒有什麼地方要花錢。 You don't really have much to spend money on anyway. • anyway 反正

你要把零用錢花在什麼上面？ What are you going to spend your allowance on?

試著不要浪費錢。 Try not to waste your money. • waste 浪費

明智地用錢是很重要的。 It's important to spend money wisely.

媽，請增加我的零用錢。 Mom, please raise my allowance.
• raise 提高

增加多少？ By how much?

增加 50 元。

By 50.

我想這太多了。
我多給你 5 元。

I think it's too much. I will raise it by 5.

如果你一直要求增加的話，我就不給你。

If you keep on asking for a raise, I won't give you one.

asking for：要求～

• keep on -ing 一直

不要忘記好好保持你的支出紀錄。

Do not forget to keep a good record of the money you spend. • record 紀錄

你已經花完你所有的零用錢了嗎？

Did you already spend all of your allowance?

媽，我的零用錢很吃緊。

Mom, my allowance is too tight for me.

• tight （時間、金錢）緊的

如果我幫你做事的話，你會給我更多的零用錢嗎？

If I do some errands, will you give me a bigger allowance? • errand 差事

我會洗碗，所以你給我些零用錢。

I will wash the dishes, so give me some money for it.

我會把剩餘的零用錢存起來。

I will save my leftover allowance.

• leftover 剩餘的

Chapter 42

交到朋友了

Who's Jenny's best friend?
誰是珍妮最好的朋友？

Bill is my best friend.
比爾是我最好的朋友

ch42-01.mp3

同班同學

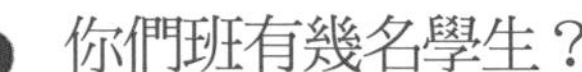

你們班有幾名學生？ How many students are in your class?

我們有 30 名。 We have thirty.

女生有幾名？ How many girls are there?

我們有 14 名女生和 16 名男生。 We have fourteen girls and sixteen boys.

我喜歡我們班所有的同學。 I like all of my classmates.

在你們班的同學中，你最喜歡誰？ | Who do you like the most among your classmates?

我最喜歡蘇娃。 | I like Suwa the most.

你知道所有同學的名字嗎？ | Do you know all of your classmates' names?

我正努力記起來。 | I'm trying to memorize them.

• memorize 記住

有一個朋友的名字跟我一樣。 | There is a friend who has the same name as me.

我們有兩個小朋友都叫敏基。 | We have two kids whose names are Minji.

我們班上有雙胞胎。 | We have twins in our class.

吉娜住在我們的公寓社區內。 | Jina lives in our apartment complex.

旻久住在我們的公寓大樓。 | Minjiu lives in our apartment building.

太好了！你們兩個早上可以一起去上學。 | Great! You can both go to school together in the morning.

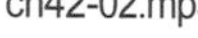

ch42-02.mp3

介紹朋友

媽媽，這是我的同學民肅。 | Mom, this is my classmate Minsu.

喔，你好。我是金宏的媽媽。 | Oh, hello. I'm Jinhong's mother.

我聽到很多有關你的事情。 | I've heard a lot about you.

叫蘇洪的同學真的很好。 | My classmate named Suhong is really nice.

我們班的哈金總是被老師責備。 | Hajin from my class always gets scolded by the teacher.

gets scolded：責備

我們班的君梭真的很聰明。 Junsuo from my class is really smart.

民浩是個非常好的學生。 Minhou is such a good student.

繼望在我們班完全是個搗蛋鬼。 Jiwong is such a troublemaker in our class.

我想跟我班上的憫所變得更親近。 I want to get closer to Minsuo from my class.
（get closer：變得更親近）

是嗎？我們何不邀請他來玩呢？ Do you? Why don't we invite him over?
（Why don't we：我們～吧（= Let's～））

我的班上有新同學。 There is a new student in my class.

喔，他叫什麼名字？ Oh, what's his name?

他從哪裡轉來的？ Where did he transfer from?
• transfer 轉學，調動

我想跟記溯更親近，但記溯只跟哈金玩。 I want to get closer to Jisu, but Jisu only plays with Hajin.

嗯，那麼，你們三個人可以一起玩。 Well, then the three of you can play together.

從明天開始，我和哈金一起去上學。 I will go to school together with Hajin from tomorrow.

蘇洪和我搭同一台公車回家。 Suhong and I ride the same bus back home.

ch42-03.mp3

朋友的問題

我跟我的朋友吵架了。 I got in a fight with my friend.
（got in a fight：打架，爭吵）

你為什麼吵架？ Why did you fight?

我們都想要同一個玩具。 We both wanted the same toy.

他搶走我的玩具。	He took my toys away. ・take away 拿走
你們應該輪流玩。	You should take turns. 輪流
我還以為你們處得很好。	I thought you two were getting along. 和睦相處
你需要學習如何一起玩。	You need to learn how to play together.
我因為朋友而感到傷心。	I'm upset because of my friend.
他一直取笑我。	He keeps making fun of me. 取笑～
他一直打我。	He keeps hitting me.
他一直說髒話	He keeps saying bad things.
他一直煩我。	He keeps annoying me. ・annoy 惹惱
你一定很難過。	You must be upset. 一定～
你不可以跟你朋友做同樣的行為。	You shouldn't act the same way as your friend.
清楚地說「不」。	Say "No," clearly.
要對朋友好。	Be nice to your friends.
試著了解你的朋友。	Try to understand your friend.
試著跟朋友好好相處。	Try to get along with your friends.
即使那樣也不要去跟老師告狀。	Don't tell on your friends to the teacher, though. 告狀
他們可能會叫你告密者。	They might call you a tattletale. ・tattletale 告密者
我想跟吉娜做朋友。	I want to make friends with Jina.
有幾個小孩欺負我。	Some kids pick on me. 欺負～
我覺得他們在霸凌我。	I feel like they are bullying me. ・bully 欺負

你需要學習怎麼保護你自己。 You need to learn how to defend yourself. •defend 防衛，保護

你們打完架後，也有可能變成更好的朋友。 You guys could become better friends after fighting.

即使是好朋友，也要保持禮貌。 There are manners to keep even among close friends. •manners 禮貌

我很高興你是個善於交際的小孩。 I am glad you're such a sociable child. •sociable 善交際的

ch42-04.mp3

集體霸凌

在你們班有人欺負你嗎？ Does anyone from your class pick on you?

季浩一直欺負我。 Jihou keeps bullying me. •bully 欺負

他怎樣欺負你？ How does he bully you?

他一直打我。 He keeps hitting me.

他一直嘲笑我。 He keeps teasing me. •tease 嘲笑

他跟我的其他朋友說我的壞話。 He says bad stuff about me to my other friends.

他用髒話對我大吼大叫。 He yells and swears at me. •yell 吼叫 •swear 罵髒話

因為他，我不想去上學了。 I don't want to go to school because of him.

我想轉到其他學校。 I want to transfer to another school.

他是從什麼時候開始的？ — Since when did he do that? (Since when：何時之後～)

從學期初。 — From the start of the school year.

甜心，不用擔心。媽媽會幫你。 — Don't worry, Sweetie. Mommy will help you.

我們告訴老師這事情。 — Let's talk to your teacher about it.

對你來說，處理這個真的太難了。 — It must've been hard for you to deal with. (deal with：應付，處理)

我的朋友一直欺負吉娜。 — My friends keep picking on Jina.

那樣很不好。你不可以那樣做，好嗎？ — That's not very nice. You should not do that. Okay?

你何不阻止你朋友去欺負她？ — Why don't you stop your friends from picking on her?

• stop A from -ing 阻止 A 做～

ch42-05.mp3

去朋友家玩

我想去吉娜家玩。 — I want to go and play at Jina's house.

媽，我可以去我朋友家玩嗎？ — Mom, can I go and play at my friend's house?

今天是我要去記溯家玩的日子，對吧？ — Today is the day I am going to play at Jisu's house, right?

我答應要去旻久的家玩了。 — I promised to go and play at Minjiu's house. (promised to：答應，承諾)

我認識她嗎？ — Do I know her?

完成你的作業後，再去玩。 — Go and play after you finish your homework.

真的嗎？旻久的媽媽也知道嗎？
Really? Does Minjiu's mom know about that?

媽咪打電話到她家一下。
Mommy will call her house.

蘇娃說她今天沒有時間。
Suwa said she does not have time today.

去玩兩個小時就回來。
Go and play for two hours.

我兩個小時之後去接你。
I'll come and pick you up in two hours.

五點之前回家。
Come home by 5 o'clock.

我可以多玩一個小時嗎？
Can I play for one more hour?

你不可以在其他人的家待太久。
You shouldn't stay at someone else's house for too long.

晚餐之前要回家。
Come home before dinner.

不要跟米娜打架，要好好玩。
Don't fight with Mina and play nicely.

要聽米娜媽媽的話。
Listen to Mina's mom.

對米娜的爸媽要有禮貌。
Be polite to Mina's parents. ‧polite 有禮貌

給我你朋友的電話號碼。
Give me your friend's number.

玩完之後，要整理乾淨。
Clean up after you play there.

下次邀請她來我們家。
Invite her to our house next time.

不要把她家弄髒亂。
Don't make a mess at her house.
製造混亂

注意你的行為舉止。
Behave yourself.

媽，我可以帶這個去嗎？
Mom, can I take this?

把這個帶去跟朋友一起吃。
Take this and eat it with your friend.

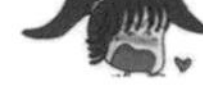
再見。等一下見。
Bye. See you later.

媽，你能帶我去那裡嗎？
Mom, can you take me there?

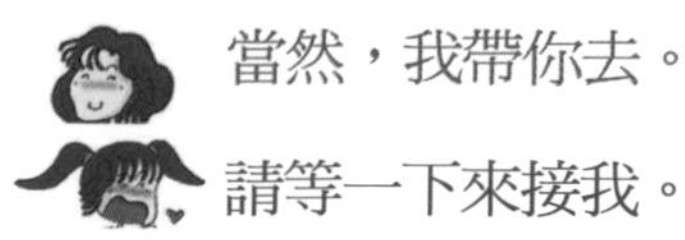

當然，我帶你去。 Sure, I will take you.

請等一下來接我。 Please come to pick me up later.

ch42-06.mp3

在朋友家睡

這個星期六，我可以在民肅家過夜嗎？ Can I sleep over at Minsu's house on Saturday?

sleep over 在別人家過夜

我收到週六睡衣派對的邀請。 I'm invited to a sleepover on Saturday.

• sleepover 過夜派對，睡衣派對

哇，是睡衣派對耶！ Wow, a pajama party!

你得到他父母的許可了嗎？ Did you get his parents' permission?

• permission 許可

是他父母邀請我的。 His parents invited me.

你把需要的東西都準備好了嗎？ Did you prepare all the things you need?

沒有媽媽，你睡得著嗎？ Can you sleep without Mommy?

媽，我現在是大人了。 Mom, I'm a grown-up now. • grown-up 成人

這是你第一次去朋友家睡。 It's your first sleepover at your friend's house.

你已經把牙刷和內衣都準備好了嗎？ Did you prepare your toothbrush and underwear already?

不要打擾民肅的父母，知道嗎？ Try not to bother Minsu's parents. Okay?

• bother 打擾

不要太吵。 Don't be too noisy. • noisy 吵鬧的

你不可以賴床。 You should not sleep in.

sleep in 睡懶覺

睡覺之前，一定要刷牙。	Be sure to brush your teeth before you go to bed.
好好享受睡衣派對！	Have a fun sleepover!
我想這將會很有趣。	I think it's going to be really fun.
我好想快點去！真的好興奮。	I can't wait! I'm so excited.
媽，明天見！	I'll see you tomorrow, Mom!
 如果有什麼事，就打電話給我。	If there's anything wrong, just call me.

Chapter 43

學校課業

ch43-01.mp3

學習

該學習了喔！	It's time to study!
預習明天要上的課程。	Study ahead for tomorrow's lesson.
你要不要複習今天的功課？	Why don't you review today's lesson?
上課的時候，要認真聽老師講課。	Listen to your teacher intensively during class. •intensively 集中地

你不應該一直拖延你的學習。	You should not keep putting off your studies. (推遲，拖延)
你習作本都寫完了嗎？	Did you finish the workbook?
你不可以看解答。	You should not be looking at the answer key.
我不想學習。	I don't want to study.
我可以先休息一下，接著再學習嗎？	Can I get some rest first and then study?
我可以休息一下嗎？	Can I take a break?
我想今天我學習得太多了。	I think I studied too much today.
學習需要堅持不懈。	Studying needs consistency! • consistency 持續，一貫
我發現學習很有趣。	I find studying to be interesting. / I enjoy studying.
我想我需要再解一次這些數學題。	I think I need to solve the math problems one more time. • solve 解題
檢查你做錯的題目。	Check over the questions that you got wrong. (做錯)
媽，我不懂這題。	Mom, I don't understand this one.
好，媽咪來幫你。	Okay, Mommy will help you.
所以，現在你理解了嗎？	So, do you understand it now?
為什麼你一直做錯相同的問題？	Why do you keep getting the same question wrong?
我知道持續學習是很辛苦的。	I know it's hard to keep on studying.
看到你努力學習，我感到很自豪。	I'm very proud to see you studying hard.

ch43-02.mp3

考試

你什麼時候考試？ When is your test?

你知道考試範圍嗎？ Do you know the test range? ‧range 範圍

當你準備考試的時候，不可以死記硬背。 You should not cram when studying for an exam. ‧cram 死記硬背

下週開始是期中／期末考試。 The midterm / final exam will begin next week.
‧midterm exam 期中考試 ‧final exam 期末考試

這週是期中／期末考試的期間。 This week is the midterm / final period.

你要認真準備考試。 Study hard for your exam.

考試包含太多章節。 The test covers too many chapters.

對於考試，我很緊張。 I'm very nervous about taking the test.
‧nervous 緊張不安的

我們今天有小考／單元考試。 We had a quiz / chapter test today.

考試考得好嗎？ Did you do well on your test?

我想我這次考試考得不錯。 I think I did well on the exam.

我想我考得不好。 I don't think I did well.

有點難。 It was a little hard. ‧hard 困難的

很簡單，但是我做錯了。 It was easy, but I made a mistake. 做錯

我沒有足夠時間。 I did not have enough time.

我不小心做錯了兩題。 I got two questions wrong by mistake. 不小心

你不應該做錯你知道的題目。 You shouldn't miss a question you know.
‧miss 未做到

我們來重溫你做錯的題目。 Let's go over the questions you missed.
重溫

再次仔細檢查你的答案。 Review your answers carefully.
• review 再檢查

再次確定你的答案。 Check over the answers to make double sure. 再次確認

你的成績將反映出你學習了多少。 Your test score will reflect how much you studied. • reflect 反映

你得到你應得的。 You get what you deserve.
• deserve 應該得到～

不要那麼失望。下次，你能做得更好。 Don't be so disappointed. You can do better next time. • disappointed 失望

下次，你會做得更好。 You'll do better next time.

如果你已經盡力了，那才是重要的。 If you did your best, that's what counts.
• do one's best 盡力 • count 重要

明天就要考試了，你怎麼還一直在玩？ How come you keep on playing around when you have a test tomorrow?

ch43-03.mp3

成績

你的成績如何？ How is your report card? 成績單

我在我們班／年級得到第一名。 I am number one in my class / grade.

我進入班上前十名。 I am in the top 10 of my class.

我不認為我可以進前十名。 I don't think I can make it into the top 10. 做到，成功

你這次考試得到幾分？ What score did you get on the test?

你的平均／總成績是多少？	What's your average / total score?
你覺得你會考幾分？	**What do you think your grade will be?**
 我的平均／總分是 82 分。	My average / total score is 82.
我數學考了 90 分。	**I got a 90 in math.** ★ 要說分數的時候，只要寫出數字，並加上不定冠詞(a, an)。
吉娜的分數比我高／低。	Jina's grade was higher / lower than mine.
我的分數提高／降低了。	**My grade went up / down.**
跟之前相比，我的分數提高／降低了 10 分。	Compared to before, my grade went up / down by 10 points.
我的成績因為數學分數被搞砸了。	**My grade is ruined because of my score on the math test.** ‧ruin 搞砸
我每科都考到很好的分數。	I got a perfect score in every subject.
我數學考了 100 分	**I got a one hundred in math.**
我想我會得到全班最高／最低分。	I think I will get the highest / lowest score in my class.
 不要太難過	**Don't be too upset.**
不要把自己跟朋友作比較。	Don't compare yourself with your friends. ‧compare A with B 比較 A 和 B
如果你盡力了，那才是最重要的。	**If you tried your best, then that's all that matters.** ‧matter 重要，問題
有可能你的學習的習慣錯了。	Your studying habits may be wrong.
 下次考試，我要考到全班第一名。	**I'm going to be the top student in my class on the next exam.**
哎，這次我已經盡全力了。	Well, I tried my best this time.
抱歉。我讓你失望了嗎？	**I'm sorry. Did I make you disappointed?**

嗯，事實上你的成績不錯了。	Well, your score is actually pretty good.
我確定你下次會考得更好，對吧？	I'm sure you can do better next time, right?
你這麼努力用功，現在來看看你考了幾分！	You studied so hard, and now look what you got on your test!
你的分數變好了一點。	Your grades improved a bit. • improve 提高
看起來，你進步了很多。	It seems like you've made a lot of progress. • make progress 進展，進步
我很高興你這次的考試進步了很多。	I'm very glad that you improved a lot this time. • improve 進步，改善
我想你要更努力一點。	I think you need to try harder.
不要太自滿。	Don't be too proud of yourself.
如果你努力，就能考到好成績。	If you try hard, you can get good grades.
當你考試的時候，你一定要集中注意力。	You need to focus when you're taking a test. • focus 集中
你很認真聽課，但考試卻考得很差。	You've done well in class, but you did badly on the test.

就因為我做錯了幾個題目，我就變成懶惰的學生了嗎？	Just because I got a few questions wrong, does that make me a lazy student? • lazy 懶惰的
那是不公平的。	That's not fair. • fair 公平的

那就是為什麼你要注意每個題目。	That's why you need to pay attention to each problem. （pay attention to）注意～
不管結果如何，我都愛你，寶貝。	Whatever the result, I love you, Honey.

我會努力的。	I'll try hard.
我考試考得不好。	I didn't do well on the test.
我下次不會再犯錯了。	I won't make any mistakes next time.

得獎

ch43-04.mp3

我得獎了。	I received an award. •award 獎
我得到大獎／次獎。	I got the grand prize / second prize.
我因為當了班上／學校代表而得獎了。	I got an award for being a class / school representative. •representative 代表
校長在全校集會上頒獎給我。	The principal gave out the award during the school assembly. •assembly 集會
得到這個獎的時候，我站在全校師生前面。	I stood in front of the whole school and got an award.
你到前面去領獎嗎？	Did you go up to the front to get the award?
我這學期在優等生名單了。	I am on the honor roll (優等生名單) this semester.
我好高興，因為我得獎了。	I was so happy because I got the award.
我得到了獎狀和獎章／獎品。	I got a certificate for the award and a medal / trophy. •certificate 證書
我也想得獎。	I want to receive an award, too.
我會盡全力去得獎。	I will try my best to get an award.
他們甚至給了我獎學金。	They even gave me a scholarship. •scholarship 獎學金

我們班只有兩位學生得獎。 It's an award given to only two students in our class.

我得獎了，所以你很開心，對吧？ You're happy because I got the award, aren't you?

寶貝，我高興得說不出話了！ I can't tell you how happy I am, Honey!

這是我真的很想得到的獎。 This is the award that I really wanted.

我想得到金牌。 I wanted the gold medal.

我得到了銅牌，有點不太滿意。 I wasn't satisfied a bit by receiving the bronze medal.

我們把獎狀掛在牆壁上吧。 Let's put the certificate for the award up on the wall.

我真以你為榮。 I'm really proud of you.

ch43-05.mp3

放假

暑假／寒假是什麼時候開始？ When does your summer / winter vacation begin?

你有任何想去旅行的地方嗎？ Do you have any place that you want to visit?

你認為放假期間做什麼好呢？ What do you think is good to do during vacation?

你的假期持續多久呢？ For how long does your vacation last?

超過一個月。 It's over a month.

我想在放假期間學游泳。 I want to learn swimming during the vacation.

既然你放假，我們去你奶奶家吧。

Let's visit your grandma's house since it's your vacation.

你不應該只因為不用去學校就睡懶覺。

You should not oversleep just because you don't go to school. •oversleep 睡懶覺

我們來訂放假生活計畫表吧。

Let's make a day planner for your vacation.

你不應該拖延你的作業。

You should not put off your homework.

整個假期我只想休息。

I just want to rest for the whole vacation.

這次的假期太短了。

The vacation is too short.

你的假日作業是什麼？

What's your vacation homework?

我要寫日記，讀幾本書，寫信，還有寫閱讀報告。

I have to keep a diary, read some books, write a letter, and write some book reports.

什麼時候開學？

When does school start again? / When do you go back to school?

我不想開學。

I don't want school to start again.

你做完所有的假日作業了嗎？

Are you finished with all of your vacation homework?

再過幾天，就要開學了。

School will start after a few days.

我還沒有做完。

I'm not finished with it yet.

我告訴過你不可以拖延的。

I told you not to put it off.

•put off 拖延，延遲

Chapter 44 學校活動

Where are you going for your field trip?
你們要去哪裡校外教學啊？

We are going to the amusement park.
我們要去遊樂園玩。

ch44-01.mp3

郊遊／校外教學

 離去郊遊還有幾天？ How many days are left till the field trip day?

郊遊，校外教學

 你還有兩天就要去了。 You only have two more days to go.

 耶！再兩天，我就要去郊遊了。 Yay! I'm going on a field trip in two days!

 你一定很開心吧！ You must be really happy!

郊遊是什麼時候？ When is your field trip?

我們下週五去。 We are going next Friday.

你要去哪裡郊遊？ Where are you going for your field trip?

我們去動物園。 We are going to the zoo.

我們會去中央公園。 We'll be going to Central Park.

我好想快點去郊遊！ I can't wait to go on the field trip!

我希望郊遊的那天快點到來。 I want the field trip day to come faster.

你想帶什麼午餐？ What do you want for your lunch?

媽，請幫我準備一些炸薯條。 Mom, please make me some fried potatoes.

媽，你也可以幫老師準備午餐嗎？ Mom, can you make lunch for my teacher, too?

你想帶什麼零食？ What do you want for a snack?

我想帶些葡萄和餅乾。 I want some grapes and cookies.

我想跟朋友們分享食物，所以請裝多一點。 I want to share my food with my friends, so please pack a lot.

下雨的話，怎麼辦？ What if it rains? ～的話，怎麼辦？

不用擔心。他們說天氣會很好。 Don't worry. The weather will be nice, they say.

老師告訴我郊遊那天要穿體育服。 My teacher told me to wear my gym clothes on the field trip day.

我要練習才藝表演。 I have to practice for a talent show.
• talent 才能

才藝表演你要表演什麼？ What are you going to do at the talent show?

你已經打包好校外教學的行李了嗎？
Did you finish packing for your field trip? / Did you put everything in your backpack?

搭巴士之前，你要先吃暈車藥。
You should take a pill for nausea before riding on the bus. •nausea 暈車

一定要一直跟著老師。
Make sure you follow your teacher all the time.

一定要好好聽老師的話，守規矩。
Be sure to listen to your teacher and behave well.

會出太陽，所以你一定要戴帽子。
It will be sunny, so be sure to wear a cap.

你什麼時候回到學校？
When do you arrive back at your school?

我會去那裡等你。
I will wait for you there.

郊遊如何？好玩嗎？
How was your field trip? Was it fun?

我想再去一次！
I want to go again!

媽，海苔卷真的很好吃。
Mom, the seaweed rolls were so delicious. •seaweed 海苔，海藻

ch44-02.mp3

運動會

你是藍隊，還是白隊？
Are you on the blue or the white team?

我是白隊。
I'm on the white team.

白隊要穿白色的襯衫。
The white team should wear white shirts.

你們是如何分組的？
How did you divide up the teams? (divide up 分配)

	我們根據班級來分。	The teams are grouped by classes. • group 把～分組
	我是接力賽的班上代表。	I'm the class representative for a relay. • representative 代表
	媽，請幫我加油。	Mom, you have to cheer for me. • cheer 加油，鼓勵
	運動會將有什麼比賽呢？	What kind of sporting events will be played on field day?
	我們有拔河。	We'll be playing tug-of-war. • tug-of-war 拔河
	我們也會有賽跑和搖呼拉圈比賽。	We'll also have a running race and a hula hoop rolling race.
	我來參加拔河。	I will participate in tug-of-war. • participate 參加
	媽，你一定要贏。	Mom, you have to win.
	對你來說什麼競賽最好玩？	What game was the most fun for you?
	我最喜歡拔河了。	I liked tug-of-war the most.
	萬歲！我們贏了。	Hooray! We won!
	媽，我賽跑贏了。	Mom, I won the running race.
	恭喜！	Congratulations!
	今年是藍隊贏了。	The blue team won this year.
	我很傷心，因為我們隊輸了。	I'm sad because our team lost.
	但是你跑得很好。	But you ran really well.
	如果你贏了就更好了，但是輸了也沒關係。	It would have been nicer if you had won, but it's okay to lose.

你應該去恭喜贏的人。 You should be able to congratulate the winners.

即使你輸給他們之後？ Even after you lose to them?

ch44-03.mp3

健康檢查

學校要我們做健康檢查。 The school told me to get a medical examination. 健康檢查

我下週之前一定要去做。 I have to do it by next week.

今天是你要做健康檢查的日子。 Today is the day of your medical examination.

我們要去哪一家醫院？ What hospital should we go to?

我做健康檢查時，要打針嗎？ Do I get a shot when I get the medical examination? 打針

我們只會做簡單的檢查。 We'll have just a simple checkup.

哇，我兒子／女兒長高很多了。 Wow, my boy / girl has grown up a lot.

你長高了 5 公分。 You've grown 5cm more.

你增加了 5 公斤。 You've gained 5kg.

你要做牙齒／身體／眼睛的檢查。 You have to get a dental / physical / an eye checkup.

• dental 牙齒的，牙科的 • physical 身體的

因為你的臼齒有蛀洞，所以你一定要去看牙醫。 You have to go to the dentist because your back tooth has a cavity. 臼齒

• cavity 蛀洞

因為你的視力不好，你需要戴眼鏡。 Since your eyesight is bad, you need to wear glasses. • eyesight 視力

媽，我是什麼血型？

Mom, what's my blood type?

你是 A 型。

Your blood type is A.

我來幫你填檢查記錄。

Let me fill out your medical record for you. [fill out 填（表格）; medical record 檢查記錄]

護士會幫你量體溫。

The nurse will take your body temperature. [body temperature 體溫]

護士也會幫你量血壓。

The nurse will take your blood pressure, too. [blood pressure 血壓]

你要用這個杯子裝尿液。你可以嗎？

You need to fill this cup with urine. Can you do it? • urine 小便

媽，我一切都正常嗎？

Mom, is everything normal with me? • normal 正常的

當然！你是個健康的小孩。

Absolutely! You are a healthy child.

如果有什麼異常，他們會告訴你的。

They will let you know if there's anything wrong with you.

ch44-04.mp3

觀摩教學

下週三我們有一個觀摩教學。

There is an observation class on next Wednesday. • observation 觀察

這是相關的通知信。

Here's the announcement letter about it.

首先，你必須要在旁聽席。

You have to be in the auditorium first. • auditorium 聽眾席

我等不及去看上課。

I can't wait to see the class.

很抱歉，我想我去不了。

I'm really sorry, but I don't think I can make it.

媽，請準時到。 | Mom, please come on time. 準時

媽，我怎麼樣？我做得好嗎？ | Mom, how did I do? Did I do well?

因為你來，我上課的時候好興奮／緊張。 | I was so excited / nervous during the class because you were there.

甜心，我太以你為榮了。你說得太好了。 | I was so proud of you, Sweetie. You were so well spoken! 說話得體的

如果我沒去，就會錯過那個場面了。 | I would have missed the scene if I hadn't been there. 當時就～了

你不能來，我感到很傷心。 | I was sad that you couldn't come.

我答應你，下次我一定去。 | I promise that I will go next time.

ch44-05.mp3

各種競賽

我想參加英文演講比賽。 | I want to participate in the English-speaking competition. • competition 競賽

我正在數學大賽與人競爭。 | I'm competing in the math competition. • compete 比賽，競爭

太棒了！被選上真的是件光榮的事。 | Great! It's a great honor to be chosen for that. • honor 光榮，名譽

比賽的準備進行得如何了？ | How's the preparation for the competition going? • preparation 準備

我必須去解為比賽所設計的幾本練習簿。 | I have to work on some workbooks designed for the contest. 為～設計

有個畫畫比賽，要畫的是我讀過的書。 | There is a drawing competition. The drawings should be about the books I read.

你要畫什麼書？ What book will your drawing be about?

我代表班上／學校去參加作文比賽。 I'm the class / school representative in the essay contest. 作文比賽

我得到了金牌／第一名。 I won the gold medal / first prize.

恭喜！讓我看看你的獎章。 Congratulations! Let me see the medal.

這個比賽有頒獎典禮。 There was an awards ceremony for the competition. 頒獎典禮

我以代表的身分走到前面去領獎。 I went up to the front and got a prize as the representative.

我不想參加這次的比賽。 I don't want to participate in the contest this time.

我想我的準備還不夠。 I don't think I'm prepared enough.

參與本身就很有意義。 Participating itself is a meaningful effort.

・meaningful 有意義的

ch44-06.mp3

家長會談

明天有一個家長會談。 There's a parent-teacher conference tomorrow. ・conference 會議

你一點之前到教室就可以了。 You can come to the classroom by 1 o'clock.

我要問你在學校的表現如何。 I'm going to ask about how you're doing at school.

媽，明天你要打扮得很漂亮。 Be sure to look pretty tomorrow, Mom!

我想知道老師會跟你說什麼。

I wonder what the teacher will say to you.

當你跟老師面談的時候，我要在哪等你？

Where should I wait while you have a talk with my teacher?

我跟老師面談時，你何不去待在圖書館呢？

Why don't you go and stay in the library while I talk to your teacher?

媽，老師說了什麼？

Mom, what did the teacher say?

老師跟我說我兒子是一個很棒的模範生。

The teacher told me that my son is such a model student.

我很高興聽到你跟朋友們都相處得很好。

I was happy to hear that you're getting along with your friends very well.

她說你在上課時很認真。

She said that you concentrate well in class. •concentrate 集中

聽到你在學校表現得不錯，我就很安心了。

It's such a relief to hear that you're doing great in school. •relief 安慰，安心

她跟我說你一直很積極和熱心。

She told me that you are always very active and enthusiastic. •enthusiastic 熱心的

你的老師很好。

Your teacher is really nice.

她跟我說了很多好話。

She told me a lot of nice things.

老師稱讚了你很多事情。

She said a lot of nice things about you.

老師跟我說你需要更多的自信。

The teacher told me that you need more confidence. •confidence 自信

她說你上課的時候好像有點分心。

好像～

She said you are likely to get distracted during class. •distracted 注意力分散的

她擔心你經常跟朋友吵架。

She was worried that you often argue with your friends.

抱歉，我會試著不再爭吵。 I'm sorry. I will try not to fight again.

ch44-07.mp3

校慶

校慶是什麼時候？ When is the school's foundation day?
‧foundation 創建

是九月五日。 It's September 5.

明天是我們學校的創校紀念日。 Tomorrow is our school's foundation day.

創校紀念日是什麼呢？ What is a school's foundation day?

那是你的學校第一天開辦的日子。 It's the date when your school first opened.

校慶的那天，你不用去學校。 You don't go to school on the school's foundation day.

我希望天天都是校慶。 I hope that every day is a foundation day.

你們學校成立多久了？ How old is your school?

因為這次是 20 週年紀念日，所以學校成立有 20 年了。 Since it's the 20th anniversary of our school, it's twenty years old now.

創校至今，已經過了 20 年了。 It's been twenty years since your school was founded. ‧found 創建；創立

ch44-08.mp3

畢業

已經是畢業的時候了。	It's already graduation. ·graduation 畢業
我不敢相信我兒子已經要畢業了。	I can't believe that my son is already graduating!
時間過得真快。	Time flies.
你出生的時候，感覺好像還是昨天。	It feels like yesterday when you were born. 感覺好似～
恭喜你畢業了！	Congratulations on your graduation! / Happy graduation!
畢業典禮幾點開始？	What time does the ceremony start?
爺爺奶奶會去參加你的畢業典禮。	Your grandma and grandpa will come to your graduation ceremony.
因為是你畢業的日子，你要穿得好看一點。	Since it's your graduation day, you have to look great.
請把這些花送給你的老師。	Please give these flowers to your teacher.
不要忘記跟老師說謝謝。	Don't forget to say thank you to your teacher.
我想我也要跟你的老師說謝謝。	I think I should say thank you to your teacher, too.
畢業典禮的期間，我差點哭了。	I almost cried during the graduation ceremony.
我想我會很想我的朋友／學校。	I think I will miss my friends / school a lot.
這是送給你的花。	Here are some flowers for you.

我來幫你跟朋友們照相。	Let me take a picture of you with your friends.
我們去吃好吃的，如何？因為這是個特別的日子。	Why don't we go to eat some delicious food? It's a special day!
哇，現在你是中學生了。	Wow, now you are a middle school student!
你在學校表現得不錯。	You've done a great job in school.
我真的很感謝你的努力。	I really appreciate your hard work.

我們不知道的美國派對

婚前派對 Wedding Shower

這是結婚前為新娘舉辦的派對。主要由和新娘很親近的人來主辦，邀請一些好朋友。被邀請的人帶來新娘所需要的禮物，主辦人則會準備豐盛的食物，大家一起來談天說笑。最近，為了避免禮物重複或者不是新娘需要的，新娘普遍都會去百貨公司等地方登記結婚用品（wedding registry），再告知朋友們，他們就可以各自負責一個禮物。

孕婦派對 Baby Shower

這是為生產前的媽媽舉辦的派對。由和孕婦的親友來主辦，被邀請的人們帶來嬰兒所需要的用品當作禮物。除了享受派對的美食之外，也會玩一些包尿布，把大人打扮成小孩子等等跟嬰兒相關的好玩遊戲。和 wedding shower 一樣，為了避免禮物重複，準媽媽會去百貨公司登記嬰兒用品（baby gift registry）。這是個既實用又好玩的活動。

和外籍老師的溝通

Chapter 45

英文幼稚園／補習班

Sorry, I forgot to bring my book.
抱歉！我忘了帶我的課本了。

Let's turn to page 10.
我們翻到第 10 頁。

ch45-01.mp3

經常使用的教室英文

● 老師經常使用的表達

大家好！	Hello, everyone!
週末過得如何？	How was your weekend?
我們來自我介紹一下吧？	Shall we introduce ourselves?
我要來點名了。	Let me take attendance. • attendance 出席，參加

該點名了。	It's time to call the roll. 點名
有人忘了帶課本了嗎？	Did anyone forget to bring their books?
上次我們學到哪裡了？	Where did we stop last time?
好，我們翻到第十頁。	Okay, let's turn to page 10.
這個的英文叫做什麼呢？	What do we call it in English?
知道答案的人，請舉手。	Anyone who knows the answer, please raise your hand.
那麼，誰想分享他／她的意見？	So who wants to share his / her opinion? • opinion 看法
誰要先說呢？	Who wants to go first?
跟著我唸一次。	Repeat after me.
仔細聽。	Listen carefully.
都清楚了嗎？	Is everything clear?
你們都懂了嗎？	Did you guys understand everything?
你怎麼想？	What do you think?
你做功課了嗎？	Did you do your homework?
請交出你們的作業。	Please turn in your homework. 提交
請在週五之前交出你的作業。	Please submit your homework by Friday. • submit 交出
請把這些練習題傳下去。	Please pass around the worksheets. • worksheet 練習題
你能把講義分給所有人嗎？	Will you pass out the handouts to everyone? • handout 講義；傳單

請把這個傳給下一個人。	Please pass this along to the next person.
拿一張，然後把其他的往後傳。	Please take one and pass the rest back.
我們來玩遊戲吧。	Let's play a game.
四個人分成一組。	Group yourselves into 4. / Make groups of 4, please.
那，現在輪到誰了？	So, whose turn is it now? • turn 順序，次序
好，今天的課就上到這裡。	Okay, this is it for today's lesson.
今天就到此結束。	Let's stop here for today.
下次見。	See you next time.
請用英文說話。	Please speak in English.

● 學生們常用的表達

我忘記把書帶來了。	I forgot to bring the book.
我還沒有完成我的作業。	I haven't finished my homework yet.
我看不清楚。	I can't see it clearly.
我有個問題。	I have a question.
老師，請幫我。	Sir / Ma'am, I need your help.
我，我！我想先回答。	Me, me! I want to go first!
這個太難／容易了。	This is too difficult / easy.
我星期一不能來上學。	I can't come to school on Monday. / I have to miss school on Monday.
我可以去廁所嗎？	Can I go to the bathroom?

我可以用中文回答嗎？	Can I speak in Chinese?
這個怎麼說？	How do I say this?
我不知道這是什麼。	I don't know what this is.
我可以得到一張貼紙嗎？	Can I get a sticker?

ch45-02.mp3

英文名字

你的英文名字是什麼？	What is your English name?
 我的名字是 Kelly。	My name is Kelly.
我根據我最喜歡的故事的主角取了這個名字。	I got this name from the main character of my favorite story. 主角
我沒有英文名字。	I don't have an English name.
我的名字很好發音。	My name is easy to say.
外國人能很輕鬆叫出我的名字。	Foreigners can say my name easily.
 你的名字很難發音。	Your name is hard to pronounce. • pronounce 發音
 我的名字是 Jennifer，但你可以叫我 Jenny。	My name is Jennifer, but you can call me Jenny.
叫我 Sophia。	Call me Sophia.
 哇，那是知名女星的名字。	Wow, it's the name of a famous actress.
那要怎樣拼呢？	How do you spell it? • spell 用字母拼；拼寫
 它拼成 S,O,P,H,I,A。	It's spelled S, O, P, H, I, A.

ch45-03.mp3

年齡

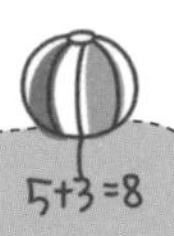

你幾歲了？	How old are you?
我六歲了。	I'm 6 years old.
你比同年齡的人高很多。	You are very tall for your age. • for one's age 就年齡來說～
你是哪一年出生的？	In what year were you born?
我是 2005 年出生的。	I was born in the year 2005.
我是 2003 年 2 月生的。	I was born in February 2003.
我是猴年出生的。	I was born in the year of the monkey.
他／她跟我同齡。	He / She is the same age as me.
我比她／他小一歲。	I'm a year younger than she / he.
你是幾年級？	What grade are you in?
我是二年級。	I'm in the second grade.
我還只有七歲，但是我已經讀一年級了。	I'm still 7 years old although I'm already in the first grade.
我提早一年入學小學。	I was enrolled in elementary school a year early. • enroll 入學

ch45-04.mp3

老師指示行動

請安靜。	Be quiet, please.
不要說話。	No talking, please.

請集中注意力。	Concentrate, please. / Pay attention, please.
請坐好。	Sit properly, please.
不要搗蛋。	Do not joke around. / Stop playing around.
不要罵髒話。	Do not swear. •swear 說髒話罵人
請小聲說話。	Please talk in a quiet voice.
不要跟旁邊的人聊天。	No chatting with the person sitting next to you. •chat 聊天
請不要玩你的手。	Do not play with your hands, please.
不要讓你的椅子發出噪音。	Try not to make any noise with your chairs. •noise 噪音
在樓梯玩是非常危險的。	It's very dangerous to play around in the stairway. •dangerous 危險的
不要在走廊上奔跑！	No running in the hallway! / Do not run in the hallway. •hallway 走廊
對大人要很有禮貌地打招呼。	Say hello to an adult in a polite way. •polite 禮貌
請把口香糖吐出來。	Please spit out (吐出) the gum.
你發言之前應該先舉手。	You should raise your hand before you talk.
先到先用。	First come, first served.
誰先舉手的？我們要依照順序。	Who raised his / her hand first? Let's follow the order. •follow 聽從；遵循 •order 順序

當你的朋友在發言時， 不要打斷他／她。	Do not interrupt your friend while he / she is talking. •interrupt 打斷；阻礙
請站成一排。	Please stand in line.
如果你打你的朋友， 我會給你一個警告。	I will give you a warning for hitting your friends. •warning 警告
請不要浪費學校用品。	Please do not waste school supplies. •waste 浪費
你應該要有禮貌地說話。	You should speak politely. / You should speak in a polite way.
請表現好一點。	Please behave well.
我們把垃圾放進垃圾桶內吧。	Let's put the trash in the trash can. •trash 垃圾
我們要節約資源和能源。	Let's conserve our resources and energy. •conserve 節省，節約

Chapter 46

和外籍老師面談

Does she understand the lesson well?
她對課程都了解嗎？

Absolutely! Jenny is a great student.
好極了！珍妮是個很棒的學生。

ch46-01.mp3

老師

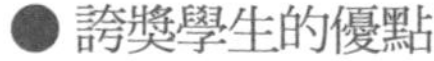

● 誇獎學生的優點

民肅上課時很專心。	Minsu concentrates well during class. • concentrate 集中
他很聰明。	He is smart / intelligent.
他在課堂上積極參與。	He participates well in class. • participate 參與

他對學習很有熱情。

He is passionate about studying.
・passionate 熱情的

他熱愛學習。

He loves learning.

他記憶力很好。

He has a good memory.

他做任何事情都很積極和熱心。

He is very active and enthusiastic in everything he does. ・enthusiastic 熱心的

他在新的環境適應得很好。

He adapts well to a new environment.
・adapt 適應 ・environment 環境

他很堅持努力。

He has a lot of perseverance.
・perseverance 堅持不懈

他好奇心很強。

He has a lot of curiosity. ・curiosity 好奇心

他很勤奮。

He is diligent. ・diligent 勤奮的

他做什麼事情都很努力。

He works hard at everything. /
He is a hard worker.

他在任何方面都比同年齡的小孩快。

He is ahead of other kids his age in everything.

他對其他人都很親切。

He is very friendly / kind to others.

他對其他人都相當細心體貼。

He is very thoughtful and considerate of others. ・thoughtful 考慮周到的 ・considerate 體貼的

他很謙虛。

He is humble / modest.
・humble 謙遜的 ・modest 謙虛的

他很活潑。

He is very active. / He is full of energy.

他很積極。

He is very positive. ・positive 積極的

他很有責任感。

He is very responsible.

他的個性很好。	He has a great personality. • personality 個性
他跟大家都處得很好。	He gets along well with everyone. (gets along well：與～和睦相處)
他有很多朋友在他身邊。	He has a lot of friends around him.
他比他的年紀還要成熟。	He is more mature than his age. • mature 成熟的

● 指出學生的缺點

她很倔強。	She is stubborn.
她非常害羞。	She is very shy.
她很容易受到驚嚇。	She is easily frightened.
她很膽小。	She is timid.
她不是很有耐心。	She is not very patient.
她很沒耐心。	She is impatient.
她很容易感到厭煩。	She gets tired / bored of things very easily.
她做任何事都消極。	She is passive at everything.
她很害怕新環境。	She is afraid of new environments.
她沒有跟朋友們和睦相處。	She does not get along with her friends.
當媽媽不在身旁時，她會很焦慮。	She gets anxious / nervous when her mother is not around. • anxious 焦慮的
她對數學有些學習障礙。	She has some difficulty with math.
她看起來對上課不感興趣。	She doesn't seem to be interested in class.

她很容易不開心。	She gets easily upset.
她在小事情上也很容易生氣。	She easily gets mad at even small things.
她不尊敬大人。	She does not show respect to adults. 尊敬～
她的話很多。	She tends to talk a lot. / She is talkative.
她太拘謹了。	She is too reserved ・reserved 拘謹的
她經常打其他人。	She often hits others.
她不會體諒其他人。	She is not considerate of others.
她不會遵守自己的順序。	She has trouble waiting for her turn.
她很容易不專心。	She is easily distracted. ・distracted 注意力分散的
她不太能專心。	She doesn't concentrate well.
她沒辦法保持注意力。	She has trouble staying focused.
她沒辦法專心做一件事。	She has a hard time staying on task.
她不喜歡單純重覆的事情。	She does not like simple repeating tasks.
她經常哭。	She often cries.
她會挑食。	She is picky about food.

ch46-02.mp3

父母

● 詢問上課態度

他的上課態度如何？	How is his behavior in class?
我想知道他是否聽你的話。	I was wondering if he listens to you. 想知道是否～

上課期間，他經常發言嗎？ Does he often speak up during class?

他有積極參與上課嗎？ Does he participate actively during class time?

他曾擾亂你上課嗎？ Does he ever disrupt the class? ‧disrupt 擾亂

他有聽懂上課內容嗎？ Does he understand the lessons well?

他有遵守學校規定嗎？ Does he follow the school rules?

有什麼地方是他需要去改善的？ Is there anything that he needs to improve on? ‧improve 改善

在學校生活中，有哪一部分是他應該多花點心思的？ Which part of his school life does he need to work on?

他很了解你的教法嗎？ Does he understand you well?

以你的看法，哪個領域是他感興趣的？ In your opinion, in which field does he show any interest? ‧opinion 看法 ‧field 領域

午餐時間，他有好好吃飯嗎？ Does he eat well during lunchtime?

我想知道他是否能好好回答你的問題。 I want to know if he answers your questions well.

他上課時有專心嗎？ Does he concentrate in class?

他跟同桌的同學沒有說太多話嗎？ Doesn't he talk with his seatmate too much?

● 詢問成績

我想跟你談談她的成績單。 I'd like to talk about her report card with you.

最近她有任何進步的表現嗎？ Is she showing any progress these days? ‧progress 進步；進展

她上課時努力學習嗎？	Is she studying hard in class?
哪一個科目是她需要更努力的？	**Which subject does she need more effort in?** ・subject 科目 ・effort 努力
我不確定她英文好不好。	I'm not sure if her English is good.
她應該增進她的閱讀和寫作能力嗎？	**Should she improve her reading and writing skills?**
她屬於哪一個等級？	In what level has she been placed? / In which level does she belong? ・place 放置，安置
她的英文精通程度如何？	**How is her English proficiency?** ・proficiency 精通，熟練
她能讀得很好嗎？	Can she read well?
我想在家裡幫助她閱讀，我應該怎樣做？	**I want to help her read at home. What should I do?**
她考試考得好嗎？	Did she do well on her tests?
她這樣的分數能讓她在班級的前段嗎？	**Does this score qualify her in the top part of her class?** ・qualify 使有資格
跟同班同學相比，她做到哪個程度了？	Compared to her classmates, how well did she do? 跟～相比
她最弱的部分是什麼？	**What is her weakest part?**
她落後她的同學嗎？	Does she fall behind her classmates? 落在後面
她上這堂課很吃力嗎？	**Does she find it hard to work in this class?**
她對課業好像感到有些困難。	She seems to have some difficulty with the classwork.
我想知道作業是否也算成績。	**I was wondering if you grade homework.**

你認為她有進資優班的潛能嗎？ Do you think she has the potential to be in the top group? • potential 潛力

● 詢問交友狀況

他跟誰特別親近？ Who is he especially close to?

他在家裡經常講民肅的事情。 He talks a lot about Minsuo at home.

他跟其他人的關係如何？ How is his relationship with others?
• relationship 關係

他跟朋友們相處得好嗎？ Does he get along with his friends?

他跟朋友們互動得好嗎？ Does he interact with his friends well?
• interact 互動，相互影響

他跟朋友們談得來嗎？ Does he talk well with his friends?

他曾經欺負過同學嗎？ Does he ever bully his classmates?
• bully 欺負

他曾經打同學嗎？ Does he not hit his classmates?

他曾跟其他朋友打架過嗎？ Has he ever fought with his other friends?

他說民肅很會欺負他。 He said that Minsuo bullies him a lot.

我想知道你是否注意到有人在欺負我的小孩。 I was wondering if you're aware that someone is bullying my child.

我想知道你是否注意到有些小朋友在欺負我的孩子。 I was wondering if you're aware that some kids are picking on my child.
欺負～

班上有新同學嗎？ Are there any new students?

最近，有學生轉學了嗎？ Has any student left school recently?

他曾告訴我他跟繼望打過架。

He once told me that he had a fight with Jiwang.

他們跟對方和好了嗎？

Did they make up with each other? (make up 和好)

他只跟吉娜一起玩。

He is only hanging around with Jina. (hanging around 到處玩)

請幫他跟其他的同學做朋友。

Please help him make friends with his other classmates.

● 詢問準備物品

明天的課程需要什麼物品嗎？

Are there any materials needed for tomorrow's class?

‧material 材料，物品

她星期一的課需要帶任何東西去嗎？

Does she need to bring anything for Monday's class?

每週三她都要穿體育服嗎？

Should she wear gym clothes every Wednesday?

請寫下來我的小孩要帶什麼去上課。

Please write down what my child needs to bring to her class.

郊遊時，她需要帶什麼去？

What does she need to bring for her field trip?

我把她早上忘記帶的用具帶來了。

I brought the supplies that she forgot to bring this morning.

我送她來時也讓她帶著東西了。請確認是否都齊全。

I sent the materials with her.
Please check if everything is there.

如果你告訴我明天的課程需要的準備物品，我會確認她都帶齊每樣東西了。

If you let me know about the materials needed for tomorrow's class, I will make sure that she brings everything.

‧let A know 讓 A 知道

ch46-03.mp3

感謝信

● 媽媽的信

________老師，

您好。我是________的媽媽。
感謝您這段時間教導我的小孩。
在老師良好的照顧與支持下，小孩表現出極大的進步。
因為他很喜歡您，所以________很喜歡去幼稚園。
感謝您對我小孩付出真誠的愛心。
我不會忘記老師對我們溫暖的微笑。
希望您明年也健健康康，一切順利。

________ 媽媽 謹上

Dear Ms. __________,

Hello! I'm ____________'s mother.
Thank you for teaching and guiding my child so far.
He has shown great progress under your excellent care and support.
__________ enjoys going to kindergarten because he loves you.
Thank you for your sincere love for my child.
I will never forget your warm smile for us.
I wish you all the best and good health in the next year.

Sincerely,

____

● 小孩的信

親愛的________ 老師，

感謝您一年以來對我的教導。
老師在每件事情上都很親切地幫助我。
因為老師，讓我喜歡去上學。
再次感謝您。

________ 謹上

Dear Mr. ________

Thank you for teaching me for the entire year.
You helped me in everything very kindly.
I loved to go to school because of you.
Thank you again.

Love,
____

ch46-04.mp3

信件用語

感謝您把我的小孩照顧得很好。 Thank you for taking good care of my child.

感謝您愛護我的小孩。	Thank you for loving my child.
我感謝您為吉娜所做的一切美好的事情。	I thank you for all the wonderful work you have done with Jina.
祝您有個好玩又愉快的假期。	Have a very fun and happy vacation.
一切都是因為有老師的幫助和支持。	It was all because of your help and support.
謝謝您整個學年辛苦的付出。	Thank you for working hard for the entire school year.
我帶了個小禮物，以表我的感謝之意。	I brought a small gift as a sign of appreciation. •sign 表示 •appreciation 感謝
我希望你健康幸福。	I wish you good health and happiness.
我的小孩會很想念你的。	My child will miss you a lot.
我會永遠感謝你的努力。	I'm always grateful for your effort.
有你當他的老師，我想我的小孩真的很幸運。	I think that my child is really lucky to have you as a teacher.
非常感謝您所做的一切。	Thank you very much for all your work.
託您的福，我的小孩才可以自在地上學。	Because of you, my child could feel at home at school.
託您的福，他的英文實力提升了許多。	Because of you, his English skills improved a lot.
我真的很感謝您幫助他學習的方法。	I really appreciate the way you helped him learn.
我感謝您鼓勵他參與上課。	I thank you for encouraging him to participate in the class. •encourage 鼓
託您的福，民肅真的很享受他的學校生活。	Minsu is really enjoying his school because of you.

因為我的英文能力有限，不能跟老師聊很多，我感到很可惜。	I feel bad for not having talked enough with you because of my limited English.
因為我的英文不好，所以沒能好好地表達出我的感謝。	**I didn't even have a chance to thank you because my English is not that good.**
我希望你未來所做的努力都會很順利。	I wish you all the best in your future endeavors. •endeavor 嘗試

ch46-05.mp3

祝賀信

● 教師節

教師節快樂！	**Happy Teacher's Day!**
在這個特別的日子裡，恭喜您，也祝福您。	Congratulations and best wishes to you on this special day.
有教師節真的很好，因為可以讓我對您表達感謝之意。	**It's nice that there is Teacher's Day because it allows me to show my appreciation to you.**
我知道太晚了，但是我一直很感謝您的付出。（教師節過後，寄出時）	I know it's too late to say this, but I'm always thankful for your work.

● 聖誕節／新年

聖誕節快樂！	**Have a very merry Christmas!**
希望你這次的聖誕節充滿和平，愛和歡樂！	Wishing you peace, love, and joy this Christmas!
希望您跟家人有個很棒的聖誕節！	**Wishing you and your family a wonderful Christmas!**

希望這個聖誕節帶給您跟您所愛的人幸福和歡樂。
May the Christmas season bring only happiness and joy to you and your loved ones.

希望聖誕節的歡樂和愉快一直延續到新的一年！
May the joy and happiness of Christmas last throughout the new year!

我希望在新的一年您萬事順利。
I hope that everything goes well in the new year.

祝您有一個幸福富裕的新年。
Best wishes for a happy and prosperous new year. ‧prosperous 繁榮的；富裕的

● 道歉信

我為我的小孩的無禮，寫信向您道歉。
I'm writing to apologize for my child's misbehavior. ‧misbehavior 沒禮貌，品行不端

我對小孩昨天所說的話表示抱歉。
I'm sorry about the things he said yesterday.

我對他的錯誤感到很抱歉。
I'm sorry for his mistakes.

我對我的小孩所犯的錯感到很抱歉。
I'm sorry for the wrongdoing that my child committed.
‧wrongdoing 做壞事 ‧commit 犯（錯）

對於我的小孩為你所製造的麻煩，我很抱歉。
I'm sorry for any trouble that my child may have caused you.

因為她確實做錯了，我向您道歉。
I apologize to you because she obviously did a poor job. ‧obviously 明顯地

我發現她對您說謊。我要對此道歉。
I found out that she lied to you. I would like to apologize for that.

我會讓她為此事向您道歉。
I'll have her apologize to you for that.

我保證不會讓這種事情再發生。
I promise I won't let this happen again.

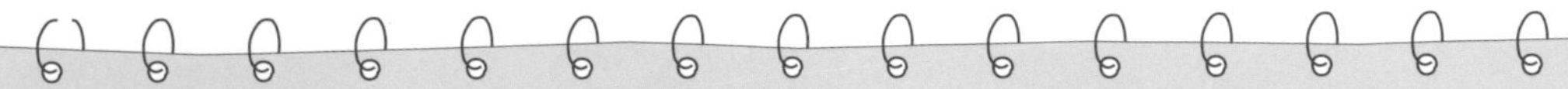

英語系國家經常使用的單位

溫度 Temperature

跟使用攝氏（Celsius）的我國不同，美國是使用華氏（Fahrenheit）。

- Celsius °C = (Fahrenheit – 32) × 5 / 9
- Fahrenheit °F = (Celsius × 1.8) + 32

長度 Length

長度用英吋 (inch)、英呎 (feet)、碼 (yard)、英哩 (mile) 來標示。

- 1 in (inch) = 2.54 cm
- 1 ft (feet) = 12 in = 30.48 cm
- 1 yd (yard) = 3 ft = 91.44 cm
- 1 mi (mile) = 1,760 yd = 1.6 km

容積 Volume

- 1 gal (gallon) = 3.8 liters

面積 Area

- 1 sq ft (square feet) = 929 sq cm = 約 1 / 36 坪
- 1 sq yd (square yard) = 9 sq ft = 約 1 / 4 坪
- 1 acre = 4,047 sq m = 約 1,227 坪

美國生活中經常使用的單位

鞋子的尺寸 Shoe Size

台灣是用公分來表示鞋子的大小，美國則是需要知道 Size 的大小。

〈男生〉

- Size 6 = 24 cm
- Size 7 = 25 cm
- Size 8 = 26 cm
- Size 9 = 27 cm

〈女生〉

- Size 5 = 22 cm
- Size 6 = 23 cm
- Size 7 = 24 cm
- Size 8 = 25 cm

衣服的大小 Clothing Size

〈男生〉

褲子的尺寸是用兩個數來表示。例如，有 28-30，34-32 這樣標示的數字。前面的數字是腰的尺寸，後面的數字則表示褲子的長度。
T-shirt 的尺寸是用 small，medium，large，extralarge 等單字來表示。

〈女生〉

女生的衣服是用 size 來表示。
（B = 胸圍，W = 腰圍，H = 臀圍）

- Size 2 = B32.5, W24.5, H35 in
- Size 4 = B33.5, W25.5, H36 in
- Size 6 = B34.5, W26.5, H37 in
- Size 8 = B35.5, W27.5, H38 in
- Size 10 = B36.5, W28.5, H39 in
- Size 12 = B38, W30, H40.5 in
- Size 14 = B39.5, W31.5, H42 in
- Size 16 = B41, W33, H43.5 in

〈T恤〉

T恤（T-shirt）的話，則用extra-small，small，medium，large 等代替 size 來表示。和 size 的關係如下。

- XS = size 2
- S = size 4 ~ size 6
- M = size 8 ~ size 10
- L = size 12 ~ size 14
- XL = size 16

〈小孩的衣服〉

小孩的衣服，如果是未滿兩歲，就會用 M（month）來表示。8M 就是指 8 個月的小孩的衣服。滿兩歲的幼兒則用 T（toddler）來表示。每個品牌都會有些不同，不過大致差異不大。3T 適合滿 3 歲的小孩，4T 則適合滿 4 歲的小孩。

Part 10

遇到疫情、緊急情況

Chapter 47 疫情／傳染病

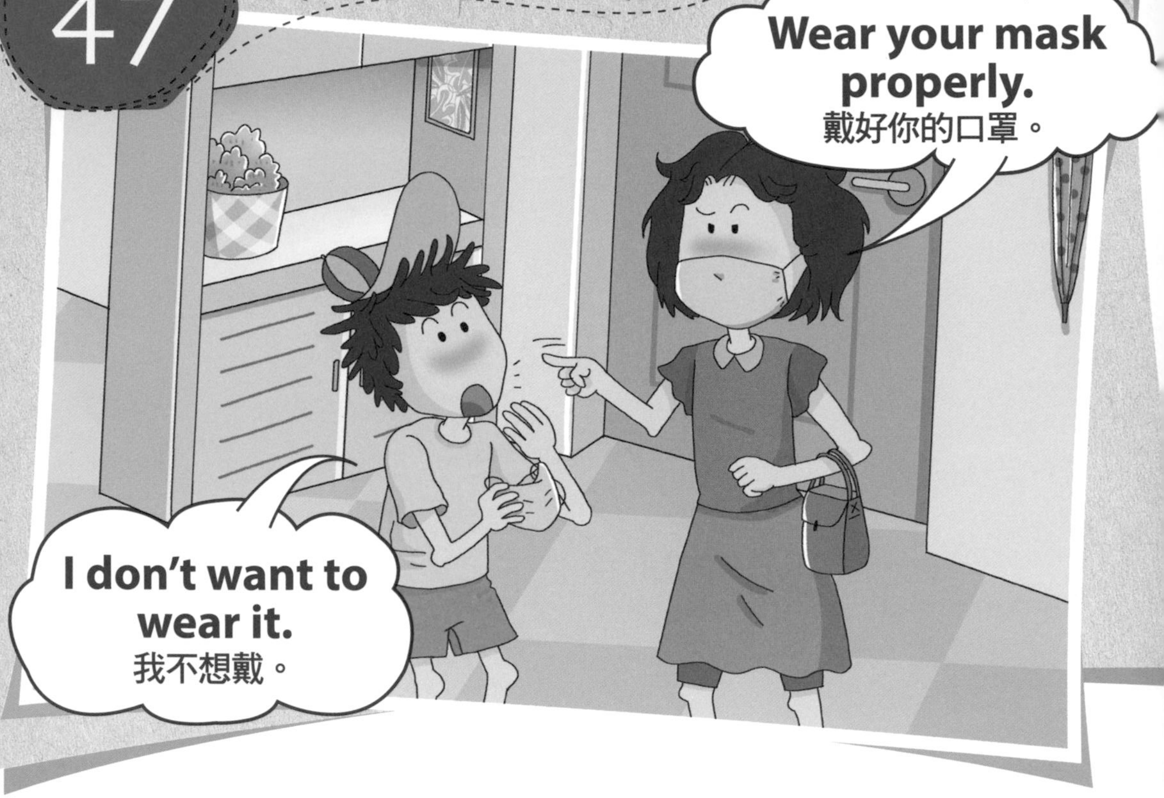

Wear your mask properly.
戴好你的口罩。

I don't want to wear it.
我不想戴。

戴口罩

ch47-01.mp3

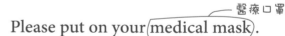

請戴上你的醫療口罩。	Please put on your medical mask. 醫療口罩
不要把口罩拿下來。	Don't take off your mask. 脫下
輕輕地捏鼻樑上的金屬條。	Pinch the metal edge of the mask gently on your nose bridge. 鼻樑 •edge 邊緣
如果你覺得不舒服，你就必須戴上口罩。	If you feel unwell, you have to wear a mask. •unwell 不舒服的

確保口罩覆蓋住鼻子和嘴巴。
Make sure the mask covers both your nose and mouth.

媽媽，我不想戴口罩。
Mom, I don't want to wear it.

戴口罩太熱了。
It's too hot to wear the mask.

我不喜歡在臉上戴東西。
I don't like to wear something on my face.

戴口罩可以預防散播高傳染疾病。
Wearing masks can prevent the spread of highly contagious diseases.
傳染疾病

忍受一下吧。
Just bear it. • bear 忍受

我們在家就不用戴口罩了。
We can take off the masks when we're at home.

ch47-02.mp3

定期更換口罩

你必須在戴口罩的前後清洗雙手。
You have to wash your hands before and after you take off the mask.

當你拿下口罩時，你必須從掛耳繩取下。
When you take off your mask, you have to remove it from the ear loops.
掛耳繩

醫療口罩只能使用一次。
Medical masks are single use only.

如果你的口罩太髒了，就要換新的。
If your mask is too dirty, replace it with a new one.

我會記得拿下口罩後去洗手。
I will remember to wash my hand after I remove the mask.

媽媽，我的口罩髒／濕掉了。你可以給我一個新的嗎？
Mom, my face mask is soiled / damp. Can you give me a new one?
• soiled 弄髒的 • damp 潮濕的

媽媽，我可以把口罩丟在哪裡？
Mom, where can I discard the face masks? ・discard 丟棄

把用過的口罩丟在可封起來的垃圾桶裡。
Discard the used masks in the closed bin. ・used 用舊的

ch47-03.mp3

洗手消毒

用肥皂和清水洗手。
Wash your hand with soap and water.

你必須洗手至少 20 秒。
You have to wash your hands for at least 20 seconds.

用擦手紙巾擦乾雙手。
Use hand paper towels to dry your hands.
擦手紙巾

把雙手擦乾淨。
Dry your hands properly.

在回家後洗手是很重要的。
It's important to wash your hands after coming back home.

請用乾洗手來清潔雙手。
Please use the hand sanitizer to clean your hands.
乾洗手

你必須在吃飯前洗手。
You have to wash your hands before eating.

在打噴嚏、咳嗽或擤鼻涕後要洗手。
Wash your hands after sneezing, coughing, or blowing nose.
擤鼻涕

雙手抹上酒精或乾洗手，並搓揉 20 秒。
Apply the alcohol or hand sanitizer on your hands and rub for 20 seconds.
・alcohol 酒精 ・rub 揉搓

乾洗手好臭。
The hand sanitizer is stinky.

媽媽，我不喜歡乾洗手的味道。
Mom, I don't like the smell of hand sanitizer.

我洗好手了，我可以吃點心了嗎？	I washed my hands. Can I have the snack?
我對乾洗手過敏。	I'm allergic to the hand sanitizer. (allergic to 對～過敏)
我可以只用肥皂嗎？	Can I just use the soap?
在學校的時候，我會記得洗手的。	I will remember to wash my hands when I'm at school.

ch47-04.mp3

確認是不是傳染病

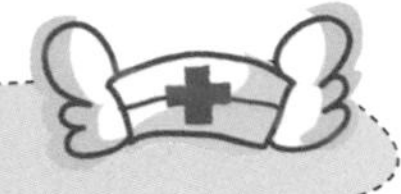

你看起來很糟，怎麼了？	You look terrible. What's wrong?
你感覺如何？	How do you feel?
有發燒嗎？	Do you have a fever?
有覺得胸口悶悶的嗎？	Do you feel pressure in your chest?
你有呼吸困難嗎？	Do you have trouble breathing?
讓我量你的體溫。	Let me measure your body temperature. (body temperature 體溫)
你有頭痛或喉嚨痛嗎？	Are you having a headache or sore throat?
我不舒服。	I don't feel well.
我頭痛。	I have a headache.
我不想喝水。	I don't want to drink water.
我有流鼻涕。	I have a running nose.
我一直咳嗽。	I keep coughing.

得到新冠肺炎的人可能會有一些症狀。	People with COVID-19 can have some symptoms. •symptom 症狀

你應該多喝水、好好休息。	You should drink plenty of water and take a good rest.

ch47-05.mp3

有同學確診了

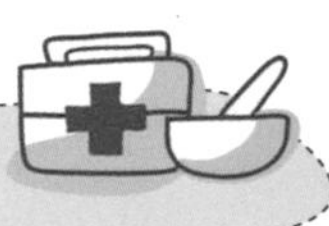

我同學得到了新冠肺炎。	**My classmate caught Covid-19.**
他跟我坐得很近。	He sat close to me.
我很怕我也會得到新冠肺炎。	**I'm afraid I will catch Covid-19, too.**
我可以怎麼做來避免生病？	What can I do to prevent from getting sick?
我可以待在家嗎？我很擔心。	**Can I stay at home? I'm worried.**
別擔心，在學校小心點就好。	Don't worry. Just be careful at school.
你會沒事的，你沒有任何症狀。	**You will be fine. You don't have any symptoms.**
不要焦慮， 這幾天好好照顧你自己。	Don't be anxious. Take good care of yourself these days. (好好照顧自己)
你在學校必須好好戴口罩。	**You have to wear masks properly at school.**
如果你擔心的話，可以做快篩。	If you're worried, you can take a rapid antigen test. (快速抗原檢測)

ch47-06.mp3

上線上課程

上線上課的時間到了。

It's time for online class.

登入線上課程的應用程式。	Log in (登入) to the online class application. • application 應用程式
現在是學習時間，把遊戲應用程式關掉。	**It's learning time. Turn off your game App.**
你的課本在哪裡？	Where is your textbook?
 **媽媽，你知道要怎麼登入線上課程嗎？**	**Mom, do you know how to log in to the online class?**
我打開鏡頭跟麥克風了嗎？	Did I turn on the webcam and microphone?
怎麼樣把麥克風靜音？	**How do I mute my microphone?**
你可以跟我說怎麼分享我的螢幕畫面嗎？	Can you tell me how to share my screen?
網路連線好糟糕。	**The Internet connection (網路連線) is poor.**
我找不到課本。	I can't find my textbooks.
我可以去廁所嗎？	**Can I go to the bathroom?**
我想要喝水。	I want to drink some water.
我不知道怎麼拼這個單字。	**I don't know how to spell this word.**
 你要專心上課。	You need to pay attention (關注～) to the class.
你還在上課，坐好。	**You're still in class. Sit properly.**
還沒下課，坐在位子上。	The class isn't over yet. Stay at your seat.
我現在在工作，回去你的座位。	**I'm working now. Go back to your seat.**
我在做家事，請不要打擾我。	I'm doing chores. Please don't disturb me.

ch47-07.mp3

做快速檢測

媽媽，我覺得我得到了新冠肺炎。

Mom, I think I got Covid-19.

我應該做快篩嗎？

Should I do the rapid test?

我需要快篩。

I need to do the rapid test.

我想知道我是不是得到新冠肺炎。

I want to know whether I got Covid-19 or not.

我去拿快篩試劑組。

Let me get the test kit.

我會幫你做快篩。

I will help you do the rapid test.

我們必須用肥皂和清水洗手。

We have to wash our hands with soap and water.

我們先來閱讀指示。

Let's read the instructions first.

把試劑條、拭子、還有萃取液試管拿出密封袋。

試劑條

Let's take the test strip, the swab, and the extraction tube out of the sealed bag.

萃取液試管

• swab 拭子 • sealed 密封的

你可以把頭抬起來一點點嗎？

Can you lift up your head a little bit?

抬起

我要把拭子放進你的鼻孔裡了。

I'm going to put the swab into your nostril. • nostril 鼻孔

我會用拭子抹你的鼻孔內側，旋轉整整十圈。

I will wipe the swap around the inside of your nostril and make 10 complete circles.

這可能會不舒服。

This might be uncomfortable.

我想打噴嚏。

I want to sneeze.

真的好痛。 It really hurt.

等等…就快好了。 Hold on… Almost done.

現在把拭子放進萃取液試管裡。 Now place the swab into the extraction tube.

我們必須把蓋子放在萃取液試管，並擠萃取液試管在試劑條上。 We have to put the cap onto the extraction tube and squeeze the extraction tube on the test strip.

現在我們必須等 15 分鐘來得到結果。 Now we have to wait 15 minutes for the result.

試劑條只有一條線，你的結果是陰性。 There's only one line on the test strip. Your result is negative.

真是鬆了一口氣。 That's a relief.

喔，不！試劑條上有兩條線，你確診新冠肺炎了。 Oh, no! There're two red lines on the test strip. You caught Covid-19.

我該怎麼做？ What should I do?

ch47-08.mp3

確診後的線上看診

我們必須聯絡診所，來進行遠端看診預約。 We have to contact the clinic to schedule a telemedicine appointment.

• telemedicine 遠距離醫學 • appointment 預約

把陽性的快篩和健保卡的照片傳給醫生。 Send the picture of your positive rapid test and healthcare card to the doctor.

健保卡

• positive 陽性的

現在，我們可以等醫生跟我們聯絡。 Now we can wait for the doctor to contact us. • contact 聯絡

做醫生告訴你的指示。	Do what the doctor told you to do.
跟醫生說你的症狀。	**Tell the doctor your symptoms.**
醫生會開藥給你。	The doctor will prescribe the medicine for you. ‧prescribe 開藥
什麼是遠端看診？	**What is telemedicine?**
你不需要去診所看醫生。	You don't have to go to the clinic to see the doctor.
我不需要去診所嗎？	**I don't have to go to the clinic?**
你可以透過視訊對話來跟醫生談話。	You can talk to the doctor through video chat. (video chat 視訊對話)
遠端看診可以降低疾病傳播的風險。	**Telemedicine can reduce the risk of spreading the disease.** ‧spread 散播
我要怎麼拿到藥？	How can I get the medicine?
媽咪會去診所拿你的藥。	**Mommy will go to the clinic to get your medicine.**
太方便了。	It's so convenient.
我不用出門就可以看醫生了。	**I can see a doctor without stepping outside.**

自己在房間隔離

ch47-09.mp3

根據政府的政策，確診新冠肺炎的人應該要待在家裡。	**According the government's policy, people who caught Covid-19 should stay at home.**

我不想要一個人。	I don't want to be alone.

我必須待在房間嗎？

Do I have to stay in the room?

隔離的天數太長了。

The isolation days are too long.

• isolation 隔離

你應該要待在家裡幾天。

You should stay in your room for a few days.

如果你必須在我們的周圍時，要戴上口罩。

Wear a mask if you have to be around us.

記得使用個別的廁所。

Remember to use the separate bathroom.

• separate 個別的

家裡只有一間廁所，所以每個人用完廁所都要清潔。

There is only one bathroom in our home, so everyone has to clean the bathroom after using it.

我們需要戴上手套，清洗馬桶和洗手槽。

We need to put on the gloves, and clean the toilet and sink.

如果你呼吸困難，要盡快跟我們說。

If you have trouble breathing, call us as soon as possible .

媽媽或爸爸會待在你附近不同的房間。

Mommy or daddy will be in a different room near you.

我要如何吃早餐、午餐和晚餐。

How can I have my breakfast, lunch and dinner?

我可以出去吃點零食嗎？

Can I go out and have some snacks?

我已經清潔好浴室了。

I've cleaned the bathroom.

我會把食物放在你的房間門口。

I will put the food in front of your door.

你吃完飯後，可以把餐盤放在房間的門口。

After you finish your meal, you can put the dishes in front of the door.

我會收集並清洗餐盤。

I will collect the dishes, and wash them.

你必須定期吃藥。

You have to take your medicine regularly.

試著在房間做些有趣的事情。

Try to do something interesting in your room.

Chapter 48

緊急情況

What do you learn from the drill?
你從演習中學到什麼？

We had an earthquake drill at school today.
今天在學校有做地震演習。

ch48-01.mp3

預防火災

火非常危險。	Fire is very dangerous.
我看到幾則火災意外的新聞。	I saw some news of fire accidents.
我們可以怎麼做來預防火災？	What can we do to prevent fire?
爸爸，什麼是煙霧探測器？	Dad, what is a smoke detector? (煙霧探測器)
你覺得我們需要安裝煙霧探測器嗎？	Do you think we need to install a smoke detector? • install 安裝

我們家有滅火器嗎？	Do we have fire extinguisher in our house? 滅火器
 確保在我們睡覺前關掉所有的爐子。	**Make sure to turn off all the stoves before we go to bed.**
記得在我們離開家前熄滅蠟燭。	Remember to blow out the candles before we leave the house. 吹熄
煙霧探測器是一種可以感測建築煙霧的裝置。	**The smoke detector is a device that senses the smoke in the building.** • sense 感覺到
它是火災的指示器。	It's an indicator of fire. • indicator 指示器
安裝煙霧探測器是預防火災的好方法。	**Installing a smoke detector is a good way to prevent fire.**
我們必須要檢查滅火器的有效日期。	We need to check the fire extinguisher's expiration date. 有效日期

ch48-02.mp3

防止一氧化碳中毒

 炎熱的夏天很容易引起火災。	**Hot summers are prone to fire.**
一氧化碳中毒的症狀有什麼？	What are the symptoms of carbon monoxide poisoning?
一氧化碳中毒的人會感到頭痛、暈眩、虛弱和呼吸急促。	**People who have carbon monoxide poisoning will feel headache, dizziness, feeling weak, and shortness of breath.** 呼吸急促 • dizziness 頭暈目眩
 什麼將會造成一氧化碳中毒？	What will cause carbon monoxide poisoning?

用在加熱和烹煮的家用電器，如果故障可能會產生一氧化碳。

Appliances used for heating and cooking might produce carbon monoxide if they are faulty.

‧appliance 家用電器 ‧faulty 有缺陷的

我們必須預防一氧化碳中毒。

We have to prevent carbon monoxide poisoning.

保持房間通風良好。

Keep the room well-ventilated.

‧well-ventilated 通風良好的

在煮飯的時候，不要把窗戶關起來。

Don't close the windows when you're cooking.

我會打開我房間的窗戶。我喜歡房間很通風。

I will open the windows in my room. I like the room being airy. ‧airy 通風的

ch48-03.mp3

制定逃生計畫

今天我們在學校有做消防演習。

Today we had a fire drill at school. (fire drill 消防演習)

我從消防演習中學到好多。

I've learned a lot from the fire drill.

你可以教爸爸媽媽在火災時要怎麼做嗎？

Can you teach mom and dad what to do during a fire?

我們需要制定火災的逃生計畫。

We need to have a plan to escape from the fire. (escape from 逃脫)

當我們聽到火災警報器時，必須保持冷靜。

When we hear fire alarm, we need to stay calm. (fire alarm 火警警報器)

大家應該要開始離開建築物。

Everyone should start moving out of the building. (moving out 搬出去)

不要忘記帶隨身物品。

Don't forget to bring your personal belongings.

把身體趴到地板的高度，並蓋住臉部。

Stay low to the ground, and cover your face.

在火災時，我們必須走樓梯而不是搭電梯。

We need to use the stairs, instead of (而不是～) taking the elevator during the fire.

去最近的逃生出口。

Go to the nearest emergency exit.

如果衣服著火，記得停住、趴下、滾動。

Remember STOP, DROP, ROLL if our clothes are catching fire.

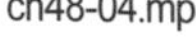

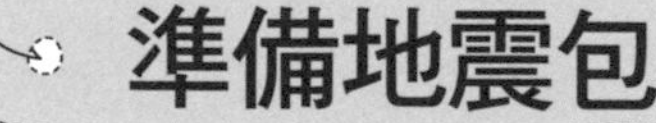

準備地震包

ch48-04.mp3

媽媽，你知道要怎麼準備地震緊急包嗎？

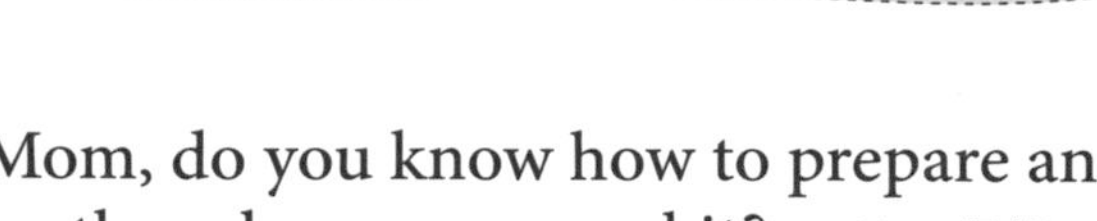

Mom, do you know how to prepare an earthquake emergency kit? ‧kit 工具箱

我們需要把一些重要物品放在地震包裡。

We need to keep some essential items in the earthquake bag. ‧essential 必要的

地震包將會幫助我們在地震中存活下來。

The earthquake kit will help us survive the earthquake.

我們必須打包水、電池、手電筒、罐頭食物、口哨還有急救箱到地震包裡。

We have to pack water, batteries, flashlights, canned food, a whistle, and a first aid kit (急救藥箱) in the earthquake bag.

我們去超市買這些物品吧。

Let's go to the supermarket to get these items.

地震了

ch48-05.mp3

我們要如何知道地震發生？

How can we know when an earthquake happens? ‧earthquake 地震

地震預警系統會透過手機通知你地震報告。

The Earthquake Early Warning system (地震預警系統) will notify you of the earthquake report through your phone. •notify of 通知某人某事

當我們收到地震警報，必須馬上採取行動。

When we receive the earthquake alert, we have to take action (採取行動) immediately.

我們必須保持冷靜，並關掉電力和瓦斯。

We have to stay calm and turn off the electricity and gas.

•electricity 電力 •gas 瓦斯

不要靠近高的傢俱、窗戶和有玻璃或重物的櫥櫃。

Don't get near the tall furniture, windows, and cabinets with glass or heavy items.

在地震當下不要奔跑。

Don't run during the earthquake.

我們在地震期間可以搭電梯嗎？

Can we take the elevator during an earthquake?

不行，我們在地震期間不能搭電梯。

No, we can't take the elevator during an earthquake.

如果我們在室外，可以怎麼做？

If we are outdoors, what can we do?

•outdoors 在戶外

走到遠離建築物的空曠地。

Go to an open space far away from buildings.

如果我們在地震期間正在開車呢？

What if we are driving a car during an earthquake?

如果我們在開車，必須靠邊停並待在車上。

If we are driving, we have to pull over (開到一邊) and stay in the car.

地震的口訣

ch48-06.mp3

地震的口訣是趴下、掩護、穩住。 The earthquake tip is Drop, Cover, and Hold on.

在原地蹲下，雙手和雙膝著地。 Drop where you are and stay on your hands and knees.

用手臂蓋住頭和頸部。 Cover your head and neck with your arms.

用單手抓住任何牢固的遮蔽處，直到搖晃停止。 Hold on to any stable shelter with one hand until the shaking stops.

• stable 牢固的 • shelter 躲避處

我會把這些指示謹記在心。 I will keep these instructions in mind.

• instruction 指示

收看颱風預報

ch48-07.mp3

我們來看天氣預報。 Let's watch the weather forecast. （天氣預報）

根據報導，有颱風要來了。 It's reported that a typhoon is coming.

• typhoon 颱風

這是輕颱／中颱／強颱／超級強颱。 It's a mild / moderate / severe / super typhoon.

• mild 輕微的 • moderate 中等的 • severe 劇烈的

那就是下大雨的原因。風吹得好強。 That's why it is raining cats and dogs. （下傾盆大雨） The wind is blowing so strongly.

這個超級颱風什麼時候會登陸？ When will this super typhoon make landfall? • landfall 登陸

後天就會來。 | It is coming the day after tomorrow.
後天

現在颱風的強度是什麼？ | What is the strength of the typhoon now? ‧strength 強度

政府在幾個小時內會發布颱風警報。 | The government will issue a typhoon warning in a few hours. ‧issue 發布
颱風警報

政府已經解除颱風警報。 | The government has lifted the typhoon warning. ‧lift 解除

我們必須延後假日的計畫嗎？ | Do we have to postpone our holiday plan? ‧postpone 推遲

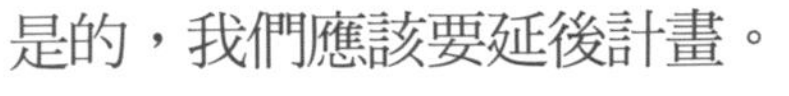

是的，我們應該要延後計畫。 | Yes, we should postpone the plan.

你覺得政府將會宣布颱風假嗎？ | Do you think the government will announce a typhoon day?

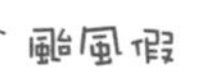

颱風假時，我們必須待在家裡。 | On typhoon day, we have to stay at home.

我們不必去工作或去上學。 | We don't have to go to work or school.

政府已經宣布繼續上班上課，所以我們還是要早點起床。 | The government has announced school and work will continue as usual, so we still have to wake up early.
照例

ch48-08.mp3

為颱風做好準備

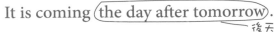

～是重要的

為颱風做好準備很重要。 | It's important to prepare for a typhoon.

我們應該要準備什麼？ | What should we prepare for it?

我們必須準備一些食物、飲水、電池和手電筒。 | We have to prepare some food, drinking water, batteries, and a flashlight.

我們需要準備急救包嗎？
Do we need to prepare an emergency kit? 急救包

我們在客廳有急救包。
We have an emergency kit in our living room.

媽媽，我們必須把陽台的花盆拿到室內，對嗎？
Mom, we have to take the flower pots on the balcony indoors, right?

是的，盆栽可能會被吹走，造成一些意外。
Yes, the plants might be blown away and cause some accidents.

還有，窗戶在颱風期間應該要關起來。
Also, the windows should be closed during typhoons.

我們應該盡快去超市，否則我們沒辦法買到足夠的食物或其他商品。
We need to go to the supermarket as soon as possible, or we can't buy enough food or other items. 盡早～

ch48-09.mp3

颱風造成的災害

颱風可能會造成什麼災害？
What damage or disaster might a typhoon cause?
• damage 損害 • disaster 災害

颱風可能會造成停電、淹水、土石流或山崩。
Typhoons might cause a power outage, flooding, debris flow, or landslide. 停電 土石流
• flooding 水災 • landslide 山崩

這個平原地區淹大水了。
There was severe flooding in this plain area. • plain 平原

我們家在颱風期間停電了。
Our house had a power outage during the typhoon.

大雨造成這個村子發生嚴重的土石流。
The heavy rain caused severe debris flow in this village.

這條路因為山崩而受損。	The road was damaged because of the landslide.

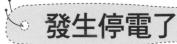

發生停電了

發生什麼事了？為什麼這麼暗？	What happened? Why is it so dark?
停電了。	The power just went out.
我覺得電力會馬上恢復。	I think the power will be back on soon.
媽媽，我很怕黑。	Mom, I'm afraid of the darkness.
別害怕，放輕鬆。	Don't panic. Take it easy.
你知道手電筒在哪裡嗎？	Do you know where the flashlight is?
這支手電筒沒有備用電池了。	There're no spare batteries for the flashlight. ・spare 備用的
讓我去拿蠟燭。	Let me get some candles.
不要觸碰蠟燭。	Don't touch the candles.
這間房間裡面好熱。	It is so hot in this room.
我們打開窗戶讓空氣循環。	Let's open the windows to make the air circulate. ・circulate 循環
停電了，所以冷氣無法運作。	The power is off, so the air conditioner is not working.
我們來完幾個遊戲吧。遊戲結束時，或許電力就回來了。	Let's play some games. When the game is over, maybe the power will be back.

ch48-11.mp3

用手機查詢停電原因

 喔，不！我的手機快要沒電了。	**Oh, no! My cell phone is running out of battery.**
 你之前應該要充電的。	You should have charged your phone.
 我從來沒有想到今天會發生停電。	**I never thought a power failure would happen today.**
 別擔心，我的手機還有電，你想要的話可以用我的手機。	Don't worry. My cellphone is still working. You can use mine if you want.
 為什麼停電了？	**Why did the power go off?** go off（機器）停止運行
 我來看一下手機的新聞。	Let me check the news on my phone.
據說是發電廠發生故障。	**It's said that the power plant had a breakdown.** It's said that 據說～ power plant 發電廠 •breakdown 故障
電力公司正在處理這項故障。	The power company is dealing with the breakdown. dealing with 處理
 我希望電力公司可以馬上恢復電力。	**I hope the power company can restore the power soon.** •restore 恢復